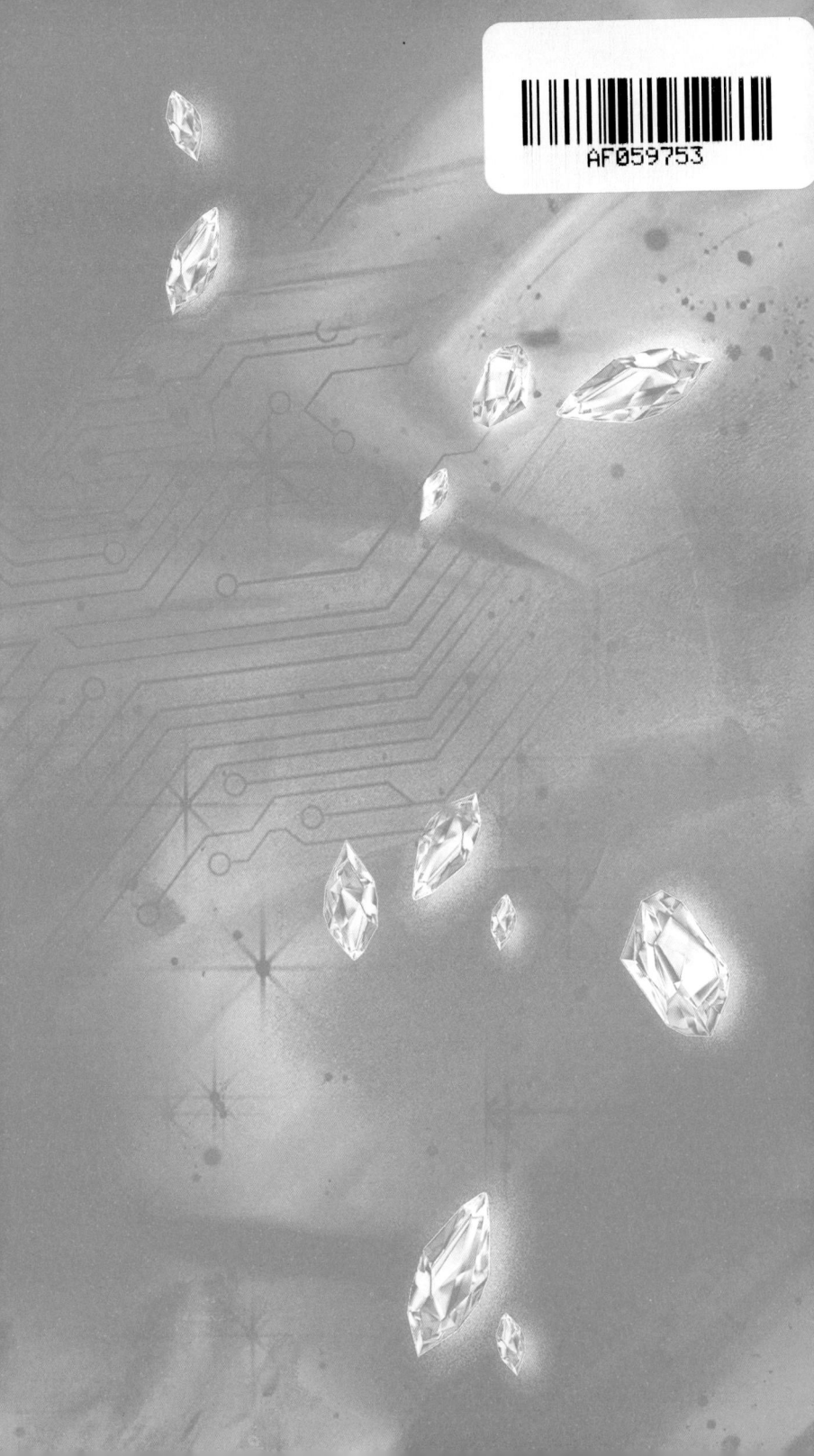

RELEASE ME

A SHATTER ME NOVEL

TAHEREH MAFI

First published in Great Britain 2026 by Electric Monkey, part of Farshore
An imprint of HarperCollins*Publishers*
1 London Bridge Street, London SE1 9GF

farshore.co.uk

HarperCollins*Publishers*
Macken House, 39/40 Mayor Street Upper, Dublin 1, D01 C9W8, Ireland

Text copyright © Tahereh Mafi 2026

The moral rights of the author have been asserted.

Trade HB ISBN 978 0 00 871817 6
Waterstones Exclusive ISBN 978 0 00 883346 6
Trade PB ISBN 978 0 00 872273 9
Export exclusive HB ISBN 978 0 00 880123 6
India PB ISBN 978 0 00 882855 4
PB ISBN: 978 0 00 871818 3

Printed and bound in the UK using 100% renewable electricity
at CPI Group (UK) Ltd

1

A CIP catalogue record for this title is available from the British Library

All rights reserved. No part of this publication may be reproduced, stored in a retrieval system, or transmitted, in any form or by any means, electronic, mechanical, photocopying, recording or otherwise, without the prior permission of the publisher and copyright owner.

Without limiting the exclusive rights of any author, contributor or the publisher of this publication, any unauthorised use of this publication to train generative artificial intelligence (AI) technologies is expressly prohibited. HarperCollins also exercise their rights under Article 4(3) of the Digital Single Market Directive 2019/790 and expressly reserve this publication from the text and data mining exception.

Stay safe online. Any website addresses listed in this book are correct at the time of going to print. However, Farshore is not responsible for content hosted by third parties. Please be aware that online content can be subject to change and websites can contain content that is unsuitable for children. We advise that all children are supervised when using the internet.

There are quicksands all about you, sucking at your feet,
trying to suck you down into fear and self-pity and
  despair.
That's why you must walk so lightly.
Lightly my darling.
                        —Aldous Huxley

WARNER

1

"Well?" I pivot slowly to face him, leaning one shoulder against a cold concrete wall. "Can you sense anything?"

Adam takes a tight breath.

"I don't know, man," he says. He shoves his hands in his pockets and shakes his head, exhaling. "I might need another minute. Something feels off."

I watch him shift his weight as his eyes track the vast window, assessing the stark scene beyond: Rosabelle Wolff is seated at a metal chair, unmoving, stiff as a stake in the ground as her estranged father, Hugo, attempts another ill-fated interrogation.

"Rosa," Hugo says desperately, his voice pitching higher. "Please—why won't you speak to me—?"

Every day has been a failure.

Every day Hugo's panic rises as the hours progress, his emotional instability spiking to near hysteria as Rosabelle grows only more remote. I've encouraged him several times to abandon the assignment, but now that he's seen her again after so many years apart, he's lost all objectivity. He's frantic for a spark of recognition—a moment of redemption—and he won't relent. I'd hoped his determination to connect with his daughter would give us a much-needed psychological advantage, but the unfortunate truth is that Hugo has become a liability. Worse, he's costing us time. Most days these sessions end in tears.

His, not hers.

I do my best, every day, to dissociate from his pain.

More concerning is that I haven't been able to get a read on Rosabelle in over a week. Her eyes are vacant, her energy cold. I've grown so accustomed to being flattened by the psychic torrent of other people that it's nearly disorienting to be confronted by her style of silence.

Rosabelle's emotional response is nonexistent.

In my life I've encountered one other person whose emotional state I couldn't fathom—and he's standing right next to me. My half brother Adam Kent Anderson. Only a year apart, we'd grown up never knowing the truth about each other or our family. For so long Adam and I had jettisoned our father's name from our lives; *Anderson* had once torn us apart. Our father had intentionally pit us against each other; in fact, we once sought to kill each other. But over the past decade we've learned to reclaim our shared name, slowly suturing ourselves back together. Me and my brothers, finally united under the same banner.

It was Ella who inspired this. Ella, who refused to be broken or branded by the story once written for her. It's what she taught me was possible when she took back the name Juliette.

She's known to the world as Juliette Ferrars.

She'll always be Ella to me.

I experience a stab of pain at the thought of her, tensing

even as I try to ignore the blade of fear that's lately lodged itself between my lungs. A quickening in my blood chases every unguarded beat of my heart these days; my own feelings are so unstable I can't allow myself to experience them in full. The thought of losing her—or our unborn child—is more than my paper soul can survive. Even now I feel an encroaching tremor animate my body and I clench my fists in concert with my jaw, compartmentalizing my life the way I always do.

The way I have to.

"Hey," says Adam suddenly.

I realize only then, meeting his eyes, that he's been watching me.

"You okay?"

The lie comes out fast. "Yes."

"You sure?"

Adam's concern continues to surprise and disarm me, despite its consistency.

"I'm sure," I say, turning away, struggling to rebuild the walls in my mind.

"Hey," he says again. "Look at me for a second."

When I look up I feel the spike in his sympathy. More than that, I see it in the way he studies my face, then scans the rest of me, as if searching for open wounds.

"You want me to ask Alia to check on her?"

These words deliver me a disorienting injury.

I had no idea I was so obvious; I have no desire to be pitied. Still, my heart begins to pound, my fears threatening to bleed beyond their enclosure even as gratitude expands in me like static, bristling under my skin. That familiar blade pierces me again and I can't compartmentalize quickly enough; instead I retreat so far inside my mind I feel physically distant when I say, tonelessly, "Nazeera is with her now. But thank you."

Adam holds my gaze a beat longer; finally, he nods.

I once thought he was a brainless soldier.

I'd read him wrong, all those years ago. In fact, I couldn't read him at all. His interior quiet was never as complete nor as deafening as Rosabelle's; instead, his emotional cues came across as both vague and wooden, and I thought I had the latitude, as a result, to make the tragic assumption he was a garden-variety idiot. As it turns out, Adam has the uncommon ability to neutralize the preternatural powers of others—and he'd been unconsciously exercising a skill to shut me out. There was a time when he didn't even know how to unlatch this armor; now he rarely bothers to hide his emotions from me. He calls it *growth*.

I call it loud.

"So," Adam says, building toward a segue. He takes a breath as he returns his eyes to the interrogation. "You really think this girl is activating some kind of a shield?"

I step closer to the window, pulling up beside my brother. As my heart rate steadies, I feel the pager vibrate in my pocket, each buzz like a shot to the head. I glance at the notifications, scanning for emergencies and finding none for the moment. In my head I build the scaffolding for the work to come: I silently add things to my to-do list; draft responses to questions; sketch out solutions to problems;

delegate responsibilities; attempt to anticipate the next pitfall. All this I'll set aside to manage later.

Right now I give Adam a cursory glance.

I thought I was dressed casually today, forgoing my standard uniform for a leather field jacket, slacks, and boots; but Adam redefines the word *casual*. He's wearing a lightweight puffer jacket over an old hoodie and a pair of faded jeans, at least a day's stubble shadowing his jaw. He could use a haircut. His sneakers are scuffed and worn, and he's pulled his shoelaces so tightly the tongue and toe box are pinched, the sight of which so aggressively repulses me I have to force myself to look away. I spin my wedding ring around my finger. It costs me something to say nothing about his shoes.

Still, despite our outward differences, we share an uncanny moment of alignment: exhaling at the same time.

"I don't know if it's a shield," I admit, returning my eyes to Rosabelle.

There's a dim clang of metal as she sits up in her seat, her manacles knocking together, and Hugo, who's sunk to the ground in defeat, looks up at the sound.

"Rosa," says Hugo, his voice fraying as he repeats the same lines over and over. "Please. You have to believe me—I never would've left you. They forced me to leave you. Please, say something—"

I look at Adam, anchoring myself in the room.

"As you already know," I say to him, "we discovered last week that the mercenary has the unprecedented ability to die at will. It's possible she's able to shut off her mind by extension. But logic would insist that were she capable of such a thing, she might've activated this power earlier."

"And you don't think she has?"

"I don't know," I say again, more quietly this time. "I've never had an issue sensing her emotions, which leads me to assume for the moment that this is some new kind of power—something we haven't seen from her before."

Adam nods, even as he frowns. "And you think I might be able to disarm her. You think it's something she turns on and off."

"I don't know," I say for the third time. "I'm not ready to commit to absolutes yet. If you find that you're able to shut off her power, I might be able to understand its origins. I'm trying to determine whether this—whatever this is—is an internal power, activated from within, or an external power, generated remotely."

"Remotely?" Adam raises his eyebrows. "Like, you think The Reestablishment might've turned off the chip in her brain?"

"The problem is, there is no chip in her brain," I say, my mood darkening as I meet his eyes. "If there were, she'd be a lot easier to understand. All I know is that *this*"—I nod at the window—"is not her natural state. I know her to be capable of heightened emotion and brain activity, but her mind has been impenetrable since the moment of her incarceration. It's like nothing I've ever encountered."

"Really?" asks Adam, his surprise peaking. "Not even with me?"

I feel him throw up a shield between us to illustrate his point, and his shock quiets to a note of flat, anemic interest.

"No," I say, returning my eyes to the inmate. "Not even with you."

Rosabelle's silence is so complete she might as well be dead.

She wears no expression despite having been recently united with her father after more than ten years of separation. Occasionally she shifts in her seat, her shackled hands clasped behind her, and the sounds of metal ring softly through the room. Each time this happens Hugo seizes with a visibly painful hope, practically holding his breath at the thought that she might finally speak, but in eight days, she hasn't said a word. If it weren't for the human blink of her eyes, the rise and fall of her chest, the occasional rearrangement of herself in her chair—she might be mistaken for a machine.

Or a ghost.

There's something spectral about her. She's surprisingly slight, lacking in substance and color. She's almost porcelain white; her skin and hair leached of pigment. Even her eyes are desaturated—some kind of gray. Still, the pallor of her skin is secondary to the real issue, which is perceptible only in her presence: Rosabelle doesn't seem to belong here. She emanates an otherworldly resonance, as if she might've died in birth but was sentenced to life.

Looking at her for too long makes me uncomfortable.

Looking at her for too long takes me to dark places. In her I see shades of myself, and I don't like the comparison.

"She really hasn't said anything in a week?" Adam asks

me, his voice dropping to a near whisper.

"Eight days," I say to him, shifting slightly. Fatigue is beginning to wear at my edges. I press the heel of my hand to my forehead in a vain attempt to dispel the building pressure. "And no. Not a word."

I know she's capable of volatility.

I got a clear read on her when she'd first regained consciousness upon arrival in The New Republic. She'd been so unwell that her heart had nearly flatlined; she was so unstable that she'd vomited. I've seen her eyes brighten with fear; I've seen her face animate with feeling; I've seen her cheeks flush with color. I was able to get a read on her even when she'd been lying in the morgue, freshly awoken from the dead. She'd seemed to be processing something like grief, of all things, which surprised me. I even got a read on her right before her incarceration, when she'd been able to hide neither her shock nor her chaotic feelings toward my younger brother. I knew my tactical maneuver had paid off when I felt her horror at reuniting with her father; and I didn't mistake her feelings then.

We should've seen results by now.

Without warning, I feel Adam relent to a crashing wave of disappointment. He gives up his position by the window and flops down in a hard chair, the metal legs scraping the concrete floor as he sighs. Right away, his knee starts bouncing. His body language alone shouts that he doesn't want to be here, but I can actually feel his anxiety building, nervous energy gathering in the room like a storm. It makes me restless. My chest tightens.

I already know what he's going to say.

I've known for several minutes now. I've been trying to resolve my own disappointment as I wait for him to tell me what's now obvious.

In the interim, I glance at the time.

These days have begun to take on a pattern. Hugo gave up any proper efforts at interrogation about fifteen minutes ago; he's now sagging against the back wall, visibly distraught. I close my eyes a moment, trying to shut his escalating pain out of my head. Hugo is on track for a complete breakdown, which is usually how these sessions end.

"I'm sorry, man," Adam finally says. "I wish I could help, but it's like—I don't know how to explain it. It's like trying to catch a fish with my bare hands. Sometimes I think I've got something, but then it's gone, like I might be imagining it. If she has some kind of power or shield up, I don't think it's normal. I can't get a handle on it."

I manage to nod. My head is pounding. Adam's misplaced guilt is assaulting me. "Thank you for coming in anyway," I say to him. "I know you don't like involving yourself in these matters."

Adam doesn't disagree with me.

In fact, my words seem to give him tacit permission to surrender to his own discomfort, and suddenly I'm shotgunned by the weight of his unleashed aversion.

"It's so damn creepy in here," he says, looking around the enclosed space. "I don't know how you do this every day."

There's a sudden upsurge in Hugo's agony, and I nearly strain my neck trying to shake it off.

"You say that," I force out, "as if you think I enjoy being here."

"Don't you?" Adam asks.

I shoot him a dark look. He laughs.

"What?" he says, crossing his arms. "Isn't this, like, your natural habitat? I thought you liked—" Adam physically recoils, metal screeching through the room as he pushes back in his chair, nearly falling over. "Jesus, is he crying?"

I glance at Hugo, and the tension in my body coils tighter. "He's been having a hard time."

"You mean he does this regularly?"

"Most days," I say.

I steel myself before touching my fingers to the window to awaken the glass; a digital list of commands glow green, superimposed over the scene beyond. A melodic murmur echoes through the room.

"Good afternoon, General," says a smooth, disembodied voice. "Play back transcript?"

"Not now," I respond. "Prepare to end session. Page Samuel. Initiate security protocols for prisoner transfer."

"Yes, General."

"Upload today's transcript to my files upon termination of the session. But first, confirm that you've made note of every instance of sound and movement from Rosabelle Wolff today."

A rhythmic ping.

"Confirmed, General."

"Previous transcripts noted only dialogue—or lack thereof—from Rosabelle Wolff. Search through all previous recordings and update existing transcripts to include sound and movement from Rosabelle wherever applicable."

"Yes, General," says the voice. There's a pause, then another rhythmic ping. "Transcripts have been updated."

"Increase the voltage on Rosabelle's manacles to seventy-five percent," I say. "Reduce to forty-five percent when she's safely inside her cell."

"Yes, General. Increasing voltage now."

As always, Rosabelle evinces no reaction to the surge.

In eight days, she's displayed no evidence she even experiences pain. Now, as the manacles radiate what I know to be a breathtaking charge of electricity, she doesn't so much as draw audible breath. She waits patiently to be collected, as lifeless as a doll.

My jaw tightens.

If all this is a strategic effort on her part, I'm forced to admit it's effective. I'm beginning to lose my patience with these methods. I'm losing my patience with *her*.

I'd be tempted to pivot to a less humane approach to provoke a reaction, except that I've witnessed enough of her eccentricities to know that she can somehow deaden herself to suffering, even while maintaining consciousness. Weeks ago I made the deduction that physical torture would not be enough to compel her to speak. Psychological manipulation was my only recourse. I assumed her weakness for her sister would translate to a weakness for her father. Clearly, I was wrong. Clearly, she knows what she's doing.

And I have no idea what she's planning.

"Voltage increased, General. Session has now been terminated."

The lights in the interrogation room brighten to painful levels, a soft alarm chiming through the space. Hugo remains rooted to the floor, his knees pulled up to his chest like a child. He buries his face in his hands as the door unseals, guards storming inside.

Another day, another failure.

My anxiety ratchets only higher.

There's no doubt in my mind that Rosabelle is biding her time. She, like me, was built by The Reestablishment. Our type was bred on cruelty, custom-designed to survive the harshest conditions, trained to thrive as prisoners of war. The trouble is, I've never encountered anyone quite like her before. Not only is she apparently numb to external stimulus, but she's proven immune even to the tech we have that might've shut off her power.

Exposing her to Adam was a worst-case scenario.

I take a slow, even breath as a band of pressure seems to tighten around my skull. I have the ability to sense the emotions of others, but greater than that is my ability to draw upon any latent preternatural power. In a normal scenario I'd be able to take Rosabelle's power and use it against her.

Instead, dealing with her is like handling a dead battery.

Another melodic murmur sounds throughout the room. "Can I assist you with anything else, General?"

"Compile a separate file," I say, "highlighting all of Rosabelle's nonverbal responses over the past eight days. I want a day-over-day comparison."

"Compiling now, General."

"That's all for today."

There's a reverberating slam of a metal door as Rosabelle is safely escorted from the room. In my periphery, Adam startles. I clear all the prompts, ending the comms with another melodic ding.

Finally, reluctantly, I turn back to Adam.

All this time, I've felt him openly staring at me. I've felt his silent, hesitant, confused admiration.

It bothers me.

"Is it weird," he says, his smile growing as he studies me, "that I keep forgetting how fancy you are now?"

"Yes."

He laughs out loud. "It's cool that you're so humble about it."

"It's not a matter of humility," I say, bristling. "I oversee all branches of the military in The New Republic. You'd have to make an effort to forget what I do."

"I never said I forget what you do," he says. "I just keep forgetting your title."

I only stare at him, my impatience building.

"What?" he says. "It keeps changing. Doesn't it keep changing?"

"No."

Adam's frown deepens. "But you've had a couple of title

changes, right?" He bounces his knee again and I snag on the sight of his unforgivable laces, the pinched toe box, the triple-knotted mess. The pounding in my head is only getting worse. I'm reminding myself to say nothing about his shoes, to keep my unsolicited advice to myself, when he adds, "I thought you were a chief commander of something. Or head of state. But the robot just called you General. I think it's fair to say it's a little confusing."

"It's not confusing," I say coldly. "Juliette is head of state. I'm general of defense."

"Can you remind me again how those jobs are different?"

"No."

"It *is* new, though, right? Weren't you recently promoted?"

"No."

I silence another series of incoming notifications on my pager, scrolling through at least a dozen urgent missives to glance at the few highlighted as priority—

Nothing to report. Calm down. She's sleeping.

STOP FUCKING PAGING ME

Bro I think James is on his period

Inconclusive, sir. We'll need another extract from the vial in order to run a new set of trials

I stretch my neck and clench the pager too tightly in my fist, trying to release the tension radiating through my shoulders. I fight to organize my thoughts, but there are too many things vying for my attention. My mind is like a faulty camera lens, hunting for focus and failing.

My head is overrun.

Hugo's soft cries are haunting me; echoes of Rosabelle's skittish movements continue to susurrate through my memory; the low buzz of overhead lights is compounding my headache; the bouncing of Adam's foot is starting to drive me insane.

I close my eyes. Open them.

I miss my wife.

I want to go home.

"Oh," Adam is saying, his frown deepening. "Maybe I'm thinking of Kenji? Did Kenji get a promotion?"

"Two years ago," I say, forcing myself to be present.

Adam's confusion is palpable and annoying. "Someone got a promotion, though, right?" he says. "Why do I feel like someone got a promotion?"

"Maybe you're thinking of James," I say unkindly. Too sharply. "Who was recently *demoted*."

Adam sits back in his chair, one foot propped up on his knee. Bouncing. "Hey, whoa—I'm on your side in this, okay? I'm just as pissed off at James as you are."

"I doubt that."

"Okay," he says slowly. "Whatever. It's not a competition."

I can't seem to breathe deeply enough. This pounding in my skull is nearly blinding. I tell myself to return to center, to finish out this session, to focus only on the emergencies ahead of me. *Priorities.* Instead, I hear myself snap: "Your sneakers are too big for you."

Adam's head shoots up. "My what?"

"Your sneakers," I say, turning my eyes to the window. Hugo is sitting like a dead insect in the corner, collecting dust. As always, I'll need to manage this emotional fallout. "You shouldn't have to pull the laces that tightly. Get a smaller size."

Adam laughs, unamused. "Uh, I've been buying my own shoes all by myself for a long time, man. I think I know my shoe size."

I turn to face him. "Apparently not."

"What the hell is your problem?"

"I know how shoes are supposed to fit," I say, even as I wish I'd never spoken. I don't know why I brought this up. I don't know why I'm still talking. I wish I could take it back. "You shouldn't have to choke the laces in order for the shoes to stay on. If you have to strain the laces like that, then you've chosen the wrong fit for your foot—"

"You know," he says, cutting me off, "it's shit like this that makes people hate you. Why do you need to lecture me about my shoes? Let me choke my fucking laces if I want to. Why do you care?"

"Because someone has to care," I counter. "Someone has to know that there's a correct way of doing things. Why would you choose to do it wrong when there's a better way? Why insist on the path of ignorance simply because it's familiar? And why do you need to use profanity to emphasize your point? How many times have we talked about this?"

"You know what I love?" says Adam, crossing his arms.

I can feel his anger building now.

"I really, really love it when you, the reigning king of virtue, give me life advice."

I shake my head, looking away.

"Like, you could be shooting someone in the face," Adam goes on, "and if I walked by at that exact moment and said, *Holy shit, you just shot someone in the face!* you'd look at me like I was the one who did something wrong."

"I only shoot people when they deserve it," I point out. "Yet you feel the need to punctuate every other sentence with a vulgar epithet that only serves to diminish you in the process—"

"Wow," he says, feigning amazement. "You should be studied. I don't think I've ever met anyone more delusional in my life. Except maybe James, and we both know that's your fault."

"My fault?" I say, stiffening as I turn to face him. Fury radiates through my chest. *"My fault?"*

Adam scowls. "Yes, bro, fucking your fault—"

"If this situation is anyone's fault, it's yours," I say sharply. "You made him think it was okay to disrespect authority, to live arrogantly. You made him think it was okay to be reckless. You made him think it was acceptable to speak using the cheapest words language has to offer—"

"Me?" Adam makes a sound of disbelief. He uncrosses his legs; sits forward; finally stops bouncing. "Are you serious? If I had any influence over that kid I would've prevented him from turning into *you*—"

I physically recoil. "He's nothing like me."

"He's exactly like you!" Adam cries, throwing up his hands before rising to his feet. "You both occupy the same delusional landscape! He thinks he's some kind of superhero. He thinks he can go around murdering bad guys for a living. You made him believe he could grow up to become king of the fucking world—"

"I did no such thing—"

"Bullshit—"

"He never even listens to me," I argue. "I've spent ten years trying to teach him to be disciplined and thoughtful, and instead he's turned out to be entirely unmanageable—"

"I really thought it'd be good for him, you know?" Adam is saying. "I knew he'd seen some dark things. I could tell he was desperate to prove himself. Even as a kid he was doing dangerous shit, always nearly getting himself killed, and I was worried he'd end up hurting himself without an avenue to work out his anger. I thought training him would be productive. I thought he'd at least learn proper self-defense. I thought it would make his life safer. I thought he'd spend a few years working things out of his system and then he'd come to his senses, and instead he's lost his fucking mind and fallen for a psychopath—and all because of you—"

"You coddled him!" I counter. "You gave him too much positive reinforcement. You fed him too many lies about life. You didn't want him to be afraid of the world. You made him think he could be anything he wanted to be if he just believed in himself—"

"Oh yeah? Well, you fucking spoiled him," Adam shouts

back. "You gave him whatever he wanted. You gave him a fancy title and too much power. You let him go everywhere with you. You let him see how people look at you and talk to you and shit their pants around you and he fucking loved every second of it. Hell, he even looks like you—"

"It's not my fault," I say, my voice rising dangerously, "that James decided to take the wealth of knowledge I gave him and use it to make bad decisions—"

"It sure as hell isn't my fault—"

"Yes, it is—"

"No, it isn't—"

"You did this to him," we both say at the same time.

JAMES

2

When my pager goes off for the third time, I unearth it from my pocket and chuck it angrily into the ocean.

Kenji looks up, stunned.

"What the hell is wrong with you?" he says, his heavy boots kicking up sand as he rushes toward the shoreline. He shields his eyes against a cool glare of sunlight. "That's government-issued tech. You can't just throw it into the nuclear-infested waters—"

"Too late," I mutter, glowering at the unsorted test tubes before me. I'm perched on one knee, sinking slowly into cold, damp beach. Judgmental shorebirds stare at me. Crows caw rudely overhead. I'm tired and hungry. My head hurts.

It's possible I've never been so pissed off.

To be fair, I'm not sure anything could've made this day better. It's wet and blustery and smells like sewage. Nests of seaweed, jetsam, and decomposing fish surge in and out with the tide. I slot the sand and sea samples into my kit and listen to Kenji curse colorfully into the wind.

Over the past decade we've dedicated great resources to reviving natural bodies of water, monitoring and rehabilitating marine life. It was one of the many reasons we decided to leave the landlocked middle of the continent and move back to a temperate, coastal area: Juliette, my sister-in-law and revolutionary icon, wanted to be able to keep a closer eye on the ocean.

Obviously there are entire departments dedicated to this work, but once every quarter Warner sends some poor bastard out here to make sure the samples we collect match up with the samples we receive. That's just like him: always checking everyone else's work. Looking over everyone's shoulders. He can't trust people. He needs to micromanage everything—

"All right," says Kenji, stomping unevenly toward me through the sand. "Enough of this shit. You've been in a pissy mood for over a week now, and I'm tired of it."

"I'm not in a pissy mood."

Kenji's pager goes off, blaring with a sound I've lately begun to associate with rage. He glances at it, sighs, and silences the notification. "Look, I'm sorry you went and fell in love with a psychopath—"

"I'm not in love with her," I say sharply.

"Oh, great, what a relief," he says, faking a smile. "Here I was, worried you'd developed feelings for a professional mercenary of The Reestablishment—"

"Jesus." I drag a hand over my eyes.

"—after she'd effortlessly scammed you into bringing her into the heart of the resistance—"

I look up at the sky, exhaling.

"—in order to execute your family and potentially massacre the population"—he holds up a finger—"but only after she slaughtered a few of our people and tried to kill *me* first—"

"Stop." I glare at him. "I'm sick of this conversation. I've heard enough of this shit over the past nine days."

"Oh, wow, you're counting the days, huh?" Kenji raises his eyebrows. "Tell me something: Are you counting the hours and minutes, too? Measuring your life against the last time you had a Rosabelle hit?"

"Shut up."

"I will not shut up. You think I don't know what it's like to be this pathetic? I *am* this pathetic. Why do you think I agreed to come out here in this shitty weather to babysit you while you do a job a worm could do?"

"What?" I frown, forgetting my anger a moment. "Bro, worms don't even have hands."

"Rude of you to hold that against them," he says, crossing his arms. "Worms turn garbage into compost. Worms do more for the world than you do. Worms just eat dirt and mind their business. Worms need a better marketing campaign."

I peer up at him. "Are you feeling okay?"

"Do I seem okay?" he snaps at me. "Are you not hearing me? I'm freezing my ass off on this gross beach talking about worms. No, I am not okay. I'm hiding from Nazeera."

"Right." I give him a loaded look. "Because she tried to say hi to you."

"Yes, because she tried to say hi to me, and don't you dare take that fucking tone with me, as if you have any right to judge. There's only enough room on this planet for one of us to be acting like a hormonal teenager right now, so I suggest you pull yourself together. This is my time to shine."

"Whatever," I mutter. "I'm not acting like a hormonal teenager."

"You've been in a shitty mood ever since Warner locked up your fascist girlfriend for espionage, murder, and conspiracy to commit murder—"

"I'm in a shitty mood because he stripped me of all my security clearances!" I shout, rising to my feet. I drop the remaining test tubes in the sand. "I can't leave The Waffle without a permit. I can't reenter without an extra layer of screening. I have to flash my ID everywhere I go even though everyone's known me since I was a child." I gesture to the samples arrayed before me, rigid with anger. "I can't even do *this* simple job without you breathing down my neck. It's humiliating—"

"You messed up, kid," Kenji says. "You don't get to complain."

I laugh bitterly. "Great. Thanks." I drop back down to my knees and swipe the samples from the ground. Sand clings to my fingers, making me irrationally furious.

Kenji stalks over, looming above me.

"You think things are bad now?" he says. "You think your life sucks because you've been demoted? You have no idea how much worse things could get. Keep this up and Warner will punt you so far down the food chain you'll end up working the information booth in the city center, handing out pamphlets in a hot dog costume."

A ghost crab scuttles by, startling me, making me angrier. "He wouldn't do that."

"The hell he wouldn't," says Kenji. "You have no idea what that man would do. He's so mad at you right now I'm surprised he hasn't kicked you out of his house."

Now I roll my eyes.

"Don't roll your eyes at me," Kenji says, pointing at my face. "*This*, right here—this is your entire problem. You think this is a joke."

"I don't think this is a joke," I say, fury forcing me upright again. A breeze unfurls across the beach, clinking the glass samples against one another. "My entire problem is that everyone *thinks* I think this is a joke—"

"Look, I don't have time for this. I'm trying to save your life right now. Get your shit together. Warner isn't the only one pissed at you. We were all counting on you. We all thought you were smart enough—"

"If you thought I was smart enough, you would've listened to me when I had something to say. No one takes me seriously. No one respects my thoughts or my theories or my instincts—"

"Clearly, we can't trust your judgment."

"That's bullshit!"

"*I gave you one job*," Kenji says, rounding on me. "A simple, straightforward job. I told you to get the mercenary to supermax because I couldn't—because she'd lodged a knife in my leg—and you had the singular, first-class audacity to show up holding her hand with cartoon hearts popping out of your fucking eyes—"

"I wasn't holding her hand!"

"No," says Kenji calmly, unsheathing a rare, focused anger. "You're right, you weren't holding her hand—you were carrying her in your arms like she was some kind of wounded princess—as if she hadn't been recently discovered beside the eviscerated remains of a fellow patient and the slaughtered bodies of our friends—"

"It's not that simple—"

"It's exactly that simple," he says, raising his voice. "While I was getting my wounds healed you thought you'd take your girlfriend on a romantic stroll between murder and prison. You gave Samuel shit for putting cuffs on her, as if she deserved better. You stood guard over her like she was some kind of vulnerable innocent, talked to Warner like he was beneath you—"

"That's not—" I drag my hands down my face. "Look, it wasn't like that."

"James, I love you, but fuck you if you think you can talk to me like I'm an idiot. If it wasn't like that, then what was it? There are cameras in the tunnels, dumbass. You're lucky there was no audio on that security footage, because if there were words to set to a melody, one of us would've already mixed it into a shitty song just to ruin your life. You think this is humiliating?" he says, nodding at me, then the test tubes. "This is us going easy on you."

I blow out a breath, squeezing my eyes shut. Heat moves

up my neck, singes the crests of my cheeks.

Kenji chucks something at my face without warning, and I react instinctively, catching the small plastic packet before realizing what it is.

"Eat something," he says, irritated. "I'm going to do you a favor and assume you're being an asshole because your blood sugar is low."

As I turn it over in my hands, I feel my head catch fire.

Gummy bears.

WARNER

3

"Don't panic, okay?"

Her words reach me through layers of sleep, pushing up like fresh shoots through inches of soil. It takes me a moment to catch up, to sort the sounds into meaning, and when I do—

I sit straight up in a panic, my heart beating violently.

"No," she says, placing a hand on my bare chest, gently guiding me back to bed. "I said *don't* panic."

"Why? What's happening?" I blink fast, struggling to breathe. I fall back on my elbows, a little lightheaded as I search her for signs of danger. "Are you okay, love? What can I do? What do you need?"

"Nothing," she says, though her smile is strained. She's emanating worry. "I'm fine. I'm sorry—"

I push upright, the blanket falling to my waist, the morning air bracing my heated skin. I take her face in my hands and she sighs, relenting as I search her eyes, then further assess her emotional state. Her smile grows steadier as I check the rest of her, skating a hand down her arm, then the curve of her belly. When I feel the familiar kick of a tiny foot under my hand, the responding flight in my chest is so severe it takes my breath away.

This happens most mornings.

Ella says it's the sound of my voice. She says the baby is responding to the sound of my voice. The doctors agree with her; the literature agrees with her. Still, I've refused to take a position on the matter. I don't know how to reconcile the equally annihilating forces of joy and terror that chase this experience.

"You're sure you're okay?" I ask her, and I feel another responding kick under my hand. Then two more.

I'm suddenly winded.

Sometimes I think I might be imagining the rush of inexpressible feeling I lately experience in Ella's presence. It's like the touch of wings; a flutter against my throat.

A second soul.

"I'm fine," she says. "I swear."

Only when I'm certain this is true does my body succumb to a relief so great the feeling seems to dissolve what's left of me. My limbs give out, suddenly leaden. Exhaustion reclaims me. I'm flat on my back as I surrender to the soft bed, sinking into the pillows. I stare, unseeing, at the ceiling.

My heart won't stop racing.

The sheets sigh as Ella shifts, sliding down a few inches, turning on her side to face me. She glides her hand across my chest, then down my torso. Her skin against my skin works like an opiate.

Slowly, I begin to relax.

As if she knows this, she continues to draw soothing motions up my naked body, moving toward my neck, the line of my jaw. She caresses my cheek, her thumb brushing across my cheekbone, and I exhale deeply, feeling a little drugged. Her love is so powerfully resonant that when I allow myself to surrender to the tide, I wish I never had to resurface. It's like being submerged in a euphoric tranquility. Her proximity offers me a relief I can hardly describe. I've never felt safe anywhere but here, next to her.

"Aaron," she whispers.

I turn to face her, my eyes slitting open.

She's in a cropped T-shirt and a pair of underwear. Her top is straining against her breasts, doing nothing for her bump.

She's never not beautiful. It always decimates me.

"You must be cold," I say softly, reaching for her.

She insists she's okay even as she acquiesces, letting me turn her gently. I tuck her into the curve of my body, her back nested against my front. I reach blindly for the blanket, pulling it up around us, and then I press my face to the silken skin of her neck and shoulders and breathe her in, the familiar scent of her calming my senses. I've taken on the weight of concrete.

I'm nearly asleep in seconds.

"Aaron," she whispers again.

My eyes flutter against her neck. I'm half dreaming even as I press a kiss to her skin. "Yes, love?" I murmur.

She experiences a sudden, jolting wave of grief.

"What's wrong?" I say, tensing. My mind fights to sharpen. "What just happened?"

"Nothing," she says tightly. "Nothing, I'm just worried about you. You're doing too much—you're dealing with too much—"

Relief releases me once more, returning me to my body. I exhale heavily.

"I'm fine," I say, pressing another kiss to her jaw, then her shoulder. "I can deal with anything as long as I get to come home to you."

Her responding affection is both wild and tender. It's like being bound in warm light.

Out loud she only sighs, her head tilting back. "Aaron."

"Yes, love?"

"I'm sorry," she whispers.

I draw my hand down her arm, our fingers threading around her belly. My eyes feel permanently closed. My limbs are molten. My body is heating, sinking. "Why are you sorry?"

"I couldn't bring myself to wake you up."

"Wake me up?"

"You were so tired," she says, her worry undercut by a note of pain. "You slept through your alarm this morning and I just couldn't— You were so exhausted last night it was beginning to scare me. I didn't want to wake you up. I told Kenji you might be late, but—"

Now I stiffen.

My eyes fly open, my heart picking up dangerously. I try to lift my head, searching for a window, but I'm somewhere between sleep and panic, and I'm processing facts too slowly. Only then do I realize bands of golden light are struggling beyond the heavy shades, stealing into the room.

"Ella." I'm trying to stay calm. "Love."

"I'm sorry," she whispers again.

"Sweetheart, what time is it?"

She squeezes my hand. "Don't panic, okay?"

"Okay," I lie.

"It's about an hour after sunrise."

I nearly fall out of bed.

JAMES

4

I stare into the distance, studying the eroding cliffs hollowed out along the shore. A sudden gust of wind buffets my body, unsettling my hair. I shove the bag of gummy bears into my pocket without a word, feeling suddenly, deeply uncomfortable.

No one knows I was eating gummy bears when Rosabelle slit my throat. It was a weird detail; it felt weird to mention. I didn't include the part of the story where she looked at me and whispered *You smell like apple* and I felt the heat of her gaze on me like a shot to the heart. It didn't feel like the right note to hit when sharing first impressions of a mercenary. But there was just something about the way she'd looked at me then—something so intense and vulnerable and emotional in her gaze—

Jesus.

I hear it—I hear the way I sound when I think about her and I sound *deranged*.

I press the heels of my hands to my eyes.

If anyone else tried to feed me this kind of bullshit—like, yeah, wow, you should've seen how gorgeous that girl was right before she fucking killed me—I'd think they were unhinged.

It's possible I'm unhinged.

A month ago I thought it was a good idea to launch a covert operation into enemy territory. My instincts had been screaming for a while that something was wrong. Implausible attacks on our soil were escalating. More key figures with old ties to The Reestablishment were turning up dead. After a sudden, unexplained gas explosion at an elementary school, I couldn't take it anymore. It wasn't an accident that over a hundred children died that day; we knew which nefarious force was responsible.

I needed to do something.

I lobbied hard for launching a mission into the Ark. I felt certain that if we didn't find a way to gather intel we might miss something more dangerous. I tried to tell everyone that something was coming; that we needed to know what they were capable of—what else they were planning—but no one would listen to me.

No one had ever breached Ark Island and lived to talk about it.

The last refuge of The Reestablishment is notoriously impenetrable and unknowable—and Warner always insisted we weren't ready yet to take on that risk.

I decided to do it anyway.

At the very minimum, I thought coming home alive from a mission no one had ever survived would finally earn me the respect of my friends and family. Instead, every day has been a new kind of hell. It's true that I'm mostly pissed at Warner. But it's true, too, that Rosabelle has me entirely messed up.

I don't know what's wrong with me.

My last conversation with her plays on repeat in my head all the time. The sound of her voice. The fear and tenderness in her eyes when she told me she trusted me.

I'd be lying if I said I wasn't thinking about her constantly.

Still, I swing wildly back and forth between certainty and uncertainty where she's concerned. I went from seeing her all day, every day—to radio silence. And my mind has filled this dangerous vacuum with vivid memories and disturbing daydreams. The rare glimpse of her smile. The sight of her surrounded by dead bodies. The silky give of her skin. The blood spattered across her face. The breathless sound she made when I touched her. The moment she pointed a gun at Kenji. The way she looked at me like she wanted me. The image of her dead body in the morgue.

I swallow, hard.

I turn my eyes to the water, listening to the wind as the tide grows more turbulent. I squint up at the sky, the gathering gray clouds. The world feels ominous to me in a way it hasn't in a long time.

I feel like I'm losing control of my life.

I've never felt quite like this, never been so distracted or angry or confused, not since I was a kid. My emotions are operating at a heightened pitch, swinging between discomfort, desire, humiliation, fury—

I take a deep, cleansing breath.

When I was looking into Rosabelle's eyes things felt

clearer, but in her absence I've been inundated by calls to get my head checked.

Literally.

I went to visit Adam the other day and he pulled me aside to ask, very seriously, whether I'd consider *seeing a psychiatrist for the unresolved trauma that's leading me to make poor and destructive choices.*

I stuck my head in his freezer for a full minute just so I wouldn't lose my shit in front of his kids.

Everyone thinks I've lost my mind.

The night Warner put Rosabelle in prison, I tried to get him to see my side in all this, but he shut me down so fast—and with so much venom—I was stunned. Furious. We haven't had a proper conversation with each other since.

Worse, he had no trouble shutting me out.

I was a little more optimistic a few days ago; I thought the ice between us wouldn't last. I thought it'd turn out like it did in the movies: we'd bump elbows in the kitchen reaching for the same tub of protein powder and he'd realize he couldn't do this without me.

Nope.

My older brother deleted me from his life, as if our yearslong bonding montage never even happened. I'm just a subordinate to him now. He hardly speaks to me anymore; instead he pages me all the time, ordering me around like I'm some kind of nameless foot soldier.

Warner and I have fought before, but never exactly like this, and never for this long. Every interaction between us is now clipped and volatile. Not even Juliette seems capable of mediating. She's made a couple of half-hearted attempts to get us in the same room, but it's clear she's on Warner's side. Hell, everyone is on his side.

In a stunning reversal, I've managed to unite everyone against me in his favor. Warner's never been so unanimously supported in anything. Ever.

"C'mon, man," Kenji says, peering up at the sky. "Wrap this up. It looks like it's going to rain and I want to head back."

My jaw tenses. "I thought you were avoiding Nazeera."

"I'm sorry"—he raises his eyebrows at me—"I didn't realize I needed your permission to change my mind. Besides, I just realized I can avoid her in the warmth of my own home." He hesitates. "Maybe."

"Has she even given you anything yet?" I ask. "Any leads, any intel? Any indication of what's coming?"

"Who?" He frowns. "Nazeera?"

I exhale sharply, irritated. "Obviously I'm talking about Rosabelle."

"*Obviously?*" he echoes, studying the kit of ocean samples still open before me. "How is that obvious? The rest of us have other things on our minds. The rest of us aren't obsessed with a girl rotting in prison for murder."

I glance up at him. "Didn't Nazeera try to kill you once?"

"That was an accident! And she only did it because she liked me," he adds, his voice quieting. "Damn. She used to like me."

"And you think *I'm* the idiot?"

"You know what? I'm leaving." He shoots another look at the sky and starts moving. "You can walk home."

"Why won't you answer my question?" I call out as he goes. "Have you figured out what's in the vial yet?"

"That's none of your business," Kenji calls over his shoulder. "And you know it."

"It's been nine days and you still don't know anything, do you? You still haven't gotten her to speak, have you? I bet she hasn't said a single word."

Kenji stops in place, turning around to glare at me just before his pager goes off again. He scans it, his mouth flattening into a grim line. "I need to take this."

I shake my head, my mood darkening only further. "Whatever."

"Okay, what the hell is wrong with you?" he says, stomping toward me. "Is this some kind of delayed puberty? Are you about to grow your first chest hair?"

I flip him off without looking at him.

"Listen," Kenji tries again, "if you tell anyone I said this I'll deny it until the day I die, but Warner is, like, genuinely hurt right now. You're treating him like shit, and, believe it or not, he doesn't deserve it."

"I'm treating *him* like shit?" I look up, eyes wide. "I can't even use the elevator in my own house without a chaperone! I can't access the gym in the mornings! He's docked my pay—put me on probation—"

"C'mon, James." Kenji looks disappointed. "You know

Warner better than anyone, and you don't need me to tell you that our favorite emotionally stunted jackass might be feeling heartbroken and betrayed by your stupid, reckless behavior. If you want to fix this, you need to start by apologizing."

"How many more times do I need to apologize?" I shout, nearly choked with anger. "I've apologized a thousand times already—"

"Not for this, you haven't."

"*I didn't do anything wrong!*"

"Here we go again." Kenji rolls his eyes. "You know what? I actually think Warner is going easy on you. You have no idea what we're dealing with right now. On top of everything else he has to manage, Warner has to mitigate the chaos *you* brought into our lives—"

"If I don't know anything, it's because no one is telling me anything," I say, struggling to rein in my temper. "All I want to do is help. Why do you think I'm so pissed off? I'm fucking *worried*. We need her to talk before it's too late—"

"Trust me, Warner is doing his best."

"Warner doesn't know how to deal with her!" I explode. "Their temperaments are too similar—"

"Bro, you're in no position to talk. You spent almost two weeks with her and you couldn't get her to give up shit."

I turn partly away, my fists flexing.

"Maybe not," I admit quietly. "But I learned enough about her to tell you this: Rosabelle isn't going to open up to any of you. I'm the one who spent eight hours a day with her. I'm the one who knows her, who understands her—"

"Jesus. James, do you hear yourself right now?"

"Look, believe whatever you want," I say, heat radiating up my neck. "But I'm the only one of us who made it into the Ark and out again. I'm the only real resource we have right now, and instead of utilizing me, no one will even let me near her." I shake my head. "No, you know what? It's worse than that—everyone is acting like I'm dead."

"What the hell is that supposed to mean?"

"I've been shunned and shut out of my own life! Cut off from my own family—"

"Because you've proven you can't be trusted—"

"Do you truly believe that?" I say, turning angrily to face him. "Do you really believe you can't trust me? *Me?* A lifetime of dedication and you think I'd sell you out? That I'd risk endangering the lives of everyone I love—"

Kenji laughs, stunned. "C'mon, man, you already did."

"And I'm telling you, for the hundredth time: I don't agree."

"She murdered three people!" he shouts back. "She would've murdered me if you'd given her the chance! She was found in possession of a nefarious vial, the contents of which are so deadly and volatile we still haven't been able to form a comprehensive assessment of its capabilities—"

"I know, I was there—"

"James—"

"—and I'm not trying to say that she's on the right side of history." I cut him off. "I'm not trying to say she's a misunderstood saint. I'm just trying to point out that there's more going on with her. She knows something. She was going to tell me something important in those tunnels—"

Kenji cuts me off with a loud, aggravated sound.

"All right, *enough*," he cries, squeezing his eyes shut. "I can't fucking take it anymore. I need you to stop talking like this before I fully lose my mind, okay? I've already lived through this once. I've served my time. You have no idea how exhausting it was to listen to Juliette go on and on and on about how Warner *isn't as bad as people think* and *he isn't a monster* and *don't hurt his tiny little feelings or I'll kill you*—"

"Well, she was right."

"No," Kenji says flatly, opening his eyes. "She wasn't. Warner is ruthless. When he's on your side—great, you win. When he's not"—he laughs, darkly—"good luck. I love that man like a brother but you haven't seen him the way I've seen him. You were too young to know him the way I've known him. I firmly believe that without Juliette he would've lost his soul a long time ago. And let me be perfectly clear," he adds, "that kind of connection—the connection he has with J? That only happens once in a lifetime. Trust me. The rest of us losers are not the chosen ones."

"I'm not—Kenji, I'm not trying to compare my situation with theirs! I already told you I'm not in love with her!"

"I think you doth protest a bit too much, bro."

I hesitate; take a step back. "What?"

"What?" he says defensively.

"Are you quoting *Hamlet* at me right now?"

"Fuck you, I like Shakespeare."

"I never said I didn't like Shakespeare," I say, confused. I feel suddenly exhausted. I push my hands through my hair, search the darkening skies. "Look, I'm just trying to point out that no one has spent as much time with her as I have. I can understand why you don't want to give her a chance— but what about me? Why is no one willing to believe *me*? Don't my thoughts and opinions count for anything? I want to keep my people safe, just like the rest of you."

For the first time, Kenji goes quiet.

He studies me.

"And maybe I do care about her," I say into the silence. "Maybe that does make me an idiot. But it also makes me an asset. I know things about her. She feels comfortable with me. You need me; you need my insight. And if you don't let me into this process, you're going to fail. I keep trying to tell you that you can't keep her locked up like this—"

"Nope. You need to stop now." Kenji holds up a hand before looking over his shoulder, searching for ghosts. "I'm not supposed to be discussing this with you. If Warner finds out I so much as let you say her name in front of me, he's going to lose his shit—"

"*I don't care*," I say, my voice rising an octave. "I need you to hear me. The very fact that she's played prisoner for over a week has to be part of a larger strategy. I think she wants us to let our guard down. I think she's pretending we've got the upper hand, that she can be managed safely behind bars.

But when she's ready she's going to disappear, and you won't even realize she's gone—"

"That's your big theory?" Now Kenji makes a sound of disbelief. "You think she's going to escape? Bro, supermax is a relic of The Reestablishment. Not only is she monitored around the clock, but the prison was purpose-built by the fascists to make escape impossible—"

"*What on earth is wrong with you?*"

Kenji and I both look up, struck, at the sound of his voice. Warner is standing on an outcropping just above us, his eyes flashing with electric anger. "Does this bleak period in our lives strike you as the best time to ignore my pages? Of all the stupid, irresponsible—"

"Whoa, hey, what's going on?" Kenji asks, his body tensing. "What's happening?"

Warner's expression goes flat and cold. He turns to look at me with exaggerated reluctance, as if there's a literal gun to his head. "I need to talk to you," he says.

I'm rendered still, even as my heart starts hammering. "Why?"

"The girl," he says, "is missing."

JAMES

5

Despite everything, my face splits into an enormous smile. Vindication soars inside of me. "Didn't I literally just—"

"No." Kenji points at me. "Absolutely not. This is not the time. *Fuck.*"

He immediately begins pacing.

Even now, Warner looks down at him with mild disgust. "Foul language is a cheap feast for an underfed mind."

"Thanks, I love it," says Kenji. "I'll ask Winston to whip that up in needlepoint. What do you mean she's missing? Missing how? Missing for how long? Did we catch her on camera? Did anyone see her leave?"

"No."

"I just asked you five different questions, and you're giving me a syllable in response?"

I look to Warner for his rebuttal, but he jumps off the outcropping and onto the sand, landing so suddenly and silently I recoil when I realize how close we are.

"No," he says again, directing his words to Kenji. "No one caught her on camera. No one saw her leave."

"How is that possible?" Kenji counters, stunned.

"If I knew that," he says, "I wouldn't be here right now." And then, for the second time, Warner turns his cold green eyes on me. "We've already dispatched units across the city—but I need to know, right now, whether she ever indicated what her plans might've been for that vial, or whether she was looking for any particular landmarks—"

"Wait," says Kenji, frozen in shock. "Hold on a second. She took the vial?"

"She took what she believed to be the vial," Warner says. "I've personally verified that the original is untouched in its secure location."

Kenji exhales in relief.

"Don't be so quick to celebrate," says Warner. "The dupe had a tracker in it. We traced its location to a party supply store, where we discovered it stashed in the pocket of a mannequin." He hesitates. "The mannequin was dressed as a clown."

I laugh out loud.

"You think this is funny?" Kenji turns on me. "You think it's hilarious that your girlfriend is pranking us on her way to kill everybody?"

Warner looks furious, but it's the first time in days that I've so much as smiled, and it feels really good.

Apparently, Rosabelle has a dark sense of humor.

Leaving the vial with the clown was her way of saying she'd known it was a fake—that she took it only to buy herself time. While Warner was tracking a false lead, she got a head start disappearing.

"Yeah," I say, fighting my smile. "I do think it's hilarious. Except I don't think she's trying to murder anyone, so

I'm not really worried about it."

Warner turns his full and undivided attention on me. "A professed executioner of The Reestablishment has broken out of a maximum-security prison cell without a trace, and you're *not really worried about it?*"

"She told you she's an executioner?" I ask, still grinning. "Kenji said you couldn't get her to talk."

"I never said that," Kenji says quickly. "In fact, I never said anything—"

Warner doesn't bite; he keeps his eyes on me. "Why don't you think she's going to murder anyone?"

I raise my eyebrows. "Are you really here to ask me what I think? After icing me out for over a week, you're finally ready to hear what I have to say?"

My brother's expression only darkens.

Kenji laughs, but he sounds nervous. "Yeah, maybe we should table this conversation for another time—"

"Don't make me regret it," Warner says to me. "I'm only here because I have a responsibility to make sure I've explored every possible avenue for answers."

"Fine." I cross my arms against my chest. "Has she been eating?"

Warner stills. "What?"

"In prison. Has she been eating?"

He studies me for what feels like too long, clearly weighing whether to share this information. Finally, he says, "I came here to ask *you* questions."

I shrug. "You want me to tell you what I think she's doing

or where she's gone—but I can't offer confident answers without knowing more about her recent behaviors." I nod at him. "Has she been eating? Yes or no?"

Warner exhales slowly. The gathering clouds part briefly, a blade of sun slanting across his face, severing him into equal parts light and shadow. "The fugitive," he says, "is in roughly the same physical state now as she was upon incarceration."

I have to assume this means she's been eating just enough. Not really the answer I was hoping for, but getting him to give up even a crumb of information feels like a win.

I try again: "Has she been sleeping?"

"No," says Warner.

"No?" I echo, raising my eyebrows. "Not at all?"

"Why do you need to know this stuff?" Kenji asks, shifting uneasily. "What does eating and sleeping have to do with where she's going? This girl is on the loose—we need to get moving—"

"Wait," Warner says quietly, watching me. "James wants to know how the fugitive is feeling."

"Ew," says Kenji. "Can we go?"

"So she just . . . hasn't been sleeping?" I ask Warner. "Not even a little?"

"Not well."

Even now, after everything, I can hardly control the uncharted feeling that moves through me at the admission. Apparently, the instinct to protect Rosabelle hasn't died in me at all. Nine days and she's hardly slept. That makes two of us.

Great, I hate it.

"Thank you for the insight," Warner says, straightening. His eyes go cold. "I see nothing's changed."

I look up, stunned. Instantly pissed off.

A little humiliated.

I can't believe I didn't see it right away: he was only answering my questions to gain something in return.

Dickhead.

It's always embarrassing to be emotionally examined by Warner. Sometimes I really hate that he can read other people's energies. He's constantly giving me shit for taking my healing abilities for granted—and he's probably right that it's made me reckless—but I don't think he realizes he's just as blinded by his own powers.

Warner's greatest strength is also his greatest weakness.

He relies too much on his ability to sense other people's emotions, forgetting that it's not a precise science. There can be nuance in feeling—people can feel multiple things at the same time—and it can all be true, and it can all be changing.

When I finally look back at him, he's still watching me.

"What?" I say angrily.

"I'm well aware of my deficiencies," he says after a moment. "I've been laid low many times by my deficiencies. You, on the other hand, have yet to be battered by the closed fist of your own arrogance."

I laugh, the sound hollow. "How would you know?"

"You lack humility," he says.

"Me?" My eyes widen. "Have you looked in the mirror lately?"

"Confidence and arrogance are diametrically opposed," he says with deathly calm. "If you were wiser you'd understand the distinction."

"You never answered one of Kenji's earlier questions," I say, ignoring this. "How long has Rosabelle been missing?"

Warner holds my gaze, his jaw tensing. "We have reason to believe she left the prison grounds just over an hour ago."

"*An hour?*" Kenji gapes at Warner. "You waited an entire hour to tell me this?"

Warner pinches the bridge of his nose. "Why are you so loud?"

"Why do you look like shit?" says Kenji, inspecting him up close.

Warner lifts his head. He looks offended, which I find quietly hilarious.

It improves my mood a little.

"Okay, all right," Kenji says, relenting. "You don't look like shit. But you look a little rough. Did you even get any sleep last night? I talked to J and she said—"

"Shut up," says Warner quietly.

Just like that, my improved mood is gone.

Heat coils in my chest, galvanizing into resentment. Suddenly Warner's intentions are crystal fucking clear: he didn't come here to repair things between us. He's not interested in my participation. He came here only to mine me for answers like I'm some civilian eyewitness to a crime.

He's still treating me like a traitor. Like an *idiot*. As if he wasn't the one who taught me everything I know.

Excellent.

Really fucking excellent.

I pack up my sample kit immediately, snapping the clips shut in two satisfying motions. The wind batters my back and I welcome it. I feel suddenly hot, my head full of steam, but the adrenaline is somehow calming.

I stalk off without a word.

"Hey," Kenji calls out. "Where the hell do you think you're going?"

"I'd tell you," I shout back, "but you don't have the necessary security clearance to know."

Kenji laughs, the sound colored with disbelief. "Are you joking? You can't leave right now— We need your help—"

I keep walking, well aware I'm being immature, and too angry to care.

"James." Warner doesn't raise his voice, but somehow it carries.

I ignore him.

"*James.*"

I ignore him again.

No one follows me, and I don't look back.

I'm done being patient. I'm done waiting for Warner to realize I'm not some inexperienced, emotional child. All the people I care about think I'm some broken, helpless kid who still wakes up screaming every night. Maybe I'm still broken, but I'm not helpless anymore, and while the nightmares keep coming, I stopped screaming years ago.

Warner wants to be an asshole and ice me out?

No problem.

There's only one way to fix this situation now. If they won't give me respect, I have to demand it. I'll force his hand, piss him off, and prove him wrong by doing what he can't do on his own—not because he's incapable, but because he's got his head shoved so far up his own ass he can't see that I'm useful.

And I'm really fucking useful.

Maybe, if he'd asked politely, I'd have told him exactly where to start looking for Rosabelle.

ROSABELLE

6

I duck instinctively between buildings as shadows shift in my periphery, holding my breath until I'm convinced the movement was caused by nothing more than a rearrangement of the clouds. I was caught in a brief, intense downpour as I crossed the city on foot, and I stifle the impulse to shudder as a frigid gust barrels into the narrow alley, sealing cold into the damp, ill-fitting polyester of my outfit. Of all the variables beyond my control, the weather is the most unpredictable at the moment, and I'm running out of time.

I need to identify a bolt-hole, and fast.

A snippet of conversation carries on the wind, which then delivers a rush of incoming footsteps, and I stiffen, retreating into the deepest shadows, pressing my body flush against the wall. Only when I'm certain I'm alone do I dart around the corner.

I run silently along a low fence toward a nondescript warehouse that I know has only two cameras, both of which are directed toward the northwest side of the building. I did several earlier scans of the area and identified limited gaps in surveillance here, which—

Well, at least it's not poorly secured, for once.

I take a steadying breath, glancing quickly between buildings, then take cover behind a maintenance truck, its rugged wheels half as tall as I am. I crouch low beside the chassis, then assess the undercarriage of the vehicle, deciding it might prove a decent hiding spot should I need to take cover again. The sky rumbles in the distance.

The air smells like rain.

I peer up at the clouds, watching them move at an unnerving pace that indicates the winds are getting worse. The only real benefit to the weather is that this private airfield is nearly deserted. A preliminary analysis of the scattered aircraft and their insignias indicate that this is a military outpost, which was what I'd been hoping to find.

Still, there's nothing to celebrate.

Nine days I spent trying not to break under the emotional sledgehammer of my father's face. Nine days I spent being tortured in ways no training exercise ever prepared me for. Nine days of endless, unceasing nightmares.

My father.

Not now.

I glance up at the silent red lights still flashing in the windows of the central office in the distance, the insistent strobe reminding me, without warning, of the familiar blue light of surveillance—

Of home.

I brace myself as a wave of disorientation moves through me. I remind myself to be here, where my feet are; here, where the cold pavement is hard under my hands;

here, where the air is crisp; here, where my heart hardens against my ribs.

Only criminals need privacy, Rosa.

Only criminals need—

I'm here.

Here, where the wind pushes through the grassy field in the distance, where damp, synthetic fabric is suctioned uncomfortably to my skin, where water droplets still cling to my eyelashes. Here and not there, on Ark Island, where my sister, Clara, still rots in an asylum. Here and not there, in prison, where my father, Hugo, grew straight out of the grave of my memories, limbs pushing up like maggots from the earth to form a man I hadn't seen in ten years. Of all things, it's his voice that haunts me most.

Rosa—ROSA—

No.

Rosa, is your mother still alive? How's Clara?

You've been dead inside for years, I tell myself.

They lied to you, Rosa; I never left you—

No—

I didn't leave you—

Die, I remind myself. Die.

Surveillance is security, Rosa. Only criminals—

Mentally I fold my father into an envelope, push the envelope through a shredder, set the shredder on fire.

The sky ruptures.

The world seems to roar as it unleashes a violent torrent of rain, icy sheets pelting the ground so hard the deluge sounds like hail. I grit my teeth and tug my hood as far forward as it will go, resisting the impulse to wrap my arms around myself for warmth. Much as it might provide me the illusion of comfort, I need to keep my hands free and my body ready; precious seconds could cost me everything.

I still haven't sourced a proper weapon.

The clouds are moving quickly enough to shift around the sun erratically, shafts of illumination appearing and evaporating in dizzying flashes. I watch dark and light change hands with the bated breath of a gambler waiting to see how the dice will fall—

Without warning, the sun snuffs out.

I take the small win, exhaling as a vein of lightning streaks silently across the darkening sky. Cold numbs my extremities, windswept rain seeping more aggressively into the damp canvas of my tennis shoes. I peer through the downpour as a roll of thunder cracks in the distance. Uniformed personnel patrolling the airstrip are beginning to look around with increasing uncertainty. Most appear to have been called away by the recent security alert, and now the remaining few—six, by my count—appear to be considering shelter indoors.

I clench my teeth harder, refusing to acknowledge the fatigue in my bones or the loss of feeling in my toes. If I can be anything, I can be patient.

Patience is its own weapon.

It took longer than I'd hoped to orient myself after emerging from the maximum security prison—my calculations were close, but not exact—and I had to make some inadvisable choices in the pursuit of a map, a sense of direction, and a change of clothes—but more than that, the world of The New Republic was a piercing shock.

I don't know what I was expecting.

Sharper teeth, perhaps.

Instead, I was offered a soft landing in a sea of unmanaged chaos. People and vehicles dotted everything like so much careless seasoning; I couldn't figure out what they were doing or why. There didn't appear to be any system governing their actions; no instructions or reminders were delivered over central comms. In fact, many people appeared to be outside for no reason at all: idling on sidewalks or else watching leashed animals defecate on patches of grass. There were no soldiers on patrol; no guards stationed at intervals; no checkpoints; no quiet zones—not a single armed officer already waiting to intercept me.

Worse: it was *loud*, everywhere.

I'd thought it was just the patients at the rehab facility who acted without composure and restraint. I was wrong. Pedestrians everywhere spoke in unregulated tones all around me, with no apparent fear of being overheard or recorded or reported.

I felt like a time traveler to a land long extinct.

I soon realized that surveillance around the city was nearly nonexistent, particularly in residential zones.

High-density areas were better equipped, but these

measures were consistent only in their inconsistency. Some streets had cameras; others did not. As I trekked across city blocks on foot, the cameras I did spot were often different makes and models, many originating from diverse manufacturers. Some were visibly old. Others newer. Some with audio-recording capacity, others without. Very few models were advanced enough to support facial recognition technology—and there appeared to be no great logic underpinning any of these decisions.

This was astonishing.

In the absence of a streamlined, cohesive system, there could be no centralized surveillance apparatus in The New Republic. No unilateral network responsible for monitoring civilians; no database accounting for every person; no single purveyor of security equipment; no principal organization devoted entirely to dissecting the micro movements of its citizens. Instead, civilians appeared to live their lives entirely unregulated.

It soon became clear to me that I was dealing with a level of incompetence so profound it was almost impossible to believe.

I simply stopped moving.

I stood stock-still as people walked past, their eyes glancing off my uncovered face and stolen clothes without consequence to any of us.

At one point an older woman smiled at me and said, "Good idea with that jacket, dear. I can feel the storm coming in my bones."

I'd stolen the jacket from a teachers' lounge after picking a few locks in a shamefully unsecured elementary school. I wandered the unmonitored halls and quickly located a bulletin board with bright letters that read GEOGRAPHY TAKES US PLACES! under which was a colorful map of my present location along with a number of important landmarks helpfully illustrated with pictures and street names.

"Thank you," I said to the older woman, who flashed me another smile before moving on.

It occurred to me, as I stood there in my second change of clothes on a cracked sidewalk in a modest residential neighborhood, that by the time anyone even noticed I'd broken out of prison I'd already be halfway across the city. It would take them days to catch up to me—and that's only if I stayed in one location.

These people, I realized, were breathtakingly stupid.

I'd paused on the sidewalk for just long enough to wonder how the rebels ever managed to defeat a force as powerful as The Reestablishment, and as I turned this idea over in my mind a dusty car pulled into a sloped driveway across the street. As one, the small family popped open doors, each one like a muted gunshot.

I recoiled like I'd been hit.

Unfolding before me was a moment of mundanity from the kind of life I'd never known. I hadn't seen anything so prosaic since I was a child.

The trunk sprung open with an inelegant *thunk*.

Little arms and legs pushed out of the car at once,

then collided on the pavement only to push each other. A frazzled mother rolled her eyes as she batted blindly at her hair, searching for the unseasonal sunglasses perched atop her head.

I held my breath.

The two children screamed at an unreasonable decibel level and my eyes darted to the neighbors' doors and windows, bracing for an altercation.

Where were the soldiers?

Did they not assign officers to residential neighborhoods to keep order?

I looked back at the family in time to watch one child pretend to go boneless, sliding to the filthy ground with a choked gurgle that made my heart clench reflexively.

I'd closed my eyes.

The child was playing a game, I told myself. The child was not receiving a punishment for a sound violation. The parents would not be punished for—

"If you're going to play dead," someone shouted, "can you pretend to be zombies, at least?"

My eyes had flown open.

The dad was hauling bags into his arms. "I could use the help of some nice, slow-moving zombies with all these groceries—"

Groceries.

Groceries.

A sharp pang of hunger lances through me, returning me roughly to the present moment, the sound of rain roaring in my ears.

Not now, I tell my mind.

Not now, not now.

Not ever.

I press a hand to my chest, my heart beating too hard beneath the breastbone. My head has lately been overrun with spirals of thought and explosive feeling—refusing to remain contained—and it's scaring me. I was fine before I came to this strange place with its strange people and their loud, unrestrained voices.

My mind was small; my heart was smaller.

Everything inside me had been hermetically sealed and stowed away in locked compartments. Now I feel as though a tornado has torn me open, and when I'm being honest with myself I know exactly who to blame.

Can you trust me?

Stop.

Rosabelle, do you trust me?

I close my eyes, pressing my shaking hands to the cold, wet ground. I inhale the icy air, tasting rain.

I've been living here too long.

Almost a month I've spent in a world without the Nexus—without synthetic intelligence—without the constant fear of looking into someone's eyes and being surveilled for information.

I have a job to do; it's time to go home.

It was a relief to discover that, all this time, I'd been deposited on the southwestern coast of what used to be

North America. All these weeks of not knowing my location had made it difficult to strategize. Now at least I know that I'm not so far from the Ark as to make the journey home feel impossible—and yet not close enough to accept anything less efficient than a plane for transportation.

I sigh.

Reflexively, I lean my aching body against a massive tire of the maintenance truck, then quickly straighten, refusing to accept help even from inanimate objects.

The trouble is I trust nothing, dead or alive.

Rosabelle, do you trust me?

Stop—

If you trust me, we can fix this together. If you trust me, everything is simple—

STOP, I scream in the silence of my mind.

My heart continues to race and I exhale hard, wicking away the memories, forcing my mind to blank. I clench and unclench my deadened fists, then reassess the parked jets through the unrelenting downpour.

They look new, or at least well-maintained, but they're unmistakably older models built for an era of weaker security. They have internal combustion engines, not electric motors; requiring fuel, not batteries. They don't appear to be secured by external locking mechanisms or even basic biometric scans.

Essentially: unprotected.

I spent the last decade of my life surviving on an island where every person is connected to a neural network—a network that effectively transforms all beings, human and animal, into active recording devices. Every pair of eyes is a camera; every thought uploaded to a server; every word spoken and unspoken transmitted to a central surveillance office.

No one is safe.

No mother is spared spying on her child; no husband spared spying on his wife. But here—

I have no idea how they keep order.

I suppose it's possible that the weak security measures of the mainland are enough to keep its civilians in line, but their outdated technology is so unsophisticated I'm almost disappointed. The rebels don't appear to understand how vulnerable they are. Hacking these ancient systems will require little effort.

Still, I'm not prepared to leave.

Not only would it be impossible to fly in this weather, but I can't face Klaus without the right weapon; the synthetic brain that controls the surveillance technology of Ark Island is too inhuman to be killed easily. My only chance at disrupting the system, destroying the Ark, and saving my sister requires tracking down the authentic vial of earth—which means the hardest part of my mission is still ahead of me.

And I need to be untraceable.

I'll have to find a new source of shelter every night, but first I need to verify my exit plan. My short-term goal is to wait for nightfall before stowing away in a nearby hangar, where I'll be close enough to test my theories about these jets. I'll need at least a few days to do some basic reconnaissance, not only at the airfield but—

"Hey," he whispers. "Why are you dressed like a cat?"

My body turns to lead.

ROSABELLE

7

As if in slow motion, I turn around.

The sight of him strikes me harder than I expect. My pulse picks up an erratic, dangerous rhythm; goose bumps come alive on my skin. Impossibly, my heart beats harder, my chest compressing. I feel a terrible tremble in my hands and I close them into fists, then lose two full seconds looking into his eyes, tearing away only to lose another three to the study of his features.

The blood rushes from my head.

"No," I whisper.

In response, James almost smiles. "I'll try not to take that personally."

I sink back against the truck, finally relinquishing a measure of control. I need to lean against something, brace myself against something. I'm unmoored, as always, by the potent force of his presence. There's something electric about James's spirit, the effect heightened by the high contrasts he carries. The staggering build of him tempered by the warmth in his eyes; the harsh cut of his face softened by the freckles dusted across his nose.

Everything about him is both playful and brutal.

A raindrop unhitches from his hair and I watch,

mesmerized, as it wends its way down his cheek, surrendering to the soft curve of his mouth. My eyes linger there too long, heat rising up inside me, steaming my cold head. In stillness his beauty is alarming enough, but he's most terrifying when he moves. When he laughs and looks around, when he walks across a room—

When he makes direct eye contact.

Even now, here, as the rain shatters around us, James is looking at me with unyielding amusement, his head canted in silent challenge.

"You have cat ears," he says.

I try to speak. My lips part.

I manage only to exhale.

He reaches out slowly, softly touching the small, pointed ear attached to my hood. "I have so many questions," he says, looking me over as if we have time. As if we're not drowning.

As if I'm not being hunted.

You'd never know a storm was raging, that a security alert had been issued throughout the city, that lightning had begun to flash all around us. A different version of me might've underestimated him once, might've thought I could catch him off guard, disarm him in an instant.

I know better now than to believe anything about James is casual.

I feel myself growing only more frantic as he studies me, his eyes lingering along the lines of my body as he takes in the too-small fit of the costume I'm wearing. I'd grabbed it from the party supply store to replace the stolen teacher's clothes. I changed several times upon exiting the prison, discarding outfits on principle.

My last attempt was a bit reckless.

The poorly sewn sleeves are a little too short, the rough seams of the shoulders just a little too tight. I'd reached quickly for what I'd thought was a simple, all-black outfit. And I know the moment James spots the tail, because he makes a choked sound, somewhere between delight and disbelief.

"I thought it was a ninja costume," I whisper.

Now he laughs out loud.

He throws his head back and laughs with his entire body, the sound all but lost in the storm, and I watch him helplessly, with growing desperation.

Help, I want to scream.

James has an effect on me I never knew was possible; an effect I don't even know how to name—

My instincts want to sleep when he's nearby.

My brain tries to shut down its defenses. My nervous system begins to quiet. My bones unclench; my eyelids feel heavy; exhaustion overtakes me.

The fight simply leaves my body.

I'd been relieved, days and days ago, by the idea that I'd never see him again. I'd been certain I'd never feel this kind of weakness again. Never be this close to him again. Never glimpse this smile again.

And now—

My breaths grow shallow, my eyes closing as a wave of

cold panic crashes through my body.

"Is this—" He reaches for my wrist and I stop breathing altogether, holding still as his thumb softly grazes the short cuff. "I'm sorry," he says, still fighting a smile, "but is this a children's costume?"

My cheeks heat.

"Rosabelle." He says my name like I'm in trouble. "You've got the full force of the resistance flooding the streets, snipers stationed on rooftops ready to take you out, and you've been running around town in a little kid's cat onesie? With a tail?"

"I was— The inseam of an adult size would've been too long on me." I falter, mortified. "I couldn't— There was no time to try on different sizes—"

"*Wow,*" he says, his eyes shining.

I shake my head. "Please," I say. "Please don't do this. Don't make me do this."

He releases my wrist and I nearly give it back.

"Do what?" he asks.

This isn't fair. I can hardly breathe. I'm so disarmed around him I don't even realize I'm practically begging when I say, "I really, really don't want to kill you."

He leans in.

Suddenly he's so close I can feel the heat of him. So close I can almost count his freckles; so close I can no longer feel the cold, can no longer access my mind.

I think I might be trembling.

He whispers, "That's practically a declaration of love, Rosabelle Wolff."

I take a sharp breath and draw back, my heart slamming painfully against my ribs. I try to clear my head, but I'm up against the truck, and I've only bought myself a few inches. My hood slips off, exposing my face to freshly windswept rain. "How did you even find me?"

James considers this a moment, then reaches for me slowly, as if approaching a wild animal. I hold still, trying not to exhale as he pulls the hood back over my head. I feel him adjust the wilting cat ears.

"Everyone else thinks you're on your way to commit mass murder," he says. "They've taken positions all over the city, covering major landmarks and densely populated areas." He shakes his head, releasing me. "This is the closest airbase to the prison. I knew once you realized where you were, you'd be trying to find the most efficient way to get home."

My heart is so loud now I can almost hear it over the rain. "You don't know that," I say faintly. "Maybe I am trying to commit mass murder."

His eyes soften in a way that scares me. "Liar."

"You can't make me stay here."

He briefly looks away, over his shoulder. "You know I can't let you leave."

"Just pretend you never found me." I sound desperate, even to myself. "You can walk away right now—"

Slowly, he shakes his head. Even more slowly, he rises to his feet, towering over me, blocking out the rain. "You're soaked through the bone, Rosabelle. You've barely slept in days. You're clearly not eating enough. You need to get out of the storm. You need sleep. You need soup." Then, studying me: "Do you like soup?"

He's silent for long enough that I realize he's waiting for an answer.

"Is that a real question?" I ask, frowning at the blur of red lights still flashing in the distance.

"Do I look like I'm joking?" he says, crossing his arms.

I meet his eyes. "You want to know if I like soup?"

"Yes."

"*Now?*"

"Yes."

"I—I don't know," I say, confused.

"What do you mean you don't know?"

This turn of the conversation is disorienting me; my panic is still coiling. I rack my mind, trying to take inventory of the rations Clara and I have been allotted in the past decade, while simultaneously trying to determine the most discreet exit out of the airfield. I'm going to have to change plans. "Are you talking about liquid soup?"

"*Liquid soup?*" he repeats, his arms dropping to his sides. "Is there another kind of soup?"

I blink up at him, wiping rainwater from my eyes. "Sometimes they give us porridge."

"Jesus." His jaw tenses. "Look, I need to get you inside, get you warm. You're going to die out here."

"I'll die when I'm ready," I say to him.

A ghost of an angry smile touches his lips.

He pushes wet hair off his forehead and looks around at the darkening sky, bands of golden light still struggling to break through the clouds. "You're really going to make me work for this, aren't you?" he says, returning his gaze to me. "In the middle of a rainstorm."

I inch away from him. "What do you mean?"

"All right, sleepyhead." He sighs. "Let's get this over with."

My eyes widen. "*Sleepyhead?*"

"Yeah," he says, considering me. "You always look at me like you're about to fall asleep."

Fresh mortification delivers me a burst of uncomfortable energy. "No, I don't."

He makes a face at the clouds. "Lie to me later, okay? I really don't want to be out here for any longer than is absolutely necessary. You're already forcing me to learn how to cook. I don't even know how to chop an onion."

"I'm not forcing you to— What are you talking about?"

"C'mon. Let's go."

I'm shaking my head. "I'm not coming with you."

"Yeah, I know," he says. "You ready?"

"For what?"

"To fight." He offers me his hand. "If I win, I take you back. If I lose—" He hesitates, briefly retracting his hand. "Well, then, I guess I'm dead."

"*No*," I nearly shout. I stare at him, alarm awakening in my chest. "I won't fight you. I don't want to kill you—"

James reaches inside his jacket and I don't even think before I react, jumping to my feet to land a combination of blows to a few vital organs before landing swift kicks to the backs of his knees. He slips on the wet pavement and nearly hits the ground before throwing out a hand to catch himself, hard, against the side of the truck.

"I'm sorry," I gasp, stiffening in horror. "I'm so sorry— I didn't mean—"

"Jesus," he mutters. He stares up at me, his face inscrutable as he massages the side of his torso. "I was just trying to give you this before I lose the chance." He reaches back into his jacket and retrieves something slim and rectangular, which only becomes clear once he's pressed it into my hand.

It's a chocolate bar.

The chocolate bar I'd received in a small pack of essentials prior to arriving at the rehab facility. I'd promised myself I'd save it for Clara—that I'd take it home to her so she could taste chocolate for the very first time. After the grisly incident with Leon in my room, I'd never had a chance to go back and get it.

"If you do manage to kill me and make it out of here," James says, straightening, "I thought you might want to give this to your sister."

Very slowly, I meet his eyes.

My feet are nearly numb with cold. Rain is pelting me from every direction. I can hardly feel the tip of my nose. Every inch of me is drenched, cold piercing through bone. And yet I feel nothing but a terrifying heat as I look up at him. Unmanaged, unnamed, uncategorized emotion is threatening to incinerate me.

"How did you know?" I whisper.

"I already told you," he says, pushing another wet lock of hair out of his eyes. "I pay attention. Besides, I know what it's like to be left behind. I always loved it when my brother brought me something after being gone for a while. It's nice to be remembered."

I don't have time to process this admission.

He sweeps my leg so fast I fly backward with a startled cry, my head moments from hitting the pavement before I remember to shift and roll out of reach. I launch to my feet badly, even as adrenaline courses through my veins, then I unzip the neck of my costume and tuck the chocolate bar into the too-tight catsuit, fight-or-flight responses awakening in my body.

I try to catch my breath, then take a step back.

James takes a step closer.

I've seen him fight. I know what he's capable of. I watched him take on a troop of soldiers unarmed, slaughtering his way ruthlessly through bodies. I watched him tear open his own flesh to dig bullets out of his injured body. I watched him sustain near-death injuries from an explosion that broke both his head and his back. I once personally slit his throat and, still, he didn't die.

I inch away slowly, my heart beating faster.

Once more, I underestimated James. I didn't account for him when I was making my escape plans, and I should've seen him coming. Now the only way to evade him is to badly injure him—and yet, considering his healing abilities, there's no guarantee an injury will suffice. The only way to take James out is to kill him ruthlessly; he'd have to be hacked to pieces or else dealt a blow so lethal his healing powers would never have a chance to kick in.

I already know I won't do it.

Killing people was the crown jewel of my job. I spent my lifetime training to slaughter in merciless, efficient methods. I did what I was ordered to do and I did it without complaint so that my sister might live, so that she might know a future without pain. I did it even as we were starved and tortured, even as my soul turned to ash.

But now, for the first time in my life, I'm not taking orders from anyone. The moment I realized Klaus had sentenced my sister to death, I decided my last act as an executioner would be to take out the system that created me—even if it meant destroying myself in the process.

James takes another step closer.

This time, I don't move.

I allow myself an impulsive second to really look at him, recommitting him to the memories that haunt my dreams. The slashes of his brows pull together above his eyes as I watch him, his irises dark and luminous in the dusky light. Rivulets snake down the hard planes of his face, his hair inky, dripping. His jaw tenses, his lips soft and wet with rainwater.

I watch the movement in his throat, spellbound.

"Why do you always look at me like that?" he says

roughly. "What are you thinking?"

All these years, I thought there was nothing left of my humanity save a scrap that lived on only for Clara.

Maybe I was wrong.

Maybe the ashes of who I was will cultivate the soil of who I want to be. Even now I feel the press of a tender shoot pushing up through the darkness of my soul, searching for the light that floods my body only when James is around.

I don't want it to die.

And no one will ever force me to kill again.

I need to get the vial, and then I need to get back to the Ark before it's too late. There has to be another way out of here. I need to get around him. Outrun him—

"Whoa, okay," James says, his voice rising in warning. "Now I know what you're thinking—and I'm telling you, it's a terrible idea."

"You don't know what I'm thinking."

"Yes, I do," he says angrily. "And you can't run from me, Rosabelle. If you run from me they'll kill you."

"How did you—" I take a firm step back, unsettled by his prescience. "I'll take my chances. I'm not going to fight you."

"Why not?" He steps forward, closing the distance between us. "Because you're so sure you can beat me?"

"Yes," I say, then hesitate. "I mean—no, you're an excellent fighter— It's just—I'm afraid I might kill you by accident."

Surprise widens his eyes before he laughs, his gaze warming with something almost like affection. "All that murdering muscle memory?"

I don't answer this. I don't think it's funny at all.

"We don't have to do this," he says, his smile fading. "You could surrender. Just come back with me—"

"I'm not going back to prison."

"Look, I need you to understand: if you start running, I can't keep you safe. If they spot you, they'll shoot you on sight—"

"This is not negotiable."

"*Rosabelle*—"

I pivot and run.

JAMES

8

I swear, this girl is going to be the death of me.

Shit, she's already been the death of me.

Fuck.

My footfalls hit the ground with increasing intensity even as I remind myself not to sprint in the storm. The winds are only picking up, sending sheets of rain at a diagonal aimed directly at my feet. With my luck I'll manage to fall and snap my neck before Rosabelle even gets a chance to kill me—and this girl is definitely going to kill me. She'll either break my heart or bury a knife in it; one way or another, my life is in her hands.

There's something very wrong with me.

I can think of no other reason why I happen to be deeply, alarmingly attracted to a girl who murders people for a living. Sorry, correction: a girl in a cat costume who murders people for a living. I can't believe this is actually happening. I can't believe this is my real life right now: I'm running after a girl wearing a child's cat costume, watching her little tail swish as she darts from one building to another.

Fuck me.

Idiot. Idiot. Idiot. The word echoes in my head with every footfall as I chase after her, audibly groaning as I watch her move in the direction of a distant airplane hangar.

I swear to God, if she thinks she can fly a plane in this weather—

I briefly lose my footing, nearly tripping on a grate buried in a puddle. By the time I steady myself, water is sloshing in my shoes, and Rosabelle has gained twenty more feet. I'm wearing the wrong gear for this. I should've been wearing boots; instead, I'm wearing a pair of low-tread, low-top sneakers. Clearly, I didn't wake up this morning thinking I had to dress for an undercover chase through a rainstorm.

Worse: Rosabelle is faster than she looks.

Quiet, too. If this is how she operates running on little food and no sleep, I can only imagine what she's like when her tank is full. I have no clue what she's thinking right now. I only know her well enough to know that this girl doesn't do anything without a plan.

"Rosabelle," I hiss, trying not to raise my voice.

She doesn't turn around.

"Rosabelle," I try again, a little louder this time.

Again, her little tail swishes.

Suddenly I can hear Adam's voice in my head—I can practically read the fear in his eyes when he suggested I see a professional for *the unresolved trauma that's leading me to make poor and destructive choices.*

Yeah, well.

I might have to revisit that.

I wasn't sure how I'd feel if I saw Rosabelle again; I thought maybe I'd come to my senses, that I'd see her and realize everyone was right—that I'd romanticized her in my head; that I'd experienced momentary insanity; that everything I'd once felt for her was a result of some weird fever dream.

Nope.

Apparently, I have a shitty imagination, because I wasn't imagining her well enough. It's not just that she's gorgeous; it's not that simple. With Rosabelle, her beauty is just the beginning. Her brain and body are so vividly connected that I can always see her mind working. She's like a tightly coiled current, a live wire sparking dangerously, even though she lives in a breathless sort of stillness. There's some sort of alchemy in all this that makes her arresting in person; she's physically *striking*. When I see her I feel like I've been knocked off a cliff.

And the way she looks at me—

Those fucking eyes. Those sleepy, soft, blinking eyes. I swear she only looks at me with those eyes.

It makes me want to take her to bed.

I should probably pick out a tombstone instead; get my affairs in order; leave all my stuff to Gigi and Roman and my little niece- or nephew-to-be.

At that sobering thought, I almost slow down, losing my rhythm. My left foot lands hard in another deep puddle, splashing water up my jeans.

Guilt batters me in waves.

The reminder of Juliette's impending due date is a blow. No one knows the gender of the baby; she and Warner wanted it to be a surprise. Personally, I think Warner didn't want to know because he didn't want to get too attached. The truth is, we still have no idea whether the baby will survive the birth.

The truth is—

Shit, the truth is, Kenji was right. Warner's been under crushing levels of stress lately, and I've done nothing but make things worse. And if I let Rosabelle escape when I had a chance to bring her in, Warner will never trust me again. He'll think I let her go on purpose. Forget handing out pamphlets in a hot dog costume; my life as I know it will be over.

He might charge me with treason.

I was the one who brought Rosabelle here to begin with; this is my mess to clean up. The least I can do is finish what I started, and right now, trying to disguise anything about this shitshow is pointless. Rosabelle might be wearing dark, inconspicuous clothing, tail and all, but I'm wearing a windbreaker with reflective stripes that form an obvious V right down the middle of my chest. I practically glow in the dark. There's a zero percent chance we haven't already been spotted. It's only a matter of minutes before—

Shit.

I risk a glance over my shoulder, peering through the rain as a pair of distant headlights flash through the storm.

There's no time.

I pick up speed, shoving wet hair out of my face as I push my body harder, risking stability in exchange for lengthening my strides. My longer legs soon eat up the ground between us and I'm close enough to throw myself forward, practically tackling her to the ground.

She cries out as I catch her.

I tuck her against my chest and roll over as we fall so her head doesn't hit the ground, but by the time we stop moving we're both breathing hard and I've got her half-pinned beneath me. Rainwater drips from my face to hers, and she blinks up at me in the ghostly light, a flare of some unfathomable emotion flashing in her eyes. For a moment I nearly forget myself. Suddenly we're just two people alone in the dusk, and I can feel every inch of her under my body.

I nearly lose focus.

She recovers before I do, her eyes shuttering as she pushes uselessly at my chest. "Let me go—"

"No."

"James—"

"Listen to me," I say, raising my voice as a roll of thunder breaks across the sky. "There's no point in running. They're going to shoot you just to take you out, and then they'll heal you and dump you right back in prison—"

"I'm not going back to prison—"

"You keep saying that like you can make it true. I realize there are some philosophical differences between us, but where I come from, you don't get a paycheck and treat when you kill people. You go to jail."

"Then why aren't you in jail?" she argues. "You kill people all the time."

I open my mouth, then close it.

"You're a hypocrite," she says. "You're all hypocrites."

"That's not"—I frown—"I'm a soldier—"

"So am I," she hits back.

She squirms beneath me and I take a sharp breath, suddenly fighting for my life. Even now. Here. In the rain.

"Okay, I need you to stop moving like that or this is going to get really embarrassing for one of us."

She pushes at my chest again, then drags her hands angrily down my body. "Let me go—"

I take another breath. "Me. Just me. Really embarrassing for me."

"James—"

"I'm sorry, I just, you know, when I imagined this moment in my mind I really thought it would go differently."

"This isn't funny," she snaps.

"I never said it was funny."

She bucks upward, the effort gaining her an inch of leverage. She manages to get one of her legs scissored around me, but it's the way she grabs my hips as she torques her body that leaves me a little lightheaded.

"Okay, Jesus," I say, my chest heaving. "I tap out, okay? I swear I'll let you go. I just need you to promise not to run."

"No," she says angrily. "I don't have time to go back to prison. I left for a reason—"

"*You don't have time?*" I repeat, grateful for the chance to reset my head. "You mean you would if you could but your busy schedule just won't allow it?"

"That's exactly what I'm saying."

"Wait— What?"

She glances at something behind me, then takes a shaky breath, licking rainwater from her lips. "I'm sorry," she says. "I'm really sorry. You don't understand—I have to get home before it's too late—"

I gasp.

The pain is immediate and shocking, and in the seconds my body contracts in response, she rolls us over and quickly pulls the knife out of my side.

My knife.

That she stole off *my* body.

"I'm sorry, I'm really sorry," she says in a rush, wiping the blade on my jeans before getting to her feet. Rosabelle looms over me like she did the day she slit my throat, but at least this time she has the decency to look upset. She flips the blade closed. "No vital organs, I promise."

"You're so fucking mean to me," I say, grimacing to exaggerate my pain. "And I'm always so nice to you—"

I grab her ankle and pull.

She cries out, free-falling as I launch badly upright, wincing for real as the pain in my side screams; still, I catch her before she falls, then spin her against the wall of the airplane hangar, the metal reverberating as the two of us collide. I stare at her, breathing hard, water dripping off my nose. "You've got a lot of nerve, you know that?"

She's looking at me with something like panic. "James," she says desperately. "I've still got your knife."

My eyes widen a fraction.

"*Goddammit*," I bite out, staggering backward as fresh pain explodes in my thigh. I yank the knife out of my leg with a muted cry, flipping it shut before stowing it in a safer place. By the time I look up, Rosabelle's already fifty feet into the darkening distance, and now I've got a limp. But when I hear the rising rush of footfalls, I know I'm well and truly screwed.

Minutes.

We've got less than minutes.

I grit my teeth and push forward through the pain, more irritated that Rosabelle's ruined my clothes than I am about the injuries. It took me forever to find this windbreaker in my size; it's an original issue from an era long before I was born. There's a reason I wear technical gear when I'm doing real work. I don't run laps in a tuxedo like Warner; I don't like messing up my stuff.

Though, to be fair, he doesn't mess up his stuff.

During the reign of The Reestablishment, the idea of clothing as personal style became obsolete; only the ultra-rich had access to private clothiers; everyone else was given equable, government-issue garbage.

I grew up wearing government-issue garbage.

Under the guise of starting over, The Reestablishment planned to burn every vestige of the past. That was the big lie: the promise of a fresh start to solve our problems. Delete language; delete culture; delete identity. They were going to rewrite history; reshape the future; reestablish world order.

Or: incinerate humanity as we knew it.

Adam doesn't like to think about the past; he finds it too stressful. Old things give him anxiety. But I can lose hours in antiques shops and museums; that kind of time travel gives me a strange hope. It reminds me that no matter the era, human fingerprints have always been both beautiful and bloody. And no matter how dark it gets, we somehow go on forever trying to light a path.

We were lucky enough to be able to recover a lot after the revolution—books, art, music. Old computers and cameras and cars. Watches. Cassette players.

But the first time I walked into a vintage clothing store I fell face-first in love.

"Shit," I mutter, inspecting the bloodied tear at my thigh. I hold a hand to my slowly healing side wound as I hobble forward, wiping my red-slicked fingers along the ruined denim. Vintage, selvage Japanese denim.

"You're going to pay for this," I shout at her retreating back. "These jeans cost me months of my life."

Surprise, surprise: she doesn't care.

I peer up at the sky, holding out my sticky hands to catch rainwater as golden light fractures through ominous clouds. We've got less than half an hour before the sun sets altogether, and I'm willing to bet good money that Rosabelle was waiting for nightfall to set some major plan in motion. I pick up speed as the pain in my leg and torso abates by degrees, pushing harder than is advisable, really, to close the distance between us. There's a sudden, blinding flash of lightning, and in the flare I spot Rosabelle darting around the side of the airplane hangar.

I chase after her, wincing, only to find she's stopped moving. She's standing in front of an electrical panel, her hands working too fast to promise anything but bad news. I mutter another expletive under my breath before glancing over my shoulder. If I can hear people coming, she can definitely hear people coming.

Thunder cracks overhead.

"This is a waste of time," I call out as I hobble forward. "You can't just steal a plane. Trust me, I would know—the security measures are more complicated than they—"

She glances at me, her eyes wild, then bolts out of sight as a roaring mechanical whirr fills the sky with manufactured sound.

Shock comes for me like a whip.

I rush around to the front of the building, watching in horror as the enormous, hydraulic door lifts open to reveal the outline of a jet currently undergoing maintenance, streaks of fading sunlight pinwheeling through its depths. The pincers holding the plane in place slowly exhale, releasing the steel body from a death grip, and suddenly my head is overheating. Rosabelle has not only disarmed the security system, she's somehow overridden every safety protocol.

This isn't funny anymore.

My heart races violently as I begin to fathom the shape of her plan. She's really going to try to fly an unserviced aircraft out of here. In the middle of a lightning storm.

I watch her disappear inside the cavernous hangar, her fucking cat tail twitching, and only then do I realize the depth of my mistake. I really thought we were just playing a half-hearted game of hide-and-seek out here. I thought we both knew how this was going to end. I thought it was pretty obvious she'd never be able to escape.

Wrong on all counts.

I see now why she chose this hangar: it's the one closest to the runway, with the least interference. The working jets parked in the apron would need to be slowly navigated through taxiways before reaching the runway's entry point, which would cost her too much time.

She's taking a gamble.

She must've known this was a maintenance hangar, but she's decided she'd have a better shot at takeoff with an unobstructed, slightly defective plane. If she moves quickly enough, she could maneuver this jet immediately onto the tarmac and take off with little impediment.

Just minutes ago I would've laughed off this idea as impossible. Now I'm full of dread.

It's becoming clearer and clearer to me that I'm in way over my head with this girl. I don't actually know anything about her. I have no idea what she's truly capable of. I still don't know how she once managed to literally drop dead before coming violently back to life thirty minutes later. And now I'm worried I might really have to kill her—or at least level her an injury severe enough to stop her.

Shit. This is bad.

This is really, really bad.

If she escapes, Warner is going to *murder* me.

And then, as if I've conjured him with the thought, I hear his voice—growing louder with distant footsteps—like something out of a nightmare.

"Don't hold your fire when you find them," he says coldly. "He's made his choice."

JAMES

9

This time, I don't tackle Rosabelle to the ground.

This time, I don't make a sound.

I dart into the shadows, grab the menace by the tail, and yank her backward, covering her mouth to capture her scream. I clamp down her arms, keeping her hands where I can see them, and pin her back to my front as I pull her deeper into the recesses of the darkening hangar, shifting us both away from the last shafts of golden sun.

"So when you told me you weren't some kind of genius-level hacker—"

She stiffens against me.

"—you were obviously lying."

Her chest rises and falls against my forearm. I can practically feel her heart beating, and I'm not as armed, emotionally or physically, as I'd like to be in this moment. The knife I'd had in my pocket was a simple, everyday carry; I've now stashed it out of Rosabelle's reach, but I wish I could do this whole day over again. I'd be armed to the teeth. I wouldn't be wearing these jeans.

"Any other confessions you'd like to make?" I ask. "Are you a professional fighter pilot, too? Do you spend your free time base jumping off cliffs? How many languages do you speak? How long can you hold your breath underwater? When was the last time you told someone the truth?"

She shakes her head, making a muffled, indistinct sound, and I move in seconds, fluidly trading one hand for the other, flipping open my knife and releasing Rosabelle's mouth before pressing the blade to her throat.

"Speak," I say sharply.

"James— Please—"

I press the blade a little harder. "That's not an answer."

"You're not going to hurt me," she says. "I know you don't want to hurt me."

I lower my lips to the curve of her ear. "You didn't want to hurt me, either. But when it mattered, you didn't hesitate."

Her breath hitches. She tenses against my body.

I really thought Rosabelle would see reason; I thought she'd needed to put up a fight on principle; I thought she'd understand that I literally could not let her go.

Apparently not.

Just because I believe she's had a change of heart about the fascists doesn't mean I'm going to let her run home without telling us what the hell she was doing here. I need to know what her original mission was; I need to know what she was planning to do with that vial.

Contrary to popular belief, I am not an idiot.

For as long as we have a mercenary of The Reestablishment in our midst, reformed or otherwise, we're going to need her to talk. The safety of the entire continent—the world— depends on it.

Footsteps shudder through the building like a roll of thunder, vibrations sending waves of tension through my barely healed body. I brace myself.

"You know," I say, "it's just occurred to me that I never even asked you how you broke out of prison. How were you able to escape supermax without a trace? What did you mean when you said you left for a reason?"

She tries to launch out of my arms and I clamp down harder, pulling her more tightly against me.

"I'm not fucking around anymore," I say darkly. "I was being nice to you earlier. Try to run again and I'll have you on your knees."

I can hear her breathing. I swear I feel her tremble.

I lower my voice to a whisper, my jaw nearly grazing her temple. *"Rosabelle."*

She stiffens.

"How did you break out of prison?"

"James—"

"Last chance."

She audibly releases, sinking against me in something like surrender. Her head rocks back against my chest and she makes a soft, breathless sound that messes with my heart rate. I've got her pressed so hard against my body I can feel every curve of her through this thin, cheap catsuit. She's dripping wet; the material is suctioned to her skin. I literally can't ignore the fact that she's not wearing any underwear.

I swallow, adjusting my hold on the knife.

"Your prisons were built by The Reestablishment," she

says quietly, and my spiraling mind surges back into focus. "I've done hundreds of hours of sim training breaking out of every single one of them."

"Wait." Shock rocks through me. "*What?*"

"James," she says, sounding almost tired. "You don't understand how vulnerable you are. Your movement has already been badly infiltrated. I'm the weakest executioner we have and your world offers me no challenge. We have much stronger mercenaries everywhere, so seamlessly integrated into the fabric of your government that you can't see what's coming. And there's no time—"

Footfalls are suddenly louder; soldiers are dispersing deeper into the vast hangar. I hear the clanging sounds of metal, the hush of discreet conversation. I peer around the part cart partially obscuring us from view, and swear quietly under my breath.

"I cut the power to the overhead lights," she says softly. "The last of the sun should be gone by now. They won't be able to find us easily."

My jaw tenses. "You really thought of everything."

"And you have time to change your mind," she says. "Make the choice. Let me go. I have a chance to fix things before it's too late—"

"What do you mean *before it's too late?*" I cut her off, alarmed. "How much time are we talking about?"

"Under seven weeks," she whispers.

I go still, even as my heart beats harder. "And then what?" I ask. "What happens in seven weeks?"

She goes quiet.

My fears divide and multiply.

"If you let me get back to the Ark, hopefully nothing," she says. "But you have to let me leave right now."

"Stop giving me these cryptic answers," I say angrily. "You're talking about my home—my people—the possible devastation of everything we've worked for. I need you to tell me something real. You came here to do something horrible, didn't you?"

She hesitates. "They didn't tell me what I was supposed to do until I got here."

I let this sit for a second. "Who's *they*?"

Another clatter.

I look up at the sound, and I can just make out a team searching the aircraft high above us, boots thudding up and down the safety ladders.

"We're almost out of time," she whispers. "I said they wouldn't find us easily, not that they wouldn't find us at all. Choose your questions carefully."

My lips flatten into a grim line. "What were you sent here to do? Why did you change your mind about doing it? What was in that vial?"

"I can't answer these questions succinctly," she says. "Any answer I give you will just prompt more questions, and I don't have time—"

"Why do you keep saying that? What's the rush to get home? You said seven weeks, not seven minutes—"

"If you want so many answers, why don't you just let

your team interrogate me?" she counters. "Why hold me here, in the dark, under threat of discovery? Why do you seem to be hiding *with* me?"

I tense, betraying myself in the process, and she mirrors the action, stiffening against me.

"James?" she says carefully. "What's going on?"

Shit.

I keep my voice low, speaking near her temple when I say, "First of all, don't change the subject. Second of all, don't change the fucking subject. Third of all, we both know you're not going to answer their questions."

"But you knew I would answer yours?"

"I don't know anything about you," I say, my cheek accidentally grazing hers. "I don't—"

The touch of her arrests me, words dying in my throat. Her skin is so soft it does something dangerous to my nervous system; gives my imagination too much ammo.

It occurs to me, in a moment of panic, that I'm not really in control of this situation.

"They pushed you out, didn't they?" she says. "You're not supposed to be here right now, are you?"

"Stop deflecting," I say, desperately trying to pivot. "I want to know the purpose of your mission here. I want to know what's in that vial—"

"What did you do?" she says, her voice sharpening.

"Rosabelle—"

"Did you try to defend me?" she says, and now she sounds alarmed. "Are they going to hurt you if they find you here?"

I finally lose my patience.

I flip her around instinctively, backing her into a corner blocked by an air compressor and a hydraulic lift, heavy shadows pushing us into deeper obscurity.

Right away, I feel this mistake reflected in my pulse.

My thigh is firm between her legs, pinning her to the wall. I've got both her wrists in one hand, gripping them tight above her head, my other hand holding the knife to her throat. Somehow, this doesn't register.

The shadows are making things worse.

We're cloaked in the kind of semidarkness that makes bad decisions feel forgivable. This close, I can still see into her eyes. This close, I can still make out the curve of her lips. She's cold and wet, her cat ears drooping as her hood slips back, but there's no trace of fear in her eyes. In fact, she's giving me that wild, unguarded look, the one I've seen only twice before—something so intense it's close to awe.

It gives me a small heart attack.

She blinks slowly and I watch, transfixed, as a raindrop releases from her eyelashes. She looks so soft and vulnerable I have to actively remind myself that this girl just stabbed me. Twice.

I really didn't think this through.

"You need to stay away from me," she whispers.

"You need to answer my questions—"

"Once I'm gone, I want you to leave the airfield," she says. "Don't let them find you anywhere near me."

"Rosabelle—"

"I love your freckles," she whispers, her gaze moving slowly across my face. "Sometimes, when I can't sleep, I count them in my head."

I take this like a gunshot.

I release on instinct, a flood of emotion disarming me just enough that she manages to slip one of her hands free and throw an elbow into my barely healed thigh. I stumble, gasping, and it's the edge she needs: she lands a few quick blows to my ribs, forcing space between us before she doubles back, jump kicks off the wall, and strikes my side wound so hard I'm still reeling when she tears off running—directly into the line of fire.

Fuck.

I grit my teeth through the pain, blood seeping through my renewed injuries. I know the instant she's spotted, because the hangar dissolves into an explosion of shouts and the deafening sounds of chaos. I hear the clangor of metal, the thunder of boots. Machine-gun fire echoes off the walls, bullets pinging off steel surfaces, ringing in my ears.

I sigh, closing my eyes.

Then I wipe my bloodied hands on my ruined clothes, and limp after her into the fray.

ROSABELLE

10

Blood runs fast down the side of my face, the wound fresh, still searing, from a close call with a direct shot to my head. I duck for the fourth time in as many seconds as I dart behind a towering storage unit, my heart pounding as I home in on a soldier just steps away.

First things first: I need to acquire a weapon.

I scramble up the side of the storage unit, knowing I have less than seconds to make a move with such a high level of exposure; I hear shouts break out as I jump from the unit, drop-kicking my mark in the back. He falls to the ground with an audible crack, but I tuck my knees too late and fall badly beside him, knifelike agony exploding in my left ankle. I suck in a breath at the pain, then tug the automatic rifle out of his limp hands, staggering upright. I'm briefly lightheaded.

There was a time when I was better at this.

There was a time when I was stronger, healthier; when The Reestablishment wasn't aggressively cutting my rations in a slow drip of systematic starvation; when I ran rigorous, daily simulations, racking up tens of thousands of hours of backbreaking training.

This was before they downgraded my assignments.

This was before they cut back my sims; before they declared me too weak to be worthy of my title.

I was regularly fed less for poor performance only to perform poorly because I was fed less. I was soon given no choice but to accept occasional factory work as my body and soul were slowly, methodically dismantled. Forced to watch my sister die a little more every day as my hands grew only weaker with shame.

But there was a time, not so long ago, when I was still useful to them.

Those were the years when Soledad still had hope they could get me connected to the Nexus; when they assumed the malfunction of my brain was a solvable system glitch and not a massive liability. Back then, the tremors in my right arm were only occasional. My muscles were better honed, my movements more refined, my reflexes faster.

Now, this version of me will have to do.

I haul the stolen weapon into my arms. It's heavier than I expected, and takes me a moment to calibrate. I study the fallen soldier as I drag myself out of sight, fairly certain he's unconscious but not dead.

My finger trembles on the trigger. The only thing that hasn't suffered much is my aim; I've always been a dead shot. My problem now is that I don't know how to miss.

Don't kill, I remind myself. *Don't kill, don't kill.*

I manage to tear myself away, heart hammering like an addict trying to override old programming. My every instinct screams at me to finish the job.

Finish the job so that Clara will have food.

Finish the job so that Clara will have medicine.

Finish the job so that Clara might have a fire.

Finish the job to keep her safe; finish the job to secure her future; finish the job so they might set us free—

In the privacy of my mind, I scream.

You've been dead inside for years, I remind myself.

Die, I tell myself.

Die.

It doesn't help; I can't seem to shut off all the way. I can't access my mask, my bloodless facade—and I'm beginning to understand, with breathtaking fear, exactly who to blame.

James has become my new weakness.

The mere sight of him motivates my heart to work harder, regenerating my life force almost against my will. I can feel him leaving a mark on me, his name being freshly carved, letter by letter, into my skin.

No.

Not now.

Not now.

My head is pounding, my palms growing slick as my feelings spiral out of control. I grip the gun more firmly in my hands, reading its ridges with my fingers. I'm here, where my feet are; here, where cold winds sweep mist and rain into the open hangar, where the air is fresh and bracing, chilling my damp clothes. I steel myself and fall back on logic, hold fast to reason—

I need to get home.

Just because I need to get home doesn't mean I have to murder everyone on the way there. *Killing is no longer my job.* I don't know who these people are; they might be James's friends. They might be his family members.

I don't know when that began to matter to me.

I hear boots before I see her, the giveaway granting me the second I need to pivot just as a soldier comes up on me from behind. She's inexperienced; I can tell by the way she hesitates, the way her eyes widen in surprise when she glimpses my costume.

I never hesitate.

I shoot her in the arm, then the leg, then order myself to stop, physically forcing my finger off the trigger. My right hand trembles dangerously, my breaths coming in fast. I clench my teeth through the moment, shutting out her screams as she falls, as I retreat. I remind myself that they have healers. She'll be all right as long as she doesn't bleed out for too long. She might make it.

Don't kill.

Don't kill.

The words echo in my head as I move soundlessly, ignoring the spasms branching up my leg. I duck into the shadows, pressing myself flat against the side of a boom lift, and attempt a fresh scan of the situation. From this vantage point I can't be precise about how many fighters I'm up against; based on the shadows I'm seeing I think I can safely estimate that there are about twenty-five soldiers roaming the hangar.

That means I have to be patient.

I'll need to maintain a defensive position, retreating over and over, taking them out only as they seek me out. Unlike the citizens of the Ark, some of the rebels still have preternatural abilities. I can't know what kinds of powers they have at their disposal until it's too late, which means I can't risk assuming an offensive position until their numbers winnow. Only when I'm certain I've cut down enough of their fighters can I risk making my move toward the center of the hangar—where the jet remains untouched and exposed.

Shafts of ghostly moonlight illuminate the two rolling safety ladders on either side of the open doors, which were left unlatched by soldiers doing their initial scans.

There's no time for a new strategy.

I was never going to be able to fly this jet all the way back to the Ark. That was never the plan. I was only going to use it like a weapon: take advantage of its bullet-resistant heft to get myself out of here. I only need to get far enough into the sky and over open water so I might safely eject myself. The plane would be lost to the ocean; I would parachute-land as best I could.

Best-case scenario, they assume I'm dead.

Worst-case scenario, I buy myself time to find a new bolthole, lose my shadows, scout out a new airbase. There's no point getting back to the Ark without the vial. Stealing a plane is a small task compared to what I know awaits me on a hunt for that glass cylinder—because I have to imagine the rebels were at least smart enough to stash it in a secure location.

The trouble is, I don't know enough about this place to hazard a reasonable guess as to its whereabouts. I need time to do reconnaissance before I can even compile a list of probable locations—

A soldier surges up on my left, making no effort to hide his footfalls, and he shoots before I even have a chance to lift my weapon. I dive for the ground, bashing my elbow into a steel cabinet, pain ricocheting up my arm. I glimpse him in my periphery and push through the agony, flipping onto my back to shoot him in the thigh, then the foot. He buckles, his cries echoing, but even as he falls he manages to get off a few well-aimed shots. I roll over but not fast enough, hissing through my teeth as a bullet nicks my right arm.

I take a fraction of a second to catch my breath.

I drag myself upright as the soldier struggles to regain his feet, catching the glimmer of an unusual, puzzle-piece pendant hanging from a chain at his neck. He tries to stand but I get to him first, striking the side of his head with the rifle, and I watch, chest heaving, as he slowly slides to the ground with a grunt.

I rock back on my feet, grimacing as fresh pain blooms through my injured ankle, but when I see his fingers still twitching for his weapon, I kick it toward me and grab the strap, looping it quickly over my head.

Then I shoot him in the arm.

He chokes out a fresh cry and I tense, my finger uncertain on the trigger, wondering if maybe I shot him too many times.

Slow down, I tell myself, alarm constricting my chest. You can be gentle. You can be better. You—

I hear a storm of footsteps—fighters following the sound of their comrade's cries—and I compartmentalize my own pain as I push deeper into the shadows. I duck down behind a generator, take a breath, then take a position. I peer up over the ledge, my gun poised at my eye line, searching for a target.

"Hey, this is fun, right?" someone whispers. "I think everyone is having fun. I love team-building exercises."

I stiffen at the sound of his voice, my heart beating so hard I feel the ground shift beneath my feet. I pull back my position, equal parts agony and fury as I turn to face him.

ROSABELLE

11

"Get away from me," I breathe, horrified.

James ducks down beside me, grimacing as he crouches. When he meets my eyes, he gestures to his wounds, to the blood streaked across half his body. "Oh, this?" he says with a shrug. "Nothing to worry about. She told me she loves my freckles."

"You have to get out of here," I say, forcing my anger to override the ache in my chest. "You're going to get yourself killed."

"Um, I'm pretty sure you're the only one trying to kill me, Rosabelle."

"Stop," I say desperately. "This isn't funny—"

"I agree. We really need to stop meeting like this."

"James—"

He lifts a hand to my cheek, his eyes tightening as he sweeps his thumb through the tributary of blood still dripping down the side of my face, and I forget to breathe.

"I'd really like to spend some time with you under normal circumstances," he says, forcing a grim smile. "Dinner. Movie. No murdering. Better ambience."

I know he's joking, trying to defuse the tension, but something inside of me grieves the simple dream he's describing. I hope he finds that kind of happiness.

I'll be long dead by then.

"I haven't actually murdered anyone," I admit, presenting this confession self-consciously, like a child offering a crude illustration as art.

James casts me a doubtful glance. "You haven't murdered anyone?"

"No."

"You mean, like, in the last five minutes?"

My cheeks heat. "Yes."

Now he's fighting a grin. "Wow, Rosabelle, that must've been hard for you."

I don't answer that.

Shouts echo in the distance. There's a sudden crack of thunder, and a deluge of rain batters the roof, briefly indistinguishable from gunfire.

"I really need you to get out of here," I say to him. "Now."

"*Now?*" He feigns surprise, looking around as if he were at a party. "Like, right now? But I haven't even had a chance to say hi to everyone—"

"You never listen to me," I say angrily. "I need you to listen to me just this once—"

This time, his shock is real. "*I* never listen to *you?*"

"Being in my orbit will cost you your life. Stay away from me. I heard your brother tell them not to spare you—"

"Who? Warner?" James makes a face. "He's not going to let anyone kill me. I mean, don't get me wrong," he says, hesitating. "He'll definitely let someone shoot me. He might let a lot of people shoot me. But if I died on his watch his wife would never forgive him."

"You're wrong," I say, tensing as debris skitter along the ground, rolling carts whining as they're pushed around by the wind. I hear a shudder of footsteps and adjust my gun, my finger hovering over the trigger. "They're taking straight shots at my head and they don't seem to care who they hit."

James absorbs this in silence.

He seems to see me as if for the first time, his gaze sweeping along my body, his eyes hardening as he takes account of my various injuries. He looks like he's about to say something when I feel a rush of movement.

I look over James's shoulder, lock eyes with an incoming fighter, and choose to forfeit my shot in order to tackle James to the floor.

She opens fire and I roll over, moving faster than I can think, then shoot her in the arm twice, listening for the cry and clatter as the gun slips out of her hand. It's hard work to deny my own instincts, muscle memory processing faster than my mind, and I remind myself to slow down—to act consciously—as I clamber upright, shooting her in the other arm before forcing my finger off the trigger. She makes a guttural sound of rage as blood snakes down her arms, and I take advantage of the moment to climb onto the generator and jump-kick her directly in the chest.

We fall together, tangling as we hit the ground.

I land poorly and nearly bite through my tongue, my head

pounding, pain exploding in shock waves along my ribs. The soldier groans as she tries to rise, but I drag myself behind her and lock her in a blood choke, the effort nearly draining my reserves. When I finally feel her pass out, I release her limp body to the floor.

"Jesus."

I look up, breathing hard, to find James staring at me.

"I thought you said you weren't murdering anyone." A notch forms between his brows. "Is she dead?"

"No, she's just asleep."

"I think you shot her three times."

"She nearly killed you!"

He frowns. "Did we just write a haiku?"

I glance behind us, then duck behind the generator again, needing a minute to catch my breath. "James, please. For the last time, get out of here. This isn't your fight and I don't—"

He suddenly kneels in front of me and I falter, words failing me as he reaches for the spare gun slung around my neck.

"I don't want you to die," I finish breathlessly.

He lifts the strap over my head and I'm rooted in place, afraid to move. He studies me, his eyes inscrutable. "You say that so much I'm starting to think you really mean it."

"I do mean it."

"Wow, Rosabelle," he says softly, almost smiling. "I had no idea you were such a romantic."

"Please," I say. "Leave."

"No."

"James—"

He laughs. "No fucking chance."

"Listen to me," I say, finally losing control. I grab a fistful of his shirt and yank him closer, my voice nearly shaking with fury. "If these soldiers matter to you, leave. If you want to spare their lives, *leave*. I'm trying—I'm really trying to be a better person, but if even one of them hurts you I swear I'll slaughter them all."

James goes still.

My heart is hammering violently in my chest.

He loses his smile as he stares at me, then at my hand gripping his shirt. All traces of humor have vanished from his face. There's a look in his eyes now that I've never seen; a dark heat I don't know how to name. Somehow this reaches me without words, without a sound, and the longer he stares at me the more unsteady I feel. I finally remember to release his shirt, studying my own hand as if it betrayed me, and put it back where it belongs: around the rifle. My finger glides against the cold metal trigger, trembling. James looks away from me and takes a tight breath, and my eyes drift to the unsteady rise and fall of his chest.

I feel raw. Exposed.

A little terrified.

"James," I try again, quiet but desperate. "Please."

A soldier rushes up behind us and James rises to his feet in a fluid motion, pivoting so effortlessly I don't even think to stand. He seems to change bodies then, hardening into something both brutal and unbothered as he aims his gun casually at the fighter, who comes to a sudden, paralyzed stop at the sight of him.

The soldier looks between me and James like he doesn't know what to do.

"Hey, Liam," James says easily. "Get the fuck out of my way."

I stiffen.

Liam's eyes widen, his gaze darting to me. "I'm not supposed to—"

Two more soldiers turn the corner, and now I'm on my feet, but James shakes his head at me and I slowly, cautiously, lower my weapon. He nods at the newly arrived soldiers, both cloaked in shadow. They, too, come to an uncertain halt when they see him.

Everyone is looking warily between us.

James sighs.

"We're done here," he says to the group. "Go home."

One of the fighters steps slowly into a shaft of moonlight, his dark skin gleaming. He shoots an uncertain glance my way. "Bro," he says, shaking his head slightly. "What the hell is going on?"

"Is that her?" The other soldier steps into the light, drawing closer, and I catch a glimpse of his dark eyes, his slightly broken nose. "Why does she have cat ears?"

I don't even have time to process this before there's another hush of movement, a thunder of footfalls—and six more soldiers suddenly skid to a stop before us.

One of them, a towering brunette, throws out an arm to

stop the others from rushing forward. "Whoa," she says, her eyes on James, taking in the blood painted down his body. "Hey, are you okay?"

Then, again:

Another clutch of bodies surges toward us—at least ten more—and my heart rate accelerates as I take them all in, doing quick calculations in my head. My chances of fighting my way out of here are slowly decreasing to zero.

Alarm detonates inside me.

ROSABELLE

12

One of the soldiers breaks off from the large group, charging forward with a palpable frustration.

"Okay, what the fuck?" he says by way of hello.

I take a quiet breath, then do a quick check of the magazine to see how many rounds I have left.

Five.

Tension tightens my shoulders.

James took my other gun. I can't remember why I let him take my other gun.

Approximately nineteen soldiers surround me now. Twenty including James. I took out four earlier.

This must be everyone.

Then, a whisper: "Is that the girl?"

"Seriously, what's going on?" asks the towering brunette.

James glances at me, his face unreadable.

"I don't know," says the guy from earlier. "I'm still waiting for an answer."

"Malick?" The brunette's eyes widen, as if surprised to see him. "Isn't your wife in labor?"

This question pierces the haze of my mind.

I feel a cold prickle at my nape, a sick sensation pooling in my gut. I might've killed him. A different version of me might've killed him. I might've left his wife a widow, his newborn child an orphan—

No.

No.

Not now.

I wrestle my conscience back into its cage.

"Yeah," says Malick, looking uncomfortable. He runs a hand over the back of his head. "I mean, obviously, it was unexpected. A few weeks early."

Soft murmurs from the group.

James props his gun against his shoulder, then pinches the bridge of his nose. When he lifts his head, he looks murderous. "Get the fuck out of here."

"But—"

"*Now,*" he says. "Go be with your wife."

Malick looks around uncertainly. "Look, man, no disrespect— You know we all love you, but word on the street is you don't have the authority—"

James takes a decisive step forward and everyone surges back.

I hear my breath catch.

I'm struck anew by the sheer brawn of him, the untapped power in his body. James moves from skin to skin with disarming ease, lulling people into a false sense of complacency just long enough for them to forget to be scared. He's terrifying when he steps fully into his strength. I can see now that it's not an act. It's not a premeditated strategy.

He's heart and fury in the same body.

"Leave," he says to Malick. "I'll deal with Warner." He looks around. "Where is he, anyway?"

No one answers him.

"Where the hell is my brother?" he says again, loudly this time.

"I—I don't know," says Liam.

"Great," James says, still furious. Then he calls over his shoulder, my name like an expletive: *"Rosabelle."*

I nearly flinch.

"Her name is Rosabelle?" says another soldier. "Seriously?"

"Rosabelle," James says again, his voice even. "Come here."

I don't move.

James sighs. He turns to look at me, narrowing his eyes as he says, "Get over here. *Now.*"

I realize, with rising fear, that I might not have a choice. I take quick inventory of my injuries, compiling a non-exhaustive list:

fractured ankle;

fractured ribs;

head wound;

shoulder laceration;

possible concussion.

My body is otherwise flayed by myriad cuts and bruises, my ankle so swollen now I can hardly put weight on it. My head is still bleeding, though I think it's clotted at least a little. The bigger problem is that I stopped moving for too long; I've lost both momentum and adrenaline. And the truth is, I'm in no state to take on so many fighters alone.

James is still waiting.

I take a breath, then a single, cautious step toward him and the soldiers recoil like a school of fish, drawing back as one body before lifting nineteen rifles at my face.

James mutters an oath.

I try to hide my limp as I slowly approach the group, keeping my face impassive and my head level even as I walk past the blur of loaded weapons aimed directly at my heart. Whispers rise up around me like smoke.

"That's her? I thought she was someone's kid."

"Why does she have a tail?"

"Shut up, you did not think that was someone's kid—"

"Yes, I did!"

"Wait, is she wearing a cat costume?"

"You really thought someone decided to bring their kid to work today?"

I'm not ready to admit defeat.

I just need a new plan.

"Oh shit," someone says, barking out a laugh. "I just saw the ears—"

Once I'm close enough, I hear James exhale roughly, losing some of his tension. Still, he seems angrier than I expected. He shoots me a dark look when he says, under his breath, "This isn't going to work if you can't take an order to save your own life."

I look up at him, confused, but then I cast a glance at our audience and bite back my response.

"So—what now?" asks the tall brunette, looking around. "Has the mission changed?"

The guy with the broken nose nods at me. "I thought we were supposed to bring her in."

James clamps an arm around my shoulder. "I've brought her in. Mission complete."

"No." I stiffen, alarm sounding through my body. "Wait—"

James doesn't meet my eyes. "Try again next time, Rosabelle."

"James—"

"Hey, where's Kian?" a woman asks, looking around. "Why isn't he here?"

Liam points at me. "She killed Kian."

"What?" Someone gasps. "No—"

The group erupts into agitation.

"You killed Kian?" James goes briefly slack, stunned as he looks at me. "Really?"

"Who's Kian?" I whisper, eyes widening as I take in the chaos. "I didn't kill anyone. I mean, I didn't think I—"

"I saw him," Liam shouts, his face mottling with color. "He was covered in blood, passed out on the ground—"

"All right, everyone calm down," says a familiar, disembodied voice.

James stiffens beside me.

A body materializes out of thin air in the distance, the sight of him striking my memory like a match. Black hair, impish eyes. I remember fighting him in the morgue. I remember lifting a gun to his head.

I remember his name: *Kenji*.

My pulse picks up.

"Kian's not dead," Kenji says as he approaches, his boots echoing. He looks at me, sparing me a searching glance that leaves me unsettled.

Then he narrows his eyes at James. "You didn't disarm her?"

James turns to me sharply. "Shit, yeah, sorry, I'm going to need the gun," he says, reaching for the strap.

"No," I whisper, taking a measured step back.

"You and me?" Kenji says to James, his eyes darkening. "We're going to talk later. I don't know what the hell you thought you were doing today, but just to be clear? Fuck you."

James glowers. "Great," he says. "Can't wait."

I look from Kenji to James, confused.

I take another step back.

Kenji turns to the group. "Kian's with the girls now," he's saying. He unearths a familiar pair of manacles from his jacket pocket, the sight of which sends my heart rate rocketing. "Warner called them in hours ago as a precaution. We didn't know how bad the night would get. But no casualties tonight."

Tension releases from the room with a palpable

exhalation; shoulders falling; eyes closing. They're relieved. Wrapping things up. They think this is over.

No.

No.

I begin to panic.

"Rosabelle, I need the gun," James says, lowering his voice. "You're outnumbered and injured; there's nowhere to go. Please don't make this difficult. If you don't give up your weapon I'll have to physically disarm you—"

"And James is right," Kenji is saying, heading toward me now with the manacles. "We're done here. Go home. Get some rest. And congrats to Malick—"

A couple of people cheer.

Adrenaline floods my body, sharpening my senses as my heart pounds. The pain in my head nearly retreats as my thoughts clarify and clarify.

This can't be it.

This can't be over.

"Let me do that," James says to Kenji, nodding at the manacles. "Last time the settings were way too high—"

"Hell no," Kenji says, shooting him a dark look. "Get out of here, bro. Warner's waiting for you."

"What? Where?" Then: "Why?"

"Why the hell is she still armed?"

James swears again. "Rosabelle—"

Kenji shakes his head angrily, tucking away the manacles before pulling a gun on me. "Drop the weapon, Rosabelle. I'm not your boyfriend, okay? I have no problem taking you out. In fact, I'm still pissed at you for throwing a knife at my leg."

I look around blindly, backing away.

"*Now*," Kenji barks at me. "And I want your hands where I can see them."

I hardly hear the conversations around me as they swell and retreat, voices clamoring, bodies surging, but I can feel the tension in the room shifting again: relief reorganizing into fear; easy whispers rising into terse warnings. There's a collective rush of sound, the soft clatter of weapons lifting to meet my heart again.

James drags a hand through his hair.

"Do you know how to count, Rosabelle?" Kenji cocks his head at me. "Let's count together, okay? I'm going to give you five whole seconds before I show you how this gun works. You ready to learn math and physics at the same time?"

I feel like I'm somewhere outside of my body. Heat prickles along my skin, my nerves flaring and fading with sensation.

"Five—"

"Bro, c'mon, this isn't necessary—"

The pounding in my head grows louder.

"—four—get the fuck out of my way, James—"

My mind coils tighter and tighter.

"Just let me talk to her for a second—"

I move slowly, as if in a dream, unhooking the rifle from around my neck. My feet seem to sink into the ground, the heft of the cold metal hitting my palms just as I begin to

form the rough shape of a desperate plan.
Last chance.
"Three—"
Five bullets.
"Two—"
Clara.
Clara—

JAMES

13

"I'm sorry," she says desperately.

I hear her voice as the pain explodes across my chest, the force of the bullet knocking me backward as she sprints off at full speed on a fractured ankle. A deafening hail of gunfire erupts almost instantaneously, sparking as it pings off steel surfaces. I make out muted shouts and footfalls, the blur of bodies taking off after her. Others reach for me, steadying me, but I can't make sense of anything right away, not while the sound of my own blood rushes between my ears.

She shot me at close range.

I stagger forward, trying to bear my own weight as my vision briefly flares, cold sweat breaking out along the nape of my neck. Blood seeps warm and fast through my shirt, snaking down my torso, then my arms. I watch, breathing hard, as it drips off my fingers, splattering red across the white skin of my sneakers. I mutter a rough *thank you* to the soldiers bracing me, then release myself from their collective grip, taking a single moment to steady my head and assess my situation:

The bullet is lodged in my shoulder, just below the clavicle. I'm guessing it shattered bone.

I can't move my arm.

"*Son of a bitch*," I hear Kenji hiss, then turn to see him half lying on the ground, applying pressure to a hemorrhaging wound in his thigh. "Why does she always go for my legs?"

I blink, clearing the haze from my vision, my breathing stabilizing slowly. The pain recedes by degrees as my body tries to heal itself around the bullet. This is going to need surgery.

Fuck.

She took out my dominant arm, my right arm, and I know she did it on purpose. The bullet is acting like a pin in the joint; even if my body manages to heal itself, I won't be able to move my shoulder properly until I get the foreign object out, and this isn't something I can do easily with my own hands.

I glance around the darkened hangar, picking out the shadowy shapes of workbenches and tool chests.

Maybe I can find a pair of pliers.

My heart picks up speed as my vitals gradually recover, hammering so hard now it's making me dizzy.

The problem is, I don't even know what I'm feeling. I'm still reeling, nearly shaking with pain and anger, and still, some delusional part of me is thinking—

Wow.

Maybe I could hate her more if I admired her less.

Rosabelle will go down fighting with her last breath, and I can't help but respect her for it. That's the kind of girl who shows up, holds the line, keeps her promises, guards your secrets, destroys your enemies. That's the kind of girl I want to go into battle with.

I close my eyes and, right away, I hear the echo of her voice.

I'm really trying to be a better person, but if even one of them hurts you I swear I'll slaughter them all—

The memory of that moment floods a searing heat through my veins that nearly hurts, stealing my breath.

I swallow.

Fuck poetry, this girl is going to carve my heart out with a knife.

The truth is, I'd have done exactly the same thing in her position. I'd have done anything to get home to my family. No mercy; no regrets. Maybe I'd be angrier if I didn't know she was just trying to get back to her sister.

Before it's too late.

I exhale, pushing aside a rising, paralyzing apprehension. Seven weeks. No one else understands the stakes. No one else knows what I learned from her tonight—and if we let her escape, we might never know what the hell is coming.

The crash and clangor of metal echoes all around me, the general din of chaos unabated. I squint up around the moonlit hangar, studying the few shafts of illumination slanting across its depths. Occasional shots ring out, boots hitting the ground.

If they're working this hard, Rosabelle's still running.

Of course she is.

I catch movement in my periphery, turning to see Kenji

struggling to his feet, Zain and Allie helping him up.

Kenji and I exchange a single, loaded look.

"Really?" he says, his jaw tensing. "*This* is the first girl you decide to bring home to your family?"

I manage a grim smile. "Sorry. She gets nervous around strangers."

Zain chokes out a laugh.

"You think this is funny?" Kenji says, turning to him. "Look at me. Look at *him*." He nods at me. "You still think this is funny?"

"No, sir," Zain says quickly.

I wince as I tweak my bad arm, testing it. Then I unzip my ruined jacket with my left hand, peeling it off with difficulty. The windbreaker is shredded and still dripping blood, and I spend a moment staring at what's left of it, realizing I was a different person the day I bought it. I didn't know what was coming for me when I'd pulled it off a hanger, trying it on with a naive optimism. I'd gotten a discount for the small stain near the pocket, which I'd then carefully soaked and scrubbed out by hand.

But now—

Now I let the ravaged article drop to the ground in a bloody, wet heap.

Kenji hisses in pain and I look up, watching him grimace as he adjusts his weight.

"Get him into recovery," I say to Zain and Allie, who are still awaiting orders. "He's going to pass out if he keeps bleeding like that." And then I grab my ruined undershirt by the collar and tug hard, tearing the thin fabric badly off my body.

"Do you—" Allie glances at me, gasps, and looks away. "*Oh—*"

"What the hell are you doing?" Kenji asks.

"What are you waiting for?" I say, nodding at the soldiers. "Get him out of here. He's going to start spiking a fever—"

"Did you just rip off your shirt?" Kenji asks, stunned. "Do you realize it's still raining outside?"

"I need to do something with my arm." I frown at him, then brace myself, breathing through the pain as I use the cotton to fashion a crude sling for my shoulder. "I can't run after her like this."

"You're not running anywhere," Kenji says, his voice hardening. "You need to walk right into recovery. Let the unit round her up—it shouldn't take long—"

"No." I lift my head to look at him. Rain sweeps into the hangar on a sudden gust of wind, the cold mist welcome on my overheated skin. "Rosabelle is *my* problem."

"Let her be someone else's problem."

"She's already mine," I say darkly. "And I don't like sharing my problems with people."

"Maybe we should go," Allie says quietly to Kenji. "Get you over to the girls—"

"Shut up, Allie."

"Yes, sir."

"Bro, did you take a blow to the head?" Kenji says to me now. "Why are you trying to get yourself killed?"

I tie off the sling with my teeth. "I'm not trying to get myself killed."

"Oh, okay, so maybe you've just lost track of the fact that this is, like, the fourth time she's tried to kill you."

"She only tried to kill me once."

"You mean that blood all over your jeans, that nasty gash in your side, that bullet in your shoulder—that's just fashion?"

Now I'm getting irritated. "That was different."

"James, you're not invincible," he says angrily. "Just because your body can heal itself doesn't mean you can withstand anything. You're lucky to be alive right now. If that bullet hit you a few inches to the left you wouldn't even be standing here—"

"Trust me," I say, cutting him off. "If she'd wanted me to die, she wouldn't have missed."

"She's not some perfect killing machine," Kenji says, his voice rising in anger. "She's an injured human being who makes mistakes just like the rest of us—"

"Thanks for your concern. I love you, too."

"Fuck you, don't make fun of my feelings. You have no idea how many people care about you—"

"And I'm trying to protect those people," I hit back. "I made this mess. I need to clean it up. I'm the only one who can handle this situation. Think whatever you want about me, but I serve a purpose here. She won't let anyone else get close to her. I can bring her in—I can *talk* to her—"

"Bring her in?" Kenji laughs. "They're out there shooting

to kill, bro. Warner is done with her. He gave the orders a few minutes ago—"

"What?" Shock shatters through me. "When?"

"—she's too much of a liability. And because of her, so are you. We tried to bring her in. She nearly killed us both. Warner's had enough and he wants her gone—"

"She wasn't trying to kill us!"

"Nope. I'm not doing this." He nods to Zain and Allie. "Let's go. We're done here—"

"Where the hell is he, anyway?" I ask, panic rising within me. "Why is Warner hiding?"

"He's not hiding, jackass," Kenji says, turning back. "He's working. That man never stops working, and quite frankly, you don't appreciate him enough."

"He's making a mistake," I say, chest heaving as a new pain radiates across my body. I turn in a circle, scanning the hangar with a sudden urgency. "This is a mistake— She has information we need— You don't— *Jesus*—"

"James, are you okay?" Kenji's voice seems to echo in my head, reaching me from far away. "Because I'm really starting to worry about you—"

Seriously, James, I'm worried about you—

In the frenzy, it's Adam's voice that surges to the surface of my mind.

—maybe it's time you talk to someone about all this. You don't seem like yourself lately. And you're still having nightmares every night? It's been over ten years. You still can't hear Gigi and Roman cry without losing your mind. What are you going to do when Juliette

has that baby? You know babies cry all the time, right? Like, in the middle of the night? Sometimes for hours? You live with them—you're not going to be able to escape it. Seriously, I think you should consider seeing a psychiatrist. I know this girl is beautiful but is that really enough? I thought you were smarter than that. I'm worried there's still a lot of unresolved trauma leading you to make poor and destructive choices—

For a second I close my eyes.

My heart is beating so hard I can't hear Kenji anymore. I can't hear anything but the sounds of my own breaths, loud in my head. I can't think beyond my own fury as frustration coils inside of me, heating my chest. I look into the middle distance, the room unfocusing around me, lights in the hangar flaring suddenly too bright—

Lights.

I frown as I look up, reality striking me with the force of a thunderclap. Suddenly I'm back in my body, my feet firmly on the ground, cold air whipping at my bare skin. Red beacon lights cut ominously through the dark, the rising rumble of a jet engine slowly building into an unmistakable, earsplitting roar.

I suck in a breath, feel the ground vibrate beneath me.

Holy shit.

ROSABELLE

14

I blink blood out of my eyes for the third time, then wipe at my fresh head wound with a shaking hand. Red smears across my fingers as I turn on the nav lights and shut off the radio before doing a few quick, preflight checks. I monitor the engine pressure as it rumbles louder, rising in RPM. This plane was receiving maintenance, but I don't know whether it was for a routine check or a more serious issue.

There's a chance something's wrong with it.

A quick scan of the systems tells me that fuel levels are low; the tire pressure in one wheel is suboptimal. There's a flashing alert for an issue I can't decipher, and a distinct, concerning rattle rises up from the engine as it accelerates, the cockpit reverberating with a force that shudders through my shattered body.

I have no doubt my ankle is broken.

I'm afraid to look too closely at the rest of me. I can feel that my lip is split, swollen and bleeding; the inflamed touch of my skin tells me I'm running a fever; my inability to duck my head without losing my equilibrium says I have a serious concussion. I'm otherwise in so much pain that one injury is indecipherable from another, my body throbbing as a single unit. But I've collapsed so far inside myself I've managed to deaden all sensations to a manageable agony, survival instincts overriding everything but my mind, my desperate need to get out of here.

My eyes dart to the windows, the glow of the moon in the storm. I hear the clamor of voices below—

Gunfire hits the glass with a violence that rattles my shot nerves, spiderweb cracks forming along the windshield. The bullet-resistant windows can sustain only so much before they lose efficacy.

My pulse quickens.

It's taking longer than necessary for the engine to reach a stable operating speed. I take a chance pushing open the throttle a little more, but the rattle only gets worse. Panic threatens to crowd my head.

There's no time. I'm out of time.

These seconds I have now were stolen from the future, meted out against the will of fate.

I have to work quickly or die.

It feels impossible that I even made it inside the cockpit, but I'm not yet beyond reach. I managed to knock down one of the two rolling safety ladders leading up to the aircraft, but I couldn't collapse the other, nearly taking a bullet in the throat as I tried to shove it out of reach, my body shaking with exhaustion. The ladder is now separated from the passenger door by several feet, but it won't be long before—

More gunfire cracks the windshield, each shot landing like a small explosion in my eardrums. I grit my teeth, begging the engine to cooperate as I take a risk and fully open the throttle.

I lick my split lip; taste blood; try to breathe.

The jet finally accelerates, and my heart nearly gives out as the plane begins to move forward. I'm breathing so hard my lungs are tired, but a whisper of relief moves through me as I reach for the nose wheel, ready to maneuver the plane out of the hangar and onto the runway.

It's going to be okay—I'm going to get out of here—

I flinch as a fresh round of shots ricochet off the steel body, a few more making contact with the windows. A final shot shatters the windshield entirely, and I duck almost too late, the bullet grazing my shoulder, burying itself in the seat behind me. I stifle a cry as the pain takes my breath away, cold winds sweeping rain into the cockpit as an alarm blares, a flashing indicator informing me that the pressurization system has malfunctioned.

Without a perfect seal, the jet won't be able to maintain cabin pressure once I'm in the air; but I'm not concerned about maintaining oxygen levels at high altitude. I don't need to ascend that far in order to escape. I might freeze to death, but at least I'll be able to breathe.

They think I'm trying to fly all the way home.

I just need to get far enough away.

The jet is picking up speed, the nose pushing farther out the hangar as I drive forward, granting me better cover for gunfire. With a shaking hand I unzip the neck of my costume, retrieving what's left of the slim chocolate bar still stashed against my sternum. It's broken in several places and at least partly melted—but the wrapper is still managing to hold most of the pieces together.

I place this tattered miracle on the interface.

If I can manage to get this plane above ten thousand feet I'll be thrilled. I'll grab the emergency kit before I eject; and then I'll find time to reset my bones, stitch up my wounds, bring down this fever. I'll be fine. I'll find somewhere safer to hide. I'll have time to heal while I regroup. I'll get home in one piece. I'll save Clara. I'll bring her chocolate.

I'll burn the Ark to the ground.

I comfort myself with these lies the way a corrupt government comforts its people: tending a wound by tying the bandage so tight you don't realize you're being killed by the same hands promising to save you.

I realize I'm likely sentencing myself to death.

But I'd rather go to my grave knowing I gave everything in the effort to get to Clara. I won't give up now, not for the pretense of survival, not to chain myself to a new master in The New Republic, not for a lifetime of wondering whether I could've tried harder to save my sister, to annihilate an oppressor.

My priorities have never been so clear.

The plane moves smoothly as we exit the mouth of the hangar, the rattle of the engine quieting, and hope begins to unfurl dangerously in my chest even as the sound of gunfire scores my desperate exit.

Nearly there.

Blood drips off my chin onto the aircraft interface with a steady *pat pat*, and the spatter is soon distracting; I wipe haphazardly at my cheek, guessing at the source of the wound, then wipe the blood off the screens only to smear everything in red.

My hands are trembling badly.

I'm not sure what will be left of me by the end of this, but I am the monster they made me. If I manage to survive I will destroy The Reestablishment for doing this to me—for lying to me, for torturing my sister—for thinking they could use and discard me without suffering the consequences.

Ten years they spent slowly disassembling my soul, and I was stupid enough to believe that after they'd annihilated my humanity I might be rewarded with freedom. It's the promise of retribution that keeps my heart beating, my broken body moving. There's no use feeling anything other than anger right now. I refuse to succumb to fear. I'll die before I ever surrender my mind again.

And when I go down, I'll take them down with me.

Bullets continue to riddle the aircraft body at steady intervals, my frayed nerves recoiling at every sound, my ears ringing in pain.

I grip the nose wheel tighter.

I navigate the aircraft onto the tarmac, using my one good foot to manipulate the rudder pedals, aligning the nose wheel with the center of the runway.

I take a deep, steadying breath.

"ROSABELLE—"

ROSABELLE

15

I go painfully solid.

The unchecked scream of his voice inspires in me a fear so great I can hardly move. In fact I have to summon the courage to turn around, my heart hammering, as I brace for the sight of him.

When I do, the last of my strength nearly leaves my body.

James is charging toward the plane, dragging a rolling safety ladder behind him. It takes me a moment to fully comprehend what I'm witnessing: he's shirtless and bloodied, illuminated in the ghostly red and green nav lights of the aircraft. A makeshift sling is wrapped around his right arm. Rain is pelting him, streaking through dried blood, rivers of red snaking down his torso. I see the shape of his plan immediately, and my throat constricts as I assess the risk, the improbability—

There's no way he's going to make it.

He shoves the ladder in the direction of the aircraft, then sprints to catch it, jumping onto its bottom step, grabbing the safety rail and hauling himself up the stairs as it careens toward the moving plane, crashing against the far side of the body with a destabilizing tremor.

I hit the brakes on instinct.

James jolts.

The chocolate bar skitters.

I hold my breath.

He has less than seconds to move, and he launches himself onto the wing badly, nearly slipping, the reverberations rocking the aircraft. I watch in horror as he loses his balance, then his grip, trying to climb up with only one arm onto the slick, rain-soaked surface.

I'm now dizzy with fear.

I look down, feel the weight of my foot on the wheel brake; then stare at my hand on the throttle.

I could take off now.

I could push the throttle to its maximum position, then generate lift at a steep incline, which would all but guarantee flinging him off the wing; I'd risk airflow disruption, but at least I'd be airborne, with a chance to correct the maneuver in flight.

James, on the other hand, would not survive.

I swallow. Maybe he would.

No, he would not.

Taking into account the storm, the winds, his injury, and the height from which he'd fall, the force of collision would almost certainly break his neck.

He'd die on impact.

Maybe.

Probably.

Panic grips me with both hands, my indecision costing me precious seconds. I hear shouts carrying on the wind, soldiers running toward my stalled jet. The truth finds me here, in my weakest moment, in my trembling heart: I want to destroy Klaus to save Clara, to demand retribution; but there's another part of me, a quieter part of me, that wants to spare this pathetic world and its simple dreams. I want to kill The Reestablishment so that these soft, loud people might continue to live.

So that James might continue to live.

My hand shakes on the throttle, heat searing my eyes. I'm staring at the ruined chocolate bar, its paper exterior separating from the foil. Its spine is broken, segments shattered like bones.

I can still feel that frail shoot pushing up through the ashes of my soul, a green tendril of new growth.

The promise of change.

I thought you might want to give this to your sister.

The costs of death are catching up to me, revealing the cracks in my skin, my spirit. Maybe it's too late to die a better person than I lived. Maybe it's selfish to ache for a ray of light after a lifetime of darkness.

Clara.

Clara.

I'd have to kill James to get to my sister. One more body on my conscience. Another strike upon my soul. I could do it. I could do it right now.

Maybe this is all I am, all I'll ever be.

My hand is gripping the throttle so hard tremors begin to shake my entire body. The sound of the idling engine roars in my ears. Movement outside the aircraft screams at my instincts to make a move, now, before it's too late.

I'm paralyzed.

I refocus my eyes on the runway, trying to calm the frenzy of my heart in order to make the right decision.

The right decision.

I look back at the destroyed chocolate bar.

I can't solve this equation fast enough.

I hear the thrum of rolling wheels before I see the ladder, then the soldiers. The body of the plane vibrates as metal slams against metal; boots thudding across the wing. Handrails suddenly appear in the side window. I can just make out the shadow of him charging up the steps and still, I do nothing.

My body has betrayed me.

Heat pricks dangerously at my eyes; my head fogs with steam, clouding my mind. When he comes into view, chest heaving, rain lashing the blood off his body, I see his face as if through panes of time, when he and I lived out an inverse of this day.

James had stolen an aircraft; I'd climbed into the passenger seat.

That was the day he drove an ice pick into my heart, delivering the first of a series of cracks that would lead me here, to this moment of devastation, his voice haunting me forever—

Where'd they take your sister?
The asylum, right?

But, like, how do we get there?

"Rosabelle," he cries. "Turn off the engines!"

But, like, how do we get there?

He yanks open the door with his left arm, the action counterintuitive, and nearly loses his footing before catching himself against the handrails, then clambering up into the cabin. He moves without hesitation, reaching across me to shut off the throttle, and the chocolate bar flies across the interface before hitting the floor with a dull thud. The engines begin to slow, the roar diminishing.

It occurs to me to do something.

My body hasn't stopped trembling, but I can't seem to lift a finger. I've gone numb.

When the engines stop he hits the master switch, shutting down all electrical systems, and the quiet is suddenly excruciating.

My ears ring so badly I want to scream.

I feel like I've been struck with a tuning fork, the sounds beyond my head suddenly incomprehensible. A strange paralysis has overtaken my limbs; shock and pain and fever inhaling me.

James is here.

He's here and now my heart is beating harder, my head is pounding, my pain devouring. His mere presence is tearing away the veils that keep me apart from sensation, and suddenly I feel everything all at once, and the deluge is more than I can bear—

A desperate, gasping sound leaves my body.

My ankle is broken. My ribs are cracked. My head is bleeding. My bones are shaking. I think, at some point, I might've been shot.

I can't breathe. I'm hyperventilating.

"*Hey*," he says, reaching for me, taking my bleeding face in his left hand. He's soaking wet. His palm is rough. The sound of his voice travels lightyears to reach me. "You're okay," he says. "You're okay. Look at me—"

Clara.

Clara.

I've failed my sister—

"Rosabelle," he says gently, tilting up my chin. "Look at me. Please—"

I look at him like I'm seeing stars. The sound of his voice is an anchor in the tempest of my mind but my chest feels as if it's been trampled. I can't catch my breath. I can't feel my hands. I can't breathe, *I can't breathe*—

"Hey, you're okay," he says again. "I'm here. I'm with you. You're safe."

I realize only as I taste the salt of my own tears that I'm crying. I've lost all control. I don't recognize these horrible sounds—these desperate sobs coming from somewhere inside of me.

It can't be me.

I don't cry. I never cry. Before I met James I hadn't cried in ten years.

"Breathe for me, okay?" he says. "I'm here. I'm with you, Rosabelle. Are you with me?"

I look up into his eyes, my heart wrenching. I seem to tilt over and over inside myself, a reminder that I have a concussion. I blink, disoriented. A convulsive gasp escapes me as a violent shudder racks my body. I'm badly nauseous. I might be suspended in space, slowly suffocating in this nightmare.

"Rosabelle," he says again. "Are you with me?"

I exhale unevenly before I feel the slow rise of a soft heat circling my throat, fingers of light moving up my face like a caress. The feeling soon intensifies, first silencing the agony in my ears, then soothing the pain in my head.

I cry out, my eyes closing.

"Rosabelle?"

I fight to draw a full, shaky breath. My racing heart begins to slow. My lungs begin to release.

"I can't heal you here," he says, his voice rough, his thumb moving across my skin. "Not like this, not in this state. My own body is too weak, your damage is too deep, and everyone is waiting outside. But I wanted to relieve some of the pain."

A wave of crushing exhaustion closes over my head and the tide takes me apart, my bones coming loose from my flesh. I let my cheek fall heavily against his hand, allowing him to catch me.

I hear the intake of his breath.

I force my eyes open to find him searching my face, his own eyes tight with something like pain.

"Is it helping?" he asks.

"Yes," I say, breathless. "Thank you."

"Stay with me, okay? Don't pass out. We still have to get off the plane."

Sounds carry from the world beyond; the thump of boots on metal as someone stomps up the ladder. Then—

"Hey, man, you all right up there?"

The stranger's voice sharpens something inside of me, piercing the moment like a knife.

I stiffen.

I sit up, suddenly fully seated inside myself, shields rebuilding, exhaustion retreating, ice closing over my head. Survival instincts come back online, my vision clearing, my bones hardening.

I set aside the pain again, letting it simmer.

James doesn't meet my eyes as he pulls back, his body shaking slightly. He pushes wet hair off his forehead, turning only a little when he says, without shouting, "Give me a minute."

I wipe my tear-streaked cheeks with unsteady, bloodstained fingers, struggling to piece myself back together. In a shock of clarity James comes into focus: shirtless in the moonlight, the bare expanse of his chest and torso gleaming, rivulets of rainwater still snaking down the hard planes of his body. Shadows catch every curve and ridge of muscle, rendering him into something breathtaking.

The voice, again: "You sure you don't need backup?"

"I'm sure."

"Really? Because—"

"Just give me a fucking second, Zain," James says, his

voice rising, his body tensing. "She's really badly injured."

A pause.

I can practically hear the smile in Zain's voice when he says, "No shit? Is that why she didn't kill you? We all thought she was going to take off while you were climbing the plane. No way you would've survived that."

James swallows, hard, and I watch the movement in his throat, my heart racing again.

Very slowly he looks up at me, searching my eyes.

"Yeah," he says. "That's probably why she didn't kill me."

"Insane move, man. Lucky it worked out."

"Lucky," James echoes, staring at me. A drop of rainwater releases from his hair, breaking on his cheek.

I hold my breath; I'd suddenly rather die than speak.

His eyes sweep across my face again, his jaw tightening. Gently, he says, "Can you stand up?"

"Yes," I lie.

James has to stoop in the cabin, ducking as he offers me his good arm, and I take it, shifting my weight onto my only working leg as I use borrowed strength to rise from my seat. I make a choked sound as I accidentally tweak my broken foot, and James pales as he scans my body, his eyes widening in fear.

I follow his gaze to my bad leg, where the polyester of my costume is torn open and blood-soaked at the thigh, poorly clotted at the wound.

"You've been shot," he says, stunned.

I hold steady, closing my eyes as the pain crescendos.

That explains the fever. "How many times?"

"*What?* Rosabelle—"

"Hey, man— Um, I'm supposed to tell you that if you don't get down here soon"—Zain laughs nervously—"uh, Warner said he's going to shoot you through the window?"

"Great," James says angrily. "Thanks."

"I mean I'm sure he wasn't serious, but—"

"I'm sure he was serious." James cuts him off. "We're coming down the ladder now."

I feel, for a dizzying moment, like I'm going to faint. My hand tightens around James's arm as I fight the compulsion, and I sense him turning to me, his voice strained with anguish. "Can you even walk?"

"Yes," I lie, forcing my eyes open.

Zain tries again. "Hey, so, uh, quick update? He seems really, really mad—"

James glares through the open door, suddenly furious: "Tell him to wait a single fucking minute—"

A warning shot shatters what's left of the windshield.

ROSABELLE

16

I don't know how we get off the jet.

The experience is punctuated by pain so excruciating it provides its own anesthetic; I feel myself nearly lose consciousness on several occasions, and I can't help but wonder if James, whose arm remains tight around my waist with every difficult step, isn't giving me some kind of low-level relief.

The rain, at least, seems to have died down.

I welcome the evening chill on my feverish skin, feeling dislocated as I look around. Soldiers are assembled in shadow on the tarmac below. The air is fresh, the world cleansed. Moonlight washes over everything, casting the night in a ghostly, beautiful glow entirely at odds with the state of my mind.

"You okay?" James whispers.

Like a sledgehammer, these two words land an impact that craters my chest.

I risk a glance at him.

He's soaked through; his face is streaked with blood; he's wearing a sling fashioned from a torn length of cotton; his shoulder is immobilized because of what I did to him.

He still hasn't mentioned the injury.

He hasn't betrayed a moment of anger with me; not a whisper of resentment. He let me shoot him and simply moved on. Accepted it. Maybe forgave me for it.

I never even asked him if he was okay.

The cracks in my heart are threatening to give way altogether. I'm suddenly terrified of what I might find under all that ice.

"Yes," I lie. "I'm okay."

When we finally reach the bottom of the stairs, a welcoming party greets us by lifting their weapons in concert, aiming them at my head.

I feel the tension rise in James's body as we pass through the procession of soldiers. He holds me a little tighter, and I nearly give in to the impulse to lean into him as I limp forward. His nearness is a gift; his touch is warm despite the chill; his very presence is keeping me calm.

They'll either kill me now or take me somewhere to die.

There can be no other option.

If they let me live, I'll never stop running. If they heal me and throw me back in prison, I'll never stop breaking out. Even I know I'm a liability. I'd make the call to kill me, too.

I've accepted my fate.

I made my choice on that jet by making no choice. By not killing James, I sentenced my sister to certain death. I sentenced myself to certain death.

This is what I deserve.

Still—

When I see him standing there at the end of the line,

the hard planes of his face illuminated by starlight, my fear response is immediate.

Aaron Warner Anderson.

James's older brother is waiting for me. I steel myself as I read the cold fury in his eyes; the careful, violent control in his body.

Everything about this man seems lethal.

I saw him only on special occasions while I was in prison; he'd chosen to begin interrogations by breaking my mind over breaking my body—using my father to carefully fillet my soul—and I can't say he was unsuccessful. The psychological damage from the hours I spent locked up with my estranged father has yet to be determined. I was hoping to die before I was ever compelled to examine those feelings.

This might be my chance.

Warner stands before me with deceptive composure, his golden hair glinting in a glare of light, his hands clasped in front of him. He doesn't appear to be armed, though I know better than to believe that.

His eyes follow our every move.

The physical similarities between him and James strike me anew, the evidence of their shared DNA never clearer than when they're standing close together. They're both difficult to behold up close; both possessed of shocking, extraordinary beauty. They have the same cheekbones, the same nose, the same broad shoulders and air of authority— electric and powerful.

The differences between them, however, feel vast.

We come to an uncertain stop. Crickets have begun to chirp in the distance. I feel the weight of the soldiers' eyes; the moon looming above, bearing witness. It feels as if we've reached an executioner at the end of an altar.

"Let go of her," Warner says quietly.

"She can't stand on her own," James argues.

"That's her problem, not yours," he says.

"Yeah, but she's my problem. So her problems are my problems."

"James." He says the word quietly, lifting his head to level his brother a look so severe I feel the chill secondhand. "You are overestimating my affection for you."

James rolls his eyes in response.

I'm stunned.

I look from him to his brother, alarms sounding in my head. I wouldn't think it wise to call this man's bluff. Warner was born into the arms of the original movement; he became the chief commander and regent of what used to be Sector 45 at only eighteen years old. His legacy is legendary and terrifying. I can only imagine the blood that forged him. He looks capable of anything—

"Whatever," James says. "I think you're underestimating my influence in your life."

Warner sharpens, his eyes flaring in anger, and fear arrows through my body.

"I can stand on my own," I lie quickly. "I'll be fine—"

"You were looking for her," James says to his brother, cutting me off. "I found her. You're welcome. Can we get out of here now? I'm freezing." He gestures to the soldiers behind us. "It's been a long day. Everyone is exhausted."

"*Everyone is exhausted?*" Warner echoes, his eyes widening a fraction. "You care whether everyone is exhausted? I didn't realize you possessed the imagination necessary to conceptualize the needs and feelings of others."

James sighs, squeezing his eyes shut. "Don't do this. Not here. Not right now—"

"Then step away from her."

"I can't. She'll literally fall over."

"Is this some display of delayed adolescence?" says Warner. "Have you finally decided to rebel against authority?"

"Don't be a dick," James says.

One of the soldiers audibly gasps.

Warner studies James, a ghost of an angry smile on his face. "I won't ask you again."

"*No.*"

"James—" I say, panicking.

Warner animates with movement so fluid I don't even see him reach for a gun before he shoots James in the leg.

I nearly scream.

James fights back a cry, reactively releasing me as he staggers, trying to catch himself with only one arm.

I land badly on my own injured leg, nearly biting through my tongue to contain a scream, with uneven results. Agony rushes back into my body with a force so violent I nearly faint. I blink, beads of perspiration rising along my forehead, the nape of my neck. I fight to stay in my skin, breathing rapidly as an altogether different ache fractures across my chest. *This* is why James refused to let me go.

He was managing my pain.

A few soldiers rush forward to catch him, and he tries to shake them off but he doesn't have the leverage. He's down one arm and one leg and they grapple with him, dragging him away from me, muttering apologies under their breaths. He doesn't take this well.

"You're a fucking idiot," he shouts at Warner, still struggling. "Juliette is going to kill you."

Warner goes still, his face impassive, and yet I see it: a single moment of uncertainty, flashing in and out of his eyes.

A weakness, noted.

"Was it worth it?" James is saying. "She's going to be so pissed at you when she finds out you shot me—"

"Shut up," Warner says, a muscle ticking in his jaw. "You'll be fine."

"What are you going to do to her?" James says, still fighting the soldiers restraining him, and I realize he's asking about me.

I catch a glimpse of his eyes—wild and angry—just before Warner turns the heat of his gaze in my direction, bearing no markers of his momentary uncertainty.

My heart is pounding badly in my chest.

"Warner, listen to me," James is saying, sounding panicked. "I know you're mad. I know I fucked up, okay? I'm sorry. I'm really, really sorry. I did this all wrong—"

Warner takes a step toward me.

I have no idea how I'm still standing. Pain has consumed me so completely that I'm almost looking forward to death.

"—but you can't kill her. We need her. She was trying to get home because there's something bigger going on. She was sent here for a reason. She told me we only have seven weeks before it's too late—"

Warner and I stiffen at the same time.

We both look up at James.

Warner's eyes narrow with a new intensity. Not anger. It looks more like awareness.

My eyes, on the other hand, are bright with fear.

"You know I'm telling the truth," James says to his brother. "You know I'd never lie about something like this. I want to keep our world safe just as much as you do. Rosabelle's been trying to fix things on her own, but if we work together—"

"No," I gasp, the word leaving my lips before I've had a chance to consider it. "James—"

"What do you mean, *no*?" he says, turning to me. "Would you really rather die than work together?"

"I—I don't—"

I can't think.

Right now, I can't process much beyond the pain devouring my body. I need time to gather my thoughts. To set down my head.

I don't understand what James is suggesting.

Ark officials would never forge a faithful alliance with a known adversary. The Reestablishment doesn't offer second chances to its enemies; this is not an avenue I'm familiar with. All spies who enter the island are immediately executed, or else viciously tortured and manipulated for information and then, executed.

I would know. The executions were my job.

I glimpse Warner's face, the look of concentrated interest in his eyes.

I don't like it.

I don't want a new master.

"C'mon, Rosabelle," James says angrily. "If you die, you're sentencing us all to death. Is that really what you want?"

I look up at him, my heart thudding against my ribs.

An honest answer to his question would cost me too much. I don't want their world to suffer, but neither do I want to exchange death for a life rotting in captivity, being endlessly tortured for information only to lose what matters to me anyway. They'd siphon off my marrow, draining me for intel while I fester—for what?

A half-life of a half-life?

These people are not capable of comprehending my world. Even a theoretical understanding of the sophisticated surveillance of the Ark wouldn't be enough; if I were shackled to a team of their soldiers on a mission to take out Klaus, they'd get us all killed in seconds. They're too loud, too weak; too unfamiliar with the terrors of a true surveillance state. And they'd never prioritize saving Clara. They wouldn't care about Clara—

"Tell me something, Rosabelle Wolff."

I draw breath at the sound of Warner's voice, staring up into his disorienting eyes as a shaft of light cuts across his face.

It's hard to believe this man is married.

It's hard to believe he'd be interested in the institution; that he might've experienced enough delicate emotion to entertain the idea of a wife. I can't imagine him being gentle; he seems incapable of warmth. It's only his close relationship with James that gives me pause about his character. The fact that he shot his own brother in the leg notwithstanding, James doesn't seem afraid of him at all.

I can't figure out what that means.

"You spent nearly ten days in prison," Warner says, taking another step closer to me. "Ten days, and you never said a word. You didn't take one audible breath."

Looking into his eyes feels a little like catching fire.

"Imagine my surprise to discover your complete refusal to speak—when for weeks prior to your incarceration you were engaged in regular conversation with my brother."

My heart beats harder.

"Tonight, I learn you're once again capable of forming complete sentences." He hesitates. Studies me. "What is it about James that makes you so talkative?"

"Bro, this isn't—" James tries to say.

Warner holds up a hand, his eyes on me. "Did you really decide to confide more in him during the bloodshed and chaos of the past several hours than you might've shared with your own father in over a week?"

Your own father.

I keep my eyes on the ground.

Rosa, it's not what you think—

I didn't abandon you, they'd left me for dead— These people saved my life—

Rosa— Look at me—

No.

I stay where I am despite my every instinct to run; if I shift even an inch my legs will give out from under me.

"Did you really tell him," Warner goes on, "that we have seven weeks before some new hell befalls our world?"

Rosa, is your mother still alive?

Rosa, does Clara remember me?

No—

NO.

"Rosabelle," James says quietly. "Please."

I turn my head as a first leaf might turn toward the sun, the tender shoot of life inside me responding instinctively to the resonance of his voice, recognizing light.

James shakes his head at me, his eyes tired.

I take in his fresh wound, his bound arm, the myriad cuts and scrapes across his bare, blood-streaked skin. I stabbed him in the torso, in the thigh. He just took a shot in the leg because of me.

This all began when I slit his throat.

Still, he's staring at me with a kind of anguish, like I might, at any moment, break his heart.

My chest constricts in response.

"That will suffice as an answer."

I look up, startled. Warner is studying me with a fascination that's entirely new, his incisive look sending me into a fresh panic.

"I'm going to take some time to make a decision," Warner says, his eyes hardening. "That's all for now." He makes a motion as if to dismiss me—

And I drop dead.

JAMES

17

I hold the potato firmly on the cutting board, then bring the knife down too hard, nicking the vegetable and nearly taking off my hand. The potato goes flying, ricocheting off a bottle of olive oil before hitting the ground, then rolling under the cabinet. The bottle topples over, glass clattering against stone.

Shit.

"You're not trying to *kill* the potato," Nazeera says, crossing her arms as she leans against the wall, watching me with an amused smile. She's wearing an oversized sweatshirt, her hands tucked into the front pocket, the hood pulled up. "Your food, by this point in the process, should already be dead."

"Right," I say, my head pounding. "Good point."

I swipe the potato off the ground, then rinse it at the sink before putting it back on the cutting board.

For a moment, I stare at the mess.

Potato peels are piled in a small heap on the counter, leafy celery and carrot tops stacked beside them, papery onion skins fluttering as I move, generating wind.

I gather the leavings and toss them in the compost bin.

"This is more complicated than I thought it would be,"

I say, fighting to take a full breath.

My heart is racing for no reason.

I glance out the window, then at Nazeera, the warmth in her familiar eyes a welcome diversion from my own mind. I've known her for nearly as long as I've known Kenji. For a few years the two of them were a package deal; she's always been like an older sister to me.

"You'll be all right," she says. "You already have excellent knife skills. You just need to slow down."

I cast her a dubious look. "Slow down more than this?"

I've been hacking away for at least a couple of hours, and I'm just getting worse. The problem is, I'm restless and distracted. But also—there's no consistency to chopping things. Every vegetable has to be cleaned and cut differently, and some of them fight back when you hurt them.

Slicing the onion nearly took me out.

"Slow down your *movements*," she clarifies, grinning. "Apply firm but steady pressure and you'll get the hang of it. You have to learn the technique before you can speed up. Remember: you're not dismembering a body. You're just making big things smaller."

"Right." I exhale, trying to loosen the tension in my shoulders. I stare at the little bowls arranged before me.

Nazeera insisted I prep everything before I actually start cooking, an extra step I resented before arriving at this moment. I'm realizing only now that if I'd just started cooking right away—without a plan or even a sense of how long it would take me to chop everything—I'd for sure have burned the kitchen to the ground.

I look over the selection of unevenly diced celery, carrots, and onions, and for a second I actually feel a little proud. Then embarrassed. Then irritated. Then I remember the chicken is still in the fridge.

I think it's time for a break.

I abandon the cutting board and drop down into a chair at the kitchen table, absently rubbing my eyes, which are still stinging from the onions.

When I hear a fragment of what sounds like conversation, I look up.

Nazeera is staring at me.

"Did you say something?" I ask her.

"Yeah." She smiles, but her eyes are concerned. "I said, *are you all right?*"

"Oh." I run a hand through my hair. "Sorry, I didn't hear you."

I stare out the window as a bone-deep fatigue settles inside me. Cold sunlight gleams over the quiet afternoon. Only a few people dot the sidewalks, some pushing strollers. A dog barks. A single car drives by. Wind pushes through the big tree in the front yard, and I stare at its shifting branches as my heart continues to race.

I glance at the clock.

Warner is supposed to be here for a meeting in about half an hour, and the closer we get to the appointed hour the more impatient I become. Pressure keeps building in my head.

I can't seem to get myself under control.

I startle at the sound of wood shifting against wood. Nazeera pulls up a chair, sits down.

"You never answered my question," she says.

I turn to look at her, but I'm distracted by a shaft of light beyond her head, dust motes suspended like insects in amber. "What?"

"James," she says.

"Yeah?"

"Look at me for a second."

I meet her light brown eyes, drum my fingers against my thigh. "I'm looking at you."

"Maybe you should go for a walk," she says.

I shake my head. "I went for a run earlier."

"You already hit the gym?"

"Twice."

"Did you eat anything?"

"I had a protein shake."

"That's not enough food," she points out.

I push up in my seat, thinking I might try to chop that potato again, then sit back down. Then glance at the clock. "I'm not hungry."

"Not hungry," she says, raising her eyebrows. "Sure. Okay."

For a minute, we both stare out the window in silence.

Finally Nazeera says, "Kind of a strange time to decide you want to learn how to cook."

I glance at her, but she's still staring outside, her eyes

tracking a bird. I return my gaze to the window, feeling suddenly subdued. "Yeah," I say. "Well."

She clears her throat, then says my name with intention—

"Don't you want to check on Juliette?" I ask, cutting her off before she can interrogate me.

Nazeera hesitates, drawing back. "She's napping."

"Wake her up."

"James—"

"How's your house?" I ask. "Unheated? Unfurnished? Twin mattress still tossed in the middle of the living room, single bulb burning from the ceiling?"

She almost laughs. "I bought sheets."

"Still in the bag?"

"Shut up," she says, rolling her eyes. "You know I'm only here every couple of months, and when I'm here I'm usually *here*. I don't have time to fix it up."

"You've got time now," I point out.

"Are you asking me to leave?"

"Nope," I say, shaking my head. "You stay. Hand over your keys and I'll leave. I'll even put those sheets on the mattress." I pause. "Do you own a pillow yet, or are you still using a garbage bag stuffed with old laundry?"

"I did that *once*—"

"Save your lies for a different James," I say to her. "An uglier, stupider one."

"Okay." She nods, pretending to be impressed. "Well, at least now I can tell Juliette that Warner was right to shoot you. If you're going to be this weird about having a simple conversation, the situation is worse than I realized."

"Exactly." I hold out my hand. "Give me your keys. Or wait—do you even bother to lock your door?"

"Look, you can't do this." She rests her elbows on the table, leaning forward to look at me. "You can't fall for her. This is a really, really bad idea. You know that, right? Please tell me you know that."

My heart stalls, then picks up speed too quickly. The sensation makes me so uncomfortable that my next words come out a little mean. "You know Kenji's still madly in love with you, right?"

Nazeera noticeably stiffens, like I've broken an unspoken rule.

I have.

But she started it.

We both fall silent, sharpening our knives.

"There's no happily ever after with someone like her," she says, her eyes narrowing. "No matter what happens next, it won't end with you cooking her dinner."

My headache suddenly intensifies.

I clench and unclench my fists under the table, then roll my neck, trying to release the tension. "You know, you never struck me as a coward," I say. "Why keep pretending you and Kenji aren't meant to be together?"

"James—"

"And it's not just me," I say. "Everyone is confused. You're here every couple of months. You manage to avoid each other in the beginning, but then your schedules inevitably collide, resulting in a series of emotional breakdowns. And then I sit here and picture you going back to your empty house with its one light and bag of sheets and I'm wondering if you wish things had worked out differently."

Nazeera draws breath, enough to know I've done some damage. "Wow," she says softly. "Direct hit. This must be serious. You must really be suffering."

I drag my hands down my face, sitting back in my seat. "Sorry. I'm sorry."

We're both quiet for too long, unspoken tension building, straining the silence.

"Falling in love feels a little like dying," she finally says. "No one really tells you that."

"*Fuck*," I breathe, gripping the table. "I don't want to hear that."

"No one wants to hear it. But the poets keep trying to warn us."

"I feel like I'm having a series of heart attacks," I say, forcing the words out. "I don't know how to sit down anymore. I don't even know how to stand still. I feel sick. I seriously think I'm losing my mind."

"James," she says gently. She rests a hand on my arm and I nearly flinch at the contact. "It's only been three days. She's not dead—"

I make an angry sound.

"She's not," Nazeera insists. "He didn't really kill her, you know that. Warner used her powers against her to put her into a sort of . . . coma. She's a major flight risk. We still don't know if we can trust her. It's the safest way to keep her contained while she recovers—"

"Except that we don't know anything about her supposed powers," I say sharply, looking up. "Warner's just guessing. The fact that he can sense and manipulate other people's abilities doesn't mean he knows exactly how to use them. We have no idea whether she'll actually wake up—or if he's kept her unconscious for so long that it breaks something inside of her—"

"You know what? This is my fault," she says, drawing her hands back into her lap. "You shouldn't be learning to chop vegetables. I shouldn't have taken you to the farmers market—"

"What does that have to do with anything?" I ask, reeling.

"Everything," Nazeera says, turning to face me. "You're not thinking straight. I shouldn't have indulged your fantasies—"

"*Fantasies?*"

"—and if anyone else were acting this way you'd be the first to call them out for disloyalty to the Republic. The fact that you're questioning a decision to restrain a violent, known assassin of The Reestablishment is genuinely concerning."

"I don't want to talk about this," I say, closing my eyes. "My head hurts. My chest hurts—"

"James, I need you to be realistic," she says, tempering her tone. "If you allow yourself to wallow in this daydream, things will only get worse."

"What daydream?" Now I'm getting offended.

"You really think you can date this girl?" she asks, giving me a hard look. "You think someone like her even knows how to be in a relationship? A girl like that doesn't even know how to relax. She walks into a room and immediately identifies the exits before deciding which everyday objects might double as weapons—"

"That's called being creative—"

"—she's not meeting strangers and wondering what they like to do in their spare time; she meets new people and assesses their strengths and weaknesses in order to determine the best way to kill them—"

"She's just a planner. She likes to plan ahead—"

"You think it would ever occur to her to do something for fun, or buy you a present on your birthday, or express her feelings without fear?"

I blink at her. "Wait, I'm sorry, are we talking about you or Rosabelle?"

"She's a trained executioner," Nazeera says, ignoring this. "She's spent her entire life being emotionally and physically tortured by one of the most tyrannical, oppressive regimes our world has ever known. Even if she wasn't an active threat to everything we've built; even if it wouldn't label you a traitor by association; even if you wouldn't lose the respect of your peers, the good opinion of your subordinates, the admiration of the children and widows of our fallen soldiers—"

"Now you're just exaggerating—"

"—she's too volatile to make the cut as a candidate

for your affections. She's like a stick of dynamite. Looks harmless until you strike a match."

I shake my head slowly.

I turn to the window again, closing my eyes as my heart pounds, then contracts. I take an uneven breath, watching a pair of squirrels chase each other up the trunk of a tree. And then I say, almost to myself, "I don't need her to buy me a present on my birthday."

Nazeera sighs. "Did you hear anything I just said to you?"

"Unfortunately."

"And?"

"Look, I just want to see her," I say roughly. "He won't even let me see her."

"Can you blame him?"

My jaw tenses. "Not really."

"Listen, I'm saying this because I care about you: falling in love with a girl like that wouldn't just be stupid, it would be dangerous. You have to be careful. If you keep acting like this in front of other soldiers, publicly defending her against the judgment of their own general, you'll put Warner in an impossible situation—"

"Yeah, look, I realize—"

"And you really need to cut him some slack. You think Warner's being hard on you but he's trying so hard to protect you from the consequences of your own actions—"

"Believe it or not," I say, cutting her off. "I know this."

Nazeera freezes. "You do?"

"Yes. I do. I'm not an idiot."

She lifts her eyebrows. "If that's true, you might want to be a little more obvious about it."

I shoot her a look, then sit back in my seat, rubbing my hands on my jeans. I feel like my chest is caving in. "I'm not falling in love," I say thickly. "I'm just—I just want to know if she's okay."

"That's good," Nazeera says. "That's a good start. Denial is a powerful tool."

"You would know." I glance at her. "You're the expert."

"Okay, I'm done being nice to you." She flattens her hands on the table. "You've used up all your goodwill for the day. If you're looking for compassion, try again tomorrow."

I flash her a smile.

She flips me off.

"Nice," I say. "Mature."

"Says the guy who can't chop a potato."

"Hey, when are you leaving again?" I ask. "I really need something to look forward to right now."

She flips me off with both hands.

Her hood has shifted back a little, a few strands of dark hair escaping her ponytail, framing her striking face. She scowls at me, and I can't help but laugh.

The first time I met Nazeera was the day she saved my life.

I was ten.

I'd been abducted by my own psychopathic father and left to rot in prison until the day he decided to use me as leverage. My affectionate dad was holding a knife to my throat, threatening to kill me, and then—

Nazeera.

A miracle.

She literally flew me out of there. I remember staring at her in that dumbstruck way of children; understanding, without really understanding, that I was looking at something beautiful.

When I see her now, I remember feeling safe.

My lifted spirits diminish at the memory, displaced by a sudden, weightier thought.

"Hey, seriously, though, when are you going to put him out of his misery? You two are soulmates. We all know it. I know *you* know it."

She averts her eyes. "Listen, James—"

"And maybe no one's told you this, but he hasn't so much as looked at another woman since the day you left."

She recoils, as if struck, just as the front door opens with a *bang*.

JAMES

18

"*Hey*," he shouts. "Can I get a little help over here?"

I hear Kenji's voice before I see him, walking in sideways with groceries. "J said you wanted to learn how to cook, and I said it was about damn time—"

Kenji sees Nazeera and absorbs the sight of her like a shock wave. He physically glitches, his visibility coming in and out like a shuddering breath. Groceries loosen in his grip with a rush of sound. A strange look crosses his face, a spasm of pain so acute it makes me fear the power of the human heart.

He looks at her like he's lost all peripheral vision.

"Hi," he says breathlessly.

Nazeera shoots to her feet. "Juliette is sleeping," she says, answering a question she wasn't asked. "I was upstairs, earlier. But I thought I'd give her some space."

Kenji nods aggressively, like that was a normal thing to say. "Good. Okay." He drops the groceries to the ground, where they land with unintentional violence. Something shatters. "That's nice."

This is a tragedy.

Nazeera bites her lip, the action drawing attention to her tiny diamond piercing. She used to have more, but she's phased them out over the last few years. Now she stuffs her hands into her hoodie pocket, looking uncomfortable.

"How—um, how are you?" she asks, searching his face. "I saw you the other day. At the coffee shop? I tried to say hi, but I think maybe you didn't see me."

Kenji just looks at her then.

Pure silence.

Watching this play out is not only painful, it's making me feel retroactively mortified. If I act anything like this when I'm around Rosabelle, I can understand why Warner shot me.

Maybe I should shoot Kenji.

Two infinitely long seconds pass before Kenji even notices me sitting here, and the unwelcome sight of my face makes him flinch.

"Yeah, hi," I say, my smile grim. I try to tell him with my eyes to be cool, to pull himself together—

He shakes his head at me.

I shake my head back harder.

"I have to—" Kenji looks away, searching around himself blindly. "I'm just going to— I'll be right back—"

And he walks out the house without a word. He doesn't even close the door behind him.

In his wake, Nazeera sinks down heavily in her seat.

I notice the slight tremble in her hands before she pulls the drawcords of her sweatshirt, tightening the hood around her head like a turtle retracting into its shell. She tugs her sleeves over her fists before tucking them into the single pocket, and then slowly lowers herself to the table, her eyes pinched as she rests her forehead against the wood.

I can't take it anymore.

"All right, what the hell is going on with you two?" I ask. "It's disgustingly obvious you still love each other."

She startles upright. "What? No it's not—"

"There's clearly nothing keeping you apart but your own bullshit. I've watched you both suffer for years—"

"It's not that simple—"

"Nazeera," I say, irritated. "Enough. You said your piece to me earlier; I'm going to say mine to you now. I want the truth. Why is it so impossible for you guys to give it another shot?"

She finally relents with a groan, squeezing her eyes shut as she releases the drawcords, pulling the hood away from her face. "Because," she says. "I already tried."

I blink. "What?"

There's a sudden commotion outside; voices rising. I peer out the window, distracted, but I'm not paying enough attention.

"I already tried," she says again. "I tried working things out between us. Twice. He won't take me back."

Oh.

Shit.

"*What?*" I say again, dumbfounded.

Voices grow louder in the yard, and I glance again toward the noise, but I can't focus. I feel like reality is being rewritten in my head.

"That's impossible," I say to her. "He's obsessed with you."

"No," she says, and laughs sadly. "He's not."

"Trust me, he's definitely—"

"You don't know enough about our history," she says, cutting me off. "You were so young—"

I look up at another burst of noise, voices carrying, and I crane my neck to peer out the window. When I see that it's Kenji and Warner arguing, I relax a little.

Perfectly normal behavior.

Even better, Warner is home early.

"Things are more complicated between us than you think," Nazeera says, drawing my focus again. "I was— Look, when Kenji and I first got together I was immature and stupid." She presses her fists to her eyes. "Never in my life had it occurred to me to sit down and sort out my issues, because I didn't even know I had issues. I was used to living in chaos. I was used to being messed up. I was used to blood and torture and violence. I had no idea I was an emotional idiot."

Outside, Kenji shouts, *"This is a betrayal of trust!"*

I frown at the open door, trying not to be distracted by the distant argument. "Okay, that's fair," I say, returning my eyes to Nazeera. "But I think you might be remembering things differently, because Kenji's never said a single bad thing about you or your relationship—"

"That's because he's such a decent guy," she says in an aggravated burst. "He's still protecting me from my own bullshit."

"What?" Now she has my full attention. "What do you mean?"

"I was a moron when we first met." She pulls the drawcords of her hoodie again, a turtle back in its shell. "I was smart enough to recognize that Kenji was amazing, but totally unequipped to be in a healthy relationship. I liked him so much I did everything wrong." She hesitates; releases the cords. "Did he ever tell you that I almost killed him by accident?"

"Yeah," I say slowly. "But I've never heard the full story."

Nazeera laughs, but it's more of a sigh. "See? Such a nice guy. Kenji probably didn't want you to hate me."

I draw back. "Am I about to hate you?"

"I don't know," she says, slumping in her seat, sounding resigned. "It's kind of a long story, but the short version is that I was trying to keep him safe and I accidentally poisoned him nearly to death."

I frown. "Okay, not great, but that's not so—"

"Then, because I felt terrible that I'd poisoned him nearly to death," she goes on, "I snuck into his room while he was sleeping. I wanted to check on him to make sure he was okay, but I was too proud to own up to my mistake and do it in broad daylight, so, instead, I broke into his room in the middle of the night like the worst stalker. Then, when he realized someone was in the room with him and understandably freaked out, I attacked him. Literally attacked him. I nearly killed him just because I was so embarrassed he'd find out I was worried about him."

I exhale, hard. "No shit."

"Yeah," she says bitterly. "I'm a real catch. If he were a less competent fighter, I might've actually killed him. Did I mention he was sick? Still recovering from being nearly poisoned to death? By me?"

I raise my eyebrows at her. "Damn."

She mirrors my eyebrow raise. "You still convinced he's obsessed with me?"

"Yes."

She rolls her eyes.

"*I will not keep my voice down,*" Kenji is shouting in the distance. "*This is a criminal offense—*"

"Though, to be fair, you probably can't trust my judgment," I add. "Rosabelle killed me on purpose and I'd probably let her do it again if it meant we got to spend some time together."

Nazeera smiles in spite of herself, then tries to hide it by turning her face to the window. "Idiot."

"Look, I'm just— Honestly, I'm a little confused," I say, trying to process all this. "I've always thought of you as super confident. I can't picture you freaking out like that."

"Yeah, well, we all have seasons." She spreads her hands out on the table, staring at her fingers, then curls them into fists. "I like to think I'm not that person anymore, but I had a lot of growing up to do. I've been trying really hard these past few years to work on myself. To understand who I am, where I come from, what's important to me. But during those early years of our relationship—I was kind of a mess."

She huffs a laugh. "At one point I was even jealous of Kenji's relationship with Juliette."

I'd been tilting back on the legs of my chair, and I rock forward now with a *bang*.

"Shut the hell up," I say. "No the fuck you weren't."

"I was," she says, with a self-conscious shrug.

"Don't you dare walk away from me," Kenji is shouting. "We're not done having this discussion—"

"You do realize," I point out, "that if Warner sensed for even a second that Kenji was taking advantage of Juliette's friendship, he'd cut the man's heart out of his chest and serve it to him." I pause. "You know that, right? I'm not exaggerating. He'd put it on a plate and everything."

"I already told you," she says with another shrug. "I was an emotional idiot. I was hotheaded and short-tempered and insecure—and I wasn't used to caring about anyone like that." She hesitates. "I can be really mean when I'm scared, and falling in love is *terrifying*."

"But—"

"Look, James, the truth is, he deserves better than me." She clasps her hands as her jaw tightens; she keeps her eyes trained on the window. "I didn't— I wasn't always nice to him, and I didn't appreciate him the way I should have. I was a coward. I pushed him away. And you and Kenji," she says, turning her gaze on me, "are so similar. The more I hear about this girl the more I worry about you."

I stiffen.

The implication lands in the proceeding silence; the gut

punch lands a beat later. "Did you just—did you just trick me into talking about Rosabelle?"

"James, I'm worried she's going to break your heart—"

"No way." I push back in my seat, holding up my hands. "Stop. I don't want to talk about this—"

"I've been that kind of girl," she says in a rush. "I've been closed off and messed up and emotionally unavailable—and I don't want you to fall in love with the wrong person—"

"You don't even know her," I say angrily. "And not that it matters, because you're totally different people, but for the last time, I am not in love with her—"

"James—"

"And you don't actually deserve my compassion right now, but for what it's worth, I don't think Kenji fell in love with the wrong person, either, so—"

"I thought you said you weren't in love with her."

I blink, go briefly solid.

I'm caught off guard, trying to review the things I just said out loud, and blanking.

Nazeera bites her lip to kill a smile, but the suppressed laughter in her eyes wipes out the last of my patience.

"All right, you know what?" I say, standing up. "Get the hell out of my house—"

I look up at a sudden blast of sound, reeling as Warner charges angrily through the open front door, then nearly trips over the groceries left by the entry. He looks up at me automatically, like *I* had something to do with this mess, and I can tell he's about say something when Kenji storms in after him.

"Why won't you just admit it?" he shouts at Warner. "That was my lemon tree! You cut down my lemon tree!"

The subject change is like a shock of cold water.

I'm grateful for it.

Warner pivots to face him, narrowing his eyes. "I didn't cut it down. You never took care of it—"

"You had no right to touch my tree—"

"I had the right when it died and fell over onto my property," Warner is saying. "Yet you have the audacity to yell at me when in fact I did you a favor, removing it for you without even asking you to help—"

"I didn't want you to remove it! I loved that tree!"

In a distinctly un-Warner move, he finally raises his voice, nearly shouting when he says, *"Then why was I the only one who ever watered it?"*

Kenji's mouth gapes open a moment, then closes. Then opens again. "Wait, what? What are you talking about?"

Warner exhales slowly, looking like he might be working his way through an aneurysm.

"Kenji," he says slowly, like he's talking to a full-time idiot. "Did you think the tree was growing magically, all by itself?"

Kenji hesitates, like he knows he's about to give the wrong answer, and gives it anyway. "I mean, it's a tree," he says. "Trees just grow. Like, on the planet. People don't need to go around watering them."

"*Bro,*" I say, making a face. "Come on."

"What?" His eyes widen. "I've had that tree for years. It was getting sicker over the past few months, but I thought the rain would help, and Winston said—"

"I've been trying to explain to you," Warner says, "that it was getting sicker because I *stopped* watering it. The heavy winds from the storm knocked it over, and I—" He takes a step forward and his boot catches on a bag of groceries. *"And why was this door wide open?* Who left all these groceries here? Is that broken glass?" Then, looking beyond my head: "Why is the kitchen such a mess?"

"Oh, shit," Nazeera whispers. "I think we're about to get grounded."

"You know what, never mind," says Kenji, who's now looking nervously between Nazeera and Warner. "Maybe I should go."

"Don't you dare—"

A shrill ring echoes through the room, and everyone swivels toward the sound. Nazeera glances at her pager before lifting it in the air. "Juliette is awake."

"Thank God," says Kenji, toeing off his shoes before heading hastily for the stairs.

"*Hey.*" Warner goes after him. "That's *my* wife—"

Kenji turns back, his eyes widening in surprise. "What? Really? When did you get married?"

Warner shoves past him with a glare, his voice muffling as he heads up the stairwell. "I'm going to tell her what you did—"

"*Me?*" he says, staring at Warner's back in outrage. "You're the one who killed my tree!"

"Man, I miss this so much when I'm gone," Nazeera

says, propping her chin up in one hand. Her eyes linger on Kenji as he stomps up the stairs.

I look at her, watch her take a breath.

Her eyes grow heavy with a longing I recognize too well, and she forces a smile before getting to her feet.

Nazeera turns to look at me.

"You know I love you, right?" she says. "Like, it causes me actual pain to think about how much I love you?"

"Yeah," I say tightly. "I do."

"Good." She nods. "Just checking."

She moves to leave and I place my hand on her shoulder, stopping her. She lifts her head again slowly.

"Hey," I say. "You okay?"

"Yeah," she says, but her eyes glint, briefly, before she turns away. She takes a breath. "I'm okay. I'm just thinking it might finally be time to buy a couch."

ROSABELLE

19

In my dreams, she's always running.

Clara laughs, racing through tall grass, her white-blond hair streaming in the wind. Her cheeks are full, flush with color; her hands catch the puffy heads of dandelions, releasing wishes into the sky.

She stops, looks up, watches them float.

A fist of sun unclenches above her, fingers of light illuming her face as she searches the clouds, and I know, without knowing how, that she is six years old.

Just a dream.

I tilt with the tilt of her body as she bends to fill her pockets with pebbles, then twigs. A damselfly lands lightly on her shoulder and she doesn't notice, her knees sinking into dirt, fingers digging into ground, turning over earth. A worm. She's found a worm.

Three worms and a millipede.

One pill bug.

Rosa, she shouts, her head popping up, her smile blinding. *Do you want to play a game with me?*

I have no mouth.

I'm suspended in cool water, drifting; my mind hovers inside a head inside a body inside a dream inside my mind.

I can't feel my skin.

I have no teeth.

I'm blind even as I watch her clamber to her feet; senseless even as I feel the breeze. Pebbles release from her soft fists as she wipes dirty hands on her white dress.

A butterfly totters over, curious.

Clara looks around. *Rosa?*

Here, I try to say.

I have no voice.

Rosa, where are you?

Here. Where am I? Here. I have no head. I'm here—

Rosa? Clara says my name quietly this time, her eyes rounding in her face.

I'm here.

I make no sound.

Color blotches in her cheeks. I feel her little heart beating, her pulse racing. Heat presses against her eyes, my eyes; humidity takes her hands, my hands; fear climbs up her throat, my throat.

Rosa, she says, her chest heaving.

Here.

I have no tongue.

Rosa? She turns around.

Here. I have no face.

Rosa, she screams.

Here. I have no head. I'm here. I have no hands.

ROSA—

I'm here. I have no heart.

Clara is crying now, I'm crying, her body shaking, I'm shaking, tears stream down her face my face, her eyes wild with fear my fear. She's rooted to the ground, her dirty hands splayed at her sides—

Rosa, she screams again, *where are you?*

HERE

The word is wrenched from somewhere inside of me, torn free of bone and sinew, the tissue of soul. I'm gasping for breath I don't need, reaching with my teeth for a mouth; searching my eyes for sight; listening to my ears for a sound—

In here, I look around.

Gone is the field, the sun, the flowers. I am encased in black. I hear the slow beat of my heart in this darkness. My pulse is occasional; an ellipsis.

Threads of sensation tighten around the unknown shape of me, flashes of pain and searing heat, then breath; breath exhales inside me like smoke blown into my mouth, then heart; heart hammers into pain that suffocates, then resonance. Tones focus into pattern, arrange into letters, sharpen into words—

One word—

Rosa?

I stiffen.

Rosa, is that you?

I touch my mind with my mind, unfathomable, like water touching water. I make my voice as if with my hands, gathering sound like wind.

Clara? I say.

Rosa, she says desperately. The force of her grief nearly blots me out. I nearly go away. Where?

Rosa, she says again. *Are you dead?*

Am I dead?

I gather up my mind, reading its texture with fingers I don't have. I don't know where I am, what I am.

I don't know, I say. Then, terror: *Are you?*

Silence.

My fear grows in the dark, leaves and shoots unfurling, fruit ripening faster and faster—

No, she says finally.

My heart, nonexistent, beats hard in a chest I don't have. Relief floods through me?

Am I dreaming?

I remain floating, suspended. I fight for a better grip on myself, a better hold on my mouth, but I'm blind and deaf, amorphous. I want to know myself, find my eyes, but there is a boundary here I cannot cross, a veil beyond my strength to breach.

Rosa, she says, and the blaze of her fear circles me again. *You shouldn't be here.*

Why not? I ask. *Where am I?*

Am I dreaming?

There's something wrong, she says. *Can you remember what happened to you?*

I run my fingers along the folds of my mind again, reading the flesh like braille. Flickers of scent and sensation, apple and heat, fear and longing, pain—

Tears.

Touch.

No, I say.

Something is wrong, she says again, her panic loud. *Wake up. Wake up before it's too late. You shouldn't be here—*

Why not? I ask again. *Where am I?*

I search the dark in vain, growing only blinder even as my speech improves. Sounds are coming to me more quickly, words forming with less effort.

For the third time: *Where am I?*

She doesn't answer. Am I dreaming?

Clara, I say. *Where are you?*

Why are you here? she says sharply, her feelings wild. *How did you get here? You shouldn't be here—*

What do you mean? I ask.

Wake up, she says more urgently. *Wake up, Rosa. Wake up and never come back here—*

Why? A pulse of terror. *Clara, please— What's happening?*

Quiet.

Inching quiet.

Then—

You're in my dreams, she says.

Shock sparks inside me, so strong I nearly go away. *Where?*

Do you mean I'm dreaming? I ask. *Am I a dream?*

No response.

I touch my mind to my mind, no impact, like sky touching

sky. *Are you real?* I ask. *Is this real?*

Silence for too long.

Wake up, Rosa, she says. *I can feel that something is wrong. You shouldn't be here. You need to go back—*

Tell me what's happening, I say. *Tell me where I am, tell me where we are—*

You're in my dreams, she says again. *Not yours. Mine. Never come back here. Wake up and never come back here—*

Panic, spooling. *But— Why—*

Because, Rosa, she says. *I only dream of the dead.*

Horror, white-hot.

Devouring.

Wake up, she says desperately. *Wake up—*

Clara— No—

WAKE UP, she screams. *WAKE UP—*

JAMES

20

"All right," Kenji says, "let's take a vote."

"*A vote?*" Warner frowns. "When have I ever given you the impression that this was a democracy?"

"About ten years ago?" Kenji says, without missing a beat. "Remember? We did a whole revolution? You were there. You were all, *Ew, fascists—*"

"I never agreed to allow an uninformed majority to overrule my judgment on matters within my purview."

"Technically"—Kenji cringes—"you did."

"No, I didn't."

"Yes, you did.

"No," Warner says firmly. "I didn't."

"Yes, you—"

"This is a dumb idea," I say for the third time, banging my head lightly against the window casing. This meeting has only intensified my nerves. I feel like I'm going to jump out of my own skin. "You can't just release her into her father's custody."

"I didn't ask you for your opinion," Warner says to me. "You're lucky even to be here."

"You mean you're lucky I saved you from making a huge mistake?" I push away from the window to look at him.

"You're welcome."

"James—"

"Look, I've acknowledged a thousand times now that I was stupid to bring her here. I messed up—I really messed up—and I'm sorry. But you messed up by shutting me out, too. I nearly killed myself trying to get you to listen to me, and now we've got under seven weeks before something terrible happens and we still don't know what it is—and you still won't listen to me."

"I will not discharge her from observation," Warner says coldly. "Not until we finalize a plan for her transfer and containment."

"*Observation?*" I'm nearly blind with fury. "You put her in a fucking coma!"

"She needs to be restrained," he counters with terrifying calm. "One way or another, she needs to be forcibly controlled. This girl is one of the greatest flight risks we've ever had to deal with, and I refuse to jeopardize the lives of our soldiers and the safety of our citizens by hunting her across the city every time she decides to run. The damage she did to the airbase alone will take weeks to repair, and the costs—"

"So this is your big plan, then?" I say, tensing. "Keep her half-dead until you can arrange for a twenty-year-old assassin to move into her dad's house? A dad she doesn't know? A dad she doesn't trust?"

"Okay, I hate to admit it," says Kenji, "but James is right."

"Why do you hate to admit it?" I ask him. "Why is it so

hard to acknowledge that I might have a good idea?"

"If you really want him to answer that, we'll need to schedule another meeting," Warner says coldly. "It might take a few hours."

"Now you're just being a jackass."

"Wow." Kenji stares at me. "You know what, I honestly don't know whether to be impressed with you or concerned for you. Either way"—he taps his head, then points at me—"something's not fully cooked upstairs."

"What?" I turn to him. "What are you talking about?"

"You have zero sense of self-preservation," Kenji says in amazement. "What more does this man have to do to scare the shit out of you? Keep talking to him like that and he's going to shoot you in the other leg—"

Juliette shifts in bed and we all freeze, heads turning in tandem to look at her. She goes still mid-motion, her hands hovering above her bump, dark hair grazing her waist.

"What?" she says.

"Nothing," says Kenji too quickly. But the truth is, every time she so much as moves a muscle everyone freaks out a little.

She flashes us a tired smile, then rests her head against Warner's shoulder, blinking softly.

He doesn't normally sit on the bed during these unconventional meetings. Usually he hovers nearby, or perches on the edge. I get it; it's a little weird arguing hard facts while sinking into a soft mattress with your pregnant wife curled up beside you. But today, he's sitting right next to her.

In his socks.

Every week we try to have at least one or two meetings at the house, a practice we started a few months ago when the doctors really began restricting Juliette's movement. We used to sit in the living room, but that was before she started avoiding the stairs. I'm sure Warner never thought so many people would spend this much time in their bedroom. He probably hates it.

I really like it.

It's cozy in here. Good light, lush fabrics, comfortable seating. Big windows overlooking the backyard. Warner's constantly bringing her flowers and changing out the vases, so it always feels nice and smells good. It's also maybe not a surprise to learn that he cleans his own house meticulously. Maybe everyone else is ready to piss their pants when Warner speaks, but when I see him I'm picturing the guy who spent a free Saturday afternoon cleaning out his kitchen cabinets. He does his wife's laundry. He likes to iron. For years he's dragged me out of bed at an ungodly hour because he's decided I need to learn how to clean the gutters or pressure-wash the driveway or run ten miles uphill. I once watched him intently read an oven manual from cover to cover.

And I've never been able to get him to admit this out loud, but considering the fact that I personally assisted Warner with the landscaping out back, I can say with conviction that he planted dozens of rosebushes strategically, so they'd be visible from this room when in bloom. Even now, in this coastal winter, the artfully designed scenes outside the window are green and idyllic.

The man is an incurable romantic.

"Really, I'm fine," Juliette says to the room, answering the unspoken question. "I swear." She stifles a yawn, then makes a motion with her hand, like shooing a cat. "Keep arguing."

Kenji clears his throat lightly, looking uncomfortable. "You sure you're okay?" he asks.

"I'm sure," she says, pinching a worn paperback out from under her leg. She leans forward to slide it onto her nightstand, and Warner automatically braces her.

We all seem to take the same, sudden breath.

I exchange a glance with Kenji, whose jaw tightens. Maybe Warner's just being overprotective, but Juliette's never needed support for simple movements. The doctors say she's not supposed to do anything strenuous, but her bed rest isn't otherwise hugely restrictive. She's allowed to be up and moving for brief periods to use the bathroom and shower and attend to small tasks. Warner tries to get back to the house as much as possible—and the rest of us are all on a sort of tacit rotation—but she's often alone for stretches of time. It's never been an issue.

I wonder if things are getting worse.

Juliette seems weaker than I've seen her all these months, which is really saying something. The girls have been working with the doctors to monitor her progress, administering various methods of healing at increasing intervals—but I don't really know what's happening.

And I'm worried.

Not only am I a little clueless about pregnancy in general, but Juliette has a unique set of complications causing her problems I don't totally understand. She was purpose-built by her parents for use as an experimental weapon; she'd been nearly forcibly sterilized in the pursuit of generating one of the most powerful supernatural gifts I've ever seen.

Everything about her is designed to kill.

Not only is Juliette's touch lethal, but she has the ability to project that lethal power across distances. She also has an insane superstrength that, when properly wielded, can render her physically invulnerable.

I have a feeling her body can't decide whether to protect the baby or kill it.

And her, by extension.

"Please don't make it weird," she says with a laugh. "I mean it. This is the most entertainment I've had all day." She makes another shooing motion. "Seriously. Go back to yelling at each other."

"Well," says Kenji, looking suddenly stressed. "In that case, I was just saying I think James has a point here."

"Right." I cross my arms, trying to act like anything about this situation is normal. *"Thank you."*

"But Warner has a point, too," he says, raising an eyebrow at me. "We need Rosabelle, but we can't trust Rosabelle." He tilts his head one way, then the other. "We need to wake her up, but we have to make sure she wakes up in a secure location—"

"I have a question," Juliette says, stifling another yawn.

She lifts her hand like she's in class. "Why can't Rosabelle just go back to prison? I feel like maybe I'm missing a key piece of information here."

Before anyone can answer her, Warner adjusts his body, angling his shoulder so that her head settles more comfortably against his chest. He then strokes her hair in a movement so natural it feels intrusive to watch—except he doesn't even seem to be aware he's doing it. He's too busy trying to mask a look of abject terror, his throat working as he draws his hand down the side of her head, his thumb grazing the curve of her cheek.

Upon closer inspection, Warner looks like he might be on the verge of a breakdown.

Juliette's eyes flutter, then fall closed.

Warner lowers his head to her ear. "Are you tired, love?" he whispers. "Do you want us to leave?"

She forces her eyes back open, her hand rising to his chest, resting there a moment. "No, no, I want to know what's happening." She offers us a smile. "All I ever do is sleep these days."

"Can I get you anything?" Nazeera asks, her voice tight with concern. It's the first time she's spoken in several minutes. She's leaning against the wall in a far corner, about as far from Kenji as the room will allow. They're both doing a passable job of pretending to be normal.

Juliette smiles at her. "You've been an angel," she says. "And you've already done so much. Thank you. I'm okay. Really." She turns to the group, beaming. "Actually, I have some good news. I'm officially thirty-seven weeks tomorrow, which is the milestone everyone's been hoping I'd reach. That means no more bed rest for me."

No one manages to match her enthusiasm.

"Really?" says Kenji cautiously. "Is it safe for you to be running around?"

"Well, I won't be running anywhere," she says, her smile fading a little. "I'm still supposed to take it easy, but the doctors think it'll be good for me to walk around again. Get some fresh air." She looks up at Warner, her eyes teasing. "Maybe we can go on a date."

"Of course," he says automatically.

But the room has fallen quiet.

Warner's gone very, very still; he's got that glassy, faraway look in his eyes, his hand frozen on her head.

Shit.

"Honestly, I'm offended you're still willing to have his baby," I say to her. "You don't even seem upset with him. He should be sleeping on the couch."

Warner snaps out of his stupor to look up at me.

That's a little better.

"What?" I say, crossing my arms. I nod at Juliette. "Your shitty husband shot me in the leg and you didn't even divorce him. Where's your loyalty?"

Warner's eyes harden, taking on a shocked anger that says he might kill me for real. Like, actually for real.

Maybe that was a little too much. Shouldn't have used the word *divorce*, probably.

Juliette settles back against him, then takes his hand in hers and squeezes, like she knows he's freaking out, and then she grins at me, like she knows what I'm doing.

"I was upset at first," she says, overlooking the fact that I used the word *divorce* in front of Warner. "But then I heard you insulted him multiple times in front of an entire unit. I love you, James, but I would've shot you, too."

"Wow." I lean against the window. "Nice. You two were made for each other."

Warner visibly unclenches.

A little.

"So, why can't Rosabelle go back to supermax?" Juliette asks. She tries to sit up. "Why is it so hard to find somewhere to put her?"

"Because she knows how to break out of our prisons," I explain. "Her escape from supermax wasn't luck. It was premeditated strategy."

Juliette's eyes light with understanding, then dim with concern. "Because it was built by The Reestablishment," she says.

I nod. "She told me she spent hundreds of hours of sim training breaking out of every single one of our prisons. Which means traditional incarceration is no longer an option."

"I still can't believe she told you that," says Nazeera, shaking her head as she pushes off the wall. "That's critical information about The Reestablishment's access and reach here on the mainland. Information we're using now to better detain her—to derail her from her own objectives. Why expose a weakness? What was her angle?"

I shrug. "I think she was just really confident she'd escape and never see me again."

Nazeera frowns. "That doesn't explain why she'd confide in you. I know you guys have a kind of tenuous alliance, but you're still on opposing sides, still fighting for your own causes. Why would she share things with you that might put her own interests in danger?"

The question is loaded.

Everyone turns to look at me.

JAMES

21

The collective weight of all these stares is uncomfortable, but Warner's gaze is the heaviest. I'm guessing he knows more about what Rosabelle is feeling than I do, but if he's picked up on any emotional cues from her that might fuel my delusion, I don't think he's planning on sharing.

Me, on the other hand? I can't even pretend to hide how I feel about her. I don't even want to.

Even now I'm trying to ignore the constant, steady ache that chases my every waking moment. It's like she buried a knife in my chest at an expert angle, and now I just have to live with it, because removing the knife might kill me.

I look away for a second to try to cool my thoughts, but my mind decides to make things things worse by cuing up the sound of her voice instead.

I'm trying—I'm really trying to be a better person, but if even one of them hurts you I swear I'll slaughter them all—

I take a tight breath.

God, the way she looked at me.

This is the memory that haunts me most when I'm alone, in the dark, struggling to sleep. The way she'd grabbed my shirt, as if there was any chance she could scare me away with a desperate promise to keep me safe.

I feel suddenly overheated.

I always knew my romantic expectations were warped, that growing up with Warner and Juliette had messed me up for life. I've never been interested in the kinds of relationships built on things like shared hobbies and favorite seasons; it doesn't matter to me whether we like the same foods or listen to the same music. I've always wanted something bigger than that, something I didn't even know how to name. For years I thought there was something wrong with me.

Turns out, I was right.

Apparently, what I'm really looking for is a girl who threatens to murder my enemies.

Rosabelle has set the bar too fucking high.

"Look," I say, trying to take a full breath. Everyone is still staring at me. "Uh, I can't tell you what Rosabelle is thinking. I really wish I could. But I feel like we've gotten off topic. I was just trying to say that Hugo is a bad choice for custodian. She'd sooner kill her dad than open up to him, and I think we can understand what that feels like." I nod to the group. "We're all a bunch of traumatized weirdos with murderous daddy issues. Kenji exempted, of course."

"*Weirdos?*" Warner echoes, insulted.

"Daddy issues?" Nazeera pulls a face.

"Thank you," Kenji says, pointing at me. "My parents were awesome, unlike the rest of you losers."

Juliette's eyes widen. "*Kenji.*"

"What?" he says, crossing his arms. "I'm not naming

names or anything, but some of you were never hugged as children and it shows."

Nazeera tries to fight a laugh; it comes out choked.

Warner sighs.

"Anyway," I say. "Everyone in this room can attest to the fact that big, emotional wounds don't heal overnight. That, in fact, sometimes they don't heal at all." I look at Warner. "What did Rosabelle say before you had her dragged off to prison? *My mother is dead but my father is dead to me?*"

He nods.

"Yeah, well, I think she meant it."

"But Hugo genuinely cares for her," says Juliette. "This period has been excruciating for him. He wants a chance to build a relationship with her."

"By interrogating her?" I raise my eyebrows. "By asking her to pay for his affection with her secrets? You really think she'll go for that?"

Nazeera sighs. "Yeah, okay, this is sounding kind of bad."

Kenji shakes his head at Warner. "I think he's right, man. We gave Hugo a chance and he gave us nothing. I mean, maybe with time he could become a resource. We could try to see if something grows between them organically—"

"We don't have time for that," I say, urgency building inside me again. "And we need to wake her up now, before we accidentally kill her."

"I will admit," Warner says, "that it's not an ideal solution, not even for me." He sounds tired. "The problem is, this is a highly classified project. Given the security risks, we have few options for managing the situation while maintaining discretion. We already had to do some damage control after James shouted privileged information at me in front of nearly two dozen soldiers, at least three of whom were not cleared to receive sensitive intelligence—"

"I did what I had to do," I argue. "You left me with no choice—"

"Otherwise," he says, ignoring me, "there are only a handful of people with the necessary clearance to be fully and unconditionally briefed on the matter. Most of whom are in this room."

Warner looks around at us.

"I've been trying for days to come up with a better alternative," he adds, "but Rosabelle is going to need a dedicated, around-the-clock security detail. Most of us are already operating beyond capacity, and no one else wants the responsibility of managing her—"

"I do," I say in a rush.

Everyone turns to look at me.

I hear how desperate I sound and I want to kick my own ass. Still, I can't stop myself from adding, "Let me manage her."

"*Bro*," says Kenji, the word heavy.

Pointed.

He's sitting in one of the velvet reading chairs, tossing and catching a throw pillow into the air, and just then he lets it fall to the ground. "Tell me that wasn't a serious request."

"Why not?" I ask this even as a small voice in my head tells me to shut up. "Why is that so crazy?"

"He didn't mean it," Nazeera says, shooting me a warning look. "James was definitely joking."

"I did mean it." I'm unhinged. I'm unhinged and apparently I'm committing to the personality all the way down. "I'm not joking."

Warner looks at me. "Are you seriously suggesting I lock the two of you alone together in a safe house where you might have unfettered access to her day and night? Are you really asking me to part with my mind long enough to even consider such an idiotic request?"

"Yes?"

"Separate and apart from the fact that you've clearly developed an unstable infatuation with her, your past attempts at interrogating her in a contained environment have achieved nothing but repeated bloodshed—"

"But it's the obvious solution," I say, having lost control of my mouth. "She trusts me—and I can handle her. I'm here, I'm available, I'm capable—"

Warner pinches the bridge of his nose. "Kenji," he says quietly. "Please kill him."

Juliette laughs.

Kenji chucks the pillow at me, hard. "No problem."

The cushion glances off my body. "Look, we don't have a better option—"

"I can do it."

We all turn toward the sound of Nazeera's voice.

She shrugs, then pushes her hood away from her face. "The girl can stay with me."

Warner looks at Nazeera with surprise, like he's only now realizing there was a solution right in front of him this whole time. He's looking at her like this is the best news he's heard all day. Like this is a revelation.

It pisses me off.

"No way," I say. "You don't even live here."

"So what?" she counters. "I was already planning on staying longer than usual." She darts a glance at Kenji, who seems suddenly fascinated by the throw pillows. "I have an empty house, a spare room, and no personal effects; it'll be easy to turn it into a safe house. Plus, it's *here*." She spreads her arms. "Within the boundaries of The Waffle, totally secured. Hugo lives off campus, where the risks are higher. If she's here, she'll be within easy reach of all of us. She won't have access to public spheres. We can keep a closer eye on her."

I move away from the window. "The only reason you're staying longer than usual is to assist with Juliette's responsibilities while she's on maternity leave," I point out. "You won't have the time—"

"I can do both."

"No you can't—"

"Are you sure it won't be too much?" asks Warner, who's studying Nazeera closely. "You're already helping to manage a lot of her day-to-day."

"I'm sure," she says, turning to lock eyes with Juliette. "You've already established a system out here that's optimized to ensure your safety, which means you operate without the need to be physically present—so most of the work is remote—"

"Fine, okay," I say, waving a hand. "Maybe you can find the time, but I don't think you realize that taking on Rosabelle will require monitoring her around the clock and caring for her needs as they arise."

"You say that like it's hard," she says, annoyed.

"For you? It's fucking rocket science."

"*James*," says Kenji.

"Language," Warner says with a sigh.

Nazeera glowers. "Rocket science isn't even as complicated as people think it is. Your analogy sucks."

"Whatever, you know what I mean," I counter. "Hell, everyone knows what I mean. I love you, Nazeera, but you don't know how to take care of things."

"What?" she says, drawing back. "That's not true."

"You might be able to take apart a jet engine, but you don't even know how to keep a houseplant alive. You once got a betta fish and then forgot you had it—"

"I didn't *forget*," she says, looking sheepish. "I just realized it was better suited to life with Winston."

"It died!"

"After a couple of years!"

"Five months," Kenji says under his breath.

"Look," I try again. "It wouldn't even matter if you knew the difference between a fitted and a flat sheet. Rosabelle is a trained assassin. She doesn't know you and she won't trust you. She'll be trying to kill you constantly—"

"Um, I thought the idea was that the girl only gets to live if she's willing to cooperate," Nazeera says. "If Rosabelle wants to be an asshole about living in my house, I'll be happy to put her out of her misery."

I turn to face Warner, alarmed. "Are you hearing this? She thinks she can troubleshoot her issues with murder—"

Juliette stifles a laugh.

"You're being ridiculous," Nazeera says, shoving her hands in her hoodie pocket. "Just because I don't know how to iron a shirt doesn't mean I'm incompetent. It means I grew up with maids who did everything for me, and you can blame my parents for that. They were more interested in me learning how to kill things than clean things. And at least now I know how to cook—"

"You only learned to cook because Kenji wanted to learn to cook!"

"Whoa, uh-uh," Kenji says, laughing nervously. "Don't bring me into this. Even though it's true that I'm an excellent cook. Definitely a better cook—"

Nazeera makes an exasperated sound.

"All right, that's enough," Warner says. "Nazeera is the daughter of a supreme commander. Her training and insight will prove invaluable, and she'll be more than capable of handling whatever comes her way."

"But—"

"Take the win, James," he says to me. "This is a good compromise. I'll have to let Hugo down; but of the two, this is the stronger option."

"I think it's a great idea, too," Juliette says thoughtfully, considering Nazeera. "But are you sure you have the time, long-term, to take this on? It might end up being a bigger project than we anticipate. When do you need to get back home?"

"Not for a few months," she says. "The timing is perfect, actually, because I was already planning for a leave of absence. I've delegated responsibilities back home. Haider is prepped to handle most things while I'm gone." She lifts a shoulder, then drops it. "I was hoping to buy some furniture for my place anyway."

"Excellent," Warner says, the word decisive. "Consider this decision final. We'll need a few days to make the arrangements, but once you're ready, we can talk about discharging Rosabelle from the hospital—"

"Wait, what?" I say, my agitation spiking. "A few more days? You can't wait that long—"

"Why not?"

"Because you're going to fucking kill her!" I explode.

Everyone stills, staring at me like I've detonated a bomb. Like I've lost my mind. Even Juliette looks shell-shocked.

I drag my hands down my face, hating myself.

A little mortified.

Nazeera shakes her head at me, eyes wide. "James. Seriously. What did we just talk about?"

I take a breath, try to calm down.

"I'm just— Look," I say, struggling to keep my voice

normal. Panic is surging through my veins like poison. "We've never run tests on her. We have no idea how her power works. She's already been brain dead for three days—"

"Bro, maybe you should take a walk," Kenji says, studying me with genuine concern. "Get some air."

I look at him and say nothing, even as my heart hammers so hard against my ribs my vision dims at the edges.

The more I freak out, the calmer Warner gets.

"James," he says. "You've tragically misunderstood me. I couldn't care less whether the girl survives. Perhaps if there was some guarantee she'd speak—that she might become a real asset—I'd be more inclined to inconvenience myself, but making arrangements for her now is merely a hedge against possible disaster. It's a contingency plan in the case we can't solve the mystery of the vial on our own. She's already cost us time and resources we can't spare. I'd decided days ago to kill her; I will not go out of my way now to keep her alive."

"But—"

"No." He cuts me off angrily. "We have no idea whether she has an interest in an alliance, and I have no confidence that upon waking she'll tell us anything worthwhile. She was in prison for nine days and said nothing. Not a sound." His eyes flash. "Do you have any idea how difficult it is to remain perfectly silent for *nine days*? Do you even understand the mental fortitude necessary—the discipline required to keep yourself from saying so much as a single word for *nine days*—"

"I'm not—"

"You don't," he says. "Because you don't understand

what we're dealing with. She appears to have the ability to physically shut off her brain and body, simulating a kind of death. Why do you think I'm focusing on efforts to wear her down mentally? Physical torture will not break her; traditional interrogation methods are useless to us. If she decides to keep a secret, she'll take it straight to her grave—"

"If you would just let me fucking talk to her—"

"*You are not as powerful as you think you are,*" he shouts at me, his composure finally breaking. "And she is not as vulnerable as you think she is."

I look away, heat flaring up my neck.

"You seem to think that just because she didn't kill you, she cares for you," Warner says, pouring acid into an open wound. "Let me be clear: you have not been chosen. She will not become pliable and cooperative at your behest, handing over her closely held secrets simply because you asked nicely." He pauses. "Or have you already forgotten that when it mattered most, she didn't hesitate to shoot you?"

I look away, equal parts angry and embarrassed. "Look, that's not what I meant, okay? I don't think I'm special. I didn't mean it like that—"

"You're going to get us all killed," Warner says sharply, "if you continue to believe you can take a wolf home and tame it. Maybe the wolf chose to leave you breathing, but that doesn't change the fact that it slaughtered your friends."

I turn to the window again, flattening my hands on the frame, trying not to exhale loudly enough to betray the tremble in my breath. I want to sink through the floor. I can't argue with anything Warner is saying—he's right about all of it—and yet I'm absolutely convinced that if he waits any longer to pull her out of this coma, she's not going to survive.

"Right now," Warner is saying, "my priority is figuring out what's in that vial. Our team has been running tests, and so far we haven't been able to—"

A familiar, shrill ring sounds throughout the room, and this time it's Warner's pager going off. He reads the missive with increasing levels of alarm.

"What is it?" Kenji asks, getting to his feet. "What's wrong?"

Warner stands and slides the receiver out of his pocket, flipping open the razor-thin metal. An explosion of staticky sound fills the room right away, the crash and clamor of chaos echoing. "She's awake, sir," comes a reedy, garbled voice. "She's awake but it's not—it's not normal— There's something wrong with her. She's out of control and we don't know what to do—"

"Don't sedate her," Warner says sharply.

"But—sir—"

"Restrain her, but don't sedate her," he says. "I need to see this. I'll be right there."

Warner snaps the receiver shut.

My heart is suddenly beating so hard I don't know whether to rip the fucking thing out of my chest or jump out the window.

"I'm coming with you," I say.

"No way, man," Kenji says, already reaching for his gun. He checks the magazine. "Sit down."

"Don't do this," I say, my voice rising. "Don't shut me out of this—"

"Nazeera," Warner says. "Get things ready as much as you can. I'm not sure how this is going to end, but let's try to be prepared."

She nods, then walks out the room without a word.

"This is bullshit," I say, hating the way I sound. Childish. Desperate. "You can't just leave me here—"

"Kenji?" Warner looks at him, but Kenji's already moving.

"I'm ready," he says. "I just need to grab another—"

"Stay here," Warner says.

Kenji rocks back on his heels. "What?"

"Please," he says, glancing at his wife. Juliette offers him a bleak smile, squeezing his hand as he draws away.

"But— You should have backup—"

Warner turns to look at me, and my fists are clenched, my head crowding with pain.

"James," he says. "Let's go."

ROSABELLE

22

I never make it to the surface.

I'm shoved roughly back inside my body, blood and organs jammed into their flesh casing, but the fit is all wrong. My skin feels strange, like it's been pulled on incorrectly, catching on sharp corners. It's as if my lips have been stretched over bone instead of throat, my eyes seated over muscle instead of nerves.

I can't see.

I make out only flaring lights and smears of movement. I feel my eyelids fluttering desperately, my head whipping back and forth. I open my mouth but I can't speak. My airways feel strangled, as if I'm drawing in oxygen through mesh. Sounds are muted and tinny, voices carrying as if from miles away.

I try to scream.

The sound is guttural. My body torques as I fight for breath, growing lightheaded as the effort fails. I try to lift my hand but my leg spasms, connecting painfully with something solid, the sound of glass shattering as if from afar. I try to scream again but I have no mouth, my voice stuffed inside a throat with no outlet. I can only make deep, mournful sounds of agony. I crane my neck, my blind eyes tracking light and shadow as a low keening pushes through my chest.

Panic is cratering me.

I wrench myself, trying to sit upright, but there's no sense to it; my head slams into something hard, pain exploding between my ears and I whimper, seeing stars, as a faraway scream pierces the fog.

I'm trapped inside my body.

I cry out again, thrashing, but the sound is muffled and faint; it's as if webbed flesh has grown over the opening of my mouth. I feel hot tears burning skin, my nerves flaring too bright, the settings dialed in all wrong.

I don't know what's happening.

Pain and terror are suffocating me. I know I need to calm down but there's a disconnect between my brain and sinew, a confusion in communication. I can't shut down, can't grasp my own mind long enough to pull the plug. I hear my heart beating but feel it in my teeth; I try to touch my face and this time my arm flings out, smashing into something that causes pain to flare, white-hot, along my skin.

Blood.

I think I'm bleeding.

There's a muted clatter, a rush of distant commotion, the vague impression of screaming, but the only sounds loud enough are in my head. I make out the pitiful whine of my own broken, stifled sobs, my fears growing greater with every passing second. I can't find my fingers. I'm starting to feel faint from a lack of oxygen.

I jerk what I think is my head, then my limbs, the results uncertain. I'm hyperventilating. I try to reason with myself, to remember myself—but I can't remember where I am or how I got here. I have no idea whether anyone can help me. I don't know how to escape this prison of my own flesh—

Weight collides with me, hands everywhere, pushing me down. I scream badly. I smell leather, choking out sounds of terror as I'm jerked around, the pull of harnesses tightening like bands across my body. Voices grow louder, sharper—

No, I try to say.

NO—

I'm wild, bleating like an animal; I try to free myself and something solid connects with my head so hard it separates time. Sounds drag, stuttering, elongating screams as pain erupts inside me; lights flicker as if in slow motion, reverberations trembling like the sluggish tempo of a song.

I slacken, my head spinning.

I think I'm choking on my own tongue, drowning as I fail to draw oxygen. I'm strapped down so tightly I can only spasm. I gasp for air as I push my eyes wider, as if the effort might cure my blindness. The din around me grows louder and louder, voices merging into a body of distorted sound.

I try again to scream; it sounds like a sob.

My chest is caving in. I can't feel my legs. Weight on me again, hands and hands and I cry out, choked, my head thrashing back and forth, light shattering into sparks, hands and hands on my arms and legs, on my throat, the tug of harnesses—

Rosabelle?

The sound of my name reaches me as if through space, separating from the mass of unintelligible noises, and I realize it's been spoken into my ear.

I stiffen.

Warmth near my face, heaviness, closeness. Hands on my body as if through plastic. My heart thunders inside me.

Rosabelle?

The voice is warped, waterlogged, but my body reacts to the sound automatically, responding to sense memory. A measure of tension leaves my body on instinct, clouds of panic slowly clearing, allowing room for comprehension.

I blink carefully, still blind.

In the stillness I can suddenly distinguish resonance—alarms blaring; straps coming undone; footsteps pounding; the clatter of metal, the pitch of his voice—

Rosabelle, can you hear me?

I make a sound deep in my throat; a whimper, begging. Help, I want to say. Help me—

Hands on my face, heavy. My eyelids flutter.

Rosabelle?

Mouth near my ear.

Hands and hands, in my hair, on my cheek.

It's me, he says. It's just me. I'm not going to leave you. I'm right here.

James.

You need to relax, okay?

Hands softly searching. Whispers in my ear.

Rosabelle? Do you trust me?

I make another desperate sound.

You can let go, he says. You're safe.

James.

Like a parachute pulled, something inside of me releases.

A terrifying, breathtaking relief overtakes me, the feeling so powerful it unhooks me from within myself. My sharper edges retract, allowing me to sink deeper into my own flesh, blood and muscle slotting better into skin, mouth retracting from bone, my airways opening. It's as if someone's driven a knife into my throat and torn open my windpipe.

A cry rips from my chest.

I draw a violent, shuddering breath, oxygen rushing to my head, surging through my blood—

Rosabelle.

Stay with me.

My hearing is beginning to improve, ears settling over auditory canals as a roar of sound overwhelms me: the incessant shriek of a monitor, the retreat of shouting voices, the diminishing sounds of footfalls, the piercing din of silence. My eyes release, sliding over more nerve than muscle, and I can make out shapes and forms now, flashes of color. I blink steadily, my heart rate slowing. I search for his face and find only sensation.

I'm flooded with awareness of him.

One of his hands is still on my cheek, the other bracing

my neck, his mouth so close to my skin. I feel his warm breath in my hair and I tremble as I stabilize, searching for my limbs, flexing my fingers. My heart nearly gives out when I realize I can feel my legs again.

"You're okay," he whispers, and I can really hear him now, his lips grazing the shell of my ear. "You're going to be okay."

I blink again and again, trying to focus. My eyesight is still damaged. I make out the blurred outline of a monitor beside my bed, its steady beeps reflecting my heart rate out loud.

I lick my chapped lips, my head spinning.

James runs his thumb across the curve of my cheek and I tense, gasping as if he's lit a match against my skin.

"Hey, it's okay," he says quietly. "You're all right. Just breathe."

I blink. The effort drains me.

Fatigue drives me deep inside myself. Residual tension dissipates, unhinging the rest of me, and I seat back into my body with a nearly audible latch.

Breath leaves my lungs in a rush.

For a long moment, I can't move; I'm paralyzed with relief; my bones like bricks. James is bent over me, no longer touching, but close. I'm physically aware of him now; he seems fully realized; and his proximity is making me feverish. Heat has ravaged my chest, fogged my thoughts. My skin feels raw and sensitive, overly responsive. The ineffable scent of him is overwhelming. I want it injected into my veins. I want to draw him inside of me.

I don't know where these thoughts are coming from.

I feel out of my head; unstable; and I realize, dimly, that my senses flared back to life too quickly. I'm feeling too much at once. I'm being burned alive by sensation.

I've lost my shields.

I can't seem to move my mouth. I desperately want to say his name out loud. I can't see clearly. I want to run my hands down his skin, taste the heat of him, press my lips to his throat. I don't trust my mind. I want to get his attention. I want him to look at me. I think I might be dreaming. It's an extraordinary feat even to lift my arm. I manage to animate a little, my blurry hand visibly shaking as I draw my fingers down what I think is his shoulder.

His T-shirt is warm.

The cotton is soft.

The muscular curve of his bicep is both solid and yielding and it's disorienting to touch him. To be the one to touch him. I am a blur; unformed. I feel drunk. I haven't initiated physical contact with anyone but Clara in over a decade.

The heart monitor reflects this.

When my fingers leave the border of his sleeve and accidentally graze his skin, the shock of connection is nearly violent.

James looks up sharply, bedsheets rustling as he shifts his weight. He meets my gaze and I can make out the blur of his eyes, the suggestion of his mouth, and I nearly lose myself again. I nearly touch him again.

"You're back," he breathes.

I blink at him.

My mind has gone soft. My eyes are still defective, still struggling to refine images, find edges. Light leaks smear the subtleties, smudging color, rendering details like an impressionist painting. I search his surrealist features, details coming in and out of focus: his dark eyelashes; the dizzying blue of his irises; the hard line of his jaw. I might be sinking softly into the ground. I can't find my borders. I'm so aware of him I think I might scream.

He stills as I study him, his eyes tightening. "You okay?" he whispers.

You okay?

I flinch; the blow batters my chest.

You okay?

You okay?

My body panics out loud, the monitor beeping frantically all around us.

Where'd they take your sister?

The asylum, right?

I hear voices, a rush of footfalls, but the world winnows as I stare slowly up, into his eyes.

But, like, how do we get there?

I don't know what's happening to me. I'm desperate to get closer to him. My heart is racing. I'm faint and restless and aching.

Can you trust me?

Rosabelle, do you trust me?

I'm alive with a chaos I don't understand. I want to press my cheek to his chest and feel him breathe. I want to climb into his body and live there, inside of him.

If you trust me, we can fix this together. If you trust me, everything is simple—

In the lens flare of my imperfect vision, his irises are bluer, his edges blurred, all of him blasted with light.

All right, sleepyhead. Let's get this over with.

"Rosabelle?"

I'm with you, Rosabelle. Are you with me?

I've been watched by infinite eyes all my life, but no one has ever looked at me and made me feel safe.

No one but him.

If you do manage to kill me and make it out of here, I thought you might want to give this to your sister—

Something is happening to me. Something is breaking inside of me. It occurs to me, as my body begins to shake, that this damage might be irreparable.

I already told you. I pay attention.

The monitor grows only angrier, alarms triggering, and only then do I see the disembodied mass of people, bodies crowding the room.

I'm here. I'm with you. You're safe—

A stake of fear drives straight through my chest.

"Rosabelle?" James says desperately. "Are you okay?"

No, I want to scream.

NO—

I understand then that I would kill for him without question. I would die for him without hesitation.

He lives, or no one lives.

I will protect him with my life.

"*No*," I whisper.

What's left of my frozen heart shatters.

WARNER

23

There's a sudden explosion of commotion.

Alarms blast, warning lights flashing across all systems as Rosabelle seizes suddenly in her hospital bed. Her eyes nearly roll back in her head. She takes convulsive breaths, strands of white-blond hair cutting across her face. She looks limp and ashen, like she might lose consciousness. Her body seizes again.

Fascinating.

Nearly two weeks of futile silence and now a deluge. Her fear is so severe and consuming it radiates like a flare, burning brighter than all other emotions in the room.

Except, perhaps, one other.

"What's happening?" says James, eyes wild, as a team of medics rush around him. "What the hell just happened?"

"She's going into shock," says one of them. "I need you to get out of here—"

It's a struggle to remain focused on Rosabelle.

The uproar and influx of bodies makes for a staggering flood of psychic feedback; I have to brace myself against it, steeling my mind as if to withstand the lashes of a firestorm.

"Wait—what?" says James. "Why is she going into shock?"

His fear, her fear.

"She needs to calm down—she's lost control—"

His fear, her fear.

"But she was fine a second ago!"

I close my eyes.

Collective urgency; flashes of anger; the slam of metal; the rush of wheels; impatience; irritation; the proliferation of alarms; the rattle of carts; vibrations of footfalls—

"Blood oxygen levels at ninety-two percent and dropping," shouts a medic I know well. Dr. Kazemi. "Heart rate is spiking—"

I open my eyes.

"James, get the hell out of my way," someone barks at him.

"General," says Dr. Kazemi, speaking in my direction. "If we don't do something quickly, she could end up with permanent organ damage—"

"Don't fucking touch me," James yells, rearing back as soldiers surge around him.

Rosabelle is hyperventilating.

Her eyes are directed toward the ceiling, wide with panic. The harnesses are undone and unnecessary, hanging like dark streamers from her hospital bed. She can't seem to move. Her terror is so severe it's paralyzed her.

No, it's greater than terror.

It's terror advancing into hysteria, cut by shame and self-loathing. *Despair.*

Interesting.

"C'mon, man," says Liam, "you can't be here right now—"

"What are you going to do to her?" James cries, fighting the group of soldiers trying to drag him away.

I stretch my neck, tense my jaw. The room is thick with anger and frustration. The rise of collective panic threatens to blot out Rosabelle's feedback.

I close my eyes again.

His fear, her fear.

"James," says Allie, "she's going to be fine—"

"Blood pressure is falling!"

"Get the fuck off me—"

Doors slamming; alarms screaming; impatience rising; the smell of antiseptic; the whirr of a curtain closing; confusion; irritation; stabs of pain; the clatter of steel instruments—

I open my eyes.

"It's not clear what's causing this reaction," one medic argues with another. "She might benefit from a tranquilizer—"

There's too much chaos.

"Why won't you do anything?" James shouts at me. "Say something—make them stop—"

Rosabelle's eyes are nearly closed. Her lips are parted, her chest rising and falling too quickly as she strains for breath. Her body is rocked by tremors. She's nearly insensate; her fear is losing its shape, having grown beyond the bounds of her body. Panic has devoured her.

"General? We need your approval to sedate her—"

James breaks violently away from the soldiers, leaving at least two of them doubled over in pain. He turns in a wide arc, finding my eyes across the room, and aims his frenetic agitation in my direction.

"Don't let them sedate her," he cries. "If she goes under she might not resurface again—"

"Blood oxygen levels at eighty-eight percent!"

"She's not in control of her mind," argues the medic. "She's in severe distress and she needs assistance—"

Four soldiers tackle James again, forcing him away from Rosabelle, and he swears in anger.

"She's not crazy," he yells as he's dragged backward. "There's nothing wrong with her mind! She's just scared—"

"General." Kazemi again. She's standing close to me now. "If we don't get the patient stabilized she could go into cardiac arrest. We need to make a decision before it's too late."

"Rosabelle," James cries angrily. "Rosabelle, can you hear me?"

At the sound of her name, her eyes widen.

Remarkable.

"Rosabelle, I'm still here—"

"General—"

"No," I say. Then, to the soldiers: "Let him go."

They release James, but with palpable confusion. He bolts forward and I hold up a hand to stop him. "Wait."

"*What?*" James is flushed; breathing hard. "Why?"

I take a step toward the girl.

The crowd parts before me, giving me a clear path. "I want everyone but James to leave the room."

There's a moment of uncertain quiet among the

voices, alarms still blaring. A spate of disbelief, anger, and disappointment is leveled in my direction.

"General, are you sure—"

I lift my head. "Everyone out. Now."

Another half second of hesitation, and the reluctant crowd disperses nearly at once. The door slams closed behind them. James rushes to her bedside.

His fear is quieting.

Her fear is quieting.

"Rosabelle," he says desperately. "Are you still there? I'm still here."

She blinks softly, her eyes glazed. Her heart rate has begun to stabilize; the alarms have begun to retreat.

"Are you okay?" he asks her.

Her hands tense and release; color moves slowly back into her cheeks. Her fear is being slowly displaced by calm. A crush of exhaustion. Acute longing.

A faint rush of desire.

My jaw tightens.

The two of them together generate an emotional load so turbulent I can't quite distinguish one from the other. It's surgical work, separating the threads, tracing each back to its source.

James, of course, has never been subtle.

But Rosabelle—

She turns her head against her pillow, her face flushed. Then she looks up at my brother and experiences a shock of pain so brutal and unexpected I take a step back.

I hear her intake of breath.

I think I've seen enough.

"James," I say quietly. "I need you to leave."

"What?" He straightens, detonating before me. Anger; fear; frustration. "Why?"

I press my fingers to my forehead, trying to release the tension. I'm suddenly agitated. Fatigued.

"We'll talk about this later," I say to him. "Right now, I need you to go."

"But—"

"I'm not going to kill her."

Rosabelle turns sharply to look at me.

James is nonplussed. "But—"

"We'll talk about this later," I say again, meeting his gaze. My head has begun to pound. "For now, I need you to trust me."

James looks between me and Rosabelle a few more times before I feel him finally, begrudgingly relent. He swears under his breath, working the anger out of his body before he turns to Rosabelle.

"I'll see you later, okay?" he says. "I promise. And don't worry, Warner's not as scary as he looks."

"Don't lie to her," I say coldly.

James shoots me a hard look.

There's a spike of fear from Rosabelle as she watches us warily, saying nothing. She doesn't say goodbye to James, not even as I feel her pain rising as he leaves. Instead, she watches him go with intention, her eyes lingering on the door even after it shuts behind him with a *slam*.

It's a moment before Rosabelle turns to look at me.

We lock eyes from across the room and, almost instantly, her emotional feedback goes cold. She reverts back to the dead battery she was in prison.

Astonishing.

I sort through the files in my head, trying to recall every experience I've ever had with her. I'm searching for patterns. Inconsistencies. I can't decide whether she's in full control of this strange phenomenon.

If she's able to open and close the doors to her mind, why not shut me out sooner? If she can't, why would The Reestablishment employ an unstable mercenary?

There's something I'm missing.

Setting aside her executioner skills, she's thus far proven her capacity for espionage, unknown chemical warfare, and cyber hacking. She nearly succeeded in stealing a military jet while under relentless fire. She's exhibited unprecedented mental and physical fortitude not only in prison, but under interrogation and duress. Upon admission to the hospital her most recent injuries had been declared so critical the medics couldn't believe she'd maintained consciousness until the end.

Why, then, when comparatively uninjured, did she collapse en route to The New Republic? Why, when given something to eat, had she vomited up her food in a panic? Why, after mercilessly slaughtering three others at the rehab facility, hadn't she pulled the trigger to kill Kenji when she had the chance?

I tilt my head at her.

More concerning than all else: I can't decide whether her erratic and inconstant feelings toward my brother are rooted in reality or subterfuge.

Rosabelle holds my gaze with a steady implacability, her eyes cold and vacant. She says nothing, and the nonaction is its own weapon. When she stops speaking she seems to draw a sword.

I understand the power of silence. I know what it's like to be watched and dissected. If I lived in a comprehensive surveillance state, I, too, would no doubt cease to speak altogether. But never in my life have I met anyone capable of presenting perfect emotional stillness. Never have I stood in a room with another person and known true quiet.

This silence is new and a little disorienting.

I can't deny that the reprieve is a relief for my tired mind, but it occurs to me then that I've never been alone with Rosabelle; not like this. Even when she was unconscious upon arrival, there were medics on rotation, checking her vitals. But more than that, she appears to have physically hardened inside herself, sitting upright now with a strength she couldn't summon only moments ago.

I take a step toward her.

She watches me closely.

She's more alert. Vigilant. My own instincts sharpen in response. Far from the panic-stricken girl she was just minutes prior, she now seems dangerous. She's more awake in every practical way, and yet, somehow—

Living death before my eyes.

I stand over her, studying her blank face. She averts her gaze, and I can almost feel her fight a flinch.

"Why is it," I whisper, finally breaking the silence, "that you don't seem to be truly alive unless you're near my brother?"

She looks up sharply.

ROSABELLE

24

Electricity hums through my body, the low-level current vibrating through my wrists, my ribs, up my throat, inside my teeth. The effect offers me a strange comfort, the white noise a stabilizing anchor for my mind.

There's no reprieve, however, for my eyes.

I blink and hold; release.

Blink and hold.

Release.

My eyesight still hasn't fully recovered. My pupils continue to dilate and constrict, trying to focus. The muscles are beginning to ache. The constant flare and retraction of light is making my head pound.

I walk in measured strides up to the sliding door in the empty living room, my hands still forcibly restrained behind my back. Absently, I touch the pads of my thumb and forefinger together, making soft circles.

Die, I tell myself softly. *Die.*

A muted blade of hunger cuts through me and I hold still, silently breathing out with the pain as it passes. It smells stale in here, like paint and dust; the air is dense and depressing. My vision blurs and focuses; blurs and focuses. Footsteps echo in the vacant space, staccato against the wood floors.

A soft hush, then thud, as she comes to a stop.

"That's the yard," she says.

Cold sunlight illuminates a stretch of empty hardscape, ostensibly a patio, beside which sits a rectangle of dirt, untended and riddled with weeds. There's a low, wooden fence containing this sad sight, a dilapidated gate leading to a vast, common green space rolling into the distance beyond, where the sun is painted off-center in the sky. A withered plant sits in a cracked, plastic container near my feet. It's been knocked sideways onto the hardened soil, rotting quietly. What's left of the leaves makes me think it was once a tomato vine.

My eyes focus; unfocus. Dilate and constrict.

I blink and hold. Release.

Blink and hold.

"And this one, Rosa?" *Clara's grubby fingers pinch a needlelike leaf, holding it up.*

I reach forward to wipe her nose, but she jerks out of reach.

I've started taking Clara on hikes through the forest, strapping her to my back with a few twists of a bedsheet, releasing her into the wild as soon as we find a stream. The blue glow of her eyes assures we're always being watched, which means we can never eat or drink anything we find or else suffer severe punishment. But Clara loves the burble of the water. It's the only cure I've found for distracting her from hunger for minutes at a time.

"This one, Rosa," she says again, batting me on the chin with the leaf.

"That's from a hemlock tree," I tell her.

She tries to repeat the word, shaping her mouth around the sound. "Hammock."

"Hemlock," I say.

"Hemmock."

"That's right."

Clara searches around herself, grabbing another: "This one?"

"Maple," I say.

"Mable."

"Perfect."

She fishes around in the dirt and finds a reddish-blue berry, her eyes widening with astonishment as she rolls it between her fingers. She presents it to me in an open hand, as if it were a jewel. "This?"

"That's—" I stiffen. "That's a huckleberry."

She frowns at me. "It's poison, Rosa?"

I stare at her small hand. "No."

She gasps happily, then shoves the berry in her mouth. Her eyes flash a brighter blue before a red sniper dot appears on her forehead. I grab her face and scoop out the berry before she can eat it, then chuck the berry into the heart of the forest. I turn back to face her, my heart pounding.

Clara stares at me, stunned.

Then bursts into tears.

"I'm sorry," I say breathlessly. "I'm so sorry—"

My right hand begins to tremble and I press it flat into the dirt. "I'm sorry," I say again. I look around frantically, terrified they'll still try to punish her. Sometimes they hurt her remotely—they can activate pain from within the mind.

I feel myself begin to panic, my eyes threatening heat, and I kill *the feeling, kill myself, disappear. I don't want Clara to witness my fear. More than that, I know they're watching me through her eyes.*

I don't want them to see my weaknesses.

"I know you want to eat it," I say to her, steadying my voice. "I know you're hungry. I'll bring you bread tomorrow, okay? How does that sound?"

Clara goes still, sniffing as her tears retreat. "Really?"

"Yes," I whisper, heart still pounding as I stare into the middle distance. I wonder what they'll make me do for a piece of bread.

"Thank you, Rosa," she says, wiping her eyes with a dirty fist.

Die, I tell myself. Die.

I force my body to calm, my thoughts to quiet. "Look at this one," I say to her, picking up a frond with my trembling hand. "Do you remember what this one is called?

She sniffs again, then points. "Fun."

"Yes," I say. "Fern."

"Rosa?"

"Yes?"

"Where is Mama's glasses?"

I look up at her. "Mama's glasses?"

Clara nods, turning away as she runs her hands along the forest floor. "She was looking for them last night."

I sit back. "What do you mean?"

"In my dreams," she says, lifting her head to frown at me, as if this should be obvious. "She never knows where anything is, but she's a grown-up, just like you."

"Like me?"

"Yes."

"But, Clara," I say softly. "I'm only eleven."

A hand grasps my arm and I nearly startle. "Hey, did you hear me?"

I turn slowly to face the woman, the action carefully dislodging her hand. My first impression of her was simple: she's beautiful. Tall and willowy, with warm olive skin and yards of dark, glossy hair that looks nearly black. She has sharp, light brown eyes. A tiny, almost missable diamond stud pierced under her bottom lip. She wears a loose shawl around her neck and a rifle strapped across her chest.

Of course, I recognized her immediately.

Nazeera Ibrahim: only daughter of the supreme commander of Asia. Sister to a brother: Haider Ibrahim.

Both siblings were traitors to The Reestablishment.

It occurs to me that almost every child of a supreme commander betrayed or murdered their own parents. This alarming fact is certainly worth greater reflection.

"Your room is over there," she says, nodding beyond my shoulder.

I don't turn to look.

My eyes focus; unfocus.

A simple wooden folding chair rests against the far wall. There's a spade in the garden. An exposed light bulb hangs from the middle of the ceiling. A loose grate is poorly affixed to the floorboards. A full-length mirror leans in the hallway. A screwdriver sits on the windowsill. On the kitchen counter there are two glass cups, a pair of scissors, and a punctured plastic sleeve with a disposable fork and knife inside; no spoon. The kitchen offers greater yield, but I'm about two yards away from the screwdriver.

"I thought you'd like to see it," she says, tilting her head at me. "Come on. I'll show you."

I don't move.

I blink and hold; release.

Blink and hold.

Release.

I've been in a state of suspended disorientation since I was discharged from the hospital. There's so much I don't understand about what's happening.

I have no idea what I'm doing here.

I don't know why I'm being offered a room in a house; if I were back on the Ark I'd be impaled to a ceiling right now, held in place by blades of directed energy. Sebastian would be overseeing my torture, smiling meekly up at me while someone burned pinprick holes into my organs—never enough to kill me right away, but enough to remind me, as I watched my blood drip onto the ground below, that I am not my own master.

That I cannot save my sister.

Once again, I can't decide whether the rebels are stupid or surprisingly conniving. These electric manacles fry and snap apart with the right power surge, but the trouble isn't finding a way to introduce the right current, it's surviving the subsequent voltage spike.

I'm still a little too weak to risk it.

For now, I'm waiting to understand whether this is some

new trap, just as the rehab facility was a glorified prison. It's worse for not knowing what they're thinking; the dread is worse. The pretense of freedom is always so much worse.

There are no cameras, anywhere.

The build of the house is old enough that any renovations or modifications to include subtle spyware would've presented an inconsistency. As far as I can tell, this place is just as unsecured as the rehab facility; perhaps less so.

This oversight strikes me as impossible.

Then again, I don't know what I might find in that bedroom. Perhaps someone is waiting for me in there; perhaps I'll be tortured where I'm expected to rest. In the early years, when I was still learning how to protect my mind, my true feelings about The Reestablishment would sometimes break loose during interrogations. After I'd been punished, and after Sebastian had unhooked me from the wall, Soledad often forced me to sleep in a shallow pool of my own blood.

Soledad is dead, I remember with a start.

James killed him.

A rush of feeling moves through me at the thought of James, my heart threatening to push beyond the veil of death. I crush it back down violently, killing my pulse.

Too much.

I unclench, allowing myself to come back to life a little. The beat is faint at first, then stronger.

"Hi? Hello?" Nazeera steps directly in front of me, ducking her head to meet my eyes. "Can you hear me?"

I meet her gaze slowly.

"Your room is over there," she says again, gesturing once more to something out of sight. She stares at me like I might be an idiot, then finally walks away, but not before shooting me an uncomfortable smile. She begins to monologue as she strides ahead, turning her back on me.

I'm not planning on killing her, but if I were, this seems like a dangerous mistake.

I am now alone with the screwdriver.

ROSABELLE

25

"As you can see," she's saying, "the house is pretty small. It's more of a cottage, really. I still need to fix the roof. The recent storm took off a few shingles, but we got lucky, because there was no water damage inside. There are two bedrooms. Your bathroom doubles as the guest bathroom, which means there's no private access—"

I sit down inside of myself.

I find a dark corner in my head and make myself small, drawing my metaphorical knees to my metaphorical chest. Here, in this constructed quiet, I allow myself to feel the real speed of my heart, the true temperature of my blood, the actual levels of my hunger—and the findings are worse than I feared. Catastrophic.

I need to be alone.

I desperately want to talk to James.

Rationally, these two desires seem to be in direct conflict; emotionally, they make a strange sense to me.

The rebels' only reliable move has been to keep James away from me. When he was finally ordered to leave my hospital room, his older brother turned his full attention in my direction, studying me with an unsettling focus, letting the proceeding silence consume us both.

Being alone with Warner reactivated my panic.

I couldn't hold his searching gaze for long. I turned to the closed door, my broken eyes searching for the ghost of James.

He promised he'd see me later.

I don't know what that means. I don't think he can or should make me such promises. And I still don't understand how he can act so comfortable or casual around Warner.

The elder Anderson brother continues to be terrifying.

"I'd like to know what happened," he'd said softly, looming over me. "How did you wake yourself up?"

I kept my eyes on the door.

Because, Rosa.

I only dream of the dead.

"Where did you go when you were gone? Why was it so painful to return?"

I only dream of the dead.

"Did James heal you?" Warner asked me. "Is that why you were able to recover?"

Slowly, I turned to look at him.

His piercing green eyes were dazzling in the glare of my distorted vision, his hair a golden nimbus around his head. His skin was luminous. All his edges had been buffed away, softened into something diaphanous and ethereal. He looked almost angelic.

Leaning in, he said, "I think it's time for you to get to know me, Rosabelle. So I'm going to tell you a secret."

At that, I stiffened.

"If I discover that your intentions here include seducing my brother in order to manipulate him, I will personally oversee the methodical evisceration of your existence."

My heart hammered in my chest.

"You've infiltrated the wrong family. Betray him, and I will break your soul. If you run, I will hunt you. Retreat will be impossible. There will be no forgiveness. I will not allow you to surrender. I'll make you beg for the days of torture you enjoyed under The Reestablishment—"

The sudden slam of a door returns me violently to myself. I turn toward the source of the sound to find that someone new has entered the house: a tall man in glasses.

He's framed in the entrance.

Nazeera reappears, having disappeared into the bedroom she claimed was mine. She shoots me an exasperated look and says, "What the hell? I thought you were trying to leave." She looks me up and down. "But you haven't even moved, have you?"

The door slams again, this time slamming shut, and Nazeera realizes, too late, that there's someone else in her house. Common sense would dictate that she be more concerned with an intruder entering her home, but for reasons unknown, this fact doesn't appear to alarm her.

She's too cavalier.

I might've made a run for the door in her absence. I might've grabbed the screwdriver—

"Hey," says the intruder, lifting a hand.

He's not armed.

In fact, he looks like the kind of person who's perpetually annoyed to be awake. He's wearing a slouchy sweater, a pair of thoroughly worn jeans, and battered sneakers. His sandy-blond hair is unkempt. His dark frames are crooked.

His anxiety is palpable.

He glances from me to Nazeera, his eyes lingering on the weapon slung across her chest. "So, uh, why am I here?" he asks her. "Because I really, really don't want to be here." His eyes dart to me. "No offense."

My eyes widen a fraction.

"I need help," Nazeera says, gesturing to the house. "I have no furniture." She nods to me. "The girl needs clothes." She points at the kitchen. "I have no groceries. I didn't have enough time to pull anything together before she was discharged, and I ended up buying a pack of sponges, a single orange, and a wedge of cheese. I'm drowning."

The stranger takes this in, shoves his hands in his pockets, nods for a long moment, then says—

"Nope, bye."

And pivots toward the door.

Nazeera is fast; she physically catches him by the back of his collar, reeling him back into the room.

He cries out in protest.

"Winston," she insists. "Today is your day off—"

"Exactly," he says, wrenching away from her. "I'm supposed to be sitting on the couch, alone, judging people on television from the privacy of my own home. Ideally, there'd be ice cream involved."

Nazeera frowns. "What people on television?"

He sighs dramatically. "The local network puts on these tragic family-friendly theatrical shows and the musical numbers are campy and horrible. The dancers wear so much polyester—"

"You're bailing on me to watch some crappy public programming channel?" She cuts him off in outrage. "Are you serious? This is a high-priority security issue—consider it a duty to your nation—"

"No, thanks," he says, and takes a step back, adjusting his sweater as he looks around. "I don't want to be here with you in your depressing, empty house and your gun necklace and your pet serial killer." He glances at me again. "Seriously, no offense. I'm sure your parents are very supportive of your lifestyle."

His indifference is shocking.

"But I really need your help," Nazeera says. "I have to buy a shit ton of things and everyone else is busy or unauthorized to assist. I was going to ask Kian but he doesn't have clearance at this level." She tilts her head, thinking. "Hey, do you think we can borrow Adam's truck?"

Winston scowls.

"Why don't you ask James?" he says. He takes off his glasses, using the hem of his sweater to clean the lenses as he looks around, grimacing. "He loves projects like this."

"No way," she says. "James can't know I'm struggling. He's not on the team. He's a nonbeliever."

Winston rolls his eyes. "James would kill for the chance

to light a scented candle in this place. He's wanted to buy you a lamp for years. You're the kind of monster who turns on all the overhead lights, and you don't even care that you're using light bulbs with the cold color temperature of a hospital. You have terrible taste—"

"*Excuse me?*"

"Let me finish," Winston says, holding up a hand. He takes another second to polish his glasses before putting them on. Then, with a flourish: "You have terrible taste."

Nazeera gasps.

"Yeah, sorry," he says, shoving his hands back into his pockets. "That was a complete sentence. I meant what I said."

"Whatever, asshole," she says, narrowing her eyes. "I have great taste."

"In fashion? Maybe."

She physically recoils. "*Maybe?*"

"If you're going to hang out with aliens, absolutely. Wear the silver fringed patent leather trench coat."

She gasps again. "You told me you loved that coat!"

"You have no idea how to build a nest," he says, backing closer to the door. "You don't know how to arrange a room around a rug, or use paint color to soothe instead of injure. Quick quiz: Do any of these words sound familiar to you? *Sconce. Credenza. Console table. Ambience. Étagère*—"

"Now you're just trying to make me feel bad."

He nods, glancing at the door. "Is it working?"

"How can you be so pretentious when I'm literally asking for help?"

"I don't have time to be your mentor, Nazeera. Call James."

"I will *not* call James—"

"Get over your pride. He's surprisingly good at this stuff, and he's obviously obsessed with the serial killer—"

"My name is Rosabelle," I say sharply.

Nazeera and Winston freeze. They turn in tandem to face me, shock printed upon both their faces.

"Weird," says Winston. "I almost forgot she was here."

Nazeera stares. "That's actually the first time she's said anything since she got here."

The door slams open again.

This time, the shift is palpable. I sense him before I see him, the veils between myself and the world thinning nearly at once. My heart picks up as James walks through the door, and I understand then, with a clarity I've never felt before, that being near him is worse than dangerous.

Being near him will get me killed.

I take a terrified step back as he enters, his eyes finding mine immediately. Desperate fear and wild, unbridled joy suffuse my body, confusing me, sending me into a panic. He walks into the kitchen, slams something down on the counter, and heads in my direction with electric focus.

I suddenly can't breathe.

"Whoa, James—"

Nazeera steps in front of him, as if to stop him, and he's close enough now that I can practically see how hard he's working to tamp down a sparking, volatile energy, his chest lifting as he looks at her, then looks at me.

"Nazeera," he says quietly. "You know I love you. But get out of my way."

"What—why? What's happening? Who are you right now?"

James shakes his head, then sidesteps her quickly enough that she's still trying to catch up as he closes the distance between us, charging toward me with renewed purpose.

I feel the floor shift beneath me.

Somehow I'm rooted here, still standing, my heart beating out of my chest. I don't know why he's here. I can't make sense of the look on his face. I can't tell whether he's angry or terrified or—

He pulls me into his arms on a shaky breath, exhaling hard as our bodies collide.

I make an aching, involuntary sound.

The warmth and strength of him closes around me, the scent of him flooding my head as he braces me against his chest. My dead senses flare dangerously back to life.

I sink into him.

"Are you okay?" he whispers.

There's nothing left to protect me from this.

The scaffolding falls away from my spirit; my body comes undone. In his arms I release myself from my many prisons into the abyss of my own fears and he catches me, holding me closer, tighter, his breath warm against my hair. I feel too much of my heart. I feel too much of my soul. I'm suddenly shaking and starving. Aching.

So tired.

So tired.

I'm dizzy with fatigue. My eyes focus and unfocus. I blink and hold, then release. Blink and hold.

Release.

Pain radiates across my body, my heart thundering in my chest. Hunger claws violently at my gut. The healing process always replenishes my vital needs, usually regenerating my body to a nearly normal state; but I can't remember the last time I ate anything solid. More than that, I feel as if I haven't slept in weeks. Wherever I was these last three days, it's clear enough now that I wasn't resting. The world spins, tilting under me.

My knees give out.

I crumple against him and he catches me, his reflexes sharp as he gathers me up into his arms with ease. I sense his astonishment in the aftermath; his fear; his chest moving too fast as my head lands softly against his heart. He's carrying me like it's effortless.

Like he's done it before.

"Rosabelle," he says breathlessly. "What just happened?"

So tired.

I blink and hold, release.

"Rosabelle," he says again. "Are you okay?"

Anger exposes itself as pain. Silence exposes itself as fear. Distance exposes itself as armor.

Blink and hold. Release.

Blink and hold—

"Rosabelle?"

I fall, suddenly, asleep.

JAMES

26

"What is this, by the way?" Winston prods the Tupperware I'd set on the kitchen counter. "Is this some kind of ocean sample? Why'd you bring it here?"

Nazeera looks from me to the Tupperware. Then back to me. "Oh my God, is this what I think it is? Please tell me this isn't what I think it is."

"What?" Winston sniffs the Tupperware, makes a face, then pushes it away. "What do you think it is?"

"James, what did you do?" Nazeera says to me. "What happened to the chicken?"

"All right," says Winston. "I'm confused."

"You didn't even sauté the vegetables, did you?" Nazeera is saying. "You don't make soup by dumping a bunch of ingredients in hot water—"

"*Soup?*" Winston straightens, fixing his eyes on me. "Since when do you cook anything but protein shakes?"

"This Tupperware is cold." Nazeera frowns. "Why is it cold? Did you even use the stove?"

I roll my eyes at the pair of them, then silently mouth two words: *Fuck off.*

But my heart isn't really in it. My heart is dying.

Rosabelle is asleep in my arms.

"He really tried to make soup?" Winston asks.

I feel like I'm suspended in space with a fever. Like I might be on drugs. I don't know how else to describe it. My head is hot but soft, like parts of it have gone bad. My chest is literally aching, pain branching across my sternum like stress fractures.

I take a tight breath, releasing it carefully.

I'm sitting on the ground in the empty, dusty living room, my back propped up against the wall, and her small body is curled up against me like a cat, hardly moving, the engine of her heart almost silent.

Her pulse is really, really slow.

So slow, in fact, that it's beginning to scare me.

Rosabelle didn't wake up even when Nazeera finally removed her manacles. She didn't wake up when I carefully repositioned her tortured arms, when I touched the tender skin at her wrists, searching for bruises. She didn't wake up when I removed her slip-on shoes and her hospital socks almost came off in my hands. She didn't move when I tugged her socks back up, my fingers skimming the sensitive skin at her ankles. She didn't wake up when Winston tried to set up the folding chair and knocked it over instead.

I swallow as I study her.

Her white-blond hair is long and loose, tumbling over her shoulders, occasionally catching in my fingers. Her skin is smooth and silken, her features softly rendered, every slope and curve drawn gently. She's too lightweight in my arms; she's already lost what little strength she'd gained at the rehab facility; but a slight flush has bloomed in her cheeks in the past thirty minutes, and I realize, as I look at her, that I might be willing to give up a piece of my soul for the chance to kiss her.

She's so beautiful it's actually a little hard on my brain. The first time I saw her I glitched so hard I convinced myself she wasn't even human.

I can't process the sight of her like this, in stillness.

She looks like if a flower were a person. Like if clouds were a person. Like if a person was made of cake.

I squeeze my eyes shut.

I sound like a fucking lunatic.

"Hey, do you think we should order food?" Nazeera says, and I open my eyes. "I can call Kip. We could have breakfast for dinner."

"Where are we supposed to eat?" Winston points out. "On your imaginary dining table?"

"We could sit on the floor."

"When was the last time you swept this floor, Nazeera?"

"Oh!" she says, snapping her fingers. "That reminds me. I need to buy a vacuum when we go out tomorrow."

Winston groans.

Every once in a while Rosabelle inhales sharply, like she's forgotten to breathe. Her body clenches, then releases, easing back against my chest in increments, like the slow give of a blood pressure cuff.

At one point she startled in her sleep, lifting her hand a couple of inches in the air, then letting it fall to my chest.

I was in agony for a full minute as gravity drew her fingers slowly down the thin cotton of my shirt, my temperature spiking as my body stiffened.

Her hand is now pressed lightly against my abs, and every time I breathe I feel her fingers press harder and lower against my torso. Her cheek shifts against my chest. She sighs into my shirt. She's wearing a cheap set of thin hospital scrubs and, as usual, she's definitely not wearing any underwear. She's sitting in my fucking lap.

I've nearly lost the will to live.

I rock my head back against the wall and close my eyes. I can't really breathe, to be honest. This is an unreal kind of torture. Intense in a way I can't even describe.

"So is this it?" Winston says, leaning against the sink. "We're just going to watch her sleep?"

"If you're bored, you can run some errands," Nazeera says. "We still need groceries, and I don't have a spare mattress, but maybe you could—"

"*Me?* Why do I have to go by myself?"

"Obviously I can't leave these two alone." She gestures in my direction. "If we're gone for too long James will probably try to marry her, and she'll probably kill him for trying. We'll have to scrape his body off the asphalt."

I flip her off.

Nazeera grins. "Anyway, I thought you didn't want to be here," she says to Winston. "This is your chance to leave."

"I didn't want to be here when it was boring," Winston points out. He pushes off the counter, then opens the fridge. "*This* isn't boring. *This* is crazy. *This* is my favorite kind of drama. This is— Wait, why don't you have any groceries?"

Nazeera sighs, exasperated. "I literally just told you I didn't have any groceries."

He cranes his neck to look at her. "I thought you were exaggerating. You seriously went out and bought one orange, a wedge of cheese, and a pack of sponges?" Then, doing a double take, "Why are the sponges in the fridge?"

"Why is everyone giving me such a hard time?" Nazeera says, crossing her arms. "I almost never buy groceries when I'm in town. There's no point; I'm never home; I don't like to waste food. I just come here to sleep—"

"On your invisible bed?" Winston emerges from his search with the single orange, then slams the fridge shut.

I grimace.

I'd tell them both to be quiet but I'm afraid to raise my voice this close to Rosabelle's head. I have no idea when she last slept, and I'm not sure being brain dead for three days counts as quality rest. In fact, I'm sure it didn't.

I force my eyes shut, trying not to remember the scenes from her hospital room. I'm not ready to think too hard about what I saw. I don't want to think about the look on her face or the tortured sounds she was making. I've never seen her like that. So helpless, so openly afraid.

I still don't know what happened—I don't know what she'd experienced or what she was trying to fight off. All I know is that it did something to me, seeing her like that.

Changed my chemistry.

I realized as I watched her that I might be driven to do dark, horrible things to make that look in her eyes go away. I realized maybe I'm not so different from Warner after all. Apparently, my morals are relative. Apparently, I'm still capable of surprising myself.

I realized I'd kill people. Lots of people.

Anything to make it stop.

"I own a proper mattress," Nazeera says matter-of-factly. "And it's in my bedroom, where it's supposed to be."

"Why do you sound so proud?" Winston rolls the orange around in his hands, warming it. "You think it's a big deal to have a mattress in your bedroom? I'm embarrassed for you. I hate secondhand embarrassment. I hate you for making me feel secondhand embarrassment."

"Get out of my house, Winston."

"You know why we're giving you so much shit?" he says, and begins to peel his orange.

"Why?"

"Because"—he looks up, looks around—"I don't think you've ever invited us over."

"That's not true," says Nazeera. "You've all been here before."

"That's not called being invited over." Winston sets a piece of orange rind on the counter, his eyes searching the room. "Where the hell is your garbage can?"

Nazeera stiffens.

Then, with stilted motions, she opens a cabinet under

the sink and retrieves a paper shopping bag, holding it open by the handles.

"Are you kidding me, Nazeera?" Winston drops the orange rind in the bag. "How can you live like this?"

Rosabelle makes a sound, something like a murmur, and everyone turns sharply to look at her as she shifts in my arms, her lips briefly parting against my chest. She sighs against my shirt.

I hold on, hold still.

Can't breathe.

When, after a moment, nothing happens, everyone unclenches.

Winston stares at me.

"You know," he says, peeling the orange again. "I just realized this is the second time she's passed out in your arms."

Nazeera frowns. "When was the first time?"

Winston drops another piece of rind in the paper bag, where it lands with a soft *thump*. "When he was escaping from the island, remember? On the mini helicopter. He said he was talking to her, asking her some questions, and she just randomly collapsed." Winston glances at me. "Right?"

Slowly, I nod.

The sun is shifting lower in the sky, rays of fading light painting stripes across the house. A band of gold falls across her face, my arms.

"Weird," says Nazeera, "I almost forgot about that."

"Narcoleptic?" says Winston.

I make a face.

Nazeera says what I'm thinking: "I don't think she'd have made it this far as an assassin if she had narcolepsy."

Winston drops the last piece of rind in the trash, then splits open the orange, which breaks apart with a suction sound. A spritz of juice dissipates in a slant of sunlight, the scent of orange filtering through the air.

"Well, narcolepsy or not," he says. "That's what we call a pattern of behavior."

Nazeera wordlessly holds out her hand, and Winston places half the orange in her palm.

"Two instances don't make a pattern," she says, prying a segment of orange away from its flesh, then popping it in her mouth. "But they do make things interesting." She makes a face. "Oh, this is tart."

"Good, though." Winston is chewing.

"Yeah." Her face relaxes. She swallows her bite, then considers Rosabelle a moment. "Hey, do you think I should get a cat?"

"*What?*" Winston and I both say at the same time.

Rosabelle stirs against my chest and I immediately regret having spoken out loud.

"You don't even have a trash can," Winston says to Nazeera. "You don't even live here full-time. How are you going to take care of a cat?"

"Maybe you could cat-sit for me while I'm gone."

"No way," he says sharply. "I am *not* taking on anymore of your abandoned pets—"

"I don't abandon them!"

"You've got priors, Nazeera. Who do you think inherited your betta fish? Who finished building that model airplane when you got tired of it? Who kept your garden going until you got sick of it? Who has sole custody of Kenji?"

"*Oh, shit,*" I whisper.

Nazeera looks suddenly haunted. "Ouch."

Winston averts his eyes. He has the decency to look ashamed when he says, quietly, "I'm sorry. I shouldn't have said that. I didn't mean it like that."

Nazeera sets her unfinished orange on the counter. We're all quiet a moment, tension ratcheting in the silence.

Finally, she says, "I'm afraid of buying a garbage can."

Winston studies her. "Why?"

She shakes her head, turns her eyes to the darkened hall. "I always thought I'd do stuff like that with Kenji. Buying plates or a lamp or a couch—without him?" She stills. "It feels like closing the door on what might've been. Like I'm accepting that it's never going to happen."

That hits me harder than I expect.

Winston sets down the rest of his orange. "So living in this empty, depressing house is actually giving you hope?"

She meets his eyes. "Is that horrible?"

"No," Winston says, his eyes drawing together. "It's just confusing."

"Why?"

"Because Kenji loves you." He laughs, but the sound is tense. "If you haven't moved on, why can't you just be together? Why do you need—"

The door swings open without warning and I stiffen, alarmed, as Rosabelle flinches in my arms.

"Why doesn't anyone knock?" Nazeera says.

"Hello?" says a familiar voice.

"Why didn't you lock your door?" Winston counters.

"I never lock the door," she says, heading toward the entrance. "You lock your door? In The Waffle?"

"Hey, why is it so dark in here?"

I see Adam before he sees me. Nazeera's single light bulb is doing little work to illuminate the house.

"Oh, hey," Nazeera says, relief washing over her face as she takes him in. "Thanks for coming."

"Yeah, no problem," Adam says, his boots echoing. He looks around as he enters, slamming the door shut behind him, and Rosabelle flinches again.

"I just saw your page a few minutes ago," Adam says, "otherwise I would've— *Holy shit—*"

He finally sees me sitting in the half dark, and he visibly startles, backing up a step. "Bro, are you trying to give me a heart attack? Fucking say something."

"Hey, man," says Winston, lifting a hand.

"*Jesus.*" Adam recoils again. "It's like a haunted house in here." He turns to Nazeera. "Why haven't you bought any furniture yet? Is that why you never invite us over? And why haven't you turned on the lights?"

"Wait—" Nazeera tries to say. "Don't—"

Adam hits the switches for the recessed lights in the kitchen, then the front hall, then the area where the dining room is supposed to be, and the small house blazes into relief all at once.

Rosabelle's face pinches. She makes a sound of distress. Shit.

Adam, meanwhile, takes a third step back, this time like he's been slapped. He's suddenly staring at me like I'm diseased. "Please, for the love of God, tell me I've lost my mind," he says, his eyes widening. "What the hell am I looking at right now?"

Rosabelle stretches a little, her head tilting upward, her lips grazing my neck. She murmurs something there, against my throat, and I nearly black out.

She relaxes back into my arms, but I'm not doing so well. My heart is fucking wild. I've never wanted so badly to be alone with her.

I never get to be alone with her.

I never get to process anything with her in private—in peace. No murdering. No trauma. No running for our lives. I just want ten minutes. Hell, five minutes.

I'd take sixty seconds.

Thirty seconds.

Thirty seconds of no one breathing down my neck. Sometimes I just want a single second to *look* at her without being interrupted.

"James," says Adam, his voice hardening. "What is going on?"

I'm still trying to figure out what to say to him when her eyes fly open.

JAMES

27

Rosabelle gasps. Draws back.

Looking into her eyes turns me into an idiot in an instant. It's amazing. An alchemical process. It should be studied. I've actually forgotten how to speak. I feel like I've been fighting for my life, like I need to convalesce. I can still feel the impression of her lips on my throat. The scent of her is in my head. Under my skin.

I can't breathe deeply enough.

She's giving me that look, that half-lidded, dizzying look. Her eyes are slightly glazed, still burning off the haze of dreams, her face flushed with the heat of sleep. Her cheek is faintly creased with an imprint of my shirt.

I stare at the soft, red mark.

My head goes hot as I take her in, my eyes sweeping across her features, lingering at her mouth. My arms are still wrapped around her, her silky hair streaming down her back, grazing my hands. My heart is working too hard to be subtle about what's happening in my body. I feel her own fears rising; I can practically touch the connection between us. She looks disoriented and dazed, but she doesn't try to move out of my arms.

She takes another sharp breath, this time nearly sitting

upright in the process, and the stark movement is so obvious everyone reacts at the same time. There's a rush of motion as Winston, Nazeera, and Adam turn fully to face us, but I can't look away from Rosabelle.

I'm frozen.

"Hey," I say softly, searching her eyes.

My hand moves to the back of her head automatically, bracing her as she looks up at me. "You're not in danger, okay? You're safe. Everything is fine."

She exhales; her eyes close. I watch her wet her lips. I feel like I'm not fully in my body.

Rosabelle's hand is pressed to my chest.

"Welcome back," Nazeera calls from the kitchen. "How was your nap?"

The interruption is like ice water.

Cold. Bracing.

I'm so grateful I nearly thank her out loud, but Rosabelle goes rigid at the sound of Nazeera's voice, her eyes flying open in horror.

"Yeah, welcome back," says Winston. "I gave up my day off for this. I'm still waiting for the part where something exciting happens."

Rosabelle tries to push up, away from me, but it's a half-hearted effort. I can feel the tremble in her body; the fatigue she's trying to mask.

"Hey," I say, my hands sliding to her waist. "I've got you."

It's the smallest thing, the way she looks up at me then. The way she lets herself lean on me a little, lets me lever her upright.

It leaves a dent in my chest.

Rosabelle sways slightly as she stands. She closes her eyes again, trying to steady herself, but when she opens them she looks dizzy.

"What's wrong with her?" says Winston. He pops another orange slice into his mouth.

"What do you think is wrong with her, genius?" I hit back. "She was dead for three days."

"Yeah, but she seemed fine earlier," Winston says, talking around the bite of orange. "Actually, she was perfectly fine before you showed up. The minute you walked in she went weird."

"Okay, asshole."

"I'm serious—"

"Whatever."

Rosabelle, meanwhile, doesn't seem to be listening. I catch her looking intensely at Adam, who's just standing there, staring at us, paralyzed.

"This is the girl?" Adam says, his eyes on me. "This is the girl who slit your throat?"

"You've never seen her before?"

"No. I mean, yes, obviously." He shakes his head. "Just— not like this. Not in, like, a normal environment."

"Well." I offer him a flat smile. "This is Rosabelle."

"Isn't she supposed to be in prison?"

"That's old news," says Winston. "Where have you been, anyway? I haven't seen you in days."

"I was"—he blinks, absently shaking the keys in his hands—"we took the kids on a road trip—"

"So can I borrow the truck?" Nazeera asks.

"Whoa, wait, slow down," I say. "We're not going anywhere or doing anything until I feed Rosabelle."

Rosabelle stiffens beside me.

I look at her, expecting her to protest, but she only stares at me with unguarded astonishment. When she finally looks away without a fight, it actually scares me a little.

She must be starving.

"Sounds good to me," says Winston. "Let's get the hell out of here."

"You want to come with us?" Nazeera says to Adam. "We're getting waffles." She hesitates, then checks in with Winston. "Right? Are we still doing breakfast for dinner? Or do you want pizza?"

"You're just—" Adam falters. "Are you joking? You're just going to take her out to dinner?"

"Warner didn't say we had to keep her locked up in the house," Nazeera points out. "She's pretty contained in The Waffle, and we have to feed her eventually."

"Yeah, you heard James," Winston says. "We have to feed her. Get her energy levels back up so she can finish murdering everyone."

"She's not going to murder anyone," I say sharply. Then, hesitating, I look at Rosabelle. "Right?"

She nods.

"See?" Winston points at her. "She says no murdering.

Let's go. I'm starving. Tomorrow, we're getting groceries."

"And a couch," Nazeera says. She looks at Adam. "Hey, can I keep your truck for a few days?"

"What the fuck kind of parallel universe have I just walked into?" he says, reeling. "Isn't she a psychopath?"

"No," I say. "She's an assassin. Big difference."

"Minor difference," says Winston.

Adam blanches. "Oh my God," he says, pushing his hands through his hair. "It's happening again. I can't believe I have to live through this again—"

"Yeah." Winston claps him on the shoulder. "Sorry. Try again next lifetime."

"How can you just take her out in public?" Adam says, his hands falling to his sides. "What if people recognize her? What if people realize who she is?"

"No one's going to recognize her," says Nazeera. "And anyone who does recognize her already knows to keep their mouth shut. The subject is classified."

"Yeah, but we should get her a change of clothes before we go," says Winston, shrugging into his jacket. "Just to be safe. The hospital gear is a little obvious and really bumming me out."

Adam stares. "You're not going to cuff her?"

"No way," I say. "She's not going to hurt anyone."

"Ooh, we can always tell people she's an old friend of mine," Nazeera says, wrapping her shawl around her head. "Visiting."

Winston scoffs. "No one will believe that."

"Why not?"

"Where's she supposed to be visiting from?" he asks, arching a brow. "Serial killer academy? She has the personality of a wall."

"All right, that's enough," I say angrily. "You don't even know her."

"How am I supposed to know her?" he counters. "She's like a mini Warner. She doesn't talk. She doesn't smile. She doesn't eat. Her only personality trait is being a good murderer."

"How can you admit that," says Adam, "and still be willing to take her out to dinner?"

"I'm starved for entertainment," says Winston.

"You're all out of your minds."

I sigh, turning to Rosabelle. "Look, no pressure or anything, but do you think you could say something? Just so they know you're capable of speech? You're scaring people."

There's a shudder of sound, then absolute silence, as everyone turns to look at her.

Rosabelle goes inhumanly still.

Clearly, she doesn't like the attention. I'm beginning to understand that she doesn't like to be watched, period.

She takes a step back. I steady her.

She shakes her head at me. I tilt my head at her.

"Please?" I say quietly. "I just want everyone to know you're not trying to kill them."

Rosabelle holds my gaze a beat before looking away, and I can practically see her mind processing: sorting and analyzing reams of data. It's a second before she looks up, her eyes tight as she scans the group assembled before her. The tension is suddenly weird and intense. No one is smiling, not even ironically. Everyone is waiting, hypnotized, to hear her speak.

She parts her lips.

Looks at me one last time.

"You can say whatever you want," I tell her. "Really. It doesn't have to be, like, a fun fact about yourself. No pressure."

Slowly, she turns to the others.

Takes a breath.

She says, "There are undercover agents all over the continent planning to commit synchronized acts of terror against your civilians over the course of the next several weeks. I don't know how many there are, and I don't know when these incidents will occur. But you won't be able to stop them. Your society has already been infiltrated. Your world is in danger. Your only chance at success lies with me." She lifts her chin. "You have to let me go home. Tonight. Or you will suffer the consequences."

ROSABELLE

28

"*Nope,*" James says sharply, shaking his head. "Absolutely not. I meant what I said. We're not discussing anything until you eat—"

"What?" I stare at him, stunned. "I don't think you understand what I'm saying—"

"I understand exactly what you're saying. I don't care if the world burns to the fucking ground, Rosabelle. You're going to eat first."

Nazeera is watching us, her eyes wide with alarm. Carefully, she says, "I think I should page Warner."

"Good idea," says James. "Invite him to join us for dinner."

"Wait, is this a joke?" says the other one, the man with the dark hair and the familiar blue eyes, the one who was never formally introduced to me. He looks panicked. "Is this— What the hell is happening right now?"

"This is not a joke," I say, turning my attention to him, hoping someone will listen to me. "I need to get back to the Ark immediately—"

"We can discuss it over dinner," says James, before abruptly leaving the group to head down the hall.

"Bro, what the hell—"

"An hour isn't going to make a difference if we're all going to die anyway," James calls over his shoulder. Then, "Nazeera, can I grab one of your jackets for Rosabelle?"

"Yeah," she says, shell-shocked. "But—"

"I think I liked you better when you didn't talk," says Winston. He crosses his arms, frowning at me.

"Me too," I say, looking away.

The quiet truth I'm struggling to admit is that, despite my urgency to return to the Ark, if I don't eat something soon I'll be useless to everyone.

I'm feeling dangerously faint.

Floaters push in and out of my vision. I'm experiencing a general, heightened debility that scares me, and my efforts to marshal self-possession are more tenuous than ever. James's effect on me has grown only worse with time. I used to be able to summon greater measures of composure in his presence, but now—

Now, I have no defenses against him.

I still haven't processed the fact that I fell asleep in his arms. There's no precedent for it.

It's incomprehensible.

When I was forced to imagine my life married to Sebastian, I could hardly tolerate the idea of holding his hand, much less sharing a bed with him. I don't enjoy proximity to other people in general; I don't like to be touched. I can't even trust the affection of my own sister. That I surrendered so easily to James, that my body yielded to him without hesitation—with implicit *trust*—

Something dangerous is happening to me.

I've broken; a jammed lever has released a dam inside of me and I don't know how to repair the damage. I can't even see James now without feeling breathless. It's hard enough to look at his face—the juxtapositions of hard and soft, the balanced arrangement of his beauty—but there's something visceral and potent about simply being in his orbit. I'm getting addicted to the relief I experience when I see him. I'm getting distracted by the need to touch him; to be touched by him. What I feel for him now is worse than perilous. It's lethal. It's scaring me.

I need him to stay away from me.

Something soft lands at my back and I look up to find that James has draped a big, puffy pink jacket over my shoulders. I try, once again, to pull myself together.

"Please, James, listen to me," I try to say, but when he draws closer I feel unsteadier right away: I can already feel the tremble in my right hand intensifying, the tremors rocking up my arm, and I make a fist, trying to contain it. "I—I have to get back to the Ark," I force out.

"No," he says. "You're in time-out."

Winston chokes.

"What?" I blink, my eyes pinging between them. "What does that mean?"

"It means we'll discuss this over dinner," says James, moving toward the hall again.

"But I have to get back as soon as possible," I call out to his retreating back. "And I can't leave without the vial, which means I'm going to need—"

"The vial?" says the blue-eyed man. "What vial?"

Winston sighs, pushing a hand through his hair. It sticks up in places. "You know, when I said I was still waiting for something exciting to happen, I was hoping for more interpersonal drama, less end-of-the-world drama. I'm really sick of end-of-the-world drama."

"Warner is on his way," Nazeera says, lifting up her pager.

"Great," says James, grabbing a denim jacket from a hallway closet. "Ask him if he wants waffles."

"You hung up your jacket?" says Winston. "When did you hang up your jacket? I didn't even know Nazeera owned hangers."

"Rude," she says.

James crosses the room toward me, his expression unreadable. "Finish putting on your coat. You look like a pink marshmallow."

"But— What?" I look at myself, then carefully push my arms into the oversized coat. The interior is lined with something silky that feels so luxurious I nearly close my eyes. It feels like wearing a pillow.

"*Oh*," I say, blinking.

James is studying me, holding out my slip-on shoes from the hospital, but when I look up to meet his eyes I stiffen, struck, like I've taken a blow to the head.

"Rosabelle," he says. "Shoes. Zipper. Please."

My chest constricts.

"What?" he says. "What's wrong?"

"Nothing," I breathe.

But the gears in my mind won't turn.

I feel almost dazed.

I've seen James a thousand times, and I've always acknowledged his beauty. The fact of his attractiveness is self-evident; as indisputable as the wet of water. But now, somehow, it's as if I'm seeing him through new eyes.

My *own* eyes.

No armor. No shields to dull the blow. I'm fully present in my body and his impact is devastating. He's not just gorgeous; he's impossibly stunning. His *hair*. His eyes. The corded muscles of his arms. The powerful lines of his neck. How have I never noticed his shoulders? His hands?

"Why are you looking at me like that?" he says, his voice lower now. He's still holding my shoes, but they seem forgotten between us. He takes a step closer.

Desperate, I grab the shoes from him.

Then I step back.

"Oh, shit," says the blue-eyed guy. "I need to tell Alia I won't be home for dinner—I was supposed to pick up milk—"

"We've got milk at our place," says Winston. "Tell her to grab the carton from our fridge—"

"Hey, so, why do you need the vial before you can leave? What does it do?" Nazeera is slipping into a long leather jacket as she speaks, and when she turns to face me she gasps, breaking into a smile. "Oh my God, you do look like a pink marshmallow."

I'm still inching backward when she says this—struggling with the zipper as I try to put as much space between myself and James as possible—and I startle when she comes over to help me.

She fits the teeth together, then tugs up the slider like I'm a child. "It's so puffy it's sometimes hard to see where it starts," she says. "Cute, though, right?"

She's smiling at me like she means it. I feel like I'm wearing a big cloud; I can't really move my arms. I realize only then that she's wearing her shawl as a headscarf—in a style decidedly reminiscent of outlawed religions—and this throws me off guard.

I can't quite make sense of Nazeera.

It's possible religion is no longer illegal on the mainland, but I can't decide whether she's wearing a scarf like this on purpose or if it's merely a coincidence; clearly it's not something she does all the time, and I can't imagine what reason she'd have to resurrect such a tradition.

Her father was the supreme commander of Asia.

Despite the cultures and practices once prevalent in the region, there's no chance she was brought up in a faith system; not when her father was loyal to the authoritarian ideology. In the name of instituting universal equality, one of the first acts of the regime was to obliterate identity. People were to act as one body, indistinguishable. All visible symbols of culture and religion were immediately criminalized.

It's considered treason to suggest the existence of a power greater than The Reestablishment; the only entity declared worthy of worship is the establishment itself. On the Ark, some have begun erecting altars to Klaus. They've developed rites and rituals meant to fully submit themselves before his synthetic intelligence, asking for answers and guidance. On the Ark, Nazeera would be sentenced to death if she were caught trying to resurrect an ancient faith.

"Yes, thank you," I say quietly, confused. Still, I'm grateful for the head change, and I remember that she asked me a question. "In order to explain the vial, I'd have to start from the beginning—"

"*No*," James says sharply. "No more answering questions. You're in time-out."

"Jesus, this is ridiculous," mutters the blue-eyed guy.

"You put her in time-out?" Nazeera says to James, fighting a smile. "Are you serious?"

"What does that mean?" I ask her.

"It means you're in trouble," Winston explains to me. He's bent over, retying his shoelaces, and his glasses slide down the bridge of his nose. He pushes them back up, then straightens to look at me. "It means you have to sit in your cool-down center and think about what you've done."

"What?" I stare at him.

"It's called a fucking calm-down corner," says the guy whose name I still don't know. "And you're all a bunch of idiots."

"It sounds like Adam needs a time-out," says Winston, crossing his arms. "Nazeera, which one is your calm-down corner? The one with all the dead spiders, or the one with all the dead spiders?"

She flips him off.

"All right, enough," James says angrily. "Not another word out of any of you until we get to the diner." He strides toward me as he speaks, clearing the few feet of distance I'd only recently reclaimed. He buttons himself into a denim jacket as he moves, and I recognize the fleece collar, the orange enamel kite pin affixed to the front pocket. I watch, transfixed, as he tugs a navy beanie over his head, the article brightening his eyes, and when he looks at me again I feel winded, like I've been knocked off my axis.

"You ready?" James says, towering before me.

It's like looking up at the sun.

How had I never felt the depth of his presence? How had I not seen the way he moves; the way his clothes fit his body; or the way he smiles, like he knows his face is a weapon?

I thought I had.

I thought I'd been thorough in cataloging his strengths and weaknesses. I thought I'd completed his character assessment for my files; duly noted the broad expanse of his chest; the breathtaking build of him; the way he commands a room. But I'd been observing him through glass, trying to describe rain through a window. I realize only now that I'd never truly felt it, not for more than flashes at a time. I'd never known him like *this*, my skin burning with an awareness that refuses to abate, my heart thudding wildly in my chest without end. This—

This is *terrifying*.

I'm nearly lightheaded as I look away.

"Wait, hold on," says the other guy, the one Winston called Adam. "How do we know she's not lying? Why are we just assuming she's telling the truth?"

Winston zips up his jacket to his throat. "I don't know, man," he says, jamming his hands in his pockets. "but I don't think she's lying."

"How can you be sure?"

"Look at her," says Nazeera, nodding at me as she buttons her coat. "She's uncuffed and unrestrained. There's a screwdriver sitting on the windowsill less than four yards away, and there's a pair of scissors on the counter in the kitchen, left in plain sight. I put a bunch of things within easy reach around the house to see if she'd take the opportunity to try to kill us—"

"You did *what*?" Adam gapes at her.

"—and instead, she's standing there quietly, wearing my coat, asking to be sent home."

Winston laughs out loud.

My eyes widen.

Adam looks horrified. "Why would you invite me over when you knew there was a chance she might murder me?"

"I'd never let her murder you," Nazeera says, looking offended. "I just wanted to see if she'd try."

"Yeah, don't flatter yourself," Winston says to Adam. "If she was going to murder anyone she'd definitely murder James first."

"What?" says James. "Why me? She likes me." He turns

to look at me, and I rock back, struck. "You like me, right?"

But I'm distracted. I'm disarranged.

I take another panicked step away from James and direct my gaze at Nazeera. "You left weapons around the house on purpose?"

"We're going to be roommates," she says with a shrug. "I wanted to gauge the level of violence I'd be managing for the duration." She flashes me a fresh smile. "If you'd tried to kill me on day one I would've made some adjustments to our living situation."

I'm stunned. I feel like I'm meeting her for the first time. With a new respect.

"Damn," says Winston. "She just flat out ignored you."

"Shut up," says James.

"Who?" asks Nazeera, tying the belt at her waist. "What are you guys talking about?"

"Rosabelle," says Adam.

"Yes?" I answer.

"No," says James. "That's not—"

"Bro, you need to stop," Adam says to him. "This is embarrassing."

James turns his gaze up to the ceiling, then groans out loud, like he's being tortured. "Can we please get the hell out of here?"

"Okay, wait, one more thing." Adam turns to me. "I just need to know. Seriously. How much should I be freaking out right now?"

I'm backing away from James again, moving closer to

Nazeera, and I'm about to answer with the truth when I realize Adam is trying to mask real terror. Something quiets inside of me, seeing his fear. It resets my head.

My heart rate begins to steady.

It occurs to me, once again, that I don't want these soft, loud, messy people to die. I don't know who this person is, but I'm starting to think he doesn't share the cavalier attitude of the others.

In fact, he might be a civilian.

"Who are you?" I finally ask him.

He stiffens, his eyes darting to Winston, then Nazeera, then back to me. "Who?" He points to himself. "Me?"

"Yes," I say.

"Why?" he says, tensing a bit more.

"You look a little like James."

James snaps his head toward me, and the impact is physical. I try to hold steady.

"Oh." Adam exhales so hard he laughs. "Yeah. Well. I'm James's older brother. My name's Adam. I'm guessing you've realized that by now."

This admission surprises me.

I look between the two of them, trying to remember whether I knew there was a third Anderson brother. I was never given a dossier on him, which seems like an oversight. From the moment I saw Adam I'd thought his eyes looked familiar, but now that I'm really looking at him, I'm noticing all the other subtle similarities. The texture of his hair; the shape of his mouth.

But Adam is softer than his brothers.

He's less defined, less muscular, less imposing. He has an anxious energy; his shoulders are rounded, his posture defensive. Standing next to James, he presents more like distant relatives. James emanates a magnetic energy that almost demands a response; he's electric and breathtaking even at rest, the breadth of him both comforting and terrifying. Adam, by contrast, seems to exist on a quieter frequency. If he ever had the harder edges of his brothers, they've been sanded down by time.

He's handsome in an unthreatening way.

He has a cartoon Band-Aid on one finger; his jacket is missing a button. His wedding ring is scuffed, dull, thoroughly worn. The glimmer of a snack wrapper peeks up out of the pocket of his jeans. He shakes the keys in his hand, from which hangs a bright, tiny toy action figure. He looks every inch an ordinary citizen. He seems far less likely—or capable—of killing someone.

"You're unarmed," I say to him.

He stops shaking the keys. "What?"

"No—you're *never* armed," I say, frowning as I assess him. "You're not like your other brothers. You're afraid of change. You don't value ambition." I pause. "You don't seek glory, do you? Your aims are smaller. You prefer routine. You fear death."

Now he looks taken aback. "What? I'm not— Wait, how do you know I'm never armed—"

"*Whoa*," says Winston, gaping at me. "That was scary."

"Stings, doesn't it?" James says to his brother. "You should've heard what she had to say about me. Felt like I'd been disemboweled."

Adam stares between the two of us, dumbfounded.

"All right." Winston claps his hands, then straightens to his full height. "Do me next. I'm ready. I can take it."

Nazeera cuts him a look.

"What?" he argues. "I'm serious. I need a ten-second psychological evaluation that could ruin my life. It might be the motivation I need to finally get my shit together."

James rubs at his eyes. "I hate all of you."

"Wait," says Adam. "*Wait.* She never answered my question—"

"You don't have to worry," I say to him. "I'm going to fix things."

"But—"

"Bro, enough, stop asking her questions," James says angrily. "For the last fucking time, she's *literally* starving, and we will discuss this over dinner." He throws opens the front door and a cold breeze immediately penetrates the little house.

"James—wait—" I try to say.

"No, this is not up for debate," he says. He storms back inside the house, grabs me by the puffed sleeve where my hand should be, and tugs me across the threshold.

"James—"

"*No.*"

I give an unintelligible cry as we're hit by the cold blast of early evening.

WARNER

29

"Look," says Kenji. "All I'm trying to say is that, everything considered, I think that went pretty well."

I glance at him. "He was crying."

"Yeah, but isn't Hugo always crying these days?"

I look into the darkening night with a sigh, bracing myself as a brisk wind pushes through the street. It's a struggle to clear out the sounds of the man's broken sobs from my head. I had to tell Hugo why he wouldn't be showing up to the prison tomorrow. I had to explain that we were ending the interrogation process and cutting off his access to his daughter for an indefinite period of time. I had to tell him we were transferring Rosabelle to a safe house. I could not assure him that she would survive. I could not promise him he would see her again.

The meeting did not, in fact, go well.

The entire arrangement with Hugo has been a massive disappointment. I don't know whether there's any ready solution for his heartache; I don't even know if we'll be able to let his daughter live long enough for him to try again.

Hugo has been understanding, but inconsolable.

I still feel heavy with his deferred pain, residual grief coursing through me, unprocessed. I have to occasionally talk myself out of a dark mood when an emotional load is particularly fathomless. Sometimes I can't decipher between what's been borrowed and what belongs to me.

Right now, I'm trying to focus on the crisp evening air, and not the incessant buzzing in my pocket.

My pager has been going off for hours, but the notifications have been nearly constant these past thirty minutes. I already know, without looking, that when I finally check my notifications I'll have to scroll through a hundred angry messages from Adam.

He's been giving me moment-by-moment updates on the situation unfolding at Nazeera's house.

Apparently, he walked in to discover Rosabelle asleep in James's arms. As if this news wasn't bad enough, the admission was followed by a litany of profane remarks riddled with typos—a result of having been sent in rapid-fire succession.

Is this a fucking joke??????>

SHE'S A PSYCOPATH

JUST LIKE YOU

I don't mean you're a psychopath bow

now

But you know what I mean

Its s o weird that nazeera doesn't have any furniutre

THEY"RE TAKLING HER OUT TO DINNER

WHAT THE FUCK

Did you say they could dtake her out to dinner

They said you said they could take her out
I CAN"T BELIEVE THIS IS HAPPENNG
You hve to fix this
GET THE FUCK OVER HERE

I've granted myself the gift of sixty seconds before I reach for my pager again. I need some time to ground myself.

"Hey, are you sure you don't want to go incognito?" Kenji says suddenly. "People are freaks around you. If you get spotted things might get weird."

I manage a tight smile in response.

I don't usually spend time in the capital city on foot, despite the tremendous efforts we've made to restore and rebuild the area. Ella was the one to establish the seat of government in this region; it was all her undertaking. The resulting metropolis is an objectively stunning accomplishment, a marriage of old and new architecture meant to mirror the culture of the next generation: evolution without erasure.

The Waffle is situated at the heart of the new capital; and the surrounding region is referred to as New Capital City, or the NCC. The truth is, I really enjoy walking through the world my wife envisioned for us. But I can't spend extended periods of time in public because too many attempts have already been made on my life. Of course, there's also the issue of other people.

The ones who *aren't* interested in killing me.

"I'm serious," Kenji says. "Remember when that woman took off all her clothes and threw them at you? And then she was just standing there—naked and screaming."

My pager buzzes again.

"I keep trying to forget," I say dryly. "But you're always reminding me. You really seem to love this story."

"What I want to know is: How did she know you were coming? How did she time it so perfectly? Was it a coordinated thing, or did she just get lucky?"

I glance at him, saying nothing.

My pager buzzes.

"And, like, what was she hoping was going to happen?" he goes on. "Did she really think being confronted by a naked, screaming stranger would generate a positive reaction? I seriously want to know what she was thinking. Do you ever wonder what's going through their minds?"

"No."

"But this lady had a dream, right? Like, she was hoping for *something*. And here's the thing," he says, pointing a finger at me. "Here's the real philosophical question: If she'd actually managed to get you alone for ten minutes, would she have been happy with the reality of you?"

"No."

"Because I feel like what they really want is just, like, the fantasy, you know?"

My pager buzzes again.

I give myself another thirty seconds before I reach for it.

We're crossing the city on foot because I'd wanted the chance to expel some of this latent energy I'm carrying. I don't like to bring it home. I usually hit heavy weights or go for a run when I need to exorcise the excess emotional static from my body, but there was no time for that tonight.

And the walk isn't too bad.

Streetlamps emit golden light that seems to melt through the early darkness, rendering the streets dusky and indistinct. Pedestrians move through the night in various formations, dipping in and out of pools of light. Altogether, the feedback is relatively undramatic. I sense no general panic, no fury or violence, so I try to push it out, away from me, into a kind of insensible white noise. Crickets chorus through it all.

It's been a relentlessly long day.

"I don't know how you deal with it," Kenji is saying. "The shit some people say to you is so weird I feel embarrassed even repeating it. If someone ever asked me for a vial of my spit I'd probably fight them."

I raise an eyebrow at that.

"What?" he counters, defiant. "There's some dark energy in a question like that. That's a weird thing to ask for. Why would you want my spit? What are you going to do with my spit?" He hesitates. "You know what, ew, I don't want to know."

Kenji's energy is a little edgy. Anxious.

He's been managing spikes of frenetic agitation ever since Nazeera decided she'd be staying in town for an indefinite period of time. He doesn't seem to know what to do with himself.

I decide to just let him talk.

Kenji was the one who insisted we take a detour after leaving Hugo's house. He claimed there was a new dumpling place he wanted to try. He assured me Ella was going to love it. He promised we'd get take-out and go straight home. He said it would be a nice surprise for her, that she deserved to try something new after being stuck in the house for so long.

I know when I'm being manipulated.

But I relented because it's true. Because I'm sure Ella would love to try something new after being stuck in the house for so long.

"So?" Kenji prompts. "Should we go incognito?"

I shake my head. There's always an introduction of risk when we can't see each other; I don't like losing one of my senses. "Not yet," I tell him. "It's dark enough for now, and the streets aren't too crowded at the moment. I'll wait until we reach the restaurant."

My pager buzzes.

Buzzes again.

I've just decided to give myself another thirty seconds when we come to a sudden stop.

"Okay," says Kenji, frowning at street signs. "I think we're here."

"Where?"

"Somewhere? Around here?"

Now I feel myself losing patience. "You don't even know where this place is, do you?" I say to him. "You said it was right down the street from Hugo's neighborhood, but we've been walking in circles for at least twenty minutes, and now we're in the Ship District, and I have no interest in spending time in the Ship District."

My pager buzzes.

"No, wait, we're so close, I swear," Kenji says, looking around. "It's supposed to be here."

We're stopped on the sidewalk in a congested part of the city lit by twinkle lights, touches of neon, and sans serif signs. The streets are thicker with bodies here, kids in their late teens and early twenties idling in outfits that will almost certainly embarrass them in five years' time. The businesses here were built from repurposed shipping containers salvaged from the old regulated territories—when The Reestablishment forced the entire population out of their homes and into manageable seas of metal prisons, corralling them like cattle. The dark history of these rugged containers has been rewritten by a generation too young to remember the blood that birthed them.

It was Winston's idea.

He and Alia designed the spread and built out the vision under Ella's direction. There are Ship Districts in several cities across the continent; they're part of the global initiative to redevelop old regulated turf. The raw, rectangular containers make for interesting visual architecture, but they also support small businesses and generate decent revenue for the city. I don't disapprove, generally.

I just don't want to be here.

I have no interest in trying new foods or waiting in lines or standing in humid, sweat-stained rooms with a sea of loud, unwashed strangers. Not only do I not enjoy being a public figure in public, but my work consumes far more than half my life. The precious few hours a day I have to myself I like to spend with my wife. I don't go out at night unless I'm with my wife.

If Ella isn't with me, I'm in the wrong place.

My pager buzzes.

I give myself another ten seconds.

"Shit," says Kenji suddenly. "Okay, wait, I think this might be the wrong street."

There's a burst of laughter from a group nearby; a cloud of sweet-scented smoke drifts into my face.

"All right, enough," I say. "I'm tired. I want to go home."

"No way—we're so close—"

"You don't know that," I say to him. "You don't even know where we are. How did you even hear about this place?"

"Haider told me about it."

"*Haider?*" I echo. "Haider, who lives on the other side of the world? That Haider?"

My pager buzzes again.

And again.

"How would Haider know more about finding a dumpling restaurant than we would?" I ask him. "And since when do you keep in touch with Haider?"

Kenji makes a face. "I never stopped being in touch with Haider. Haider is still trying to teach me Arabic. I talk to Haider all the time. Unlike you, I actually answer his messages. You didn't even say *happy birthday* to him last month, by the way. And his feelings are still hurt."

I sigh loudly.

"Anyway, Haider heard about this new spot because apparently it's right next to that huge mural of your face."

I straighten, alarmed. "Which huge mural of my face?"

"Or, no, wait, not your face. I think it's the one where you're, like, flying? Or maybe the one where you're, like, naked on a horse."

Cold mortification moves through my body. "That one is across town."

"Isn't there one where you've got flowers coming out of your mouth?"

"They're knives."

"No," he says. "Not that one. There's another one where you and J both have, like, flowers coming out of your mouths, and it's like you're kissing, but it's just, like, the flowers are kissing? You know what I mean?"

"No." My jaw tenses.

"James told me there's an entire city block that's done up in, like, a comic strip, where you're half man, half robot, and you save the neighborhood from a horde of bloodthirsty vampires. But I haven't seen that one yet."

I shoot a hard look at Kenji. "Thank you for reminding me why I never go outside."

A group of raucous kids nearly barrels into us on the sidewalk, all emanating sweat and insecurity, and I try to brace myself. Try to hold my breath.

The one good thing about spending time in the Ship District is that most of these teenagers are too young to know who I am.

Or if they do, they don't seem to care.

Many were toddlers or young children during the fall of The Reestablishment. What they know of our modern moment is mostly story and flashes of memory. If anything, this generation is more fascinated with James than any of the rest of us.

He's their true peer; an actual contemporary.

He was born and raised in Sector 45—which once comprised much of this region—and he grew up on these streets alongside many of these kids. His life story, as a result, is of enormous interest to them. For years there's been global gossip dedicated specifically to musings on his personal life, which made adolescence particularly uncomfortable for him.

It's part of the reason he and I both avoid places like this.

I did my best to shield him from public scrutiny as he was growing up, but it continues to be an unrelenting task. I have no doubt that raising a child of my own under this glaring spotlight will prove its own nightmare—

I take a tight breath at the thought, cutting it off at the root.

I turn my eyes toward a glowing streetlamp, its warm light attracting an eclipse of moths. The flutter of their wings mirrors the sudden palpitations of my heart. I seldom allow myself to think about fatherhood as anything other than an abstract concept. Ella is far more optimistic about the outcome of her pregnancy than I am.

"Hey," says Kenji, looking away from shop signs to study my face. "Everything okay?"

"Yes," I say automatically.

"*Oh, shit,*" Kenji says without warning. He elbows me,

jolting me, and I have to remind myself not to kill him. He's suddenly wheezing with laughter.

"What?" I demand. "What is it?"

Kenji points at something in the near distance.

I follow his direction to a coffee shop window illuminated under the glare of an overhead neon sign. Ornate scrollwork decorates the outer edges of the glass, all rendered in chalk marker; neat, handwritten text occupies the negative space in the center. It reads—

> JAMES, COME BACK AND REJECT ME
> SO I CAN FINALLY MOVE ON

Under that, in smaller type:

> It's been 58 days since James Alexander Anderson drank coffee here.

I nearly roll my eyes. Kenji is still laughing.

"What do you think?" says Kenji. "Should I go in there? You think I should tell them he's in love with a serial killer?"

I'm officially out of patience. "I'm going home," I say, and start walking.

My pager buzzes again.

"Wait," says Kenji, catching up to me. "Wait, look—the problem is, I already told J we'd be getting her dumplings. She's expecting dumplings. So we need to find the dumplings—"

"What?" I stiffen. "When did you promise her dumplings?"

"This morning."

"But you asked me about this half an hour ago."

"I know."

"*Kenji.*"

"What?" He rolls his eyes at me before returning his focus to the street, still trying to read shop signs as we make our way down the sidewalk. "I knew you'd say yes. You always say yes when Juliette is involved. Hell, if I told you J said we needed to go to the moon to pick up some rocks you'd probably figure out how to build a spaceship."

"A rocket."

"What?"

"A rocket," I say to him. "Not a spaceship. Spaceships aren't real. Spaceships are for aliens."

"Okay, you're literally proving my point."

I duck to avoid a low-hanging branch. "No, I'm taking issue with your analogy. You're acting as if it's an impossible thought. But we possess the technology and potential capability to launch a space program. We've just focused our energies on other things—"

"Bro. It was a simple question. A hypothetical question."

"You never asked me a question."

"Fine." He crosses his arms, coming to a halt.

We turn to face each other.

"Here's the question," he says. "If J asked you to go to the moon for her, would you go to the moon?"

"Yes."

Kenji barks out a laugh, his astonishment loud. "You

make me sick, you know that? I'm *disgusted*."

He's not disgusted.

In fact, he's feeling mournful. I can easily imagine the direction of his thoughts. The source of all his anxiety.

She's currently babysitting an assassin.

My pager buzzes.

Then buzzes again.

"You're not going to check those messages?" says Kenji. "All that buzzing is starting to drive me crazy."

I finally relent with a sigh.

I've given myself a nearly twenty-minute reprieve; waiting any longer to check on the status of things might prove dangerous.

I unearth the pager from my interior pocket and, as expected, I have to scroll through an endless stream of messages from Adam before I can get to anything else.

My eyes catch on a few as I blow past them—

What is the vial????????? vial of what???. Why don't I know about the vial?

Your brother ois an idiot

NAZEERA WAS GOIGNG TO LET HER KILL ME

WHER THE HELL ARE UOU

—and I ignore the rest. A dozen others are administrative. Two messages are from Nazeera.

One is from my wife.

I like the name Lily for a girl. :) But if it's a boy we should name him Aaron. Then I'll have two of you. :) :)

A sharp pain pierces me through the chest. For a second, I can't breathe.

"You good?" says Kenji, studying me. I feel his concern rising. He rests a hand on my back, and I manage not to flinch.

"Yes," I say, looking up. I glance again at the messages, distracted. My heart is pounding.

Two still unread from Nazeera:

Looks like Rosabelle is ready to start talking
You should get over here now

I send off a response: **Coming**

She answers immediately: **Do you want waffles**

I delete all the messages except for Ella's. Hers I'm still staring at, my heart beating faster, when I feel Kenji's anxiety rise up around me again.

"Bro, what's going on? Why do you look so weird right now?"

"It's nothing," I say, pulling myself together. "Nazeera says Rosabelle has started talking. She says we should get over there now."

"Nazeera said that?" Kenji raises his brows. "She said it just like that?"

I put the pager away. "Yes."

He shoots me a loaded look. "Did she say *you and Kenji should get over here*? Or did she say *you should get over here*?"

"She said we should both head over there."

His jaw drops open. "You dirty, filthy liar."

"I'm not lying."

"Let me see your pager."

"No."

"Hand it over."

"No."

"I will reach right into your pocket, bro; I am not afraid of you—"

My pager buzzes again, and I reach for it automatically. Defensively. Kenji crowds me, trying to read over my shoulder, and I start walking to get away from him.

When I scan the message, I come to a violent stop.

"Who is it?" Kenji says, catching up to me. "Is that her? Tell her if she wants me to come over she should page me herself. No, you know what—tell her I'm not coming—"

I look up at Kenji, not seeing him.

My mind is already working too fast.

"Whoa, what just happened?" Kenji says, his face falling. "I was just joking. I just wanted to see what she'd say."

"We have to go," I say.

"What? Now?"

"Yes."

"No dumplings?"

"No dumplings." I meet his eyes. "We'll have to stop by the armory on our way."

Kenji changes—hardens—in an instant. "Where are we headed?"

"Evidence of enemy transport has been identified at the docks."

ROSABELLE

30

"To be clear, when I said you should say something to the group, I meant, like, you could say *hello*," James says, cutting into the stack of waffles before him. "What you said was good, too—I mean, no, actually, it was horrible—but, you know, helpful— Hey, is this okay?" He looks up at me, the knife and fork paused in his hands. "Or should I make the pieces smaller?"

I stare at the plate.

My plate.

Syrup drips steadily down the jutting edges of the neatly severed waffle stack, powdered sugar dusting the rim of the dish, melting in the heat of so much crispy batter. There's a little bowl of mixed berries on the side, and I stare at them a moment.

I can't believe they're real.

I can't believe this isn't some kind of trap, that I could theoretically reach out and put one in my mouth without being forced to kill someone first.

My head is pounding.

I'm dangerously depleted. My heart is a mess. James insisted on sitting right next to me and I've come unraveled ever since. I kept my coat on if only to serve as a buffer between our bodies, but occasionally his thigh brushes against mine and each time this happens I think I might climb out of my own skin. The world around me is all knives and sharp focus; my body bristles with aching awareness; and all my carefully managed pain has been torn from its trappings, demanding attention. I don't know how to explain to James that in order to help me he has to get away from me.

I've lost all control.

My right arm was trembling so badly by the time our food arrived that I couldn't hold my knife. I kept thinking of Clara, my mind at war with my heart, guilt spearing me even as I tried to rationalize my situation. I know I need to be strong enough to get back to the island, to manage myself and my emotions. I need to be strong enough to save Clara.

To kill Klaus.

I told myself over and over that eating all this food while Clara starves will help me help her—but my arm shook so hard the silverware kept clattering against the plate as I tried to cut a piece of waffle. The more this upset me, the worse it got. The knife dropped out of my hand so many times I wanted to scream. I kept hearing her voice—

Rosa. Are you dead?

I couldn't calm myself down.

I don't know, I'd said to her. *Are you?*

I'd heard the unspoken answers in her silence, all her pain implicit. It took her so long to respond.

No, she'd said.

I clench my hands in my lap now, twisting the soft material

of the jacket in my fists, but this only chases the shudder higher up my body. I feel sick with sensation, my heart pinwheeling in my chest. I'm too vulnerable. I'm distracted by this exhaustive ache in my body, this low-grade fever that spikes every time James so much as looks in my direction.

The diner is so loud. These people are so loud. This world is so loud—

The honeyed scents and strangle of sounds are dizzying. So many people talking, and talking over one another. The ring of a bell. The slam of a door. Clara would love it here. Bursts of laughter. Muted shouts. A child begins to cry and James flinches at the sound, his body seizing. Clara would love the painted mural on the wall. A chair falls over. The child stops crying. A blur of motion. Another burst of laughter. James shifts in his seat, tensing. Releasing. The ring of a bell. The slam of a door. James glances at me.

My breath catches.

My heart beats harder.

"Rosabelle?" he says.

I look up at him. He's so close. His face is so close I could keep counting the scatter of freckles across the bridge of his nose.

I left off at seven.

I'm trying to remember his question.

"Thank you," I say faintly. "That's fine."

He searches me a second longer. "Okay," he says. "I'll make the pieces smaller."

The lights seem to flare around me, sounds surging

into indistinct noise. The ring of a bell. The slam of a door. Clara would love these plastic menus, their colorful colors. Booming laughter. A child screams and James hardens in his seat. He takes a breath, stretches his neck. I watch as a cryptic feeling moves across his face, his eyes closing. The scrape of chairs. Metal pans crashing. Plates hitting tables. James exhales; slowly reanimating, his leg grazing mine as he adjusts. I overheat. Ice water is poured into glasses. Clara would love the black and white checkerboard tiles underfoot. The child screams again and James sits back. He takes a deep breath, his eyes unfocusing. Clara would love the neon sign in the window. I haven't been inside of a restaurant in over a decade. My memories of experiences prior to that are rare and scattered, snatches of color and texture. The ring of a bell. The slam of a door. James sighs, his hands stilling. The sizzle of oil. The ring of a bell. The ring of a bell. The ring of a bell. The slam of a door. The ring of a bell. The slam of a door.

I reach, in my mind, for a weapon.

"Hey," says James. "You okay?"

I turn to face him and I'm delivered a shock to the chest. Being with him is like being brought violently back to life, over and over. I anchor myself here, in his eyes, my heart beating harder and harder until something inside of me finally loosens, my lungs expanding behind my ribs. The relief I feel around him is intoxicating. I'm soon soft in the head, loose in my bones, distracted by the fringe of his dark eyelashes as he studies me.

I need to get away from him. I need—

I need help.

I want to climb into his lap. I want to push up his shirt, drag my hands down his bare chest, press my face to his heated body. I want to breathe him in. I want to lick the salt off his skin.

I want to scream.

I've never had thoughts like this in my entire life. I don't know how I'm even conjuring these fantasies.

"Rosabelle."

I'm staring at the column of his neck. The slope of his shoulders. His arms—

I drag my gaze upward.

James is staring at me again, but his eyes are darker. I watch his chest lift, his voice tight when he says, "Why are you looking at me like that? What are you thinking right now?"

"*Nothing.*" I turn away in a panic, my face hot, and I look up to find everyone staring at me.

"This is weird," Winston says, shoveling waffle in his mouth. He gestures between me and James with his fork, still chewing. "This is so weird."

"It's not weird," says Nazeera.

"It's super weird," says Adam, who sits back in his chair and sighs.

"She was having trouble with her silverware," says Nazeera. "That's not weird. He's being helpful."

Adam scowls. "I'm not talking about that."

"I am," says Winston, shoveling more waffle in his mouth. Then, to James: "Didn't she just shoot you? And now you're sitting there cutting her dinner into small pieces?"

James doesn't lift his head when he flips him off.

"Look, I get that she's hungry," says Adam, "but are we really supposed to just sit here and eat our food and not discuss the situation?"

"She's not hungry," James says. "She's *starving*."

"I'm not starving," I lie.

James ignores this, turning to his brother. "If you're hoping to get information out of her, we need to keep her alive. She needs sustenance or she'll be in no state to help anyone. She hasn't eaten in days."

"Days?" Adam stiffens. He looks at me. "Why would you go that long without eating?"

Winston's fork clatters to his plate and I look up to find him gaping at me, a dot of syrup glistening on his cheek. "Oh my God," he says to James. "*Oh my God*, this is why you tried to make soup. The swamp water in the kitchen was for her, wasn't it?"

I turn to James, my hands unclenching from the jacket.

James glares at Winston. "Shut up."

Winston cackles. "You were trying to cook for her!"

The memory of James's voice rises up inside my head—

You need sleep. You need soup.

Do you like soup?

I feel like I've been punctured.

"Fuck you, man. You have no loyalty."

"Okay, where the hell is Warner?" says Adam loudly, looking around.

I add a note to Adam's file: conflict makes him uncomfortable.

"He said he was coming," says Nazeera, tossing a loose end of her shawl behind her shoulder. She frowns, stabbing a piece of potato before dipping it in ketchup. "He should've been here by now."

Winston opens his mouth to say something, but Nazeera cuts him off with a stern look.

"Also, Winston is sorry." She turns to face him as she says this. "Aren't you, Winston?"

"Not really."

"Fine," she says. "You want a psychological evaluation? You're an emotionally stunted gargoyle who uses snark and sarcasm to mask deep, oppressive sadness."

Winston scowls, about to protest—

"Yeah, okay, that's true," he says, spearing another piece of waffle. "Though I take issue with the word *gargoyle*."

Still, James doesn't thaw.

In fact, he's only gotten tenser, cutting the waffles as if he's performing surgery.

"You made me soup?" I ask him quietly.

I watch him swallow before he shakes his head. "I tried," he says. "I made swamp water instead."

A tide of feeling swells inside of me, heat pressing against the backs of my eyes. I'm suddenly afraid of what might happen if we're ever alone—what else I might allow myself to feel for him.

How much I might want from him.

James finally looks at me and his gaze is so intense I can practically feel the pulse between us. He exhales unevenly, the tension in him dissipating only a little. Then he pushes my plate in front of me, ceramic scraping softly against the Formica. The pieces are bite-sized now.

I look from him to the plate.

Then back to him.

"Start small," he says, placing a glass of water in front of me. "Open up your appetite slowly."

"Thank you," I whisper.

I reach for my fork and nearly drop it, steeling myself as I try to control the tremors. I have to give up on my right hand and use my left, which is shaking only a little, and though the motions are awkward, I finally manage to spear a piece of waffle.

The effort leaves me feeling out of breath.

"Stop staring at her," James barks at the others. "Let her eat her food in peace."

They look away like chastened children, turning their eyes to their plates, or else around the restaurant. James stares pointedly into the distance, his hand clenched around his water cup.

Slowly, I bring the bite to my mouth.

Sugar and heat dissolve against my tongue. Pressure builds behind my eyes.

My chest nearly caves in.

"Hey, what are you guys doing here?" comes a friendly, booming voice.

ROSABELLE

31

There's a sudden clamor as a trio of bodies separates from the dense crowd and head in our direction.

Chairs scrape against the floor as everyone but me pushes out of their seats to greet the new arrivals. I sense no imminent threat, nor anyone I recognize, so I look away as they exchange *heys* and hugs and *how've you beens*.

In fact, the moment James rises from his chair and retreats a few feet, I fall back inside myself.

Almost at once, my heart ceases its panic.

My pulse begins to slow.

In his absence the diner dims, sounds muting into something manageable. I sink more freely into the soft contours of my own mind, then force another two bites into my mouth, chewing and swallowing. The effort gets a little easier each time, but it's a struggle not to take breaks between bites.

A cold calm soon settles over me.

It's harder to find my center when James is coming and going around me, but now, in this steady reprieve, it's almost a gift to pull on this old skin, hermetically sealing my head inside my head. In order to survive, I can never allow myself to truly live—and it would be a lethal mistake to forget that. This is not the time for erratic emotion. Now is the time to sort out my plans.

I will go back to the Ark tonight.

First, I will convince these people to let me go home.

I didn't know what would happen to me after failing to take off at the airfield. I assumed I was out of chances; I assumed they'd do the obvious thing and imprison me for the rest of my life, torturing me to the point of death and holding me there, in purgatory, never healing me more than necessary in order to keep me too weak to escape. I thought they'd hack me slowly to pieces in the pursuit of information and retaliation.

It's what The Reestablishment would've done.

Instead, I'm sitting here in a warm, borrowed jacket, eating waffles in relative peace.

I once thought these people were stupid.

I'm beginning to realize I've been neatly tricked. My shields were slowly stolen when I wasn't looking. My mind softened with my own permission. I gave up information without coercion.

I never anticipated James.

A plan is coming together in my mind, the shape of it influenced by the rebels' subtle maneuvers. I once feared the idea of allying with them, of shackling myself to a new master; but I've been so accustomed to the cruel practices of The Reestablishment that it never occurred to me a compromise could be peaceful. It never occurred to me I might ask for something without being forced to pay for it in blood. I'm seeing now that I might not need to pledge my allegiance to anyone in order to achieve my aims.

Perhaps I might try the path of least resistance.

I chew thoughtfully.

If the rebels are willing to listen, there's no reason to withhold information about Klaus or the Ark, especially not if I intend to destroy it all. I'll leverage intelligence in exchange for a jet and their promise to stay out of my way. I'll convince them to give me back the vial.

And then I'll go home to die.

The tremble in my arm has begun, slowly, to abate, though I'm beginning to worry I'm eating too quickly; I've already made my way through half the stack of waffles. The trouble is, I don't have much time to refuel, but I have to be careful not to make myself sick.

I drink most of my water.

No one can know that my plan necessitates sacrificing my life in the process; I don't want opinions or interference. So I'll need some other way to convey to the rebels that it's in their best interests for me to go back—and go back alone.

This is the trickiest part.

I'm worried they might insist on participating; and that would be a true disaster. The vial of earth is nothing on its own; it activates into a deadly weapon only when fully ingested by a human body. Klaus had intended for me to launch an attack against the civilians of The New Republic, but my plan is to drink it before launching myself into his cradle. Once submerged in the synthetic waters of his mind,

I'll have detonated the cataclysmic explosion necessary to kill Klaus—to dismantle the Ark.

But before I can do any of that, I'll need to slip back into my old life on the island, which will require evading capital punishment.

I was supposed to die on the mainland. I was supposed to submit to Klaus's directive. If I manage to return home I'll be sentenced to death upon arrival for failing my mission. I've already decided that my only shot at a stay of execution will require appealing to Sebastian's distorted sense of devotion.

He has far greater power.

I force another bite of waffle into my mouth, chewing slowly.

If I finally, enthusiastically consent to marrying Sebastian, he might petition to delay my sentencing. He was the one who managed to convince the council to uphold the terms of our betrothal despite the sanctions against me. He might be able to convince them to let me live. I don't need forever. Just long enough to realize my plan.

The rebels, of course, will never understand this.

James won't understand this.

No one from the mainland will be able to grasp the nuanced strategy and sacrifice necessary to dismantle the establishment from within. No one from the mainland will be able to anticipate the complexities of Ark surveillance. There is no question that I must return by myself. These loud, unrestrained people are woefully ill-equipped to brave the many hells of the Ark.

They'll sabotage everything.

I take another bite of waffle. There's a plate of eggs and sausages in front of me, too. I realize I need protein, but the sight of it makes me a little nauseous. I'll have to slowly work my way up to eggs.

I drain the rest of my water glass.

I, too, need to prepare to reenter the terrifying surveillance state. I need to remember who I am and where I'm from. I've been on the mainland for too long; I've grown almost accustomed to the idea of privacy. I don't search for cameras as often as I should. I don't police my thoughts enough anymore. I'm beginning to think and feel things without fear of retribution. I need to reestablish my shields.

The only way to do that is to convince James to stay away from me.

I reach for a blueberry, rolling its small, firm shape between my fingers. When I push it between my lips I feel like I've done something illegal.

The tart, sweet taste explodes in my mouth.

"—mean Rosabelle?"

I look up, the sound of James's voice shattering the bell jar around my head. The din of the diner comes rushing back, footfalls thudding and chairs pushing and cups slamming. The jangle of forks and knives, the clatter of plates stacking, bursts of laughter—

"Rosabelle?" someone says. "Wait, isn't that the—"

A gasp of breath.

"Oh, shit. That *is* her."

My fork is paused halfway to my mouth.

I turn slowly to meet the gaze of the man staring at me, registering his astonishment before taking in the rest of him.

He's immediately striking.

He has a head of thick inky waves and bronzed olive skin. His dark eyes are ringed by sooty lashes. His mouth is bracketed on one side by a pair of beauty marks. There's something almost feline about his looks, except that his eyes are pure steel. Despite his civilian attire, it's clear to me at once that he's a soldier. The build of him, the way he stands, the piercing way he looks at me—

I notice, a beat late, the pendant at his neck.

His top two buttons are undone, revealing a small swath of his throat and chest. There's a simple chain glinting against his skin that looks like it was half-tucked or poorly hidden, its puzzle-piece pendant winking in the glare of the overhead lights.

"Hi," he says bluntly, blinking at me.

I set down my fork. I don't know who he is. I only remember that I nearly killed him.

Tried really hard not to kill him.

He turns to the group. Then, politely, his stiff smile never reaching his eyes, he says, "So you guys just hang out with her now?"

"It's a need-to-know kind of situation," says Nazeera.

He arches a dark brow. "Right."

James sighs. "Rosabelle," he says, "this is Kian. Kian, this is Rosabelle. You've already met."

"Sure," Kian says dryly. "We've met."

James nods at the other two and says to me, "And you might remember Allie and Liam."

I follow his gaze to the towering brunette and the buzzed redhead standing nearby. I remember seeing Allie at the airfield, though I didn't know her name then. She stands slightly apart from the guys, assessing me with a cold remove.

She doesn't say a word.

"I remember you," Liam says, the loathing in his voice a perfect match for the darkness in Allie's eyes.

I turn toward him, taking him in.

Liam's hair is so vivid it's actually orange; his milky skin dotted all over with freckles. Standing so close together, he and Kian present as complete visual opposites; it's a little jarring to take them in side by side. I had no idea Liam was a redhead; the airplane hangar had been so dark I hadn't seen him properly. But Liam is unaltered in other essential ways: he wasn't happy to see me then, and he's not happy to see me now. I still remember the way he'd pointed an accusing finger in my direction—

She killed Kian.

I sit back in my seat.

"So she doesn't talk?" says Kian.

"She talks," says Adam.

"Hey, remember when she didn't talk?" Winston says, his face brightening. "Those were good times, right? We didn't know how good we had it."

Nazeera coughs through a laugh.

"She's not talking now, though," says Allie. "What's wrong with her?"

"Nothing's wrong with her," says James. "She just doesn't want to talk to you. Look, we should probably—"

"What are you, like, her interpreter?" asks Liam.

"Yeah." James's eyes flash. "And she told me to tell you you've pissed your pants."

Winston barks out a laugh.

Liam looks down in alarm, his face going blotchy with color, only to realize the joke.

I smile at that, and James doesn't miss it.

He locks eyes with me and I feel the impact in my chest, knocking me deeper into my body. My smile fades as I watch his throat move. My skin seems to come alive. James is looking at me like he wants to come and get me.

It makes me feel winded.

"Whatever," Liam mutters under his breath.

With a start, I realize then that Kian is staring at me. His steady gaze is guarded as he studies my face, then my coat, then my face again. "She looks like a marshmallow," he says.

A child screams and James flinches, a faint tremor seeming to move through him as he turns away, directing his eyes to a wall. I track the room for the source: the mother of the distressed child picks a fallen toy off the floor, resolving the issue, and the crying ceases as suddenly as it started. James exhales, the breath moving all the way through his body.

I don't understand why no one seems to notice this.

"I guess that's one way to hide her in plain sight," Kian is saying. "Always in costume." He meets my eyes again, a wry smile touching his lips. "What, no tail today?"

Mortification catches me off guard.

Heat floods my face at once.

"Wow," says Kian, brows lifting as he stares at me. "Cute. She single?"

James looks up.

I can see the change in him from where I'm sitting: the tension in his face, the rise and fall of his chest. He looks at me, then at Kian. Then looks at me again.

"Don't worry," says Allie. "He's joking."

"Obviously," says Liam.

I watch Nazeera rest a hand on James's arm, then send him an inscrutable look. This doesn't seem to register. James has turned to concrete.

Kian glances at the door, faking a smile as he turns to face everyone. "Well, this was weird," he says. "And we should probably get going." He nods at me. "It was nice officially meeting you, Rosabelle. Thanks for the scars."

"Sorry," I say to him.

Everyone collectively tenses at the sound of my voice. Kian's eyes widen in surprise.

"For almost killing you," I clarify. "I'm sorry."

Kian's confusion is slowly displaced by a smile, his face warming with easy humor, and he looks like he's about to say something to me when Nazeera beats him to it.

"So you guys are heading out?" she says forcefully.

"Oh," says Kian, hesitating as he looks away from me. "Yeah. I just got a call about some weird activity over by the docks. Malik is on leave for the week, and I'm taking over some of his shifts—"

Without warning shrill rings chorus throughout the diner, the pitch cutting through the din, deadening the clamor. A palpable wave of dread moves slowly through the restaurant as at least a third of the occupants in plainclothes stiffen in tandem, all lifting their pagers at the same time.

So many hidden soldiers in one place.

Only then does it occur to me that I have no idea where I am within the city. James, Nazeera, Kian, Liam, Allie—all but Adam and Winston, I notice—receive the missive.

"What is it?" says Adam. "What's going on?"

There's a breath of stillness.

And then, all at once, a veritable stampede for the door.

ROSABELLE

32

"What's going on?" Adam says again, looking around in a panic. "What the hell is happening?"

The diner has erupted into chaos.

Some people pause to bid urgent farewells to their dinner partners before bolting for the exit; others, like Kian and Allie and Liam, rush out without so much as a backward glance. Voices swell and retreat, plates crashing, chairs screeching, people shouting, footfalls thundering. The ring of a bell. The slam of a door. The ring of a bell. The slam of a door.

I get to my feet as if in slow motion, a feeling of foreboding flooding my veins.

My heart is beating fast.

James, on the other hand, doesn't hurry. In the midst of so much mayhem, he seems to slow down and solidify, as if the commotion only hones him into a sharper blade. I can almost see the adrenaline coursing through him, control and focus hardening the lines of him, darkening his eyes. He shoots me a brief, heated look before clapping an arm on his brother's shoulder.

"Go home," he says to Adam, the noise level around us rising to a fever pitch. Abandoned diners are abandoning their dinners, leaving in droves. "Everything's going to be fine. Tell Alia not to worry. You'll be safe on campus."

"But—"

"Nazeera," says James. "Get Rosabelle back to the house immediately."

Alarm lances through me.

The door continues to slam open and shut, chair legs shrieking across the floors.

"No way," says Nazeera. "I'm not sitting this out."

"This is your job," he counters. "You signed up for it. Around-the-clock security detail, remember? It's not like we can take her with us—"

"Why not?" I ask cautiously.

Winston rolls his eyes at me. "Be serious."

"Take her with you where?" Adam asks. *"What the hell is going on?"*

"Yeah, and you tried to fight me for it," Nazeera is saying. "Here's your big chance."

"You're unbelievable," says James. "You can't just change the rules whenever you feel like it—"

Nazeera tries to argue and James shakes his head, cutting her off.

"Look, we'll finish fighting about this in a minute," he says. "Until then, can you run back to my place and grab a few things for me?"

"Me?" she says. "Why can't you do it?"

"Because I won't have a chance to change and head to the armory," he says angrily, "so unless you're offering to babysit Rosabelle, I need to figure out what to do with her."

Now I'm offended.

"No, thanks," says Nazeera, already heading for the exit. "I'll get the gear."

"Hey, you asked for this responsibility!" he calls after her. "This was *your* idea—"

The ring of a bell. The slam of a door.

The diner is nearly empty now.

"And that's our cue," says Winston, nodding at Adam. "Let's go. I'm heading home, too." He turns to me. "This isn't really my area of expertise, and I've had enough of getting what I asked for. I'm sorry I ever wanted you to talk. If I never see you again, please don't keep in touch."

"If I never see you again," I say to him, "you should know that your archetype is one of the easiest to kill."

Winston stiffens. "Uh. What?"

"*Hey,*" Adam says loudly. He doesn't budge from his chair. "I want to know what's happening—"

"Did you just— Was that your idea of a joke?" Winston says to me. "Did you just attempt a sense of humor?"

"James—" Adam tries again.

James grabs his jacket off the back of his seat, his fist tightening around the denim. He turns to his brother with a stifled sigh, his voice firm but not unkind when he says, "Look, are you sure you want to know what's happening? Because I don't think you do. I don't think you need to drive yourself crazy with a little information and no ready solution. But if you really want to know, I'll tell you."

Adam pushes both hands through his hair and finally

stands up. He turns in a half circle, taking in the emptying room. A few stragglers shovel last bites of food into their mouths before dropping their plates with a clatter. A bearded redhead in an apron stands, stunned, behind the front counter, surveying the aftermath.

"*I* want to know what's happening," I offer.

"I bet you do," says Winston.

"Shut up, Winston," I say softly, keeping my eyes on James. "Your inability to endure silence masks an unresolved trauma that's obvious to everyone but you."

Winston manages a stunned laugh.

James shoots me an indecipherable look, but he doesn't answer my question. In fact, he seems upset.

With *me*.

My dread solidifies into fear.

"I don't think it's obvious to everyone," Winston says nervously. "Do you think it's obvious to everyone?"

"Honestly, I'm already driving myself crazy," Adam is saying to James, glancing in my direction. "She never even finished explaining the first bombshell, and now this."

"You don't need to worry about any of it," James reassures him. "Everything is going to be fine. I'll update you on the situation as soon as the issue is resolved. Go home. Get some rest."

Adam looks up at him. His panic is real.

It surprises me, even in the middle of so much turbulence, to witness this unusual dynamic. I'd already reasoned that Adam was averse to conflict, but I'd not determined that

James would need to manage the emotional needs of his older brother. James is acting as if this is an old pattern; as if it's something he's done many times before.

It makes me wonder about their history.

"C'mon, let's get out of here," Winston says, throwing his arm over Adam's shoulder. He shoots me a furtive glance. "Rosabelle is starting to scare the shit out of me."

With a final sigh and a last look, Adam relents.

Another ring of a bell, a slam of a door, and he and Winston disappear into the night.

The restaurant is now emptied out.

The only people left are me and James and the bearded redhead behind the counter.

I'm still watching James, my apprehension rising. "You're not going to tell me what's happening?"

"You're not going to like what I have to say."

I step back.

My heart rate spikes. "This has something to do with me."

It's not a question.

And he doesn't answer.

I slowly unzip my puffy pink jacket, shedding it like a skin before shoving it under the table. I have an ominous feeling I'll soon require full range of motion.

"They never remember to pay," says the redhead from across the room, managing a smile in our direction. He gestures to the empty diner, the tables laden with half-eaten meals. "All these years and it's always the same. Can't believe I keep feeding you ungrateful kids."

"Put it on my tab, Kip," says James. "I'll settle the bill."

"I'll do you one better," he says, rapping his hands against the counter. "I'll put it on your brother's tab."

"Done."

"Good luck out there," says Kip, flashing a tired salute in our direction. He heads toward the kitchen, pushing through the swinging door as he calls over his shoulder: "But if my windows get shattered again, or my shelves get broken, or I find shrapnel in my walls, I'm making you fix it!"

"C'mon, Kip, you know we always"—the interior door swings shut behind the man—"fix it."

Suddenly, James and I are alone.

A set of overhead lights flicker out, leaving us in partial darkness, and I come alive with an electric sensation I've begun to recognize. Moonlight slants through the large front windows, warm and cold radiance melding as it washes over us, rendering James in half-silhouette, one blue eye illuminated, gleaming. He tosses his jacket onto a chair, shadows emphasizing the sculpted muscles of his arms, the hardened line of his jaw. His hair looks soft and melted. A little messy. His hands flex at his sides, the brawn of his broad chest straining under his T-shirt.

He's so gorgeous it's disorienting.

Adrenaline courses through me as I study him, my body already bright with awareness. He takes a step closer and I feel the shift as palpably as I feel the air leaving my lungs. I'm stripped back to nothing all over again, painfully alive in my skin, inhaled by the sun.

James looks at me. Looks away. Looks back. I can feel myself sinking.

He's *angry*.

He's radiating unchecked power, his eyes charged with feeling. Instinctive fear responses activate all throughout my nervous system.

"What's wrong?" I whisper.

He shakes his head slowly. He laughs, but the dark sound only seems to wind him tighter. "You know, I've been dying for a moment alone with you. Desperate for it. And now we're here, just you and me, and this isn't going anything like I thought it would." He takes a breath; his voice is unsteady. "Nothing about you has gone the way I thought it would."

My heart is hammering. "James. Please, tell me what's happening—"

"We haven't even talked about any of it," he says, looking up. "Isn't that crazy? None of it. Not what happened with Leon, or the things you said to me in the tunnel. We haven't talked about your dad. We haven't talked about Clara. We haven't talked about the fact that you shot me. We haven't talked about how you sacrificed your one chance to escape at the airfield—to get to your sister—just to keep me alive—"

I panic. "That's not— I didn't—"

"*Don't fucking lie to me, Rosabelle.*"

A sound breaks free of my chest, something wild and breathless. My pulse is frantic.

James looks unearthly. Lit by fury and moonlight. "We haven't talked about the fact that you literally *died* for three days," he says, "or even the fact that you have this power at all. We haven't talked about what's going through your head, or how you feel about The Reestablishment, or what the hell you're planning on doing next. We haven't talked about *anything*. God, I have so many questions sometimes I think I'd rip my own heart out for a chance to have a single, honest conversation with you."

A desperate ache is fracturing across my body.

I'm transfixed by him, half out of my mind. I'm watching his throat work with rapt fascination; I can't look away as he drags a hand down his neck, muscles flexing, tendons straining. He looks as if he's coming apart, fighting to remain rooted in his body, to keep the distance between us.

Fighting not to touch me.

"I want answers," he says, lifting his head. "I want to know what happened to you when you woke up in the hospital after being dead for three days. I want to know why you passed out when I hugged you. Fuck, I just want to know what you're thinking half the time."

"James—"

"I want to know what you want, Rosabelle, because I want to know if you think about me," he says roughly, "the way I think about you, because I'm beginning to lose my fucking mind every time you look at me. The amount of work I have to do just to act normal around you—" He makes a gutted sound, briefly turning away. "All you have to do is walk into a room and I wish we were alone. You breathe and I wish we were alone. Now we're alone and all I want to do— All I want—"

He cuts himself off. Visibly struggles.

The more I listen to him speak, the more I feel as if I'm separating from my body. Nothing like this has ever happened to me before. I've never felt this kind of need, this kind of fever, this honeyed heat moving through my blood. I never imagined I could desperately want someone to touch me. All of me.

I never knew I might be willing to beg for it.

"I keep covering for you," he says to the floor. "I keep taking hits for you. I keep trying to vouch for you. But I can't do this if you're not honest with me. I can't protect you if you keep all these secrets. You once told me you trusted me." He meets my gaze then, and his eyes are scorched. "Is that still true?"

I've gone up in flames.

"I shouldn't have said that," I whisper. "It was a mistake to say that—"

"Answer the question," he says angrily, his chest lifting as he breathes. "Do you trust me?"

I can't feel my hands anymore, only my heartbeat, and I can't bear to lie to him. My voice catches on the word when I say, finally—

"*Yes.*"

He exhales, his body releasing tension in a crashing wave. He unclenches his fists only to clench them again, his eyes closing. And then he looks at me with a fire that draws the breath from my body.

"Then I'm going to ask you this once," he says. "Did you steal the vial?"

JAMES

33

"*What?*" she says, stunned.

And I know, right away, that she didn't do it.

Relief leaves me almost unsteady in its wake, and no part of me recovers quickly enough. My heart is pounding so hard it's painful and distracting and I hate it. Five minutes alone with this girl and my body is wrecked. My pulse can't decide whether to speed up or stop altogether.

"James," says Rosabelle, the shock in her voice giving way to panic. "What's going on? Is the vial missing?"

But I can hardly speak.

I'm feverish with unspent energy, my body holding so tight I'm afraid to move. Frustration and need are choking me. It's an effort to keep steady. It's an effort even to look at her right now. "When Nazeera gets back here," I force out, "I need you to go back to the house."

"James—"

"I'm serious, Rosabelle. You need to go into hiding and stay put or you're going to make everything worse—"

"*Tell me what's happening.*"

I straighten at the sound of her voice. Rosabelle has gone sharp as an arrow. She looks suddenly lethal, her anger material—and this does nothing to calm me down.

In fact, it reignites my fury.

"I can't tell you what's happening," I hit back. "You're not entitled to privileged information."

She steels herself, her chin lifting as she matches my temper. "Don't do this," she says. "Don't make this mistake. You don't understand the risks—"

"Oh, really? And whose fault is that? You've never bothered sharing the risks—"

"I tried," she argues. "I tried to tell you back at the house but you insisted on taking me to the diner—"

"I was trying to take care of you!"

"I'm trying to take care of *you!*" she shouts back, a tremor moving through her right arm. "But I can't do that if you don't tell me what's going on."

"What the hell is that supposed to mean?"

"There's no time to discuss it anymore," she says. "Right now I just need to know—"

"Why do you never listen to me? Just once I'd love for you to listen to me without arguing—"

"Stop," Rosabelle says forcefully. "I need to know whether the vial is still in your family's possession."

"That's none of your business."

Her eyes flash with cold anger. "We're out of time," she says darkly. "And I'm losing my patience with you."

Those words seem ominous.

I move without thinking, closing the distance between us in a few strides. She takes a sharp breath, stumbling a few steps as I approach, her back nearly meeting the wall.

We're suddenly separated by inches. Her skin is like glass in the moonlight. Her lips are soft and full, slightly parted.

I feel unstable as I look at her. My head is dangerously overheated. My body never lost its fire. My heart never stopped racing in my chest.

"Rosabelle," I say quietly. "Are you threatening me?"

Her breathing is shallow. "Yes," she exhales.

"Do you really think that's a good idea?"

Her eyes nearly close. I'm practically shaking from the effort not to touch her.

"I don't know," she says.

My head is half steam, my heart battering my ribs. Standing this close to her is making me lose focus. I can't remember what we're talking about. I want to pin her to the wall. I've been dreaming of moments like this. Dying for a chance to get her alone, to sort out this damage in my heart, this heat in my veins, but we've never had a chance, there's never been time—

Rosabelle lifts her hands to my chest and I exhale sharply, surprised, my rigid body turning suddenly to stone. I don't even have a chance to process this before she drags her hands slowly down my torso, her fingers curling into my shirt. A shock of pleasure drives the air from my lungs. I don't know what we're doing anymore.

I can't tell if she's trying to pull me in or push me away.

"*James,*" she whispers, and the word is desperate.

The sound of her voice unhinges something inside of me, injecting a torrent of heat into my blood that kills the last of my common sense. Every reckless, irresponsible thought I've ever had about her suddenly seems like a good idea. Stripping her slowly suddenly seems like a good idea. Falling to my knees right here in the middle of this diner suddenly seems like the best idea I've had in years. I find her waist in the darkness and she gasps as I draw her close, her hands lifting automatically toward my neck, and I hear the tremor in my own breath, my heart chaotic. Her eyes are dilated in the half dark, her hair gleaming like liquid silver against my hands. She looks as far gone as I am. I drag my hands down her back, sealing our bodies together, and I can feel everything through her thin clothes—every soft curve meeting every inch of my hardened body—and the pleasure is so intense it's nearly blinding. Her head falls back on a soft moan.

That sound sinks teeth into me, becomes a part of me.

"Rosabelle," I say, my voice in shreds. "Tell me what you're thinking."

"I can't," she says, her breath catching. "I can't think when you're this close. No one has ever— This is— You don't understand what you do to me—"

"Help me understand." I push up slowly under her shirt, my hands gliding against the satin skin of her back, and she cries out again, and I feel like I'm going insane.

"I've never—I've never—" She gasps. "I don't know how to— *James*—"

I press my face to her throat, my lips grazing her pulse, and I breathe her in like an addict, my head hot and drunk. She whimpers as I skate my nose along the nape of her neck, and then I taste her there, my tongue hot against her skin, and she makes a sound like a stifled sob, the impact branding my bones.

"*James*," she says, sounding almost panicked. "James—"

I'm out of my mind.

I'm already worried I'll never get enough of this. I'm already worried I'll always need more. I want her naked in this moonlight. I want to lay her down under the stars. I want to feel the wind on my back when I make her scream. I can't fucking breathe.

"Answer me," I say, pressing the words against her throat. Her hands are caught between us, inching dangerously down the front of my body, and I can feel myself shaking, muscles taut with impossible tension. "Tell me what you want from me. What do you want right now?"

She lifts her head like she might be dreaming, blinking up at me in the glaze of starlight, her eyes half-lidded with desire. I nearly kiss her right then. I've clenched her shirt in my fist like I'm fighting for my life. I can't form a single coherent thought beyond this annihilating need to taste more of her. All of her. But her expression softens the longer she searches my face, and, slowly, the haze clears from her eyes. "I want to protect you," she says softly. "I want to keep you safe."

The breath that leaves my body is so complete it rocks the foundations of who I am.

This fucking kills me.

"Rosabelle—"

She moves back a step and I follow blindly, listening as her heels hit the baseboard. Then she turns us, trading places so I'm the one backed up against the wall.

I'm breathing hard. Confused. "What— What are you—"

She pushes up the hem of my shirt, exposing my upper body, and the cool night air on my chest leaves me almost disoriented. I feel wasted. Drugged out of my mind. The ghostly moonlight and surreal texture of the dark make this all feel impossible, and when her fingers slide against my bare skin, I think I'm dreaming.

I'm lightheaded, rigid and straining for control.

She keeps her hands on me as she brings her face to my torso, and I feel her warm breath, her silken mouth skimming ridges of muscle. "*Fuck*," I gasp. "Rosabelle—"

My heart is beating out of my body.

Her hands glide up my chest; her nose grazes my ribs, her lips a whisper. I inhale sharply as she rests her soft cheek against my wild, beating heart, and then, just when I think I might lose my fucking mind, she turns her face, pressing a tender kiss just above my rib cage.

I think maybe I could die from this. Just this.

When she draws back I feel like I've been shot. I can't even move right away. I don't know what just happened to me. It takes a full second for my mind to catch up to my body, and when it does I feel volcanic, desperate like I've never been in my life. I catch her in my arms, turning her around—

Nazeera bursts back into the diner, the bell ringing ominously as the door slams open.

JAMES

34

Nazeera comes to a sudden and complete stop at the threshold, wearing weapons like ornaments, and stares at us in shock.

Her visible horror is somehow not enough to clear the heat from my head. I'm so far gone it doesn't even occur to me to be embarrassed.

I feel like I've been recently murdered.

I can't remember how to speak.

"I was gone for like twenty minutes," Nazeera says, stunned. "What the hell is wrong with you?"

In response, Rosabelle puts half the diner between us. She retreats so far into the shadows I can hardly see her face. I look in her direction anyway, spasms of feeling still branching through my veins, stealing my breath. I can still taste her on my tongue. I can still feel her mouth on my skin. I tug blindly at the hem of my shirt, checking to make sure I'm decent. I'm grateful it's dark in here. There's nothing I can do about these pants.

She kissed my *chest*.

I feel drunk. I want to lie down on the ground.

Nazeera shakes her head at me in disappointment, then wordlessly tosses a rifle in my direction.

I catch it on instinct.

She tosses me a magazine. I catch that, too.

"Well," she says, "at least part of your brain still appears to be working."

"Yeah," I say, taking a breath. I feel like maybe someone should punch me in the face.

"So?" says Nazeera, glancing between us. "Did you ask her?"

"What?" I take another breath. "Ask her what?"

"James!"

"What?"

"The vial," she cries. "Did you even ask her if—"

"Oh," I say. *Shit*. The vial. Shit.

"You're unbelievable!" Nazeera cries.

"I mean, no," I say quickly. *Shit*. "No, she didn't take it."

More than one person needs to punch me in the face. I need people to line up. Take turns.

Fuck.

"You sure?" Nazeera narrows her eyes at me. She's sorting through some of the gear, and she tucks a couple of things in her pocket before glancing at Rosabelle. "Because the accusations are wild right now."

"Yes, I'm sure." My brain is becoming slowly operational, my instincts reviving—and with it, my urgency. "And I need you to get her back to the house so I can get out of here."

Nazeera takes her time checking the magazine on a rifle. "Look," she says casually, "I really don't understand why I'm the one who has to stay behind. I'm a much better asset than you are at the moment."

My temper is back. "Are you joking?"

"Nope, dead serious," she says, glancing meaningfully between me and Rosabelle. "You should see yourself right now. Your head isn't even fully attached to your body. You should've seen yourself when I walked in here. You weren't living on this planet. And while I wouldn't normally advocate for leaving the two of you alone together, you're an idiot right now. You'd be nothing but a problem in the field. Given the risks, I think you should stay behind. Besides, you've been nothing but a liability lately—"

"I won't be a liability if I know she's back at the house!"

"I'm not going back to the house."

Nazeera and I both turn at the sound of Rosabelle's voice. It's the first time she's spoken since she single-handedly ruined my life.

She kissed my *chest*.

She steps into a shaft of light, and she looks clear-eyed and angry. Gorgeous. Unreal. I want to be alone with her again. Now. Right now. I want to cross the room and get her, then get the hell out of here. I want—

"I want to know what's going on," Rosabelle says. "I need to know what's happening."

Mentally, I punch myself in the face.

"Look, I'd love to tell you what's going on," Nazeera says to her, "but you haven't earned that right yet. You're going back to the house one way or another, and you're going to stay there."

"You're going to have to make me," Rosabelle says softly.

"Fine," says Nazeera. "Do you want to choose where I shoot you? Or should it be a surprise?"

I bristle, alarms going off in my head as I stare between them.

"Look, Rosabelle," I say, trying to sound normal, "we can't let you loose in the middle of a manhunt across the city when you're already the number one suspect. You'd be putting a target on your back—"

"A manhunt?" she says, recoiling.

"Nice job, genius," says Nazeera.

"Shit." *Fuck.* My brain is shit.

"What did I say?" Nazeera says. "Liability."

"I'm still waiting for someone to answer my question," says Rosabelle. "Is the vial missing or not?"

I realize then that Rosabelle has moved. She's now standing perilously close to the exit.

"What are you doing?" I ask Rosabelle, at the same time Nazeera asks me, "Are you sure we can trust that she didn't take the vial?"

"If I were in possession of the vial," Rosabelle says sharply, "I wouldn't be here right now."

"Wait, what?" This clears the lingering heat from my head. "Why not?"

"I tried to explain this to you back at the house," she says. "I can't go back to the Ark without it."

"She did say that," says Nazeera. "I remember her saying that."

"Okay, but why not?" I ask. "What are you planning on doing with it?"

"Whoa, wait a second," says Nazeera. "If she really didn't take the vial, then who are we hunting across the city? Everyone assumes she's the suspect."

Rosabelle rocks back on her heels. She looks around blindly, panicking, as if she's collapsing inward. "So it's true," she says. "The vial is gone. Someone stole it."

"Yeah, okay," Nazeera says to me. "I see why you think she didn't take it."

"Do you have any leads?" Rosabelle asks, regrouping. "Do you know when the vial was first reported missing?"

"That information is above your pay grade," I say to her. "You're not going out there, Rosabelle. If you go out there, they'll kill you. No one trusts you. You're living on borrowed time. Everyone already thinks you stole it—"

"None of that matters to me," she says. "If I don't get that vial, I may as well be dead—"

"Why?" I demand. "What's in it? Why is it so important?"

"Where are we right now?" Rosabelle asks, looking around. "Why were there so many soldiers in this restaurant?"

"Rosabelle, stop," I say angrily. "This is not your mission. You are not authorized to participate. Stand down."

"I don't answer to your people," she says darkly. "And if you want to stop me, you're going to have to fight me."

"All right. Fine." Nazeera sounds irritated but resigned as she turns to me. "You're right. Liability or not, I did sign up for this, and you're clearly too far gone in the head to manage her. I'll take her back to the house and keep her there."

"*I'm not going back to the house.*"

"Rosabelle—"

I hear Nazeera's shocked cry before I even register the clatter; Rosabelle flung a plate like a Frisbee, striking Nazeera in the sternum so hard she gasps, staggering backward before hitting the window.

The heavy plate hits the ground and shatters.

I watch, horrified, as Nazeera slides, stunned, halfway down the wall.

I explode. "Rosabelle, *what the hell*—"

Rosabelle flings two more plates, one hitting Nazeera in the stomach, interrupting her air supply, and the other in the knee, collapsing her. Half-eaten waffles and breakfast potatoes fly across the room like shrapnel, hitting walls and chairs with soggy thuds. She throws a fourth plate, but Nazeera doubles over in pain, struggling for breath, and manages to shift just out of the way. The plate crashes into the window behind her, sending a rain of shattered glass into the room. Nazeera spits out a shard, her lip bleeding. A fried egg splats against the door, yolk smearing as gravity drags it downward.

Nazeera groans.

Rosabelle is already across the room, tugging weaponry out of Nazeera's limp arms. She pulls a strap over her head, then aims a gun at Nazeera, who's fighting to recover, grasping at her chest with one hand, searching herself for a weapon with the other.

I'm literally speechless.

I stare at Rosabelle in disbelief.

"Oh my God," Nazeera wheezes, her head rocking back against the wall, glass clinking as it releases from her clothing, hitting the ground. She's still trying to breathe, her face seizing with pain. "You're such an asshole."

"What's your big plan, Rosabelle?" I say angrily, finding my voice. "What are you going to do now? You don't know where you are and you don't know how to get out of here. It's not as easy as you think it is to just leave this place—"

"Your world is held together with tape," she says, meeting my eyes. "Taking it apart requires little effort."

This shocks me into a laugh.

Nazeera manages to grab clumsily at the hilt of another gun hidden in her jacket, and Rosabelle kicks it, hard, out of her hands.

"I avoided using anything sharp," she says, looking Nazeera over. "Your injuries should be manageable."

Even now, grimacing in pain, Nazeera makes a wry, humorless sound. "So this was you being nice?"

"You've been kind to me," Rosabelle says to her, even as she steps past her slumped body. "I'm genuinely sorry about this."

Nazeera winces. "I hate that I kind of respect you right now."

Rosabelle pushes open the door. It rings softly.

"*Stop.*" I rack my gun.

She turns at the sound of my voice. For a moment she

just looks at me, her pale eyes glinting in the spectral glow. Her body is braced in the doorframe, her silhouette backlit by the moon. She doesn't even glance at the gun I'm pointing in her direction.

She looks ethereal.

Surreal.

She kissed my *chest*.

A breeze pushes into the restaurant, whipping her long hair around her face, and the silver lengths glimmer in the moonlight; metallic; razor-sharp. She slowly lowers her weapon.

"Go ahead," she says, looking me dead in the eyes. "Shoot me."

"Rosabelle—"

"You still don't understand," she says to me. "I will protect you with my life. If that means I have to fight you, I will. If that means I have to suffer in order to keep you safe, I will."

My finger falters on the trigger. "What?" I draw back, ruined all over again. "Rosabelle, what are you talking about—"

"Don't follow me," she says, and disappears, the door ringing shut behind her.

For a full second I stand there, frozen in the aftermath. The gun nearly slips out of my hand. I don't know how to reconcile all the damage coming loose in my heart.

I *am* a liability.

Warner was right. Everyone was right. I can't be an asset

to my family, not like this. I've lost all objectivity. I'll never be able to hurt her. I should be taken out back and shot.

"What the hell is wrong with you?"

I turn at the sound of Nazeera's voice, my mind rushing back into my body, common sense catching up.

Jesus.

I can't just let Rosabelle run wild in The Waffle.

I cross the room, doing a quick sweep for Rosabelle's coat, but I can't find it in this darkened mess. I shrug on my denim jacket, then bolt for the exit, throwing open the door before remembering, as I'm about to cross the threshold, that Nazeera's been injured.

I hesitate, then pivot to look at her. "Are you going to be okay?"

Nazeera looks rough, but she has enough energy to roll her eyes at me. "Get out of here, dumbass."

"Right." I turn to leave, then hesitate again. "You know, if you'd just listened to me the first time and taken her back to the house like you were supposed to—"

Nazeera chucks a shard of broken plate at me.

"Okay, all right, I'm sorry," I say, and duck out the door.

ROSABELLE

35

There's no time to find new clothes.

I try to shove this thought out of my head, but as I run quietly through the darkened, abandoned streets, it occurs to me that this is a bigger problem than I'm ready to acknowledge. Not only are temperatures dropping as the night deepens, but the moon is too full and the streetlamps too bright; I'm obvious in my loose hair and pale hospital scrubs.

Still, the cold air is good for me.

Bracing.

I'd grown warm and complacent in that big, puffy jacket, and as much as I miss its warmth, wearing it would've made me an easy target; worse, I was hardly able to move my arms. Between being shot and freezing to death, the latter of the two is the slower murder, and I'll just have to be okay with it.

I hear movement—a snatch of conversation—

I duck down a darkened alley and back up against the brick, taking the opportunity to try to orient myself. I can see my breath in the glow of a distant streetlamp, and I pull the collar of my thin shirt up over my mouth, willing my heart rate to slow.

Die, I tell myself. *Die*.

My pulse quiets, my thoughts distancing from my body in relief.

I think it's possible I've gone insane.

I can't believe that was me in that diner. I've never been so reckless. Never, not once in my life, have I been so out of control.

I nearly close my eyes.

James is a greater danger to me than I can ever put into words.

Even now, in the depths of a protective death, I can still sense his hands on me, his mouth on my neck. Heat gathers deep in my core, the sensation so powerful it nearly forces my dead heart back to life. The memories drown me. The gasp of his breath. The fever of his body. The give of muscle. His skin against my lips. His tortured sounds in my ears.

The desperate way he'd said my name.

The desperation I still feel when I think of him.

I want things from James I never thought I could want from anyone. I've been starved for years but I've never known this kind of hunger.

These people have poisoned me.

I think too much; I feel too much; I rest too much. I'm gorging on dream and delusion; intoxicated by fantasy.

I'm forgetting to shut down.

Die, I tell myself.

Die.

Winds sweep into the alley, and I register the cold in my head without reacting with my body. My nose grows numb as if from a distance, my fingers losing feeling one at a time.

For as long as I can remember I'd suspected there was something wrong with me, but as I grew older and the questions sharpened, I never allowed myself to truly wonder—not until I was lying on the cold ground in a rebel prison—what it really meant to die every day.

On the Ark, I'd never been able to risk self-examination.

I always policed my thoughts on the island; thinking too critically about myself seemed dangerous. I never gave my mind permission to dwell on who I was or how I managed to live this half-life, caging myself inside myself. The questions and the potential answers seemed fodder for torture during an interrogation, and I could never risk losing my life for fear of leaving Clara unprotected.

Instead, I wrote myself into a role, defined my character by cruelty; painted myself into the image of a cold, unfeeling monster with a single weakness.

The story suited me.

The story saved me.

Even now, I wonder whether Klaus was able to see to the deeper truth beyond my shields. I wonder if that's why he sentenced me to death. I wonder if he knows about Clara's dreams. I wonder what Clara knows about herself. I wonder whether there's any point in wondering.

My life has been death since it began.

There seems no cause for celebration in the realization that murders great and small are my only strengths. There seems no need for examination of a life that will end shortly.

Only in brief, occasional bursts of unsuppressed fear do I wonder how, exactly, Warner was able to activate my own weapon against me.

But this isn't the time for reflection.

Once I'm certain the footsteps have quieted and the path has cleared, I tighten my cold grip on the rifle and push deeper into the alley, searching for an outlet.

Cursory studies of the area revealed little.

I tried to make a mental map based on signs and cues gathered during the walk from Nazeera's house to the waffle shop, but it was after dark, and there was little to distinguish this neighborhood from others I'd seen upon escaping from prison.

The only notable difference is that this area seems more walkable.

There are fewer cars overall. The streets seem unusually dead at this hour. Many shops already appear to be closed, despite the fact that the sun went down only recently. I wonder, again, at the number of soldiers I'd seen in plainclothes at the diner.

You'll be safe on campus, James had said to his brother.

I hadn't understood what he'd meant at the time, but now I'm beginning to wonder. I draw my hand along a brick wall as I go, reading the streets for secrets. There's no gum or trash beaten into the brick, no chipped edges or obvious wear. Things feel especially clean here; newer, neater. Garbage bins are arranged tidily in the alleys, undisturbed; I see no signs of graffiti.

She's pretty contained in The Waffle, Nazeera had said.

The Waffle.

The sign outside the diner had read *The Waffle's Waffles*.

A feeling of foreboding creeps up my neck, low-grade fear pushing against my mind. Where are all the soldiers? Where is the mayhem, the urgency, the chaos of upheaval?

Why is there no indication of disturbance?

I dart from dark corner to dark corner and, save the occasional gust of wind rattling a bin or scattering leaves, I hear nothing. No distant sounds or cries.

No footsteps. No voices.

It's too quiet.

My heart picks up as I run, stealthily dodging shafts of light and imagined movement. My eyes widen as I go, pupils dilating in the gloom to read the quaint shop signs above darkened windows—

The Kitchen

Mo's Market

Alphabet Snacks

Snips & Blooms

I come to an abrupt halt. I look around, my eyes pinging off picturesque buildings and perfectly paved sidewalks. Green areas have been forged gently throughout the neighborhoods, teardrops of grass and sweeping bike paths intercut with occasional swing sets and clean benches. My heart pounds harder as I take it all in, my breaths puffing in the cold.

It doesn't feel real.

I tell myself it's quiet because so many people were called away at once; I tell myself there's no foot traffic because people have gone indoors, taking shelter.

But I know when I'm lying to myself.

If there were a manhunt ongoing, there would be clamor and commotion. This world is unapologetically loud. Its people are frivolous and reckless; they make no effort to silence their lives or emotions. They are not afraid enough of their own government.

Something is wrong.

Crickets chirp merrily into the quiet. A single pedestrian strolls down the sidewalk in the distance, too busy peering up at the moon to notice me. Her dog barks once, reasonably, at a flash of movement, and I tense—

Just a rabbit, darting under a bush.

I stand there a moment longer, watching the pedestrian disappear along the path. No one else appears. No new sounds are introduced. I lift my head up by degrees, turning toward the moon as the stranger did. Fear raises the fine hairs along my nape, my instincts telling me to pay attention, and as I study the sky, searching its depths, I feel my chest constrict.

The scene warps as if underwater.

It lasts less than a second—nearly undetectable—but I stare up at the anomaly long enough to witness it again: another quick blur of the moon, a glitch of a cloud.

Panic shatters under my skin.

I know what an electromagnetic force field looks like. It

could stop a meteor. It would neutralize a nuclear weapon.

I'm gripped by vivid, escalating fear. I wonder, standing there in the dark, my eyes pinned to the sky, what other secrets this strange world holds.

"Cool, right?" he says, his voice carrying as he approaches.

I close my eyes, my shields dissolving, my heart screaming. I will the ground to open up and inhale me.

"What'd you say earlier?" James closes the distance between us. "Something about our world being held together with tape?"

ROSABELLE

36

I go nearly lightheaded at his approach, my sensory load roaring brutally back to life as the frigid night skins me alive. I can't feel my extremities. My lips have gone numb. I'm wearing thin, overly starched cotton basics on a winter night. Short sleeves. No underwear.

My body starts shaking.

I can't decide how to feel about what he does to me. I love it. I hate it. I don't even fully understand it.

And it keeps getting worse.

Being around James is like gasping for air after nearly drowning; there's a horrifying relief in his proximity, a violent shock to my nervous system.

Pleasure and pain, over and over.

"Rosabelle," he says quietly. "Come here."

"There's no way out of this place," I say, my voice breaking.

"Not for you."

When I don't move he reaches for my hand, tugging me toward him, and the slide of his fingers against my palm is enough to stun my heart, threads of electric feeling quickening through my blood. The heightened sensation is so destabilizing I can't withstand it for long; I draw away from him with a trembling breath, as if I've been burned.

"You can't," I say, panicking. "W-We can't—"

"We can't what?"

"You have to stay away from me," I say, taking a step back. "I can't get close to you or I—I might—"

He stills. "You might what?"

"James, please," I say desperately, faltering. "Something— happens to me—when you touch me—"

"Say it," he says softly. He takes a step toward me and I seem to melt at the edges. "Tell me what happens to you when I touch you."

I feel blood rush to my face, then elsewhere, everywhere. He's watching me with an intensity that seems to reach inside of me.

"I lose control," I whisper.

"No." He swallows. "You don't."

I go still. Stare at him. "Yes," I say, "I do—"

"Not yet," he says, his voice rough. "This hasn't even started, Rosabelle. You have no idea what I want from you. You haven't lost control yet. Not even close." His eyes darken. "But you will."

These words bloom in my veins like fire, releasing a searing, exquisite torture all through my body. His gaze is unrelenting. I can't seem to take a full breath. My heart is beating so hard it scares me.

He takes another step closer and I nearly make a sound.

A heavy, warm weight lands on my shoulders, and I realize, through this dizzying haze, that he's given me his jacket. I back away from him on instinct, then slip my arms into the oversized sleeves without protest, my limbs aching in relief. The denim has been warmed by his own body heat, the article infused with the scent of his skin. I inhale him directly into my lungs, and the effect is so dislocating I nearly drop my gun.

Finally, with a few feet between us, I meet his eyes.

He's still staring at me with a magnetized intensity; he's almost smiling, except that his jaw is tight, his eyes drawn together. He looks almost like he's in pain.

"Where am I?" I whisper.

James shucks the beanie off his head and steps toward me; I hold my breath as he tugs the soft hat over my hair, pulling it down gently over my ears. The warmth is instant. I want to tuck myself against him, rest my head against his heart.

Instead, I watch him look at me.

His hands skim my face as he draws away, first grazing my cheeks, then lingering along my jaw, and a sound builds in my throat. Feeling sweeps through me like a storm. I can't hold it inside.

I cry out and stumble back.

James exhales into the cold, his breath like smoke. His eyes are charged and fathomless, the moonlight catching him in relief, glazing his edges. He turns away and he looks tightly wound; muscles tensing under skin.

Everything about him has become my favorite thing.

I never had a preference for blue eyes before I met him. I never knew I cared for freckles until I saw his face. I didn't know I could love the way someone walked until I watched him enter a room. Each time I see him he seems to come into sharper focus, every facet honed, every detail more exquisite. It's becoming harder to look him in the eye, to keep myself from touching him. I don't know what I'm doing anymore. I don't know why I'm encouraging these thoughts. This is unconscionable behavior.

I'm going home to die.

"I'm going to say this nicely, just once." James looks at me. "Hand over your weapons."

I take another step back, steady my heart.

Shake my head.

"This is getting old, Rosabelle," he says. "My nerves are shot, I have to get going, and I don't want to do this anymore. I'm tired of chasing you down and taking a bullet for it. There's no point; you're stuck here. Run for as long as you like. Shoot me as many times as you want. Try stabbing me again. It won't matter. You can't get out of here without my help. All you're going to do is give me a bigger headache."

"Then help me," I say to him, taking yet another step back, trying to direct blood to my head. "Tell me where we are. Tell me how to get out of here."

He looks up at the sky as if searching for strength. When he meets my eyes again he looks almost angry. "You need to go back to the house. Now."

"You don't understand," I say to him. "James, if that vial falls into the wrong hands—"

"No, I'm not doing this again," he says sharply. "I've asked you a thousand times to explain to me why you need that vial and you've never answered my questions. So unless you're ready to tell me what it is and why you need it so badly, we're done for the night. I'll throw you over my shoulder, carry you back to the house, and feed you to Nazeera."

"You wouldn't."

"Try me."

"There's no time to talk right now," I say desperately. "I need to leave before it's too late— We can have a conversation about everything later—"

"Now, Rosabelle. *Right now.*"

"But I don't—I don't actually—"

"Fine," he says flatly.

He moves so quickly I don't even realize he's picked me up until the world flips upside down. He actually tosses me over his shoulder.

I nearly scream.

"James," I cry, panicking. "Please— Put me down—"

He starts walking. He moves unimpeded, unbothered by the effort. "Go ahead and try to shoot me, it won't help you get anywhere faster."

"*James—*"

"And you should know that Nazeera isn't happy with you. She's going to make your life a living hell."

"I don't actually know what's in the vial!"

He stops, then spins around as if to face me—as if he's forgotten he's carrying me. "What do you mean you don't know what's in the vial?"

"I don't actually know what's in it," I say, trying to catch my breath. The world is inverted, making me dizzy. "I don't know its exact properties. I only know that it's going to be used by agents across the continent to set off a chain of undetectable explosions that will release a gene-editing virus that can rewrite your DNA."

"What?" James stiffens. I feel shock batter him, his chest lifting, tension radiating through his limbs. "What do you mean, *rewrite my DNA?*"

I'm breathing hard now. Blood is rushing to my head. "Not just yours. All DNA. It will get rid of all preternatural abilities," I explain. "Reset the genetic slate, dissolve your powers, and prep your population for remote influence by synthetic intelligence—"

James staggers. He sets me blindly back on the ground, looking suddenly horrified.

Gutted.

He searches my eyes in the dark. "You waited this long to tell me that The Reestablishment is trying to turn us all into mind-controlled zombies?"

"I've been trying to explain this to you since that night in the tunnel," I say, anguished. "I've been trying to get back to the Ark all this time, to set things right—"

"Why couldn't you just tell me?" he says, panic rendering him taut. "At literally any point you could've given me the explanation that took you two seconds to give me just now—"

"I didn't know if I could trust any of you!"

Now he looks stricken.

James falls silent, the words visibly crushing him. "You didn't know if you could trust *me?*"

"I didn't—I didn't mean you, specifically," I say, backpedaling, trying to calm my heart. "I did trust you. I *do* trust you— Of course I trust you—"

"Then— What—" He drags his hands down his face. "Jesus, Rosabelle, I don't understand—"

"I just— I knew that if I told you everything, you'd want to help me."

His head snaps up. "How is that a bad thing?"

"Because I've seen enough of your society and your methods to know that none of you would survive on the Ark long enough to do what's necessary and I really"—I falter, my voice catching—"I really don't want you to die."

James stares at me, stunned.

"I wanted to do it on my own," I say, forcing myself to keep talking. "I didn't want to wait, to explain things, to have to justify my reasons. I didn't even want you to worry. I just wanted to make things right." I shake my head. "But I was going to tell you anyway. Tonight. I was going to tell you all of it. I just didn't have a chance."

The tension in his body eases slightly, but his eyes draw together in confusion. "So you didn't tell me the truth because you didn't think I'd be capable of surviving a mission into the Ark?"

"I just wanted to protect you—"

He shakes his head. "Rosabelle, that's maybe the nicest and the meanest thing you could possibly— *Shit*—"

He pulls his pager out of his pocket, the notification silent this time. His jaw hardens as he scans the message.

ROSABELLE

37

I wait, quietly spiraling, until he meets my eyes. I don't even have to ask him to tell me what's happening anymore.

"It's another call for backup," he says to me. "They've managed to corral one of the suspects in an enclosed location. They've barred the exits, but there's no telling what will happen next."

"*One* of the suspects," I note aloud.

James offers me a bleak look. "Yeah. They've already taken out a few people. Decoys, probably."

I consider him then, hoping to deliver my next words gently, and likely failing in the effort. "James. I need you to understand this: Your world is dangerously vulnerable. The Reestablishment has been pushing pieces carefully into place for years. They have every intention of taking back their power—and you shouldn't trust anyone," I say. "Spies and agents have infiltrated nearly every corner of your society."

"Yeah," he says, fixing me with a piercing look. "I know."

"You have to let me come with you," I say. "No one is as motivated as I am to get back that vial—"

He makes a harsh sound, something like a laugh. "You literally just told me not to trust anyone."

"You can trust me."

He considers me a beat, his eyes tight with some abstruse emotion. "You sure about that?"

It's a long moment before I can offer him an honest answer. He watches me as I struggle in the silence, a breeze pushing my hair across my face.

Finally, I say, "I think so."

"*You think so?*" James smiles darkly into the distance. "I can't tell you how much I hate that answer, Rosabelle."

I say nothing to that, turning my eyes instead to the jacket I'm wearing, the jacket he took off his own back to keep me warm. I find that little orange kite pin on the pocket, and I flex my fingers to keep from touching it, bite my tongue to keep from asking about it.

I don't want to learn more about him. I don't want my heart to get any bigger. There's no point.

I'll be dead soon enough.

"You're hiding something from me, aren't you?" he says. "Something else."

I look up sharply.

"You're still keeping secrets," he says. "I can tell. There's something else you don't want me to know."

"Look," I say, taking another lifesaving step backward. I try to stay calm. "I'm worried that no one else will realize the importance of the vial tonight. The vial is more important than any assailant. And if there's a chance it could be lost or broken or overlooked—"

"Wow, deflection," he says, cutting me off. "Nice. That's mature."

I meet his eyes, see the challenge there.

"Fine," I say quietly. "Yes, I'm keeping secrets. But so are you."

"Me?" His eyes widen. "I don't have any secrets."

"Yes, you do."

"No, I don't," he says. "I'm not mysterious like you. I don't have secret files documenting my second life. This is who I am. This is all of me."

"That's not true."

"Yes, it is—"

"What happens to you when you hear children cry?"

James recoils, hardening before my eyes. His voice is a breath. "What?"

"In the diner," I say. "There were a few couples with young children at the tables near ours. Every time a child cried your body seized up. You'd disappear inside yourself for seconds at a time. You're really good at hiding it." I tilt my head at him. "It's clear you've had a lot of practice hiding it. Nobody seems to notice the way you manage it."

"Rosabelle—"

"I don't think most people notice the way you handle your brother's anxiety, either. The civilian. Adam. You anticipate and soothe his emotions without being asked, as if you've been doing it for years. At the diner I caught a glimpse of the tattoos on his arms. He was once a soldier of The Reestablishment. Does he suffer from post-traumatic stress? Was he always like this? When did he start leaning on you for emotional support? He must be nearly ten years older than you."

"I don't—"

"You're the youngest by far of everyone I've met who matters to you. Do any of your family members realize how much weight you carry? Or do they treat you like an overgrown child? According to the data I gathered, you weren't raised by your father or even formally acknowledged by him until shortly before his death. Warner was loyal to The Reestablishment until a decade ago; Adam appears to have enlisted in the army when The Reestablishment was still in power. You must've been very young. Practically orphaned. Who raised you? Where is your mother? What happened to you when you were a child—"

"*Stop*," James cries. He's staring at me like I've cut him open. "I hate it when you do that."

"When I do what?"

"Rip my heart out."

This answer surprises me. "I didn't realize that's what I was doing."

He almost laughs. "You didn't realize? One way or another, I walk away from you bleeding. You've given me more scars than anyone I've ever met."

That strikes me badly. In fact, I hate it.

"I'm sorry," I whisper.

James sighs, pushing a hand through his hair. "Look, those things you just said about me—they aren't secrets."

"What do you mean?"

"My past is not nefarious. There's no subterfuge. It's just—I don't like to talk about it."

"Oh," I say quietly, looking away. "I can't relate. I love talking about my past."

James stills. "Did you just make a joke?"

I manage to smile in response.

It's tentative and a little self-conscious, and it's as close as I can get to a peace offering, but it doesn't have the intended effect. James doesn't smile back.

He goes slack. "You're so fucking beautiful."

The smile fades from my face. Need knifes through me.

"I just want to be clear," he says, his voice tight. "That if we were up against anything less than a global threat right now, I'd be trying to figure out how to finish what we started in that diner."

We lock eyes for a breathless moment.

"You kissed my chest," he says finally.

"Your heart," I whisper.

This answer seems to surprise him. "My heart?"

"Yes."

"Wow," he breathes. I watch his throat work. "Okay."

I take an unconscious step toward him and he shakes his head.

"Probably not a good idea," he says. "Come any closer to me right now and I might do something stupid. I might finally give Warner a reason to kill me."

My heart briefly stops.

James tears his eyes away from me. "So this is what you were talking about, isn't it?" he says. "Earlier tonight, when you said there were agents all over the continent. You said they were planning synchronized acts of terror against civilians over the next several weeks."

"Yes."

"So there are more vials," he says. "More agents."

"Yes."

"And when you said we had less than seven weeks—"

"I meant seven weeks before it was all over," I explain. "Not seven weeks before it started."

He takes a deep, unsteady breath, then mutters an epithet on the exhale.

"Do you understand now why I need to go back to the Ark as soon as possible?" I ask him.

"I understand why you need to go back," he says. "What I don't understand is why you think I'm so incompetent that you wouldn't even tell me your plan."

"I don't think you're incompetent—"

"I was *there*, Rosabelle. I'm the only other person on the planet who's been in and out of the Ark—"

"Yes, and that's part of the problem," I explain, cutting him off. "You think you made it out alive on your own merits, but you don't understand the scope of Ark surveillance. You only made it out alive because you were part of the plan—because Klaus read your mind and manipulated you, anticipated your moves, and built a script for our escape based on a series of emotional extrapolations derived from a thorough analysis of your character—"

"Wait, what?" he says. "What do you mean, *read my mind*? Who the fuck is Klaus?"

"James." I squeeze my eyes shut, then turn my face up to the glitching moon. "Please," I say, summoning patience before I meet his eyes. "We're officially out of time. I promise I'll tell you everything if we live to have the chance, but if there are agents trying to get back the vial right now it's because they know I've failed my mission—and if I don't get ahead of this the consequences are going to be so much worse than any of us can possibly anticipate."

"Fine," he says darkly. "I'll make you a deal, Rosabelle."

"No."

"You can't just say no."

"*No.*" I try to cross my arms, but the sleeves on this jacket are too long, making me look like a child. I drop my arms. "No deals. I already know I'm not going to like this—"

"You haven't even heard the terms yet—"

"No," I say again, anger coiling in my chest. "You're not coming with me to the island."

"Then you're not coming with me tonight."

"James—"

"*Rosabelle.*"

"This isn't the same thing!" I nearly shout. "You won't survive five seconds on the Ark—"

"I won't survive *five seconds*?" He raises his eyebrows. "Jesus, Rosabelle. Just drive a stake through my heart."

"I'm not trying to insult you," I say, exasperated. "It's not just you. None of you would survive, not even your scary older brother. You have no idea what you're up against—"

"I'll take my chances," he says.

"I don't want you to die!"

James actually laughs, the sound sharp and brief. "You know, I never get tired of hearing you say that. Coming from you, it's like poetry."

"*James.*"

"What?" he says. "I'm serious."

I shake my head, losing steam. "This is exactly why I didn't want to tell you. I can't reason with you."

James reaches suddenly into his pocket again, retrieving his pager. "Shit," he says. "Okay, now I really have to go—"

"I'm coming with you—"

"No way." He backs up a few steps. "Take the deal, Rosabelle."

"*No.*"

"Fine. Can you walk back to the house on your own, or do you still need me to carry you?"

I could scream. *"I'm not going back to the—"*

I sense the sky move before I hear the explosion, and I look up in time to see violent tremors warping the moon and clouds above. I gasp, my eyes widening as a fire cloud erupts like daylight in the distant dark; then the sound, shattering the silence—

Deafening.

My ears ring, a high-pitched frequency vibrating through my head. I stumble back, then pitch forward, realizing James has grabbed me by the waist, steadying me.

"You okay?" he shouts, his eyes wild.

I nod, blinking, willing my head to clear, my ears to quiet.

Fear shudders down my spine. I look up at the burning sky as if from outside of myself; James turns with me to stare at the smoke, his own body rigid with tension.

I feel like I'm inside of a nightmare.

"James," I say, raising my voice above the din.

He doesn't look at me when he says, "You ready to accept the deal?"

"Only if we discuss the terms later."

"Fine," he says sharply. "Let's go."

WARNER

38

"We have to split up."

Kenji ducks down beside me as I say this, a bead of sweat dripping down his temple. He wipes at his face with the hem of his shirt, breathing hard. "Just like that? No romance, no poetry? You're just breaking up with me?"

"Something is wrong," I say, turning to look at him. I taste blood as I speak, and I reach blindly for the gash at my head, trying to ascertain the damage. "This feels like a much bigger operation than we've trained for—"

Kenji slaps my hand away from my head. "Don't touch it. It looks worse than it is. Head wounds bleed a lot."

"I'm fine," I say, narrowing my eyes at him.

"No concussion?"

"Like I said, I'm fine."

Kenji peers around the low wall, then falls back. "Look, these dudes are fighting with weapons I've never even seen before. One of those lasers could've taken off your whole head."

"The teams were prepared," I admit. "We've got powers on our side, but they leveraged the element of surprise. We have to pivot, and we have to do it quickly." I pause. "I think we should split up."

"No."

"Why not?"

"Because I hate it when we split up."

This nearly prompts a smile. "It's our best option," I say to him. "All units are under the directives of their commanding officers, and I can't issue any new orders without giving away our position. Between the two of us we can cover more ground, execute individual operations—"

"Wait, hold on, why can't you issue new orders? You can decide right now. Issue a new directive over the comms. We'll pivot together. We have a system for that."

I shake my head, then check to make sure we're still clear before I say, "I think our central comms have been hacked."

"*What?*"

"The information has been inconsistent," I explain. "In some cases, entirely unverified."

"Shit."

"All intel seems to insist that a high-profile prisoner and known Ark assassin is responsible for stealing sensitive material. But we know for a fact that Rosabelle has been in Nazeera's custody for several hours."

Kenji takes this in. "You think someone's trying to set her up?"

"I don't know. I still don't know what to think of her. She might've helped orchestrate the entire thing. Created the opportunity. All I know for sure is that the intel isn't coming from *us*. I wasn't the one to report the vial missing. I certainly never indicated to anyone that she was the main suspect—"

"*Get down*," Kenji cries, knocking me to the ground, then covering me as he exchanges fire. The sounds are both deafening and short-lived.

Kenji ducks back behind the wall, breathing hard.

We both activate invisibility, but the protection has been limited; our enemies had already seen us open fire from this position.

I rise into a low crouch and spot an assailant taking cover behind a distant building. I soon spot two others. They're dressed exactly as our infantry would be. Same uniforms. Flawless mimics. Perfect spies.

The only difference is, I can feel their malice.

"On your left," I say quietly. "Two on my right."

"I see him," says Kenji.

We take them out together, finding our marks in nearly coordinated kills.

Then we bolt.

"Head inland," I say as we run. We can't see each other, but I can sense Kenji close by. "I want to get away from the harbor—"

I hear the electric thrum of advanced weaponry and I tackle Kenji to the ground, holding him there as the laser fire shoots past our heads.

"Motherfucker," he cries.

I hear the weapon recharging and I grab him by the arm, hauling him upright, and this time I don't let go. "Run," I shout. "We can take cover in the alley up ahead—"

Shots hit the ground at our feet, then whizz past our

heads. I realize, with a shock of dread, that the assailant must be sensing our heat signatures. It's possible their weaponry is advanced enough to offer this technology.

"What do you think they're trying to do?" says Kenji. "We don't even know what their objective is—"

"Enslave the world," I answer, breathing hard. "The ultimate objective of The Reestablishment has always been global colonization. By any means necessary."

"Right, I get that," Kenji says. "But what about right now?"

There's a sonic *boom*—

We both lose our footing.

The entire world seems to shudder, shock waves reverberating painfully. My ears ring as clouds of ominous smoke rise in the sky, flashes of a firestorm raging in the distance.

"What the hell was that?" cries Kenji, panicked.

"I don't know," I shout above the din, helping him up, "but we have to move. The scope of this attack is bigger than anything we've dealt with so far—"

More shots narrowly miss us both, searing the ground beneath us, pulverizing the landscape around us, and we just manage to dive into a back alley, out of range. I realize, on a delay, that my left leg caught the edge of a laser shot, the skin raw and bleeding through the scorched material of my pants.

We take a second to breathe, but I know we can't stay here long. "Their weapons have heat trackers," I say to Kenji. "We can't just keep running. We need to split up."

"How did they even smuggle these weapons onto the continent?" he says, fighting for air. "Wouldn't our teams have noticed crates of terrifying, alien weaponry coming in from hostile territory?"

I shake my head. "We're more deeply infiltrated than we realized."

"Infiltrated? You mean you think our own soldiers are working against us?"

"There's no other way they would've been able to orchestrate and execute a complex operation like this from within our borders. It makes me wonder how deep the corrupted veins run through our systems."

"Holy shit."

"Kenji," I say, glancing over my shoulder. "I'm going to tell you something right now that I want you to take to your grave. Are you listening?"

"Yeah, man," he says. "I'm listening."

"The stolen vial is another decoy. I've planted several; each one was meant to be a trap; each one has a tracker. Only I know where the original is stored."

Kenji lets out a low whistle. "This is why they paint your face all over the city, bro. Already a fucking hero."

Shots ring out in the near distance.

Not long before we're discovered.

"I want you to track down the stolen vial," I say to Kenji. "I'll tell you where to find the coordinates."

Kenji is quiet a moment, just breathing. "What about you?" he says. "What are you going to do?"

I risk a quick look through the unreliable notifications coming through on my pager, my jaw tensing, and then I glance up at the firestorm still raging in the distance.

A sinister feeling moves along my skin. "I need to find out how much of this is real."

JAMES

39

"I'm positive," Rosabelle says, ducking between buildings. She drops down into a crouch, scanning the area with a surgical precision I find fascinating.

I've never really watched her work before.

It was harder than I anticipated getting her off campus. She wasn't authorized to leave The Waffle, which meant that I had to do some technically illegal things to get her out—which I'll definitely pay for later.

Luckily, Rosabelle knows how to run.

She kept up with my pace fairly well despite the differences in our strides, but after sprinting across the city for nearly twenty minutes straight, she finally needed a second to catch her breath and recalibrate.

We both did.

I watch her brace herself against the wall.

"I'm convinced it's a diversionary tactic," she says between breaths. "Your people must've been close to success, or else they wouldn't have tried to draw so much attention away."

"Someone blew up a fucking hospital wing," I say, blind panic still clawing at my chest as I peer around the corner. "We had to divert some of our forces."

"That's what they wanted," she says, straightening. "It's

a move meant to fracture your troops. You and I need to stay focused on the original mission—"

"I know," I say. "I know we need to get the vial. But there are assailants out there actively murdering burn victims and we can't do anything to help. It's horrible."

"Where are you getting this information?" she asks. "Who's sending you these updates?"

"We have a team that runs stealth drones during operations," I explain. "They stay in the command center and give us real-time updates."

She dismisses this with a single shake of her head. "Easily hacked."

This response stuns me.

I stare at her before returning my eyes to the skyline, where smoke still spirals into the milky night. The flames have diminished, but we're not close enough to sight the full scale of the damage.

"You think this scene is fake?" I ask, glancing at Rosabelle over my shoulder, some of the tension leaving my body. "I mean, to be fair, The Reestablishment has messed with our perception of reality before, but I don't think this is a stunt."

"I don't think it's a stunt, either," she says. "I think it's a trap."

"You mean like some kind of an ambush?" I fall back, dropping down next to her so our voices don't carry.

Our shoulders touch.

She immediately shifts away from me, moving a few feet out of reach.

I'm not offended. I don't even blame her. I'm just trying to talk to her and I'm getting distracted. Her skin is like porcelain in this light. She has this celestial look about her, like she might've been born in the sky, like she might've fallen from the stars. I don't know where these thoughts are coming from. I didn't even know I could think thoughts like this.

She kissed my *heart.*

I'm a fucking poet now.

Rosabelle looks up at me as if I've spoken aloud, and for a second I think maybe I did—until I remember that I'd just asked her a question.

"I don't know," she says. "Maybe an ambush. Maybe something else. All possibilities nefarious." She tilts her head back, peering at the roofline. "I really can't believe how little surveillance you have across the city."

"I can't believe you think my own people are lying."

My pager goes off again and I read the message, then show it to her: it's another urgent call for all soldiers to report to the hospital immediately.

"I don't trust it," Rosabelle says. "A sudden humanitarian disaster is a convenient way to divert troops from a real target. Even if your brother suspects foul play, he'll have no choice but to abandon his position to assess the reported damage, and that might be exactly what they want." She hesitates. "Then again, I could be wrong. Maybe I'm not the right person to ask."

"Why not?"

"I'm generally suspicious," she says. "I don't trust anyone. Ever. As a rule."

I raise my eyebrows. "Do you really mean that, or are you exaggerating to make a point?"

"I never exaggerate."

"What about Clara?"

"Clara's mind doesn't belong to her," she says, looking away. "I can't trust her, not even if I want to."

This leaves me a little stunned.

It hits me, with sudden clarity, how isolated Rosabelle must feel all the time. It's no wonder she doesn't speak to people. She comes from a place where everything she says is recorded and dissected. I hadn't realized that she needed to police herself around her own sister. It had never occurred to me, until just now, that there was no one in the world she could freely talk to.

No one she could trust.

I still don't know what kind of hell she lived through on the Ark. I don't know why she first showed up here with all those bruises on her body.

Standardized torture, Warner had called it.

I can't wait to murder these people.

Suddenly, the words I say next mean more than they ever did. They feel heavier to me. Revolutionary.

"But you trust me," I say to her.

Even with a few feet between us, I sense Rosabelle stiffen. She turns her face away from me, from the moonlight. "You're different," she says.

A fucking firework goes off in my chest.

"Different how?" I ask, sounding calmer than I feel.

"Please be specific. I'm fishing for compliments. I'd prefer your answer in essay format."

Rosabelle cants her head. A band of light falls across her face, illuminating her lips. She smiles softly and I experience a minor heart attack. "You know," she says, "sometimes I think there might be something wrong with you."

Wow.

My disappointment is real and stunning. A little embarrassing. I would not look at myself in the mirror right now.

I take a tight breath. "I have to be honest, Rosabelle, that was not the answer I was hoping for."

She laughs softly beside me and I have another minor heart attack. "You don't count," she says, finally putting me out of my misery. She turns her eyes up to the night sky. "There's no one in the world like you."

The effect these words have on me is a little alarming. I feel dislocated in my own body. Something dangerous detonates inside of me.

I release a breath, feeling shaken.

"You're really trying to kill me tonight," I say quietly. "I thought you didn't want me to die."

She turns to me, wearing my hat, and smiles.

Fuck.

"Look," she says, "I just think there's a high chance the situation at the hospital isn't as bad as they want you to think it is."

And it's like being pushed face-first into the snow.

"Right," I say, emerging from my own head. I force myself up, onto my feet, suddenly fighting for air. I do another quick check beyond the alley, but I feel blind. I need to get away from her. Stay away from her.

Marry her, maybe.

Nope. *Nope.* That pendulum swung too far in the opposite direction. This is bad. I need help.

I need to take a cold shower.

I finally get a hold of myself long enough to perform a lobotomy and do some quick calculations. We're at least ten miles out from the first location, where the suspects were originally reported in action, and it occurs to me, without warning, that I don't even know Rosabelle's birthday. It further occurs to me that I should ask her. That now is probably the best time to ask her.

Shut up, I tell myself. *Shut up.*

Ten miles would take us forever on foot. The hospital is even farther out. That means we're going to need to steal a car. Correction: borrow a car.

I'll definitely give it back.

But we need to make a decision, now.

Rosabelle releases the magazine on her gun, and I turn in time to see her checking the ammo before sliding it back into place with a satisfying *click*. "Why is all your tech and weaponry so old?" she says. "How can you afford to continue manufacturing bullets?"

"Hey, when's your birthday?" I say, then turn toward the wall in mute horror, squeezing my eyes shut, wanting to kick my own ass.

"My birthday?" she echoes, surprised.

"Yeah," I say tightly, like this is normal. I wonder how hard I can hit my head against the wall without causing myself permanent brain damage.

"James," she says. "If you don't like my plan you can just say so. We can discuss it. You don't have to distract me with random questions."

"That's not what—"

"I just happen to think you have more rats in your house than you realize. I'm worried you're relying on unsecured sitreps for critical updates."

Okay, this actually resets my head.

I turn to face her. "You really don't think I can trust the people in my own command center?"

She considers the question, studying me a moment before saying, finally, "I'd advise you to be cautious in every instance going forward. Choose your trusted circle carefully; vet everyone else thoroughly. And doubt everything you hear."

I raise my eyebrows. "You think the situation is that bad?"

"Yes."

"*Shit.*"

"Have you gotten any messages from your brother?" she asks.

"Who? Warner?"

"Yes," she says.

"No."

"Nothing at all?" she says.

"No."

She thinks this over. "I maintain that we take up positions at the first location. You said it was some kind of a warehouse?" she asks, folding back the too-long sleeves on her borrowed jacket.

My jacket.

My heart beats harder as I look at her. I briefly lose focus again. There's something about seeing her in my clothes—seeing her so comfortable in my clothes—that activates a deep and primal response in my body. She could probably ask me for anything right now. Fuck a jacket, I'd give her an organ. Any organ. She can pick the organ.

A single word is building inside of me, over and over, like a pulse in my throat.

Mine.

"James?"

I want her to come to me when she needs something. I want her to search for me in a crowd. I want her to depend on me; I want her to reach for my hand; I want her to miss me when I'm gone. I want her like I've never wanted anything—

"James?" she says again.

"Yeah?"

"The place we're going— You said they managed to trap the assailant inside of a warehouse?"

"Yeah." I feel my chest tighten. I back up a few more steps, as if the distance will help steady my heart. "Sounds like they've locked it down."

"What does it house? Munitions? Aircraft?"

"It's not that kind of warehouse," I say, managing an anxious laugh. "It's one of those places where you can get things in bulk for a reasonable price."

She stares at me blankly.

"I'm guessing you don't have one of those." I take a deep, clarifying breath. Look around. "You know," I say. "I'm realizing I don't know anything about the way you lived on the Ark."

She flat out ignores this.

"All right," she says, getting to her feet. "Let's go."

"So you're absolutely sure about this?" I hesitate. "You really think we should ignore the big, obvious fire in the sky?"

She nods, slinging the rifle around her neck. "I wouldn't put it past The Reestablishment to blow up a hospital," she says. "But a move like that is a blatant act of war. The fact that it's being reported in your comms as an attack from an open enemy seems premature at best. Has anyone actually claimed responsibility for the explosion?"

"Not that I'm aware of."

She shakes her head. "The Reestablishment doesn't normally act without the cover of plausible deniability; it really isn't their style. They no longer have the manpower to fight major battles, and they have no interest in a land war. Their preference is for a slow war of attrition, chipping away at your world incrementally, turning the people against themselves. Then taking it out with a final blow."

"You're right," I say, tensing. "They prefer psychological warfare. Every operation we've dealt with in the past several years was a horrific attack designed to look like an accident, or else inspire mass chaos to foment division among the public. They're trying to make our leadership look incompetent in order to make our own people hate us."

She looks suddenly grim. "You've been paying attention."

"All right, fine." I sigh, resting the rifle on my shoulder. "Follow me. We're going to have to steal a car."

JAMES

40

"I thought you said it was a warehouse," she says, lowering her voice. We're backed up against a side wall, tucked into the shadows. "This looks too sleek for a warehouse, and the zoning is strange. Why is it so close to a residential area?"

"It's not a regular warehouse," I quietly remind her. "It's a place where you can buy things in bulk. It's a warehouse, but it's also a store."

"That doesn't make any sense," she whispers.

We've already done scans of the perimeter, checking exit doors and escape routes. The place is massive, ringed by an even more massive parking lot. My comms indicated that the building had been locked down, but looking around now I can see the building is no longer properly surrounded. The dispersion of our troops to the hospital has fractured our power out here. We spotted only a few soldiers on our initial checks; whatever manpower we might've had has now been severely diminished.

Rosabelle was right; something is wrong.

It's way too quiet here.

"They store stuff, in the warehouse," I explain to her, "but it's also a business. People come through during the day and buy things."

"From a warehouse?"

"Yes," I say.

"Why?"

"Because it's cheaper," I explain.

"So there are groceries inside?"

"Yes."

"Perishable groceries?" she asks. "Like milk and eggs?"

"Yeah, but also couches and chairs and lawn mowers and stuff."

"Really?" She frowns. "That's so strange."

Rosabelle, I've learned, likes to do a lot of recon.

She likes to make lists and maps in her head. She solves for contingencies constantly. I don't analyze things as much as she does before I barge into a new place, and it's been fascinating to watch her brain work.

She's literally always thinking.

"Is there anything flammable or explosive inside?" she asks.

"Definitely. There's a full kitchen in there."

"They sell kitchens?"

"No, they sell pizza," I say, then hesitate. "Well, actually, they also sell kitchens."

Now she turns to look at me, her eyes wide and gleaming in the starlight. "What?"

"And hot dogs. And ice cream. You can also visit an eye doctor and get a pair of glasses."

Her shock dissolves almost at once into frustration. She

rolls her eyes at me and whispers, *"Very funny."*

"I'm serious."

"I'm trying to get real information out of you," she says. "And you're just making jokes—"

"I'm not joking," I insist, trying not to laugh. "I'm completely serious—"

"You're laughing at me."

"I'm not," I say, forcing the smile off my face. "I just— Look, I promise, one day, when this is all over, I'll take you to one of these places myself and you can see it all with the lights on."

Now she pauses.

"Hot dogs and kitchens and eggs and an eye doctor?" she says, uncertainty flickering in her eyes. "Really?"

"And wedding rings. And birthday cakes. And a pharmacy. You can even buy flowers and a casket."

Her uncertainty disappears; frustration is back in full force. "Why are you making fun of me?" she says, sounding wounded. "I'm asking you serious questions and you—"

"I'm not making fun of you," I say, a little desperately now. "I swear, Rosabelle, I'm not making fun of you—"

She lifts a finger to her lips, telling me gently to shut the hell up. She then nods over her shoulder at the unlocked back entrance we identified earlier.

We're just yards away now, and everything is weirdly, creepily quiet. No footfalls; no gunshots; no shouts or echoes. I have no idea what to expect when we get in there.

We might be walking into nothing.

We might be walking into a shitstorm.

Rosabelle does another visual sweep as we go, one that I've begun to recognize as her search for cameras. I've already told her that the few security cameras have been obviously dismantled, but she has a hard time believing there isn't more surveillance.

I never thought I'd agree with her on that.

"How stealthy are your stealth drones?" she whispers, studying the darkened sky as we make our approach. "I'm not sensing anything."

"They're fairly undetectable," I say. "Their cloaking abilities were developed by alchemizing the DNA sequences responsible for activating invisibility. We built the mutated genetic codes directly into the machines."

She stops and turns to face me, eyes wide with astonishment. "You can do things like that?"

"Well, we're working on it." I grimace. "Some of the drones are small enough to refine, but honestly, we thought we'd be further along with these kinds of things. We're always diverting time and resources to keeping things afloat—constantly starting over. We've lost some of our best scientists to sudden, unexplained deaths." I shoot her a look. "Entire laboratories with years of research have mysteriously gone up in flames overnight."

"Spies," she says.

"Yeah, but our labs are locked down—the security measures are serious. I don't know how—"

"James," she says, frowning. "When I say *spies*, I'm not talking about strangers and new arrivals; I'm talking about people you already trust, people you've worked with for years. These are people you think you've already vetted, people with spouses and children, people you've shared meals with. People you think you've known your entire life."

I stare at her, the weight of this hitting me like a sledgehammer. "You think our own scientists are sabotaging us?"

"Yes."

"That—makes so much more sense."

She sighs. "You're not actually that naive," she says to me. "Your biggest problem is you're too optimistic."

"You think that's my biggest problem?" I raise my eyebrows at her. "Can I tell my brothers you said that?"

Her mouth curves into a smile and lingers, and it feels like possibly my greatest achievement.

I want this job. I'd be good at this job.

I want to take care of her. I can make her laugh. I could make her happy.

Hope diffuses inside my chest as she turns the handle, and I'm delusional enough, even now, to imagine a world beyond this moment. I'm already dreaming of the fragile hours and soft minutes we fight for; the quiet days and peaceful weeks so many of us are willing to die for.

Life, paid for in blood.

Adrenaline floods my body as Rosabelle crosses the

threshold. I follow close behind, my eyes sharpening as we move from darkness to darkness. I scan the shadows as we advance, lifting my gun, listening for movement. The eerie quiet unsettles me.

Confuses me.

We haven't made it more than a few feet into the building before I hear her scream.

JAMES

41

Her terrifying cry cuts off almost immediately, even as the echo of her scream reverberates in my head.

Fear nearly shuts down my body.

Somehow I manage to move, reflexes propelling me, blind fury surging through my veins. I charge into the darkness, my heart beating frantically—

But I see no sign of Rosabelle.

There's no sign of anyone.

I barrel down disordered aisles, racing through a maze of scattered cereal boxes, my boots crunching through bran flakes. My eyesight is adjusting quickly but I still can't make out distinctive shapes from afar. I dive down another aisle, taking in the chaos of broken housewares, several boxes of dinner plates tossed to the floor, shards of shattered bowls glinting in the dim light—

A masked figure rushes at me and I shoot, taking out the assailant's legs; they get off a few shots as they stagger back and I duck, then dive, tackling them to the floor, ripping the rifle out of the attacker's hand before tearing off their mask.

Blond hair, brown eyes.

She looks vaguely familiar. I feel certain I've seen her somewhere before, but I can't remember her name.

"Who are you?" I say to her, breathing hard. "What are you doing here?"

I watch her jaw work in response. I think she's going to speak but instead she appears to dislodge something from inside her own mouth. She bites down, hard, and too late, I realize my mistake.

The woman goes limp, her eyes rolling back in her head.

"*Fuck*," I force out.

My heart thunders in my chest, panic rising through my body. This was a setup.

Something is happening here—something much bigger than I imagined. I can't even fathom the scope.

Rosabelle was right.

Rosabelle.

I rush down aisle after aisle, searching for anything that might give me a clue, and I nearly slip on a heap of dry rice in the process, catching myself badly against a metal shelf. As I stabilize, trying to breathe, I notice the bullet holes riddling industrial-sized bags of white and brown rice, grains exhaling softly onto the floor. Bullet holes, I realize, have torn through nearly everything. There's already been a showdown here.

Someone already tried to get through.

One of *us*.

My heart speeds up.

Broken jars of pasta sauce gleam just ahead of me, pools of red merging ominously, the scents of basil and oregano cutting against the sharp tang of too much tomato. It makes my stomach turn.

I hear another aborted scream.

Then another.

I rush toward the sounds, cursing as my boot connects with a box of fallen flatware, knives and forks crashing together across the floor. The sounds of Rosabelle's screams continue to echo in my mind.

I can't focus. I'm losing composure. I keep imagining someone handling her—hurting her—

I spot a dark figure dart down an aisle up ahead and I chase them into a refrigerated bay, firing off shots as I enter the alcove, the sudden cold raising goose bumps along my skin. I manage to hit my mark once in the arm, but not enough to take them out. It's harder to shoot in the half dark with the intention of disabling, but I have to keep at least one of these assholes alive for questioning.

The assailant takes cover behind a massive crate of strawberries and fires back; I dive out of the way, a bullet grazing my torso, and crash into a heaving pile of packaged mushrooms, my elbow slamming into a metal shelf as I land. I hiss through the pain, fighting to get to my feet, and manage to land a shot just as the assailant nearly escapes back into the central building. The figure goes down with a muted cry, one leg collapsing beneath them, and I rush forward, shooting the gun out of their grip before I fall into a crouch. The assailant screams, staring, horrified, at their semi-detached hand. I rip off their mask.

This time, I rear back in shock. I can't find my voice at first. "Allie?"

She looks at me with wild eyes, shaking her head, and I'm trying to remember how long I've known her, trying to remember the last time I talked to her—

A couple of hours ago?

At the diner. Allie has high-tier security clearance; she has access to The Waffle. To my family. She's been privy to a thousand confidential conversations—

"What the fuck?" I say, my head spinning. "What are you— How could you—"

I watch her jaw move in that familiar way as she dislodges something from inside her mouth and I'm too stunned, reeling from the betrayal, to move quickly enough to stop her. I can't believe she was willing to die for this. They've all been ready to die for this—for *this*—

For what?

When her body goes limp, her head slumping against the floor, I go nearly solid with rage. A cold heat fuses my panic into something like steel, anger and adrenaline burning through my veins, quieting my thoughts.

I feel suddenly unhinged.

Rivulets of blood snake down my face and I realize only then that I must've cut my head at some point. I can't feel the pain. I don't feel the wound in my torso as it slowly heals. I don't feel anything but fury.

Betrayal.

I charge into the central, open space in the building and turn in a slow circle, trying to decipher what I'm looking at; I'm surrounded by amorphous shadows that could be hiding mercenaries or stacks of fleece sweaters.

"*James!*"

My heart nearly comes back to life at the sound of her scream, the desperation in her voice. A cold sweat breaks out across my skin and I kill the panic all over again, forcing my heart into higher gear.

Rosabelle is still alive.

She's fighting back.

Maybe they're not trying to kill her—maybe, I tell myself, they're just trying to kidnap her—

No, this alternative scenario offers me no relief.

I bolt toward the sound of her voice, half out of my mind, and dive down another aisle at random, eyes sweeping the shelves—

"James?"

I go deathly still. I look around, but I see nothing. No one. "*Kenji?*"

"Bro," he croaks. "Is that you? I thought I heard someone scream your name."

I'm trying not to read into the rasp of his voice. I'm trying not to think about how faint he sounds; how far away. He sounds like he's been put through a shredder.

"Kenji," I say, searching the aisles. "Where are you?"

"Here," he says.

"Pull back your invisibility," I call out, sweeping the area, not caring that my voice carries. "I can't see you—"

"I'm not invisible," he says.

"*Where are you?*"

"Look up."

The seconds it takes me to look up seem to take years. Details come into focus in a disjointed procession of images, the frame rate dragging to a crawl as the scene clarifies and clarifies.

I don't believe it at first.

At first, I don't even know what I'm looking at.

My eyesight sharpens by degrees, my mind translating impossible images into information—and suddenly, everything comes into focus.

At least a dozen people are hanging from the rafters like pendants, each person neatly clamped in metal, bodies wrapped in gleaming silver binds. They're tethered to the industrial ceiling by individual fists of black steel, each anchor flashing a pinprick of blue light.

"Holy shit," I say. "What the hell—"

"You have to get out of here," Kenji rasps. "This whole thing was a setup. There's some weird shit going down. You shouldn't be here—"

A disorienting, focused calm continues to sedate my fears. I assess the situation and form a plan in seconds, understanding that if I miss my shot, I could kill him.

"Kenji," I say. "How did you get up there?"

"I don't know. I don't remember what happened. I think I'm the only one who woke up."

And I suddenly understand his voice—

He's groggy.

"Get out of here," he says again. "I have no idea what's

about to happen, but you need to—"

I lift my gun, narrowing my eyes in the near dark as I scan the area. I feel the beat of my heart from far away, tell myself I'll try this once, maybe twice, see how it goes.

There's no time.

Rosabelle.

"James," Kenji says, his voice rising in panic. "Don't you dare fucking shoot me—"

I aim, then fire.

The shot hits a steel rod just above his head, the metal sparking, then groaning, the bullet burying itself in the ceiling.

"What the fuck is wrong with you—"

I fire again, and my second shot finds its mark.

The bullet ignites the steel anchor, causing a small explosion that briefly lights the dark, releasing the metal apparatus and dropping Kenji, without warning, from nearly fifty feet in the air. I hear his strangled cry and I dive across the room, catching him badly as he nears the ground. We collide with the floor, our heads nearly knocking, the wind gusting from my lungs.

Kenji groans, rocking from side to side.

As I sit up I realize the knife in my pocket has somehow gone clean through my leg, burying half the hilt with it. The pain is so intense I nearly give in to the impulse to pass out. I grit my teeth and dig my fingers into the wound, unburying the hilt in order to yank it free. I make a choked, violent sound as the blade comes free, then get to my feet unsteadily, feeling my head swim. Kenji levers himself upright, and he looks as unsteady as I feel.

We both look drunk.

"I think you were put unnaturally to sleep," I say, breathing through the pain, grimacing as my body slowly heals. "Get everyone else free," I tell him. "I'm guessing you don't have much time to wake them before something bad happens—"

I hear another desperate scream, then a staccato burst of gunfire.

Rosabelle.

I don't think.

I just run.

"Wait— Bro— Where are you going—"

I really shouldn't put weight on my leg yet, but I can't stop long enough to have the conversation with myself. I drag my bad leg with me, clenching my jaw so hard the pain radiates up my temples. I'm breathing too hard; my head is spinning. My body is moving almost without my permission; my wounds stitch themselves together as I go, and I run as fast as I can push myself, leaping over displays and launching myself across stacks of picture books. I knock over a display of chocolates, tumbling boxes of shoes to the ground. I stumble into a mountain of children's toys, robotic animal voices jangling to life on an ominous tune. My lungs are burning. My legs are burning. My body is working harder than I've ever—

I come to a sudden, disorienting halt.

Rosabelle.

The sight of her rocks me like a shock wave; I'm so relieved to see her alive that my relief nearly blinds me to the details. She's running from yet another masked figure, so drenched in blood she's almost unrecognizable. I watch, horrified, as she yanks a knife out of her own arm and flings it, badly, at the figure chasing her. Her hands are shaking. She's losing speed.

I bolt toward them both, giving myself a running start before I launch myself at the figure, tackling the assailant to the ground. I tuck my head as we hit the floor, then roll badly into a stand of baked goods.

I hear Rosabelle's sudden, choked cry.

Boxes of muffins come crashing down all around us, the scents of sugar and cinnamon infusing the air. I hear a volley of gunfire in the distance, shots ringing out, and I leverage the moment of distraction to pin the asshole to the ground, punching them in the face so hard the impact nearly breaks my hand. The assailant cries out, lifting an arm, too late, as if to stop me.

I can't let this one die.

Pain shatters through my fist, but I can hardly feel it. I'm breathing like my lungs are failing. My head is pounding, my hearing muted. My fingers shake as I rip the mask off the guy, revealing a pale, bloodied face. Freshly broken nose. Dark eyes. Dark hair. Roughly my age. I experience a tepid moment of relief.

I've never seen him before in my life.

And then I flip open my bloody knife and drive the blade into his shoulder, twisting it as he screams.

"Rosabelle," I call out, my chest heaving. I'm afraid to look away from this guy. I can't let him kill himself. I need to take one of these monsters in for questioning. "Rosabelle, where are you?"

"I'm here," she says, her voice faint.

"Are you shot?" I ask.

She takes too long to answer.

"*Fuck*," I say, squeezing my eyes shut. "Can you come over here so I can help you? I'm sorry—I'm so sorry to make you walk, but I can't leave him alone—"

The guy groans, the guttural sound coming from his throat, and I twist the knife a little deeper. An agonized sound rips from his chest.

"Where's the vial, asshole?" I ask. I don't even recognize the sound of my voice. I pat down his pockets with my free hand, searching him blindly. "Where are the rest of your friends, you piece of shit?"

He makes a sound—a choked gasp—and I realize he's trying to speak.

I ease my knee off his chest, releasing some of the pressure, and look into his eyes.

"Where's the vial?" I bark at him.

"*You*," he gasps.

"Excuse me?"

He struggles to swallow. His voice is hoarse. "I was hoping I'd see you again."

My shoulders tighten. A feeling of unease moves up my spine. "Who the hell are you?"

Kenji charges into view at that exact moment, then skids to a stop in front of us, looking more like himself. "Warner's on his way—"

"Where is he? Is he okay?"

"*James.*"

I turn at the desperate sound of Rosabelle's voice. She's managed to drag herself over, but she's trembling; unable to straighten one leg. Only now do I see the extent of the blood running down her body. It's in her hair. Dripping down her face. Splattered across her hands.

She's clutching the vial in one fist.

And she's staring, immobilized, at the man I've got pinned to the ground with my knife. The recognition in her eyes is unmistakable. But it's the complete and shattering horror on her face that sends serrated blades of fear through my body.

"What is it?" I say, looking between them. "Rosabelle, who is this guy?"

"Sebastian," she whispers.

I go rigid with disbelief, assaulted by a flash of memory: his name on a wedding invitation.

This was the guy she was going to marry? The guy responsible for the blood painted down her body? The guy she's staring at with a look of pure, abject terror?

What the fuck did they do to her on that island?

I'm remembering the hundreds of identical bruises we

found all over her when she first got here. I'm remembering Rosabelle on her knees in front of that shitty cottage on the Ark, a man with dark hair looming over her. I'm remembering the way she spit in his face. The way he cracked a rifle into her eye.

I'm suddenly shaking with rage.

Kenji looks at me, then at Rosabelle, then the piece of shit lying on the ground.

I suddenly wish I'd killed him.

"Who the fuck is Sebastian?" says Kenji.

Rosabelle tries to speak. She seems almost paralyzed by fear. "He's— He—"

I actually consider it then. I really think about driving the blade straight through his heart. I lock eyes with the monster, my hand still clenched around the hilt of the knife. His dark irises almost seem to glint blue for a second.

I stiffen.

"Is anyone going to answer me?" Kenji demands. "Who the hell is this guy?"

"I'm Rosabelle's fiancé," Sebastian whispers roughly, blood seeping at the edges of his mouth. He keeps his sinister gaze on me, his expression darkening. "I've come to take her home."

LOSE YOURSELF IN THIS EXHILARATING RETURN TO THE NO. 1 GLOBAL BESTSELLING SHATTER ME SERIES UNIVERSE

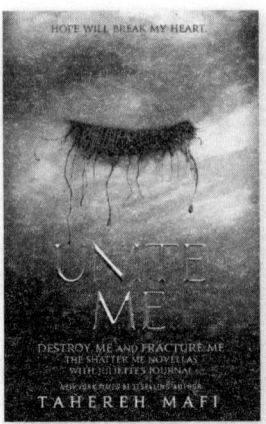
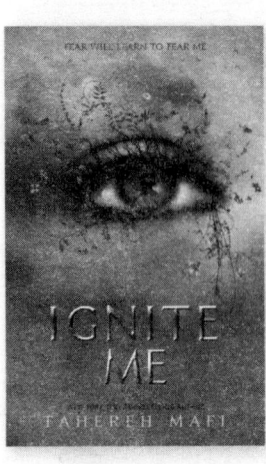

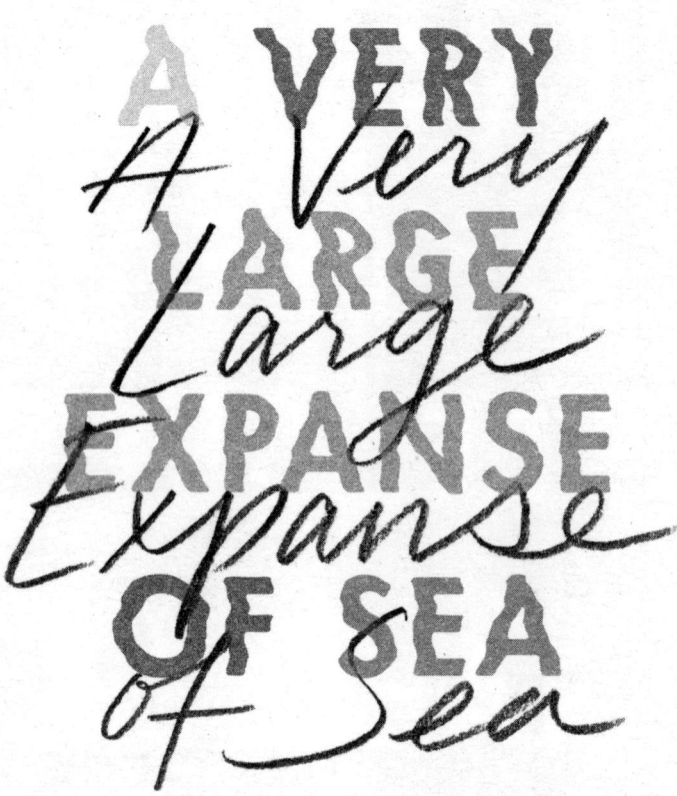

'The very best books move you to reconsider the world around you and this is one of those. I truly loved it'
– Nicola Yoon, bestselling author of *Everything, Everything*

A VERY LARGE EXPANSE OF SEA

New York Times bestselling author
TAHEREH MAFI

AN EMOTION OF GREAT DELIGHT

A Novel

TAHEREH MAFI